IN YOUR EYES

Ruth Axtell

For His Glory
WINTER HARBOR, ME

Copyright © 2013 by Ruth Axtell

All rights reserved. No part of this publication may be reproduced, distributed or transmitted in any form or by any means, including photocopying, recording, or other electronic or mechanical methods, without the prior written permission of the publisher, except in the case of brief quotations embodied in critical reviews and certain other noncommercial uses permitted by copyright law. For permission requests, write to the publisher, addressed "Attention: Permissions Coordinator," at the address below.

Ruth Axtell/For His Glory Publishing
P.O. Box 423
Winter Harbor, ME/04693
www.ruthaxtell.com

Publisher's Note: This is a work of fiction. Names, characters, places, and incidents are a product of the author's imagination. Locales and public names are sometimes used for atmospheric purposes. Any resemblance to actual people, living or dead, or to businesses, companies, events, institutions, or locales is completely coincidental.

Book Layout ©2013 BookDesignTemplates.com
Book cover design: Cheryl Casey Ramirez

Ordering Information:
Quantity sales. Special discounts are available on quantity purchases by corporations, associations, and others. For details, contact the author at the address above.

In Your Eyes/ Ruth Axtell – 2nd ed.
ISBN 13: 978-1-5237459-6-8
ISBN 10: 1523-745-967

For my mother.

Thank you for believing in God's call on my life.

GLOSSARY AND PRONUNCIATION GUIDE

Characters (in order of appearance):

Dirk Vredeman (di-rik Fray-duh-mun)
Grietje (ghreet-chuh)
Jaap Janzoon (yahp yahn sohne)
Jacob van Diemen (Yah-kub vahn Dee-mun)
Joost (Yohst)
Francesca di Paolo (Fran-chesca dee Paw-loh) "Cesca" (chesca)
Katryn (kah-trin)
Leentje (lane-tchuh)
Tante Blankaart (tan-tah blan-kahrt)

Dutch and Italian words (alphabetically):

beurs (burce) = stock exchange
Bloemtje (bloom-chuh) little flower
boers (boors) = farmers
Bruin Biertje (brown beer-chuh) = little brown beer
de heer (duh hair) = lord, sir, mister (title of great respect)
dominee (dominay) = pastor
Druifje (drowf-yuh) = little grape
gracht (guttural "g" and "ch": ghrahght) = canal
Herengracht (Hayren-gracht) = with aspirated 'ch'
Ij (eye) = a bay, formerly a lake, forming Amsterdam harbor
juffrouw (yu-frow) = miss
mynheer (min-air) = mister
Nieuwmarkt (nee-u markt) = new market (square)
pakhuis (pahk-house) = warehouse
poffertjes (pofferchus) = small puffy pancakes
Prinsengracht (prinzen-ghracht) with aspirated 'ch' = one of the principal canals ringing Amsterdam in a U shape

schoutsmen (scouts-men with aspirated "sc") = waterway police
stuiver (stou-ver) = penny
tesorina (teh-soh-reena) = little treasure
trekschuit (trek-skowt) = canal barge
trekvaart (trek-fahrt) = 17th century canal for public transport and mail, with the barge usually pulled by a horse adjacent to the canal
Zandvoort (sahnd-fort) = Dutch coastal town along the sand dunes

One

Farm outside Amsterdam, June 1641

One look at the bound, blindfolded woman told Dirk Vredeman his men had abducted the wrong female.

A string of curses that would have curdled the hardiest seaman's blood rushed through his mind, but that was all the rage he permitted himself. He'd learned the wisdom of self-control long ago.

At the moment, there were more crucial things to consider.

For one, who the devil was this black-clad woman, whose hair was plastered to her head in swirling black waves, and why had his men abducted her? And what had she been doing on van Diemen's barge?

She was certainly not the fair-haired, robustly-built Holland's maiden he had been informed would be traveling the trekvaart to Amsterdam.

Serve him right for not overseeing the abduction himself but trusting a couple of his thick-skulled sailors to waylay the Amsterdam-bound vessel. For all he knew they'd held up the wrong barge and van Diemen's daughter had long since arrived safely home.

But Dirk had thought it prudent not to be anywhere in the vicinity, thus in no way implicated with the vile deed should anything go amiss. Which clearly it had.

A sudden gust of wind hit the side of the dilapidated farmhouse, bringing with it a renewed onslaught of rain, reminding Dirk of everything that had gone wrong that afternoon.

With a brisk nod to Jaap and Willem, he gave them the order to proceed, then bit back an oath as they yanked the woman forward by the arms. Didn't they see she wasn't a sack of meal to be hauled so?

They held her before the lantern, and Dirk took a step forward. Against the dark, wet blindfold and cloak, the woman's face had the same pale cast as the ivory tusks he bought and sold on the China coast.

Disguising his voice with the coarse Amsterdam street accent he had grown up with, he growled, "Who are you, lass?"

At the sight of her trembling lip, he squelched any inclination to speak softly. Too much hung in the balance. "Speak up, I say!"

"F—Francesca di Paolo."

A foreigner. He turned away in disgust. Probably a lady's maid at that. 'Twould be good for naught, not even a ransom. "Search her goods. See what valuables she has." Better to keep up the pretense of a robbery. They'd leave her to be found in the morning by a local farmer.

He planted his feet apart and folded his arms across his chest, already impatient to be gone. Jaap dumped the contents of her leather satchel onto the floor.

Dirk started when the woman flung herself from Willem's grasp. She fumbled sightlessly among the jumble, her movements hindered by her bound wrists. Dirk clenched his fists to keep from going to her aid. How he detested the sight of human bondage.

"I beg of you, leave my things! There's nothing of value here." Despite her kneeling position and entreaties, there was a dignity to her gestures, like that of a mother protecting her child. Her speech, though not distinctly accented, had a quaint formality, as that of a foreigner, who has learned the language too precisely.

Ignoring his distaste for the task at hand, Dirk nodded for his man to continue. Jaap shuffled a muddy boot among the papers strewn about the tile floor and chuckled, clearly not minding his job a bit. "Must be some jewels or coin here somewhere."

"Please, mynheer!" The woman turned her face upward in Dirk's direction, captivating him with the sight of her long, pale throat.

He shifted position, unable to bear her supplication. "Hold her, Willem."

Finding nothing on the ground, Jaap took the satchel in his thick hands and pulled it inside out. Empty. He then tore out the lining, pawing at the material, which had nothing more to surrender. Like a starving dog, intent on getting the last morsel out of a dish, Jaap worried at the leather until it finally came apart at the seams.

"Enough!"

The woman, her movements limited, and by sense of touch alone, had gathered some of the papers in her hands. Dirk reached for them. She resisted for an instant before letting them go, turning away from him, her shoulders slumped.

She pleaded no more, her arms resting in front of her. He noted her clenched fists and paused. Despite her fragility, there was some fight in her.

He eyed the soiled, crumpled papers in his hand. Mayhap some valuable deeds to property, receipts to a local lottery, or bills of sale for a precious commodity—something that would justify a hold-up.

He rubbed his forehead, his curiosity turning to confusion at the realization that he held only unfinished drawings of human figures and faces. He glanced at the woman. Perhaps not a lady's maid, but a young lady out with her sketch pad. But what had she been doing unaccompanied?

With a frustrated sigh, he tossed the drawings back to the floor. "Enough, men, she has naught of worth. Let's be off and leave her to her fate." She'd be found when the sun came up and could claim she'd been set upon by thieves. Her boatman would doubtless tell the same tale. No real harm had been done, and no one would be the wiser.

"You will rue the day you have done this deed. Mynheer van Diemen is an important man in the city."

Dirk's footsteps froze. Had his men held up the right barge after all? He turned slowly to face the kneeling, blindfolded woman.

Who was this dark-haired maiden who used van Diemen's name as if he were her protector?

Mayhap all was not lost this ill-fated day.

"My guardian has powerful acquaintances. They'll hunt you down."

Dirk rocked back on his heels, his fingers stroking his beard. So Jacob van Diemen was her guardian.

Dirk had gone after the man's daughter and ended up with his ward. Satisfied he hadn't revealed his own identity in any way, Dirk turned to his men, a decision taken. "What're ye waiting for? We must be gone!" He'd do the rest of the work on his own.

Leaving the woman, they made their way through the long farmhouse into the connecting barn where they'd left their horses. In a low voice he gave instructions to his men about their return.

Willem frowned at him. "Aren't you coming with us?"

Dirk shook his head, flashing a brief smile. "Nay. This day may prove profitable yet."

He made sure his men made plenty of noise in their departure, although he doubted much could be heard above the din of the storm.

After they'd left, Dirk settled himself on the floor to wait. He'd give the maiden sufficient time to believe the men who'd abducted her were truly gone.

When the gray world had given way to black gloom, he rose from his position and stretched his stiff legs. The rain still came down in buckets. All the better. No trace of their horses would remain.

He took up his bag of provisions, wrapped his cape around his shoulders, and ventured outside.

Cold droplets stung his face. The wind whipped at his hat and cloak as it whistled down the flat lowlands from the North Sea. He stood there only long enough to look sufficiently soaked, as if he'd been out traveling.

Then he reentered the barn, took up the lantern he'd left hanging there, and retraced his route through the connecting rooms to the farmhouse's front room. Wanting to announce his entry well ahead of time, he banged doors back against walls, his boots thumping against the cracked tile floors.

He heard a rustle of movement from the next room. "Who is there?" Panic edged the words.

He hurried his footsteps, then stopped at the threshold, eyeing the woman they'd left scarcely an hour before.

"Good heavens!" In a few strides he reached the huddled figure. Kneeling down and depositing the lantern on the floor, he began to loosen her blindfold. "Who's done this to you?" he asked in outrage, affecting the cultivated tones he'd learned over time, to erase all evidence of his past.

"Bandits. Oh, thank you, mynheer," she gasped as soon as the blindfold was off, her eyes blinking into the light.

Dirk drew back a fraction, mesmerized. Gray irises, as velvety silver as a fox's tail, were rimmed by inky black lashes. Finely arched black eyebrows were all the more striking against pale skin. What jewel had his men captured? An exquisite South Sea pearl to his jaded eye.

He frowned. "Scoundrels! They left you here alone?" As he spoke, he freed her wrists. Her icy hands were slim and delicate, he noted. He remembered the sketches, which still littered the floor.

"Yes," she replied, cradling her wrists.

"Here, permit me, juffrouw." She didn't look older than eighteen. Gently, he took her hands in his. "Looks as if these were bound for an age." He began to massage her wrists, ignoring her attempt to pull away. When that proved fruitless, she sat still, like an obedient child. Too still. He quirked an eyebrow, studying her. Was she scared of him?

But she seemed to be studying him in turn. For a

moment, his heart pummeled against his chest. Would she recognize him?

But immediately her gaze fell, and he was at the mercy of her inky lashes. Inexplicably, he felt a flush creep up his neck. Clearing his throat, he looked down at their hands.

His sun-bronzed ones accentuated the fragility of her wrists. A sudden protectiveness swelled in him. No common maid was she. "Tell me how you came to be here," he asked softly, bracing himself for another look into those amazing eyes.

She tugged gently on her wrists, and he let them go. She scooted away from him to lean against the wall, her knees drawn up. "We—that is, a servant and I—were on our way back to Amsterdam on the Haarlemmermeer Canal. When we disembarked at Halfweg to change barges, the storm rose. We could hardly see around us. The waves on the Spiering Meer had whipped up to a frenzy." She hugged her knees. "There was hardly a soul about. Of a sudden, a band of men rode up, saying they had come to fetch me."

She shuddered, looking away as if reliving the terror. "Before I could question them, one of them swooped me up onto his horse. I could scarcely gather breath to scream before he covered my head...my face with a hood." Her hand cupped her mouth to hide her trembling lips. "I couldn't breathe. It was horrible. They r—rode for what seemed f—forever—"

He restrained the urge to take her in his arms and comfort her. Wishing the foul deed could have been avoided, he merely shook his head. "There, there, juffrouw. You're safe now." He frowned. "You're shivering. I'll build up a fire before you catch your death."

When he began to leave the room, she stood. "W—where are you going?"

He realized how scared she must be. He motioned down the long dark passageway. "Just to the barn. I'm sure there'll be some peat I can burn. Don't fear, you're safe now."

She nodded, and again he felt a wave of protectiveness, this time coupled with admiration, at her attempt to put up a brave front. He smiled gently. "I shan't be but a moment."

He returned with a load of peat to find she had gathered her scattered possessions back into her satchel.

When the smoldering fire on the hearth was emitting sufficient heat, Dirk turned to the young woman. "Come, stand here where it's warm."

As she drew near, he put out a hand. "Let me take your cloak. It's soaked through."

After a second's hesitation, she reached for the clasp. "Thank you."

He drew a chair forward to the fire. When she sat down, she began to rub one of her shoulders.

"Are you hurt?" He'd have his men's hides if they had mishandled her.

She shook her head. "Sore from that horse ride."

How he rued being the cause of her discomfort, but he could do naught about what was done. "Did the men...harm you?" So, help him, if Jaap or Willem had misused her in any way before he'd met up with them, he'd kill them.

She shook her head. "They seemed intent on finding some valuables on me, and when that proved in vain, they abandoned me here."

Clearly, she hadn't understood his meaning. She must be as innocent as she looked. So much the better. It shouldn't prove too difficult to maintain the charade of rescuer. "Mayhap they thought you were a lady of means traveling unaccompanied. A fair target." He noted her gown, though black and austere, was velvet with fine Flemish lace edging her collar.

She smiled at the description, and Dirk stared, again captivated. Her color had returned, giving her face a delightful contrast of crimson and cream, from lips the color of velvety roses to the soft diffusion of pink across her cheeks. Her irises were like the Zuiderzee on this storm-tossed night, a roiling swirl of gray ringed in black. Her damp hair was a mass of dark waves falling around her shoulders. A wisp of it brushed her cheek. Dirk almost reached out to smooth the wayward strand.

He caught himself in time. What was he thinking? Too much was at stake to risk losing his wits over a woman now, no matter how comely.

"They were doomed to disappointment if that was the case." Her tone contained that same soft elegance that had caught his attention earlier.

Dirk smiled, deciding it was as good a time as any to discover more about her. "No cache of jewels sewn into your hem?"

"Not even one. All they managed to abduct was a penniless dependent of an Amsterdam burgher."

Van Diemen. Just then he caught her shiver and cursed himself for his impatience. "Are your garments truly dry?" He made his tone deliberately gruff as he reached out to touch her velvet dress, not wanting to alarm her. She'd had enough of an ordeal, and all he wanted to do now was earn her trust until he could figure out how to use her in his game against van Diemen.

"I...I think only the hem is soaked. It will dry well enough if I just sit here close to the fire." She placed her feet near the hearth and spread her skirts out.

Dirk brought the rickety table close to the fire's warmth and brushed off its dusty surface, then rummaged through his bag.

The woman began to rise. "Let me help you—"

"Stay put while your garments dry," he ordered in the tone he was accustomed to using aboard ship. "I trust you're hungry?" He quirked an eyebrow at her and caught another heart-stopping smile.

"Ravenous."

⁂

Francesca stared at her golden-eyed rescuer. From the moment he'd taken off her blindfold, she had been entranced by his tawny looks and regal bearing.

The tall, broad-shouldered gentleman had taken command at once, loosing her bonds, building a fire to warm her, and setting about preparing her a meal. Unaccustomed to being waited on, she sat, too stunned by the events of the afternoon, to do little more than study the man and wonder how to capture such vitality upon a two-dimensional surface.

He reminded her of a lion, from the deep golden locks brushing his shoulders, to the narrow beard outlining his strong jaw line. Most of all, it was his eyes, amber-hued beneath burnished golden eyebrows. His skin was honey-toned as if he spent much time out of doors. Perhaps he was a ship's captain.

She took pleasure in the way he wielded the broad knife, crackling through the crust of bread, then sinking it into the round half of cheese. Deftly, he lopped a few slices off the joint of ham. With a grace that belied his large hands, he set a plate before her. Sliced bread overlaid with sweet-cured ham and cumin-studded cheese never looked so good. He smiled, the corners of his eyes crinkling with humor, one eyebrow raised.

"T-thank you," she stuttered, her stomach growling at the appetizing array. It had been many hours since her last meal.

He brought out two pewter goblets from his satchel and uncorked a bottle of wine. "This will take the remaining chill from your bones," he said, presenting her with a half-filled cup.

She smiled at him gratefully, then found herself blushing under his gaze. To escape it, she ducked her head and said grace.

When she looked up, he was already eating. As she took her first tentative bite of bread and cheese, the thought that had been simmering in her mind since she'd first beheld him resurfaced. How she would love to paint him.

But first she would need to fill pages with sketches to

see how best to capture the mix of raw strength and vitality with the gentleness of his touch and the discernment in his eye.

As she ate, she took in the rest of him. From the brown velvet doublet and breeches down to the soft, crushed leather of his boots, he was the picture of an elegant, wealthy merchant.

When she reached for her goblet, she found him watching her.

What did he see in her? Doubtless exactly what she'd told him—a penniless dependent, the kind of woman waiting on an elderly relative or helping watch a kin's children.

He tore off a chunk of bread. "Whom do I have the pleasure of rescuing this wild night?"

She flushed. "How remiss of me—"

A glint of amusement lit his eyes. "You have merely been abducted and left to perish of cold." The teasing smile beneath the toasted almond of his moustache made her smile in return.

"My name is Francesca di Paolo."

He quirked an eyebrow. "You are not a Holland's maid?"

She shook her head. "My father was Florentine, my mother Dutch. He came to Amsterdam to seek refuge from the persecution."

"Was? He is—?"

She lowered her eyes. "A fever took them both five winters past within days of each other."

"I'm sorry." He took a sip from the goblet before setting it down carefully. "And you continue to reside in Amsterdam? With family?"

She shook her head. "Mynheer Jacob van Diemen took me in after my parents' demise. He is my guardian."

He was regarding her so steadily, she felt self-conscious. Since her parents' death, she had grown accustomed to being always in the background, unnoticed. She put a hand up to her hair, feeling again the shame of having it unbound about her shoulders. She'd lost her lace cap somewhere along the way. No respectable woman would appear before a stranger like this. What a scandalous fright she must look.

"You needn't worry. You have beautiful hair. 'Twould be a shame to hide it."

Again, her face grew warm. No man had ever paid her such compliments. She drew her brows together, wondering if the gentleman was behaving improperly. He did not appear to be a libertine by his manner. Suddenly, she looked around at the dim shadows of the room. Was she to spend the night here, alone with him?

As if sensing her dismay, he asked more seriously, "How came—van Diemen, is it?—to be your guardian?"

She breathed more easily at the stranger's matter-of-fact tone. "He and my father were business partners."

He took another bite of his bread and chewed it thoughtfully, as if mulling over the information she had given him. "So your father went into business with van Diemen?" he asked at last.

She nodded slowly, wondering at his interest in her. "That is correct."

His tiger's-eye gaze perused her until she felt he saw every inch of her face. "You are very young."

She gave a rueful shake of her head. "Not so young. Five-and-twenty this past March." Old enough to have been long married. Instead, her future stretched out before her as one of endless servitude.

A brow lifted as he eyed her hands clasped atop the table. "As yet unmarried?"

She curled her fingers inward, flustered at how his train of thought mirrored hers. "Yes."

He pulled at his short beard. "And you fare well under your guardian?"

She gave a quick nod of her head, unused to having anyone take such a particular interest in her. "Yes, mynheer. He is a God-fearing man of rectitude and honor. My f-father entrusted me to his care."

He nodded, his eyes never leaving hers. To take the focus off of herself, she asked, "Excuse me, sir, but whom have I the honor of addressing?"

"My pardon." With a graceful bow of his head, he said, "Dirk Vredeman, at your service."

She found herself blushing again beneath his lazy smile. "I can never repay you enough, sir, for your rescue—"

He waved away her words. "I thank the Lord I happened by on this road when I did. I, too, was on my return to Amsterdam after a day on the polder."

She took a small swallow of wine and felt its warmth spread through her. "You are from Amsterdam?" Perhaps she could now have some of her curiosity over her rescuer satisfied.

He didn't reply right away. He washed down a healthy bite of bread and cheese with a long swallow from his goblet. He set it down, then wiped his mouth with a cloth. "Yes."

When she wondered if he would tell her any more, he added, "It's been many years since I've called Amsterdam my home."

She waited, her breath caught.

"I have but recently returned from the East Indies."

Her breath released. That explained the exotic air about him. Perhaps he was a sea captain as she'd first conjectured.

"I made my fortune in the Indies, and now I have returned to my native shores to set some things a right."

The words held her spellbound. What could he mean? Her imagination took flight and once again her fingers itched to take up her sketchpad and capture his likeness.

The night stretched before Dirk. He sat before the fire in one chair, his ankles crossed atop the other one. For a long time he stared into the flames, considering his next course.

As the hour grew late and sleep was not forthcoming, he arranged his body one way and another, but his mind remained fully awake. Curse this night, he fumed to himself. What an impossible situation in which to find himself. It didn't set well with him to feel such a blasted fool for the error made.

How Jacob van Diemen would laugh at him if he knew of his blunder. Thank heaven the man still had no inkling of his existence.

The Orient had taught Dirk well the value of biding his time when dealing with an enemy. This afternoon's botched abduction only meant a new stratagem was required.

He fingered his moustache slowly. All, perchance, was not lost. Indeed not. His glance strayed to the sleeping figure lying curled on her side a few feet from him before the hearth.

He'd made up a pallet for her from his own cloak and a saddle blanket. Fate had cast the comely lass in his path.

But what to do about Juffrouw Francesca di Paolo?

That was the question he'd plagued himself with since he'd bid her good night. As he shifted his body in the confining chair, the girl's words came back to him. Somehow, the thought of Mynheer Jacob's taking in his partner's orphaned child didn't fit with the man Dirk had known long ago. Could van Diemen have changed so much from the cold-hearted, calculating burgher of Dirk's youth?

Dirk stared unseeing at the slumbering girl before he gave an abrupt shake of his head.

There must be more to the story. Mayhap a by-blow of his?

Dirk frowned, not thinking it likely. She looked nothing like van Diemen. And it was clear she'd had two parents, of whom she spoke fondly.

But if Mynheer Jacob had made her his ward, clearly she must be of value to him. Could she be—Dirk didn't finish the thought it so sickened him.

No! The girl was an innocent—that was evident from her blushing manner. Van Diemen had not used her the way he'd used Dirk's own mother.

Bile rose in his throat. He turned away from the girl and stared once more into the flames, desperate to cleanse his mind of his dark thoughts.

He would need a clear head come morning if he hoped to accomplish what he'd returned from the Indies to do.

Dirk had set about this day to bring disgrace to van Diemen's only child, a girl of marriageable age with a sizeable portion and, by all accounts, fair of face. He had planned to return her on the morn, the innocent dove apparently soiled beyond repair. Let van Diemen see then if her marriage portion was enough to entice one of the respectable burghers' sons to have her to wife. Dirk gave a mirthless laugh. Fitting retribution for a man who had robbed a young maiden of her virtue so many years ago.

Instead, Dirk's men had kidnapped an innocent woman, who'd been in the wrong place at the wrong moment. It fell to Dirk to salvage the situation and turn it to his advantage.

He shifted once more on the hard chair. Clearly, the first thing to do was return this young lady to van Diemen, untouched and unharmed. At least it would serve Dirk for an introduction to his foe.

Since his arrival in Amsterdam after so many years away, Dirk had kept his distance from van Diemen, employing others to shadow the man and inform him of everything about him.

Van Diemen had done well for himself. From his modest beginnings as a young clerk in a cloth firm, today, Jacob van Diemen owned his own firm. He'd become a man of influence, held in high regard by merchants and church alike. He was known for giving sizeable alms to the orphanage. Dirk snorted. Did he think that would blot out his past sin?

Miss di Paolo stirred in her sleep, a soft sigh escaping her lips.

She was certainly a striking young lady. Nothing like the big-boned, blond Holland's maids. More like the fine-boned Oriental women he had grown accustomed to—except for those dark-fringed eyes. Eyes that seemed to look right into the core of a man's soul. They had unnerved him at first, as if she could see what he was about.

He shook aside the foolish thought, brought about no doubt by the stormy night and isolated spot.

No time for sentiment now. If anything, this young maiden should fit right into his plans like a sun-ripened peach, fallen into his hands for his use.

What if he were to call upon her as an admirer? Dirk rubbed his beard, musing. It would certainly gain him access to Jacob's household. With access he could find another weak spot in the burgher's armor.

It would be no hardship to pay court to this delightfully shy creature, whose porcelain cheeks blushed crimson at the slightest compliment. Her gentle manners and quiet modesty would make it an easy—nay, pleasurable—task.

Dirk smiled as the idea grew on him, a perfect scheme, then swore as his elbow hit the arm of the chair. Drat it, when would this night be over?

⁂

Francesca awoke shivering. Disoriented, she hugged the cloak closer. The floor felt dank and cold, her body stiff and sore.

The previous day's events came back to her in a rush...hours of darkness, hoisted upon a horse and taken through drenching rain, her belongings mauled, her sketches destroyed. A wave of outrage rose to the surface again. She was thankful for it, as it helped to smother the wave of terror threatening to break over the surface of her newfound calm.

If it had not been for her rescuer—

Or had she dreamed him?

She sat up, her eyes searching for him in the pre-dawn light. A breath of relief escaped her at the sight of his slumbering form. He lay sprawled in the chairs near her, his long legs stretched out before him, his booted feet on the chair opposite. His head was bent, forcing his neck to an awkward angle. She marveled he could find rest in such a position.

Like a cat drawn to something new, she rose, wrapping the cloak around herself, and approached him on stocking feet. His deep, even breathing reassured her that he still slept, even as his blunt manner the previous evening had quelled her urge to give way to blind panic.

She was safe because of this man, this angel sent from heaven itself. He'd given her warmth and food and fixed a comfortable pallet for her. He'd promised to return her to her family as soon as the weather cleared.

She listened a moment. Hearing nothing, she sighed with relief. The rain had stopped. Soon, she would be home again.

She worried her lip with a new fear. What would Mynheer Jacob say? How to explain she had had no control of events? She shuddered, pulling the cloak closer to herself, already anticipating her guardian's displeasure. Whenever she was a mere few minutes late from an errand, he would chastise her. She dreaded that icy demeanor and those biting words.

She shook away the thought. Time enough to face it by daylight. She moved away from her rescuer and knelt by the dying embers of the hearth. After stirring it up and adding more peat, she sat hunched before it, hugging her knees. Strange how her rescuer—Dirk Vredeman—she mouthed the syllables, marveling how the name evoked the strength and purpose of the man—strange how much this man now knew about her.

He'd proved a sympathetic listener last night over their simple supper. Gradually, she had felt at ease with him. He'd seemed so genuinely interested in her simple life. It had been a long time since she had spoken to anyone of her mother and father. Mynheer Dirk seemed to understand what it was like to lose those dear to one.

As the fire warmed her limbs, her artist's eye was once more drawn to Mynheer Dirk's slumbering form. It was second nature to her to note proportion and depth of anyone she met. This man's presence dominated the mean room, and she knew that if it had been filled with a dozen people, he would still have been in command.

Now, in the stillness before a new day, Francesca crept back toward his chair. In the emerging light, he looked younger than he had by candlelight. His cheeks were flushed above the narrow beard, his deep golden locks falling over his collar.

Her gaze roamed downward to the hand curved loosely over the chair's arm. She knew how strong and capable it was. Earlier the same hand had loosened her bonds in a thrice and steadied her when her legs threatened to give way beneath her. And with a shiver, she remembered its gentleness when he had massaged her wrists with his fingertips.

Francesca glanced toward the window. There just might be sufficient time and light.

Two

Dirk awoke to a jab of pain at the side of his neck. Years of catching a few winks of sleep any way he could made his body adaptable to a variety of sleeping accommodations, but it didn't mean his muscles didn't make their presence felt in the morning.

Yet he felt snug, as if wrapped in a cocoon of warmth. He rubbed his eyes before opening them. A bright fire burned in the hearth. His own cloak was tucked around him.

His eyes darted around the room until he spotted Francesca di Paolo seated at the only window. Had she covered him? He remembered having left her wrapped up in his cloak last evening.

A wave of remorse swept through him at what the poor girl had been subjected to the prior day, and then a cold night on a hard floor. All because of him.

Every muscle groaned in protest as he unfurled his length from the chairs. He stretched fully before taking a few steps toward the young lady.

He paused and ran his fingers through his unruly hair to bring some semblance of order to his appearance before meeting her gaze.

A shy smile touched her lips. "Good morning," she said softly. Her polished voice contained no relic of sleep. Neither did any marks of sleep disturb her appearance.

Her glorious mane of hair which had cascaded about her like some steamy waterfall deep in a Javanese jungle the night before was now bound at her nape. Her complexion, if anything, looked fresher than on the eve. Evidence of a sound night's sleep, he thought, suddenly disgruntled, remembering his hours spent in thought before the fire. Well, she deserved a better night than he.

"Good—ahem—morning." His voice sounded as rough as gravel. Not even a swallow of ale before he had to face the evidence of yesterday's debacle.

He scratched his beard, feeling at a distinct disadvantage by her clear countenance and self-possessed manner. "You appear to have fared well this night."

"I slept quite well in fact, thanks to you." It occurred to him that her voice, like the lapping of a calm sea against the prow, was pleasing to a man's ear first thing in the morning.

"I fear to ask you the same," she added with a sympathetic smile.

His lips crooked upward. "Do I owe you thanks for wrapping me up against the chill this morning?"

Her glance slid away from his again, the color rising in her cheeks. "I...I awoke rather early as is my custom. The room was quite cold. You did not look overly comfortable on those chairs." Abruptly she fell silent.

He gestured toward the papers in her lap, held beneath her clasped hands. "What have you there?"

She attempted to put them aside. "Nothing—" Before she could finish, he reached down and took them from her. Immediately, she grabbed his wrist. Her gaze locked with his, and Dirk thought how naked she looked, as if he had torn some veil from across her silvery eyes.

As rapidly as she had touched him, she dropped her hand, curling it into a ball.

Dirk stepped back, still feeling the imprint of her fingers on the back of his wrist. He should have laughed at her ludicrous attempt to wrest the papers away, but instead felt shaken by the sudden contact of both eye and hand.

To hide his reaction, Dirk glanced down, expecting to see the smudged sketches Jaap had thrown out of her satchel the night before.

Instead the topmost sheet was covered with half-finished images of him. He shuffled through the rest. All were of his slumbering form.

"Please—they're private." A hint of desperation disturbed her fine voice. She had stood and now attempted to retrieve the papers, but Dirk moved them out of her reach.

Confused by the renderings of himself, he frowned. No one had ever sketched him. It was clear the young lady had a modicum of talent, but these images were not the man he knew.

The faces of the sleeping man on the paper before him looked like babes—nay, worse—dimpled cherubs!

"What callow youths have you sketched here?" He jabbed his forefinger at one particularly offensive one, voicing his displeasure. "This isn't a man! 'Tis a babe who should be suckling a wet nurse." He narrowed his eyes at her. "Is that what you were doing this morn? Tiptoeing 'round my sleeping form?"

"You had no right to see those!" Her voice trembled as she succeeded in snatching the sketches from him. "'Tis clear you know nothing of art."

"Oh-ho, 'tis art you're about." He snorted. "It appears more a caricature to me."

"I've sketched you as I saw you." Her pointed chin revealed the pride beneath that delicate facade.

He rocked back on his heels, folding his arms in front of him. "Without my permission?"

"Would you have given it?" Her gray eyes flashed at him, each word thrust forth like a dagger. "Besides, I was not 'tiptoeing' around you." She tossed back her head. "If you think so, your conceit is great indeed. Your...your figure merely interested me for its artistic merit."

Her outrage made him forget his own. "I can hardly imagine the 'artistic merit' of a man draped on a pair of chairs in the dismal light of dawn." His voice grew warm, his anger dissipating as quickly as it had arisen. "Miss Francesca," he teased, taking a step closer to her, aware that his looming height forced her to tilt her neck to meet his eye, "You're very brave to go creeping 'round a sleeping man."

Her gaze dropped, only to meet his chest. "Nonsense," she answered with a shade too much conviction. "I simply viewed you as a subject for a composition. It took no more bravery than if you'd been that table or chair."

She turned away from him and walked toward the mentioned objects, her brisk step matching the tone of her voice. "If you think my talent so little in rendering your likeness, I'll remind you, you had no business looking at my work. No one looks at an artist's work in progress without permission."

Before he could reply, she folded up the papers and thrust them into her tattered satchel. Facing him from her safe distance, she looked him in the eye, a far cry from last night's damsel in distress. "Now then, when can we leave for Amsterdam?"

Dirk stood, torn between amusement and interest. Last night, she'd been a frightened sparrow. This morning, a bantam hen, her feathers ruffled.

It would be a delightful challenge to explore the many sides to the lady artist's temperament. And, if she truly thought he was as harmless as that table and chair, she would not be on her guard while he carried out his plans.

His intention to call on her should prove pleasurable indeed.

By the time they arrived back in Amsterdam, Francesca was fighting exhaustion. Feeling bruised and unkempt from the previous day's events, she'd also lost the rapport with her rescuer that they'd achieved the evening before.

Except for the most essential discourse, she'd hardly exchanged a word with Mynheer Dirk during the barge ride back to the walled city.

Ever since he'd seen her sketches—and offered such scathing criticism—she'd wanted to hide away somewhere. Her initial anger had only masked the chagrin that he'd thought so little of her efforts.

Each time her glance crossed his on their journey back to Amsterdam, her face burned anew at the recollection of his words—babes, dimpled cherubs, caricatures! What had made her think she'd found a kindred soul in him?

She hugged her satchel to herself, although he had offered more than once to carry it for her. Each time, she'd politely refused.

Perhaps she was not well-trained and her shortcomings were many, but her art had been her only solace for so long. It was all she had to call her own.

When they arrived at the tall brick townhouse, Francesca led Mynheer Dirk up the front steps, even though she was more accustomed to using the walkway to the kitchen entrance at the back.

To her surprise, she found the door barred. She tried it again, but it didn't yield to her push. In exasperation she pulled at the bell cord. Had Marta forgotten to unlock the door this morning? That hardly seemed possible since she washed the stoop every day.

"Is it customary for van Diemen to guard against intruders in the middle of the day?" Mynheer Dirk asked in a dry tone behind her.

"Of course not." She knew her tone was short, but she still had not forgiven him for his disparaging remarks though he had exhibited a remarked courtesy during their journey.

She frowned and rang the bell again. "'Tis strange indeed," she murmured. "For one, my guardian has his business to run from here."

Marta, the young serving maid, wearing a starched white cap and striped apron, opened the door at last. Her relief at seeing Francesca turned almost immediately to fear. With a quick look behind her, she stepped onto the front stoop and closed the door behind her. "Oh, Miss Francesca, 'tis you at last! Katryn and I were worried sick when you didn't appear last night."

"Oh, Marta, have I a tale to tell. But thank the good Lord I am safe and sound, thanks in good measure to this gentleman"—She half-turned to Mynheer Dirk—"who rescued me." She laughed at the confusion on Marta's well-scrubbed face as the maid looked up at Dirk. "What's the matter, did you forget to unbar the door this morning?"

Marta didn't smile at her chiding. Instead, she glanced behind her shoulder in fear. "No, indeed, miss." Her eyes grew round as she peered at Francesca. "Oh, miss, 'tis terrible what happened!"

Francesca grew alarmed. "What is it? Is it Mynheer Jacob or Lisbet? Has something happened to one of them?"

"Oh, no, miss!"

Mynheer Dirk stepped up beside Francesca. "For all that's holy, wench, pull yourself together and tell us what has transpired."

Marta gave him one terrified look and stepped back with a yelp, bumping against the door behind her.

Ignoring Mynheer Dirk, Francesca took hold of one of Marta's plump arms. "There now, don't mind the gentleman. He is pressed for time."

"I'm s—sorry, miss. 'Tis all so distressing."

"Please, Marta, just tell me what is wrong."

"That's just it, miss. 'T—'tis you, miss!"

"Me?" Francesca looked at her at a loss for a second before smiling in relief. "You see I'm safe and sound. I'm sorry if you were worried about my whereabouts."

"Katryn and I were dreadfully worried when you didn't come home yesterday eve. We pictured all sorts of disasters. But when Joost returned and told us the tale of highway robbers, why, we could scarcely credit it. It sounded so frightening. And to think the Haarlemmermeer Canal is normally so safe." Marta stopped, her gaze dropping. "And then—to know the worst." Her voice fell to a whisper. "Oh, Miss Francesca." The maid shuddered, not looking at her.

"I came to no harm, Marta." Uncomfortable with having her adventure discussed on the busy canal street, Francesca motioned to the door. "Why don't we go in and I shall tell you all about it?" She turned to Mynheer Dirk, doubly embarrassed by the display. "If you will excuse us, sir. I am most grateful for all you've done for me. I will be all right now, I assure you. I know you have much to do—"

Mynheer Dirk made no move. "I'm not leaving until I see you safe into your house."

With an uncertain look at Marta who made no move to open the door, Francesca nodded. "Very well, but, pray, let us continue this indoors."

Marta wiped at her eyes with the corner of her apron. "That's just it, miss. You can't!"

Mynheer Dirk loomed over her. "What do you mean, she can't enter her own house?"

The sharp question seemed to shock Marta into obedience. "'Tis Mynheer Jacob, sir. H—he's given orders." Her pale blue eyes turned to Francesca. "Miss, he'll throw me out if I disobey. You know what he is like."

Francesca tried to shush her. "That's all right. You mustn't disobey Mynheer Jacob. Now, what did he tell you to do?"

"Why—oh—'tis dreadful, miss. You're not to be admitted!" Marta threw her apron over her face and began to weep.

A familiar leaden sensation weighed in the pit of Francesca's stomach. Before she could think what to do or say, her maid sniffed and continued. "When Joost told Mynheer that the men had boasted that they would not be content to merely rob you but would have their way with you all the night, Mynheer Jacob vowed you mustn't be admitted—on account of Lisbet, he told Katryn."

Francesca grasped the balustrade, a wave of dizziness washing over her. Have their way with her? She remembered the men's rough treatment of her and her belongings. What would have happened to her if they had kept her hostage all night? She must clarify things immediately with her guardian. Icy fingers of dread crept up her spine. What if he didn't believe her?

Mynheer Dirk laid a hand on her shoulder as if to steady her, even as he addressed Marta. "What nonsense do you speak, girl?"

Marta swallowed, her eyes round with fear. "Mynheer called Katryn and me into his office. He told us that Miss Francesca had met with a tragic accident." Her voice lowered. "With a fate worse than death." She dragged her gaze to Francesca in horrified fascination as if she'd broken out in the pox. "He said he couldn't permit a 'soiled' woman to reside under the same roof as his chaste Lisbet. Those were his very words, mynheer."

Francesca stood in stunned silence as the full import of Marta's words sank in. How could her guardian have refused her entry? How could he have believed such a story? It didn't bear thinking on. Once again, her knees threatened to buckle.

The feel of Mynheer Dirk's strong fingers on her shoulders, instead of comforting her this time, reminded her afresh of the witness to her disgrace. How could she face this gentleman who had been so kind to her? Yet—perhaps he would vouch for how she had spent the night.

"Marta—"

Mynheer Dirk's words cut her off. "Where is your master?"

"H—he's in his office, mynheer," Marta whispered with another curtsy, her gaze never leaving his face.

"Please convey my greetings. Tell him Dirk Vredeman wishes to speak with him."

"H—he said he's not to be disturbed today."

"If that is the case, you may tell him that Francesca's future husband will be around tomorrow at this same time to settle the terms of the marriage contract."

Francesca turned like one in a dream to stare at him. "Mynheer, what are you saying?" she whispered. Surely, he must be teasing her once again. But his set jaw and unsmiling lips told another tale.

What would Mynheer Jacob do to her if such an imposing figure as Dirk Vredeman used that commanding tone with him? "Please, mynheer, 'tis better that you leave. I can take care of this myself."

His amber eyes met hers, and she shivered. It struck her that he could be as ferocious in protecting someone as he could in devouring them.

"I think not," he said quietly before turning his attention back to Marta. "Tell your master that I must insist Francesca remain under his protection until he and I have had a chance to speak." He paused. "Tell him it will be worth his while."

Marta didn't move but continued to stare at him.

"Marta, do you think you are capable of conveying this message to your master just as I have told you?" Although his tone was soft, there was a thread of steel to it.

The serving maid backed against the door once more, her head bobbing up and down. "Yes, mynheer."

"I shall await here until you return." With those words, he planted his feet apart and folded his arms across his chest.

When Marta had reentered the house, Francesca stared at the closed door, too mortified to face her rescuer.

"Am I to have to stare at your back for however long your maidservant dallies with my message?"

Swallowing, she turned to face Mynheer Dirk. His dark, wide-brimmed hat was worn at an angle, the brim folded up on one side. It effectively hid the expression of his eyes, but his tone told her without mistake that he was angry.

She shivered, reminded of her guardian's cold way of speaking when he was displeased. Would Mynheer Dirk treat her in the same manner?

She flinched when his gloved hand came up to her chin. "Steady lass, I'm not going to strike you."

She forced herself to continue breathing even though her heart was thundering against her chest.

"Does van Diemen ever strike you?"

She gasped and shook her head vehemently. "Indeed not,

sir!"

"Yet he bars the door to you when you have encountered a mishap." His dry tone softened. "Don't fear, I shall make everything right again."

She swallowed, all her senses focused on the soft feel of the suede glove anchoring her chin. "You...you needn't—" She couldn't even say the word, much less think it. He could not have been serious!

"Marry you?" He tilted his head to one side, his eyes perusing her face. "What do you find so strange about that? People are betrothed every day barely knowing one another."

"Why...why should you? You had nothing to do with—with—"

"Your abduction?" He continued to study her face. "No, but then neither did you. I cannot stand by and see you suffer the consequences all by yourself." His voice hardened once more. "Clearly, your guardian will not believe that you return to him chaste and unsullied."

"C—can you not tell him?"

His forefinger lightly stroked her jaw so that she could hardly focus on his words for the feel of it. "If he will not believe you, I doubt very much he will believe any story I tell him...for he has never met me," he murmured.

"But you could try, mynheer. After all, you are a gentleman. He will be impressed by your...your bearing."

He cocked an eyebrow. "Will he? So much the better." He sighed and took a step away from her, letting her face go. "I fear a betrothal it must be."

She bristled at his tone of resignation. She didn't want a man who was forced into marrying her because of some misguided sense of responsibility. She would prefer to take her chances on the street. "I see no reason why. Before last night you'd never seen me. It's preposterous. You don't know me. I don't know you. I—I have no marriage portion!" There, she'd stated the worst. Surely, now he would drop the idea.

He chuckled. "Is that what has you worried?"

She stared at him. "No—but, it should have you worried!" Was he daft?

Instead, he threw back his head and laughed, a rich sound that had a passing couple look up at them from the street. "I care naught what material wealth you bring with you. You are comely enough and of pleasing character to satisfy any man, I warrant."

The words reverberated through her, forcing her to face the grim realities of marriage. To satisfy any man.

Before she could offer any more arguments, the door opened. Francesca whirled around to find Marta once again facing her. This time the maid wore a tiny smile.

She curtsied to Mynheer Dirk. "My master says Francesca may be admitted." Her smile disappeared. "For one night only—that is, until you return on the morrow, sir."

Mynheer Dirk nodded. "Very well. I shall call again at this time. Let us hope your master is more amenable then." He took Francesca's hand and bowed over it. "Until tomorrow, juffrouw."

Francesca watched him turn and descend the steps. With a brisk stride, he disappeared down the brick walk beside the placid canal.

Would he appear on the morrow? Or, had he vanished from her life as if he'd never been?

The following morning, Dirk arrived once again at Jacob van Diemen's residence on the Prinsengracht, one of the principal canals curving like a U around the city. This time he paused at the bottom of the steps and let his gaze roam over the brick façade of the townhouse. On the previous day his attention had been elsewhere, and he had not given the house its proper attention.

The four-story canal house with its Corinthian pilasters and marble molding signaled the prosperity of a wealthy burgher. Although van Diemen had not achieved the prominence of a Herengracht address, the so-called "gentleman's canal" parallel to this one, the Prinsengracht was by no means a shabby locale. The very bricks of the houses fronting the canal proclaimed the security of solidly accumulated wealth.

Dirk grasped the limestone balustrade beneath his hand as he took the steps upward. He felt like an outsider laying siege to a mighty fortress. The rows of long, gleaming windows facing him hid their interiors behind sheer white lace. His lip curled, thinking how the thin barrier was a veil shielding the occupants within from the filth without. Catching his reflection in the shiny brass knocker, Dirk straightened and assumed a bland expression before rapping on the heavy walnut door.

"Hello, Marta." He smiled at the maid when she answered. By the wide look of her eyes, she still had not gotten over the accumulated shocks of yesterday.

She clutched the edges of her pristine white apron and dipped a curtsy. "Good day, mynheer."

"What's the matter, good maid? Didn't you think to see me around again?"

Marta opened her mouth, then closed it. "No, mynheer, I mean, yes, mynheer, no, that is—"

"No matter. Is your master prepared to see me today?"

"Oh, yes, mynheer! Please follow me." The kerchiefed girl entered the shadowy anteroom.

With a deep breath, Dirk stepped over the threshold.

Giving him no time to look around the entryway, the maid led him across the black and white marble lozenges of its floor and up a steep, carpeted staircase. With another curtsy, she left him in a side chamber at the top of the stairs.

His hands clasped behind his back, Dirk wandered the perimeter of the small room. He peered at the heavy Flemish tapestries depicting hunting scenes, which were dully illuminated by the scant sunlight filtering in through the lace curtains.

He walked past the half-dozen sturdy oaken chairs with

crimson leather seats and backs that lined one wall. A long table covered by a Persian carpet stood against another wall. Above it hung dark oil paintings framed in gilt.

The furnishings hadn't changed much since his mother's short sojourn in this house. From her descriptions, what Dirk had imagined as a boy was what he saw now in person for the first time—stately, elegant, and forbidding.

He stooped before a small, gold-framed painting and forced his thoughts to the forthcoming interview. He mustn't allow himself to become distracted with the past, not when a resolution was so near his grasp.

And a resolution which involved an unforeseen prize.

Francesca di Paolo.

He smiled, remembering her outrage at the fact of her own pennilessness. As if he needed protection from himself.

She didn't know him very well if she thought his decision irrational or mad. It was true, he hadn't planned upon entering into a betrothal so quickly when he'd walked up the steps yesterday.

At three-and-thirty, he had seen a variety of women, from the streets of Amsterdam to the jungles of Java. Francesco di Paolo, he concluded after a night and morning in her company, was a rare gem.

And the fact that a betrothal to her facilitated entry into Jacob's residence—well, that was an added benefit. Yes, indeed, once the details of the betrothal contract between Miss Francesca and himself were negotiated satisfactorily, Dirk didn't have any doubt but he would be a frequent visitor to van Diemen's house.

He turned from the painting and walked to the next.

It was time, moreover, that he wed and produced some offspring. He certainly had accumulated enough wealth in the Indies to be able to provide for a brood. Unlike him, they would be able to enjoy the fruits of their father's labor.

Up until that moment Dirk had never given marriage any serious thought. He'd been too busy trying to survive. His own mother had not had the benefit of this luxury. Which was why Dirk had been engulfed with pure, blind rage when he'd witnessed how Jacob intended to throw his ward into the street. The man had not changed since treating Dirk's mother in the same cavalier fashion so many years ago.

He turned at the sound of a low cough.

"If you please, mynheer, come with me."

He followed Marta down the corridor lined with trunks and more straight-backed chairs to a partially-opened door at the end. At the threshold the maid paused and announced Dirk's name.

"Bid him enter."

Dirk felt a queer sensation go through him at the sound of the peremptory tone. At long last, his moment had arrived.

Pulling his shoulders back, Dirk dismissed any doubts and entered the oak paneled room. A brief glance took in its burgundy and brown tones, from book-lined walls to a globe in one corner. He strode straight to the man seated behind a desk.

Jacob van Diemen continued writing, the scratching of his quill across the vellum the only sound in the room.

"Mynheer Jacob, I trust I am not inconveniencing you in any way," he said to the man's bowed head.

Van Diemen set down his pen and raised his head, then steepled his fingers beneath his chin before meeting Dirk's eyes.

For a moment, Dirk could only stare at the features that had been branded into his memory since boyhood. The features of the man who had sired him...and who knew nothing of his existence.

An altered face looked back at him. Dirk had to seek hard to find traces of that other, younger visage. But yes, the once-handsome features remained. A couple of deep lines creased the same high, wide forehead. Gray strands now diluted the swept back dark hair, which was secured into a queue at the nape. The straight nose had retained its autocratic slant. A closely-cropped moustache did not succeed in completely covering the two slashes on either side of his mouth, giving his bloodless lips a downward cast. A short, pointy beard covered his chin.

It was the dark, hooded eyes that drew the most recognition. They were as cold and haughty as he remembered the one time they had moved in his direction. Impassive, giving nothing away, they returned Dirk's look without blinking. Yet, there was also an emptiness in them now that Dirk did not remember. They conveyed a man with few illusions. The observation surprised Dirk. He had come expecting to see a self-satisfied individual who had everything Dirk until now had lacked.

Van Diemen made no overtures, as if waiting for Dirk to state his case.

Dirk had to fight the feeling of inadequacy and remind himself of his position. Likely he owned double what this man possessed.

Van Diemen held up a pale hand. "Before you begin, mynheer, I must warn you I agreed to see you merely to satisfy my curiosity. I can get no straight answer from my ward. She insists this betrothal is all a figment of my serving maid's imagination." He looked away, muttering, "She can be a pigheaded girl at times."

Van Diemen cleared his throat, before continuing in a measured cadence. "Since few men enter into a betrothal lightly, I ask you whether this is all indeed a figment of Marta's imagination, or is there some basis in fact?" His tone sounded almost bored.

So Miss Francesca intended to contradict Dirk at this early stage? He smiled, liking the fact that his shy bride-to-be had some spirit—and pride. "'Tis not very flattering to have one's intentions disavowed by one's future wife. Be that as it may, let me assure you, Mynheer Jacob, I fully intend to wed your ward."

Dirk rocked back on his heels. "I came here today to settle things to our mutual satisfaction as quickly as possible. As a man of business, I am sure you can understand my wish to bring this matter to a conclusion. I have little time for quibbling over a marriage contract."

Mynheer Jacob made a slight motion forward with his steepled fingers. "Please be seated, mynheer, and tell me exactly how you came to be with my ward yesterday."

Instead of taking the chair indicated, Dirk took a step towards its companion beside it and pulled it forward. "I made your ward's acquaintance in an abandoned farmhouse during that storm we had the night before last. She had been left there by a band of ruffians. Apart from being a bit chilled and frightened, she was otherwise unharmed and untouched." He stressed the last word.

Mynheer Jacob pursed his lips, and contining to regard Dirk under dark eyebrows. "Mynheer Dirk, do not expect me to believe Francesca was untouched, as you put it, by those thieves after what my servant reported to me. Do not think me so gullible. Before you waste your time and mine further in vain pursuits, let me state that I have made no provision for my ward's marriage." He eyed Dirk before proceeding. "Francesca has no marriage portion. Her father died a penniless foreigner."

Dirk clenched his hands over the chair's sturdy wooden arms. The penny-pinching blackguard! With all his guilders, he couldn't spare his own ward a decent marriage portion? Well, he would discover Dirk was no fortune hunter. His contempt for his enemy deepened.

"Mynheer Jacob," he replied smoothly. "Let me state my position. I am newly returned to Amsterdam after an absence of some years. What interests me is taking a wife. My time is limited, my acquaintances here few. Your ward struck me as a modest, well-mannered lass, with all the attributes to make a satisfactory wife."

When Mynheer Jacob would interrupt, Dirk held up a hand and leaned over the desk. "Furthermore, while I can vouch for Miss Francesca's virtue when I came to her aid the other night, I cannot do so now." He paused, letting the implications sink in. "I have offered for your ward's hand because it is the only honorable thing for me to do after spending the night in her company." With his words, Juffrouw Francesca's fate was sealed.

If his little sparrow thought she could upset Dirk's plans in any way on the grounds that nothing had occurred between them, he would show her he was one step ahead of her.

Mynheer Jacob sat up a fraction. "Am I to understand you have compromised my ward?"

"Whatever has transpired between Miss Francesca and myself is an accomplished fact. I have offered for her and am not interested in her financial status. I am interested in wedding her as soon as is permissible. I would not bring a bastard into this world." Dirk watched Jacob's reaction to the last words, but the man showed no signs that they meant anything to him. So, it had been too long to remember the event? Although he had expected no less, Dirk could not control the bitter gall that rose in his throat at the sudden, virulent hatred he felt for the man who had begotten him.

How little van Diemen realized how close Dirk was to grabbing him by the throat and extinguishing the life's breath from his miserable body.

"And your prospects?" Van Diemen's tone conveyed only skepticism.

"Excellent." Dirk sat back in his chair, prepared for the real negotiations to begin.

Mynheer Jacob arched an eyebrow.

"Excellent, because I speak of an accomplished fact. I sailed out to Batavia several years ago a penniless youth, and am come back to my native shores the owner of a spice plantation that brings me a healthy income. Furthermore, I am a shareholder in the East India Company and, as such, reap the profits of all the cargo coming in from the Far East."

Mynheer Jacob straightened in his chair a fraction. "You have documents to substantiate these claims, I presume?"

"Naturally. I shall have my solicitor send you all the

proper documentation. I, in turn, would like to be assured that the girl has no prior attachments, is of sound health, and, in short, that she will make a suitable wife." Dirk stifled a sigh. In truth, he wasn't overly concerned with Jacob's replies. What he had seen in Francesca had satisfied him, but he must maintain some semblance of the interested suitor for her guardian's benefit.

Mynheer Jacob reached toward a long, ivory-inlaid box and lifted its lid. From it he extracted his clay pipe and proceeded to fill it. "Francesca meets all the criteria." After lighting it from a taper and taking a puff, he spoke again. "Mynheer Dirk, however attractive your suit appears, I will only agree to a betrothal when I have received proof of your claims."

"That is understood." Dirk rose as he spoke and slapped his leather gloves against his palm. "You shall have your proof by the morrow. I, for my part, would be assured that Francesca continue under your roof until the wedding."

"If your claims prove truthful, Francesca is permitted to remain until that day." Jacob stood up from his desk, holding the pipe by its bowl. "Mynheer Dirk, I await your documents. If all proves satisfactory to my mind, I invite you to call on us, let us say a week hence in the mid-afternoon, to proceed with your suit." He bowed in dismissal.

Dirk stifled a sense of disappointment that he must wait so long to call on Francesca as her suitor. No matter, he'd manage to see her some other way before then. First, to allay van Diemen's fears. Now that he had met him, he had no wish to remain in the man's presence any longer than necessary. "Agreed then for Tuesday, a week."

Three

Francesca paced her room, wondering what was being transacted below stairs between her guardian and Mynheer Dirk at that very moment.

She stopped before the filmy lace curtain covering her window. Her room faced the courtyard in the back of the house. Bringing her palms up to her face, she cringed once more at the memory of her humiliation the day before.

How could she face Mynheer Dirk again?

How could so fine a gentleman offer for her just like that, having only known her for the space of a night?

Unbidden, a vision of Dirk's sleeping form rose up...his flushed cheeks, the way the first rays of the morning sun had bounced off his tousled locks. His face had been burnished, like a sailor's. Everything about him embodied raw strength and suppressed energy.

She shook her head, in vain trying to cast aside the images after his scornful words about her sketches. But his face and form refused to budge from her mind's eye.

She was only dwelling on his physique with an artist's eye, she told herself, ignoring the sensations swirling through her like the thick, creamy paints upon her palette.

What if he were serious? What if he did intend to marry her? What would it be like to be married to such a man as Dirk Vredeman?

Her hands fell to her sides as she tried to grasp the reality of it. She'd never imagined a suitor so strong and...larger than life. With no marriage portion she realized she would probably end a spinster, fetching and carrying for van Diemen's daughter, Lisbet, until she married. And then what? Where would Francesca go? Would she have to take care of her guardian in his old age? She chastised herself, knowing she must be grateful to him for having offered her a home after her father had died. She'd never be able to repay all that her father had cost Mynheer Jacob.

Sometimes she dreamed she would be able to sustain herself by painting. She and the old housekeeper, Katryn, would be able to buy a little farmhouse somewhere in the country.

But she knew it was only wishful thinking, indulged in when she was feeling particularly unhappy in her situation.

Her thoughts turned once again to what was transpiring in van Diemen's study. Marta had run up as soon as she'd ushered Mynheer Dirk to her guardian's office.

Francesca's rescuer had kept his word and appeared promptly at the appointed hour.

Perhaps he was only telling her guardian the truth about the previous night. But would Mynheer Jacob believe him?

But something about Mynheer Dirk's tone on the stoop yesterday belied a man who would take back his promise. I shall make everything right, he'd told her. Whatever it meant, he'd spoken with a self-assurance that Francesca envied.

If he did keep to his purpose—what then? She took a fistful of the lace curtain in her hand. It could only be out of pity. And that was worse than being branded by her guardian "used goods."

If only she had somewhere else to go. Her fingers twisted in the lacy material.

But she was penniless and without family. Her father, dear man that he was, had been no businessman and left her with nothing when he'd died. Only Mynheer Jacob's kindness as his business partner had kept her from the streets.

But in spite of his ruin, Papà had been dignified and gentlemanly to the end. He'd told her to respect Mynheer Jacob and repay the man's benevolence with her service.

Francesca let go of the curtain and knotted her hands together, unable to bear the thought of being rescued yet again, like some poor waif.

To shake away these thoughts, Francesca went over to her cabinet and pulled open a drawer. From it she took out the sheets of crumpled, soiled drawing paper and smoothed them anew beneath her palms. As she gazed at the quick sketches of Mynheer Dirk, she felt once again his golden-haired wrist when she'd tried in vain to wrest her drawings away from him.

He had belittled her attempts to capture his sleeping form. Now that her outrage had passed, the artist in her took over and judged the sketches critically. Had her hand accurately captured the qualities she had seen in his sleeping face in the dawn light?

Dissatisfaction assailed her. If only she'd had more time. If only she'd been able to draw his face awake—vibrant, animated, his gaze laced with amused irony. Something was missing in these sleeping images. He'd been right, the sketches were but a pale imitation of the man.

She pictured him at the stern of his ship, issuing commands. Forgetting everything else for the moment, she sat down and drew a fresh piece of paper towards her. Taking pen and ink, she began a sketch.

When she heard the church tower clock strike the quarter hour, she sat back, still not satisfied. She would really have to see her subject again firsthand. How else could she ever hope to render that mixture of vitality and repose? Remembering the color of Dirk's eyes when they had darkened with anger at the first sight of the sketches, Francesca wished she could do Dirk's portrait in oils. A rich mixture of browns and gold...

Virility. She shook her head as if to dispel the immodest word. 'Twas all her fault for dwelling on the idea of painting the man. This was one portrait 'twould best be forgotten!

Her thoughts returned to the meeting between her guardian and her would-be suitor. By now, it should be over.

What was to be her fate?

If only she had someone to confide in. She thought of Katryn, who'd been her closest friend and ally for the five years Francesca had spent under her guardian's roof.

But Katryn would only be overjoyed to hear of Francesca's good fortune in securing a wealthy husband. Marriages were arranged every day. Whether Francesca was in love with her suitor or not was hardly the point.

In love with a man like Dirk Vredeman? Francesca shook her head slowly, the notion was too farfetched. It was like the moon and sun—she the waxen globe beside the fiery orb. A man like that would likely soon tire of her pale glow—if not consume it in short order.

Francesca stood from her desk and collected the sketches. It would not do to have Lisbet snooping in her room and come across them.

If Francesca had no family to turn to, at least she did have one friend outside the house. She brightened at the thought of her former drawing master, Pieter. Although Mynheer Jacob had ended her lessons, Francesca managed to continue the friendship with the drawing master. A talented, though impoverished, young man, he hoped to gain success in Amsterdam at one of the ateliers of the well-known painters.

Whenever Pieter came to give Lisbet her drawing lessons, he managed to review Francesca's sketches secretly.

If Francesca walked to the market, perhaps she would see him. He frequently sat there to sketch scenes of everyday life among the hausfraus of the city.

Mayhap he could offer her some advice on her new sketches.

Having made her decision, Francesca hurried down the stairs to the basement to let Katryn know she was leaving.

Once in the kitchen, she took a reed basket from the hook on the wall.

"I'm running to the market, Katryn." Francesca knew she would not approve of her seeing Pieter. The housekeeper was suspicious of artists. "Do you need anything?"

"See if they have any nice strawberries," the older woman answered, looking up from peeling some onions. "I want to make a tart for dinner. Are you sure you want to leave before finding out how the gentleman fared with mynheer?" She smiled, setting down her knife. "If Marta is to be trusted, he is an imposing fellow, as handsome and rich as a prince."

Francesca swallowed and looked down, realizing she was running away rather than face the answer.

"How I've prayed for this day for you, for your own prince to come marching through that door upstairs and sweep you away. When Mynheer threatened to dismiss Marta and me if we let you into the house, goodness, how I prayed for some divine help." She wiped the corner of her eye with the back of her wrist. "There was no reasoning with mynheer that day." She sighed deeply. "But all's well now. Thank the good Lord for the deliverer He has sent you, Frannie dear."

For a moment, Francesca wanted to believe the fairy story Katryn painted. But then she remembered the circumstances. She shook the fantasy away. "This man is only offering for me out of pity. For all I know, he believes that awful tale Joost brought home!" She shuddered.

"Well, if he is pitying you, 'twouldn't be a bad thing. Too long you've been at Mynheer's beck and call. Time you had your own home."

Francesca turned away, knowing Katryn would never understand her pride. Bad enough she'd had to live under Mynheer Jacob's generosity for so many years, trying to repay her father's debt and the very food and clothing on her back by her service. She wouldn't trade one form of servitude for another.

As if reading her thoughts, the housekeeper said, "Your

notions are too high, my dear, that's always been your trouble." With a sigh, she picked up her knife and continued peeling the onions.

Francesca went to the door, hiding her disappointment. Her ideals—"notions"—were all she had left of Mamma and Papà. "I'm sure the two of them will come to some understanding that doesn't compel Mynheer Dirk to wed me. As I told you, it was all a great misunderstanding."

"That's not the way I heard it. Why to hear Marta, Mynheer Dirk was both very determined and very explicit. It didn't sound like a misunderstanding to me."

Francesca tightened her hold on the basket handle. "Well, I'm off."

She fumbled with the latch. Despite her careless words to Katryn, she was worried indeed about the outcome of the meeting between her guardian and her rescuer.

She hurried up the steps to the street and almost tripped at the sight of brown leather boots at the top.

A strong hand reached down to steady her. "Playing the efficient housekeeper, I see." The voice held an undercurrent of amusement. "I was wondering where you might be keeping yourself while your future was being decided."

⁂

Dirk planted his feet at the top of the steps and waited for his future bride to address him. Despite his cool demeanor, his heartbeat accelerated at the sight of her.

Her dark-fringed gray eyes widened at the sight of him.

Though her mass of hair was now tightly bound at her nape and covered by a clean white cap, her beauty struck him anew.

"Has it perhaps occurred to you, mynheer, that I don't wish having my future decided for me without my permission?"

Dirk chuckled. The asperity in Miss Francesca's tone was belied by the shy, downward gaze. She attempted to move around him without giving him a chance to reply. Dirk reached out and took hold of the handle of her basket.

"Has it occurred to you, Miss Francesca, that your future was taken out of your hands the moment you were abducted?"

He was surprised that the words brought a bright flush to her cheeks and a tug on her basket. "Excuse me, mynheer, I'm in a bit of a hurry today." Again, she made to move around him.

Refusing to be put off, he let her go but fell into step with her. "Then I shan't hold you up. Just tell me in which direction you are heading and I shall accompany you."

"That's not necessary. I—I'm going to the market—not at all the place a gentleman would be found, I'm sure."

He glanced sidelong at her, wondering what she would think if she knew of his less-than-gentlemanly origins. "I've learned to be at home in many realms."

She shot him a look but made no reply. Seeing she offered no more protest, he contented himself with walking by her side. The day was a glorious summer one, the trees lining the canal offering a dappled shade.

They reached the Westermarkt, a large plaza in the shadow of the new Westerkerk, its tall steeple easily soaring higher than any other landmark in the city. He tilted his head back to look at the imposing edifice, only the second Protestant church to be built in the city.

Amsterdam had grown much in his nineteen-year absence. The ornately decorated exterior of the red-brick and sandstone church was evidence of the growing wealth of the city's Protestant burghers since the townspeople had revolted from the Spanish empire.

"I only need to purchase a few things," his companion said. "You needn't stay with me."

Dirk turned his attention back to Miss Francesca. She was behaving as jumpy as a hare. He had assumed after their evening together of companionable conversation she would be at ease with him. Perhaps the thought of marriage threw her. She was, after all, a gently-brought-up young lady and would know little of marriage. Certain aspects of it, at any rate.

He knew little of gentlewomen. When he'd left Holland, even tavern wenches had been beyond his reach. The only women to give him a glance had been women of the street. And he wouldn't touch those.

Dirk looked down at his future bride, comparing her to those wretched women who plied their trade in back alleys. Miss Francesca certainly couldn't be more different in appearance. Despite her different coloring and petite stature, she was dressed in conformity with the housewives milling about them in the market square. In her severe black dress, starched white collar and apron, she looked like the most devout Reformist or a Mennonite lady of some means. Her hair—what little was visible from that skull-hugging linen cap—was tucked in so efficiently, Dirk could scarcely believe it to be the same springy mass he had seen unbound.

Dirk's years in the Indies had given him an appreciation for the small, finely hewn women of the Orient. They had also taught him to look at the minutest detail.

Against the bright afternoon sunlight, he noticed a rich coppery luster shining from what he had first taken to be dark ebony locks.

"'Tis a pity to hide your hair so."

She dropped the strawberry she was inspecting at a market stall and blinked up at him. "Excuse me, mynheer?"

He reached across her and picked up the fallen berry. Instead of placing it in her basket, his fingers turned it around absently, considering how best to broach the topic of their forthcoming marriage. He needed to allay her fears and reassure her that he would be a considerate husband.

But he'd never had experience courting a fine lady.

Pondering the question, he examined the plump fruit he still held. It was at the peak of ripeness. If he exerted the barest pressure, it would stain his forefinger and thumb with crimson juice. He handled it gently, leaving not even an imprint on its taut skin. His glance rose to Miss Francesca, realizing how fragile she, too, must be.

She was staring at the fruit in his hand. As if roused from a dream, she gave a quick shake of her head. "This is absurd, mynheer. Pray, what are you about?"

"At the moment, sampling the fruit." He smiled lazily, his eyes fixed on her lips, thinking how sweet they must taste. On sudden impulse, he brought the strawberry to her lips and gently popped it into her half-opened mouth, his forefinger touching her bottom lip. "Succulent, isn't it?"

In another second he would bend down and kiss her. But before he could move, she jumped back as if burned, her expression of shock almost comical.

"Easy there." He steadied her with a hand to her shoulder.

Dirk's jaw hardened when she removed a lace handkerchief from her apron pocket and began wiping at her mouth. Was he so distasteful to her? Any other maiden would be proud to have secured the betrothal to a wealthy, still-young man with all the appearance of a gentleman.

Miss Francesca turned back to her examination of the fruit. "I appreciate all you've done for me, truly I do. But this—this— farce has gone on long enough."

Gratitude would be too much to hope for, but he had been expecting something more than the officious young lady, who behaved as if she had no time for her suitor.

He tossed another berry into her basket. "This 'farce,' as you term it, is real indeed. If anyone is suffering from delusions, 'tis perhaps yourself." His men would have recognized his soft tone immediately and known he used it only when he was closest to anger.

She huffed. "I am not given to flights of fancy."

"I didn't think so." Dirk's finger once again came up to the corner of her lips, this time to wipe a drop of berry juice she had missed. "In fact I was counting on that wonderful self-possession you exhibited the other night to see you through until our marriage." He held her gaze, daring her to move away from his fingertip.

She remained motionless, though Dirk would wager it cost her a good degree of that self-possession.

"Such a rare thing to find such fortitude in a woman," he murmured, removing his finger at last. "Robbed, abducted, a night spent in company of a strange man, refused admittance into her own home. And yet you balk at a simple betrothal. Forgive me, but as a young, dowerless woman, as you yourself described, I would think the idea of marriage would have its advantages."

"Well, you thought wrong." Up came that little chin of hers.

As she fumbled through her pocket for money, Dirk tossed some coins to the vendor and took Francesca's basket from her.

She walked away at a rapid pace, scarcely giving the other stalls a glance. After a few minutes when he made it clear he wasn't going to leave her side, she addressed him without slowing her stride. "My reputation is of no consequence to you."

He lifted an eyebrow, forgetting his intention of begging her pardon. "Of no consequence? Rash words for a young lady. It could ruin all chances of any other suitable marriage for you."

"Since I don't intend to marry, 'tis of little importance to me."

"Not intend to marry?" She was full of strange notions. Dirk chuckled more deeply. "What will you do, continue to live on van Diemen's largesse? Or do you not recall that he barred his door to you?"

"That was a misunderstanding. You could tell my guardian th—that nothing happened the night of my abduction." She turned to him, a plea in her eyes. Any softer-hearted man would find it hard to resist.

He picked up a quince from another fruit stand. "I would gladly do so if I could vouchsafe it to be the truth."

"Wh-what do you mean?"

He turned the yellow fruit around in his hand. "I know not what transpired before I arrived at that farmhouse."

It took her a few seconds to understand his meaning. The plea in her eyes transformed to outrage, deepening their silvery hue to smoky gray. "How can you say that?" she whispered. "Nothing happened. You saw my bonds!"

He shrugged, laying the fruit back atop its pyramid. "Since I was not present earlier, I cannot attest with all certainty of your fate in those scoundrels' hands. I can only offer my protection in the form of marriage."

With a quick motion of dismissal, she turned from him and walked on. "It is all a misunderstanding. If you would only vouchsafe for me, all would be well. Mynheer Jacob has been good to me. He would accept me back if you but told him the truth."

He ignored her request, more intrigued than ever by her position in van Diemen's household. The man he'd known wasn't generous without exacting a price. "So good that he would take a stranger's word over your character and behavior of years?"

"I...I could have handled things on my own. You had no need to interfere. I was perfectly capable of explaining things."

She sounded more as if she were trying to convince herself than him. He shook his head in wonder. He'd never had such trouble trying to help a woman in need. Of course, he'd only ever helped street women. He had no experience with young ladies. Matters had been a vast deal simpler in the East. He tried another tack. "I've been told your guardian's daughter, Lisbet, was supposed to have been on that barge. Why wasn't she?"

She waved a hand as if at a loss. "I-she pleaded indisposition at the last moment and asked me to visit her aunt in her place. Lisbet d—doesn't like to visit her aunt."

"So, the dutiful ward obeyed. Just think, if you hadn't changed places with her, you wouldn't find yourself in your current predicament. Or would your guardian have barred his daughter's entry as well, without a chance to explain?"

"Of course not! Lisbet is his daughter."

"Of course," he echoed. "His only child."

Her pace slowed. "That is so." After a moment, she said, "Tell me, mynheer, do you always act so impetuously?" He was relieved to see her anger had cooled.

"Dirk, if you please. After all, we did spend an entire night together." Before she could get her hackles up, he continued. "Now, if you refer to our betrothal, inevitable would be a more apt description. When you get to know me better, you'll realize there are very few things I do without forethought."

"I can scarce believe that."

He looked at her profile, surprised at how he was enjoying the give and take of their conversation. "Francesca, why did you tell your guardian that our betrothal was all a figment of the maid's imagination?"

She shrugged, keeping her eyes straight in front of her as they walked. "I wanted to prepare him for when you didn't come back—"

Dirk pulled her to a stop. "Do you mean to say you didn't think I'd keep my appointment with your guardian?" he asked softly.

She did not reply, but he could see the answer in the gray eyes regarding him.

"Francesca, there is another thing you should know about me."

"What is that?" Her gaze hadn't wavered but her voice sounded breathless. Dirk felt as if they were standing all alone on the crowded street.

"Once I set a course for myself, there's very little that can dissuade me from pursuing it."

Their gazes held and for the first time Dirk understood the meaning of eternity. He could scarce remember what they had been talking about. The only important things were the proximity of her flawless skin and the awakening he read in her silvery eyes.

Before he could explore this discovery further, she looked down.

A second later, he felt a tug on the basket.

"Give me that, please! You look much too fine a gentleman to be carrying a market basket."

He eyed his bottle-green doublet with a chuckle. "Fine? That's an odd way of describing me." He was surprised when she giggled. He smiled back at her, intrigued by her sudden change in mood. In her distraction, she didn't realize their hands were still touching on the basket handle.

"You are a far cry from the sleep-rumpled figure of the other morn. Why, look at you, in your splendid doublet and hat with that luxurious ostrich plume. I would love to pai—" She bit her lower lip, her smile disappearing. Just as quickly, she removed her hand from the basket, apparently no longer worried whether he carried it or not.

Before he could ask her what she had been about to say, she was gone. Dirk allowed her to escape.

The next moment he frowned, as she hurried over to a dark-haired young man sitting before an easel at the edge of the market square. From the look of joy crossing her features, it was clear Francesca had already forgotten what had been on her mind.

※

With a sense of relief, Francesca spied Pieter at his usual spot. She'd almost blurted out to Mynheer Dirk her desire to paint him. Paint him! When she'd never attempted a full-fledged portrait of anyone, she would hardly begin with a man who had ridiculed her talent.

She forgot about Mynheer Dirk as Pieter looked up from his canvas and smiled. She had been so hoping to see him today.

The next moment her joy turned to worry as she remembered the presence of Mynheer Dirk. In her haste to escape him, she'd given no thought to the two men meeting. What could she tell Pieter?

"Good day, Francesca." Pieter sat back on his stool, laying aside his piece of charcoal. "Hello," he added, looking beyond her.

She knew that Mynheer Dirk had approached. She dared look behind her, then blinked at the fierce way he was eyeing her friend. "Mynheer Dirk, Pieter de Brune is— was—my drawing master. Lisbet's drawing master," she amended. Her smile faded. How was she going to explain Dirk to Pieter? "Mynheer Dirk is—"

"Francesca's future husband," Dirk filled in for her. Pieter gave him a startled glance, his gentle brown eyes wide.

She could feel Dirk looking at her, waiting for her reply and felt a shiver of fear. She gave Pieter a quick, nervous smile. "It's rather sudden—"

"But nevertheless true," Mynheer Dirk put in, giving her no chance to finish.

Surprise gave way to a smile on Pieter's lean face. "Congratulations!" With a hesitant look toward Mynheer Dirk, Pieter stood and leaned forward, giving Francesca a quick kiss on her cheek.

Francesca could feel her cheeks grow warm. A glance at Mynheer Dirk revealed a frown creasing his brow. Hastily, she steered the conversation away from the betrothal. "I wanted to ask your advice about some sketches."

His face grew somber. "Your guardian informed me that he no longer wishes my services. So, I wasn't sure when I'd be able to stop by your house again."

She gasped. "Pieter, no! Whatever happened?"

"I believe it has something to do with Miss Lisbet's going out in society more. Mynheer Jacob feels she will have no more time for drawing and painting. I'm sorry, truly sorry." His eyes were full of sympathy.

Francesca's shoulders slumped. What would she do without Pieter's encouragement?

"'Tis unthinkable you should stop your art." Pieter ran a hand through his shaggy brown hair. "If there is any way I can help—"

Francesca glanced at Mynheer Dirk, feeling more and more constrained in her conversation. He was looming over them, looking at them as if they were involved in a conspiracy. "P—perhaps I...I could come to the studio from time to time?" she asked.

Pieter nodded. "Of course. You said you had something new to show me?"

Suddenly afraid of showing her poor attempts to sketch Dirk, she debated. "There is an idea I have been working on—"

"Why don't you come by, let's see...Friday afternoon, sometime after two?"

She moistened her lips, still unsure. He would be able to tell her if there was any merit to the sketches she had done that morning. "Very well. Thank you."

"Ahem." They both looked at Dirk. "Where is this studio?"

"I don't actually have my own atelier." Pieter shrugged his thin shoulders and smiled. "Just a garret off Nieuwmarkt Square. I'm but a journeyman painter for Master Vondel."

Francesca frowned at Mynheer Dirk. "What is your interest in Pieter's studio?" Did he intend to prohibit her visit on the grounds that she was now betrothed to him? A claim she could still not fully believe...or accept.

"Mayhap he could show me some of his work. I believe an artist is always interested in making a sale?" He cocked an eyebrow at Pieter.

Remembering his ridicule of her sketches, Francesca couldn't help commenting, "I had quite forgotten your interest in art, Mynheer Dirk."

He turned his golden eyes to her. "Indeed? I am surprised. I recall I was quite in a passion over it the last time we met."

Francesca's own eyes widened. Could it be, or was he

making sport of himself?

Dirk turned back to Pieter. "Where did you say you had this garret?"

"On Kloveniers Quay, right off Nieuwmarkt Square. Stop in anytime." He stood and began to collect his things.

When Pieter had left, Francesca turned to find Dirk looking at her.

"What are you glowering at?"

"Nothing, merely observing." His arms were folded across his chest, market basket swinging gently, as he rocked back on his heels.

If the picture he painted had not been so incongruous, she would have been intimidated indeed.

⁂

Miss Lisbet van Diemen gave Dirk an assessing look. "What did you say your business was, Mynheer Dirk?"

Dirk sat back on the leather chair in the van Diemen salon and eyed his half-sister, finding little resemblance to himself. "I have various undertakings, Miss Lisbet. Ships, a plantation in the East, a few businesses here in your fair city, but at the moment I'm particularly occupied with trading on the stock exchange."

Van Diemen's daughter leaned forward on the velvet sofa, resting her chin on a plump, jeweled hand. "Indeed?"

Unlike Francesca, whom Dirk had only seen dressed in black, Lisbet wore a silvery-blue brocade gown, feminine in the extreme. Her coloring was also a contrast to Francesca's, her hair a dark golden blond to Francesca's ebony. Pearl earrings dangled from her earlobes and two long strands of pearls were looped about her pale neck. Clearly, van Diemen lavished his wealth upon his only child.

Miss Lisbet smiled at him. "I've heard it said that it takes a gamester's spirit to play the beurs."

Dirk gave a mirthless smile, remembering the mixture of anticipation and hunger in Lisbet's eyes when he had been introduced to her on this, his first social visit to his betrothed's home.

His glance traveled to the other end of the dim room, which let in very little of the sunshine from outside, and paused at Francesca's kerchiefed head bowed over a piece of embroidery. She sat at an elaborately carved window seat, catching the scant ray of light, which pierced the crack in the lace curtains.

Ever since his walk with her to the market, Dirk had been counting the hours since seeing her again. Unfortunately, first he had to go through the motions of this social visit with the van Diemens. After all, the real reason for his return to Amsterdam lay in this very room. He must never let his focus shift from his avowed purpose.

Setting aside his anticipation of sparring once again with his intended, Dirk turned his attention back to van Diemen, who sat beside his daughter on the couch. He was busy filling his clay pipe with some shag and tamping it down with his thumb. He replaced the lid on his tobacco box before settling back in his seat and addressing Dirk.

"You are a gaming man, mynheer?" His tone expressed disapproval.

"Without risk there is no profit." Dirk stretched his legs out before him, attempting to make himself at ease in Mynheer Jacob's ornate salon. No matter that he was more at home in the familiar surroundings of tavern, sailing ship, or Javanese plantation, his life was now in Amsterdam. If it meant playing the part of a wealthy burgher, so be it. He met van Diemen's stare. "The challenge is to minimize the risks without diminishing the profit when buying and selling shares."

"I have done well for myself and my family without courting Mistress Fate on the exchange. Look around you." Mynheer Jacob jabbed the air with his long thin pipe. "I have insured my daughter's future step by step. Oh, I know what many say about me." He gave a dry bark of laughter.

"Plodding Jacob. But you know the saying...little drops of water the ocean make."

"Indeed." Dirk's gaze roamed around the room's carved wooden cupboards, thick Persian carpets, and gilt-framed paintings with just the right measure of admiration and appraisal. "You seem to have done well enough, I grant you." He paused before giving a careless shrug as if to say "if that is all you aspire to."

"To each man his method," he continued, his gaze assessing van Diemen. "I, too, know well the merit of toil from my years in the East. I find, however, that once a certain wealth has been attained, a greater challenge is to be found in the calculated risk."

Once again he gave Jacob a moment to absorb the subtle challenge he was throwing him before resuming, "To attain significant wealth, to be a power to be reckoned with in the city, requires more than toil."

Dirk hid a smile of satisfaction at the intent look in Van Diemen's eye. Dirk glanced from father to daughter. Curiosity mingled with outright admiration was evident in Miss Lisbet's blue eyes. He would not want to lay odds on Mynheer Jacob's daughter being still chaste.

"Howbeit, many an overly ambitious man have lost all speculating on the stock exchange." Mynheer Jacob would not let himself be drawn in so easily. He must first struggle a bit on the line. But oh, he wanted to know more. Dirk could see it from the wary look that sought to hide the desire to own more. Dirk recognized the look. He saw it every day in the shrewd merchants he traded with—and more often than not—bested.

He dismissed the losers with a flick of a finger upon the sleeve of his royal blue doublet. "Ignorant novices who rush in ill-informed." He leaned toward his prey. "The real trick is to predict the future worth of a commodity, be it peppercorns or dyewood, months before it reaches port. There you have the potential for great gain."

Van Diemen took a puff on his pipe. "Yes...I've heard there are quite some profits to be made while the ships are en route. It does nothing but create a lot of speculation."

Dirk let his gaze roam to Francesca, who had let her embroidery drop to her knee, and now studied each man's face. Did she sense more between her guardian and him than mere talk of speculation? He mustn't be too obvious. Patience.

He nodded to van Diemen as if considering his words. "There are many factors affecting the outcome...the state's negotiations with the Portuguese, our fight with the Spanish, the pesky English privateers seeking to waylay our ships...a hundred and one vagaries upon the seas."

He settled back in the chair, beginning to enjoy himself the way he always did when driving a hard bargain. "Take the last fleet that arrived from Batavia. I had an interest in a shipment of nutmeg. Long before it was due in port, the cargo had been bought and sold a dozen times. The price increased moderately with each transaction. Suddenly, there was a rumor of trouble with the Portuguese off the Malabar Coast and danger that our fleet would be a target of their cannons. When word came that our convoy had been attacked, the price dropped to the floor."

He could feel the tension in the room. Lisbet's lips parted. Even Francesca's gaze was riveted on him.

"And you lost a pretty packet, I'll be bound," Jacob interrupted with morbid satisfaction.

"Quite the contrary."

"Pray, continue." Jacob made a gesture of impatience with his pipe.

"Speculation began anew as merchants feared a shortage of nutmeg." Dirk's lip curled upward, feeling like a master Javanese shadow puppeteer unfolding a tale. "The ships arrived in port safe and sound. From the time the panic began to the arrival of the cargo in Amsterdam harbor, the price quadrupled."

"And was the profit worth the risk?" Francesca spoke up for the first time since her initial greeting.

Jacob frowned at the interruption but Dirk's smile in her direction caused her guardian to smooth his features and say nothing.

Dirk fingered his beard, drawing out the drama. "With the profits I realized on that cargo I purchased a villa by the sea."

Amidst Lisbet's gasp and the jerk of van Diemen's pipe in mid-puff, Dirk's smile deepened. "I was planning to hold our nuptials there. That is, if Mynheer Jacob hasn't set his heart on holding the ceremony here at his canal house." He flicked a glance about the room before returning his attention to Francesca.

A delicate flush covered her cheeks before she looked down at her embroidery again. He let his gaze linger on her. For all Lisbet's finery, Francesca was ten times the beauty, as delicate as the silk threads being pulled through the burlap on her lap. Yet, like silk strands, Francesca was also proving strong and resilient.

"And if you hadn't been so lucky?" Mynheer Jacob's dubious tones interrupted him. Dirk hid a smile at the man's sour expression, like one who'd just been required to swallow a particularly bitter portion of gall.

Dirk chuckled with just the right measure of scorn. "I put little reliance on luck. Everything depends on your knowledge of the cargo and your information en route."

"Just how do you obtain your information?" van Diemen asked, his attention fixed on his pipe, as if he didn't really care about the answer.

Oh, I think you do, Dirk told him silently. "I have a network of reliable informants at various ports, so I am usually in a good position to calculate the time of arrival and condition of the shipment here in Amsterdam. I had received word of the safety of this particular fleet well before it arrived in Amsterdam."

The other man pursed his lips around his pipe and puffed before replying. "There are so many uncertainties. It is impossible to know of everything that can befall a shipment."

Dirk acknowledged the truth of this with a bow of his head. "I also keep informed of political and military maneuvers through the courants that are published here."

Mynheer Jacob continued puffing on his pipe. Finally, he set it down on a ceramic dish of Delftware. "By everything I've heard, it's an unsavory business at best with these...what do you call them, punters, running about risking other people's money."

Dirk dismissed them with a hand. "Those are for the small investors, who can hardly afford a share of stock. I have my own broker who has a seat on the exchange. I tell him when to buy and sell."

"It's a game of chasing the wind as far as I'm concerned," the older man insisted.

"Trading in blanco, you mean?" Dirk rubbed his hands together as he sat forward, ready to administer the coup de grace. "That's where the real profits are to be made, on paper. One needn't put up any money at all. All it takes is perceived demand for something.

"Take this tea." He gestured toward the porcelain jar he had brought them as a gift. It was filled with an aromatic blend of dried leaves. "It's an Oriental beverage. 'Tis only drunk by the more well-to-do and adventurous here in the Provinces, but wait." His slow smile traveled around the room. "Wait and see what happens over the next few years. Maybe it will take a decade, but before long it will be drunk by everyone, the way coffee has caught on. The trick is to create the demand. Those who take the risk now stand to make a fortune."

Lisbet looked enthralled as she took the jar in her hands and removed the lid, sniffing at its contents. "I am very fond of coffee, but this smells nothing like it."

Van Diemen's eyes narrowed at the jar as if it held some suspicious witch's potion.

"But look what happened to those buying tulip bulbs," Francesca said. "So many people ruined."

Dirk was impressed by her knowledge of the market. He shrugged. "Fools. You have to know when to sell."

"Francesca! See to our guest." Van Diemen motioned toward the refreshments.

"Of course, mynheer."

Dirk frowned as Francesca laid down her embroidery and hurried toward the table. He would have to put a stop to that servitude soon enough.

As he took a second helping of the candied ginger cake Francesca held out to him on a platter, Dirk could see van Diemen's interest grow in the idea of profits to be made on paper. His host's manner remained critical, but he continued questioning him closely. By the time Dirk got up to leave, he went so far as to invite him to accompany them to church on Sunday.

Dirk lingered over Francesca's hand in farewell. He would have to find another time to be alone in her company.

He frowned, remembering her promise to visit the painter. He didn't like the idea of his betrothed visiting a handsome young painter's atelier unaccompanied.

Even if he did look poor and underfed, hadn't he put a sparkle in Francesca's eye when she'd spoken to him? Sufficient reason for Dirk to find out just who this man was to his future wife.

Four

Francesca strode over the cobblestones of Nieuwmarkt Square toward St. Anthony's Gate. As the city had expanded and the old walls torn down, the ancient gatehouse had been transformed into a weigh house and surgeon's guild. Now, the tall turreted brick building with its conical slate roofs stood over the bustling market square as if surveying it with a jaded air, like one who has seen it all.

Each excursion into this quarter of the city fascinated Francesca. The canals and crooked alleys held all the richness and freedom her own life lacked. Her forthcoming marriage was a good example, she thought with a resurgence of frustration. Mynheer Jacob had informed her only yesterday that the betrothal agreement had been signed. A marriage was as good as performed. Only the direst circumstances could extricate an individual from a betrothal contract.

Francesca scanned the crowds around her. Every time she spied a tall blond gentleman, she stopped, her breath held—whether in fear or anticipation—she hardly knew herself. But then she realized the man was not tall enough or broad-shouldered enough to be Mynheer Dirk.

The way he'd questioned Pieter so closely about his lodgings had made her fear he would dog her footsteps again this afternoon on her way to her appointment with Pieter.

She resumed her steps, breathing deeply of the scent of warm bread emanating from the Jewish bake shops around her. She eyed the market stalls, where all manner of goods were sold, including used clothing and braying and bleating animals.

But what enthralled Francesca most in the quarter were the painters' and engravers' studios. On this very street Master Rembrandt had his atelier. Along many of the narrow side streets and alleys, owners let rooms out to apprentice painters.

Pieter lived on one of these side streets fronting a smaller canal, in one of the tall brick houses topped with the distinctive step-and-bell gables that formed a gingerbread pattern against the sky.

With a last look over her shoulder toward the shadows cast by the row of houses fronting both sides of the canal, she knocked on the door, annoyed with herself that she was behaving as if she had something to hide.

Yet...she did. If Mynheer Jacob were to know she had visited the drawing master's lodgings—this after that awful misconstrued abduction—what would he do to her? Would betrothal to Mynheer Dirk be enough? Would Mynheer Dirk still want her? Would he decide she was indeed too tainted to marry?

However much she disliked the notion of having been forced into a betrothal under the false assumption that she had been violated by those vile abductors, what would her life be like now without Mynheer's Dirk's protection?

Before she could pursue this thought, a dour-looking woman with salt-and-pepper hair under a gray cap opened the door. With a glance at the portfolio under Francesca's arm, the woman nodded toward the dim staircase behind her. "Looking for the painter?"

"Yes, mevrouw," Francesca said meekly.

"Top floor."

The narrow staircase became darker and steeper the higher Francesca climbed. Pieter's rooms were in what should have been the attic, where stores of grain could be hauled up from the canal below by a large hook suspended from the gable. The stairs ended in a trap door which stood open.

"Hello! Pieter, are you home?" she called out as she climbed the final steps and peered over the edge of the opening in the floor.

Pieter turned from his easel by the window.

"Francesca." His gentle smile, though welcoming, was always tinged with a certain melancholy. He rose and came toward her, giving her a hand up the last steps.

She looked around as she caught her breath. She had never been to an artist's studio before. Naked rafters came down on either side of the room. What kept the space feeling airy was the large open window at the front end and the marked absence of all but the most necessary furnishings. The steeply-pitched roof rose over her head and a smooth wooden plank floor was swept clean. The only clutter was stacked canvasses, jars of paints and brushes, and piles of books and engravings against the eaves.

"Don't let me disturb you," she began but he waved away her concerns.

"If you can wait a few moments, I shall continue working a bit longer." He turned back to his easel as he spoke. "I want to finish while the light is right."

"Yes, please do so. I shall be content to wait as long as you need." Francesca trod softly on the planks to stand behind him.

He'd arranged a still life on a table beside his easel. A crystal roemer of pale wine stood on a starched white napkin. Beside it sat a round loaf of bread that had a couple of pieces broken off at one end. On a pewter plate lay three opened oysters in their gray shells flanked by a lemon, its bright yellow peel falling in a spiral off the plate onto the white damask cloth. On closer inspection Francesca noticed the bread was moldy.

"I suppose you must finish it before your shellfish goes off."

Pieter laughed. "That's all part of the effect, the surfeit of our wealth, decaying before our very eyes."

"Ah, yes, the transience of life and the worthlessness of earthly treasures," she quoted a line she'd read about a recent artist's work.

"Something like that," he murmured, his smile lingering. "Is it too obvious?"

The smile left her face as she studied his work in progress with care. "Nay. What I see are exquisite objects. I see the fine cut of the goblet's crystal and I can almost taste the oysters."

"Good," he replied, then stuck a brush between his teeth in order to pick up another. He dabbed at the image of the wine glass with some white paint to create the reflection of light against its surface.

Francesca kept her eyes on his work a few minutes longer. Then, not wishing to disturb him, she gazed about the atelier. To her, it was like a glimpse of heaven. She felt she should tiptoe around. Even the air around her was part of the wonder of creation. This was where a real artist worked. It made her own efforts seem amateurish.

She walked to some stretched canvasses stacked along the wall and flipped through them. Whereas she preferred the human form, Pieter's specialty was landscapes. She saw farm fields and canal scenes in winter and summer. Pieter's was a wide-ranging talent. He had done still lifes, portraits, histories, and religious subjects. Many were unfinished. She knew most of his time was spent working on Master Vondel's canvasses. Between that and his private lessons he had little time for his own work.

She paused at a painting of a young raven-haired woman rising from a cupboard bed, the effects of sleep still evident in her flushed cheeks and tousled locks. A soldier's cloak hung at one end of the bed.

Francesca knew from the conventions of the day that the viewer was intended to be her lover. Already having risen and dressed, he stood ready to depart, taking one last look at his mistress's nakedness. No hint of shame clouded the subject's features as she looked boldly at the viewer.

Francesca swallowed, suddenly thinking of Mynheer Dirk. Would he look at her like that on their wedding night?

For the first time, the reality of the physical intimacies of her upcoming nuptials sank in. Soon, this strange and fearsome man would stand before her and she would be completely at his mercy.

Before she could examine her own feelings, Pieter sat back with a loud sigh and she jumped, half-believing he had read her thoughts.

"I can do no more on it today," he said, turning to her, appearing not to have noticed her reaction. "Now then! Let's have a look at what you have brought me." Without waiting for Francesca, he reached over and took the portfolio she had carried with her and laid against a chair.

"Wait, I've arranged some—" Francesca flew to his side, suddenly regretting her decision to bring those sketches of Mynheer Dirk. Thankfully, she had brought other sketches as well.

But when she arrived at Pieter's side, she saw that he had already found her crumpled sketches as well as the more recent ones she'd done of her intended.

She stood at Pieter's elbow, holding her breath, as he studied each sketch for what seemed a very long time.

When he said nothing, but carefully set aside each one, she finally spoke. "They're only rough sketches as you can see—"

Finally, he looked up. "I like them." He nodded, smiling up at her. "You've captured a wonderful mixture of qualities: strength, dominance, and yet he looks as gentle as a lamb."

Francesca returned the smile, experiencing a joy such as she'd never felt before in her drawing. To have an expert declare that she had succeeded in portraying what she had wished to in a few simple sketches—that made everything else bearable. "He'd be a wonderful subject for a portrait, wouldn't he?" she asked softly, almost afraid of voicing the thought that had been playing in her mind since she'd first met Mynheer Dirk.

Pieter looked back down at the sketches. "Indeed he would."

Encouraged, Francesca's voice quickened in enthusiasm. "I'd been contemplating a pen-and-ink drawing of the subject awake, but I'm afraid he would never countenance posing for me again. As you can see, I caught him unawares. Those others are purely from memory."

Pieter grinned back at her. "I did hesitate to ask you how you found your subject." He snapped his fingers. "Isn't this the gentleman who accompanied you—your betrothed?" he added as if just remembering.

At her reluctant nod, he continued. "I thought he looked familiar. So, he knows of your aspirations to paint?"

She turned away. "I'm not sure about that. He certainly didn't appreciate my efforts at the time."

"Didn't he like these?"

"Not a whit. In fact, he quite disagreed about my having any talent."

Pieter quirked an eyebrow. "Is that so? I can't imagine anyone thinking that. Don't worry, the man likely knows nothing about art. Many people are uncomfortable when posing and then seek to criticize the artist for what they perceive as not doing them justice."

"That is true enough." She folded her arms and gave a decided nod to her head. "Have no fear, his opinion is the least one I'm concerned with." But was that true?

Pieter gave her a sharp glance before shuffling her sketches into a stack. "You should really continue your lessons."

"Alas, 'tis not possible. I couldn't pay for lessons on my own, and my guardian no longer wishes to. I shall continue sketching, never fear." Her glance shifted away. "I...I would be grateful for any advice you could give me from time to time."

"I'd enjoy helping you. You've got a talent that needs to be developed. 'Tis a shame you can't afford the apprentice fees, or I would try to get you into Vondel's studio with me. I wonder..." He tapped a finger against his lips as he gazed down at a still life she had done of flowers in a vase, which now rested on the top of the stack. "He might consider lowering the fee if I showed him some of your work."

"You are a dear man to try, but I am afraid even that wouldn't help." She smiled at him sadly. "You see, I haven't even a stuiver to call my own. Besides, you forget, I'm soon to be wed. I can hardly imagine Mynheer Dirk consenting to my becoming an apprentice."

Pieter laughed. "No, I should hardly think so." He sat in thought a moment before turning back to her, a light in his eye. "I know! You can come here and receive lessons from me. Private lessons! At least until you are wed and your great bear of a husband doesn't let you out of his sight."

The image gave her a shiver.

"And your lessons shall be for nothing." He held up a hand before she could object. "After all, I'm not a master painter yet, only a journeyman." He pointed a brush at her with a smile. "Someday, though, I shall have my own studio with dozens of apprentices. Consider yourself my first."

"With this," Francesca waved an arm over his room, "your first studio."

"Done." They clasped hands.

Dirk released an impatient breath when he finally spotted Francesca leaving de Brune's lodgings. How long did it take a person to consult over a few drawings? She'd been up there long enough to paint a dozen pictures. His future wife had a strange idea of propriety, he fumed for the countless time, going up to a man's rooms, never mind that the man looked about as harmless as a peahen.

He'd kept silent when she and de Brune had brazenly cooked up this scheme, standing there in front of him as if he were some brutish lout, who didn't know what a paintbrush was. He'd been foolish not to lay down the law right then and there. Probably from some silly notion of not wanting to offend his fragile-looking bride-to-be.

But for all her timidity and reserve, Francesca was proving to have a streak of independence as wide as a ship's beam.

He cleared his throat and stepped from the shadow of the alley when she walked by without seeing him.

She jumped in fright. "Oh, there you are!"

"You sound as if you were expecting me."

She looked away. "I did. That is, I didn't see you—I mean, of course not!"

"As a matter of fact, I've been waiting for you for some time." He indicated the large portfolio she carried under her arm with a jut of his chin. "Your sketches?"

"Yes." She seemed nervous, and it only increased his own suspicions over her time spent alone with the painter.

"May I?"

"What?" Her glance shot up to his. "Here? No."

He finally understood that she thought he had asked to see her portfolio. "I meant, may I carry it for you?"

"Oh." She didn't meet his gaze. "I—if you'd like."

He took the leather case from under her arm and they walked along the narrow street until they came back out to the Kloveniers Quay. He took her elbow and guided her over a canal bridge. The sun sparkled on the dark water. Barges and canal boats lined the quay.

Midway across the bridge he paused at a parapet. "Are you in a rush to return home?"

"I should get back to help Katryn."

"I shall have to speak to your guardian about lessening your kitchen duties now that you are betrothed to me."

"You needn't. I enjoy helping Katryn. She has been good to me."

He stared at her a moment before saying, "Very well, as long as your household duties do not take away time with me."

They stared at one another a long moment before she

jerked her head in what he took to be assent.

"Good." He turned his back on the bridge traffic and looked out at the water. "You said you were expecting me. What did you mean by that?"

"I—" She took a deep breath and began again. "The way you were questioning Pieter the other day at the market made me think you meant to present yourself at his atelier today—when I had my appointment with him." She lifted her chin, her gray eyes meeting his with a touch of defiance. "As if you meant to stop me."

"Why should I stop you? I am not your guardian to put an end to your lessons if that is where your talents lie. I merely wished to know where my future wife was spending her time, especially if she was doing so in the company of another man."

"You mean you thought Pieter and I—? But Pieter is my drawing master. There is nothing unseemly in visiting his studio." She shook her head as if the idea were preposterous.

He was somewhat reassured but not completely convinced. "I may have been absent from Amsterdam for some years, but I do not think so much has changed in that regard. A young lady going to visit a young man in his lodgings?" He shook his head. "No. And when the lady is betrothed to another, it is not seemly at all."

"You will recall, mynheer, this betrothal was no idea of mine. And according to my guardian, I am so fallen from grace as to be beyond redemption. So you must forgive me if I go about my business not taking your sensibilities into account."

He liked her spirit. "In spite of her past record, I do expect my future wife to behave herself with decorum."

Her nostrils flared. "So, you do think me disgraced! Does that mean you expect I shall behave like a harlot? I am a God-fearing woman, mynheer, not some lost creature who plies her trade by the water's edge."

The words hit him like a jab right above his gut. He shook his head. She could not possibly know that he was a bastard son of such a woman or that he was the last person who could expect a chaste bride. With a sigh he looked away from her. "Be thankful nothing worse happened to you during your abduction than an uncomfortable night spent on the floor. Despite your scorn of those women on the shore, you little realize what the loss of your virtue means."

"So, you do believe I remained untouched the day of my abduction?"

Was his opinion so important to her? He found his anger and uncertainties disappearing. "Yes." He could give her no more than that, for fear he would give his own role in her abduction away. He smiled ruefully. "What is perhaps more surprising is that nothing happened afterwards."

He watched her initial relief turn to incomprehension. He explained, "You spent the night in the company of a man who finds you very beautiful."

At once, her gaze slid away from his.

He brought her regard back to his with a nudge of his fingertip to her cheek. It was as soft and delicate as a peach.

His fingers strayed to her chin, anchoring it between thumb and forefinger, enjoying for the moment the pleasure of touching her and watching her shy reaction. "Do you realize how tempting you are to a man, Francesca di Paolo?"

Her inky black lashes fluttered downward. "What nonsense you speak, mynheer." But her voice was unsteady.

"I thought I asked you to call me by my given name."

She made no reply and continued looking down. Dirk noticed once again the coppery sheen to her tightly bound hair, the few strands he could see peeking from beneath her snowy white cap. "You call yourself a painter. Haven't you ever taken a look at yourself in the glass?"

She held her face stubbornly down. He could force her chin up, but he preferred she do so of her own volition.

"The marriage contract states you are five-and-twenty," he continued. "It only shows you haven't experienced the least things you want to paint."

At the mention of her painting, her eyes flashed up at

him. "What do you know of painting?"

He chuckled and let her go. It all came back to her painting. With another sigh, he rested his forearms against the parapet overlooking the busy canal. At the end of it stood the imposing St. Anthony's Gate above the wide market square.

Though it wasn't visible from where he stood, he knew beyond the square lay another canal, one that led to his world.

Abruptly, he turned to her. "What you need is a day at the sea."

"The sea? Why to the sea?"

"Why not?" Suppressing his disappointment at her lack of enthusiasm—unlike the eagerness she'd shown her sketching master—he straightened from the parapet. "Forgive my lack of eloquence in delivering my invitation. If I were a sensitive lad like Pieter the painter, I should no doubt know how to word my invitation. But alas, I'm a rude and unpolished man with no talents in the finer arts. Instead, I must be direct in my speech. Though it ofttimes offends sensitive natures. Those whose complexion cannot hide their reactions." He touched her cheek again.

When she made not reply but only moved away a fraction and held her gaze stubbornly away from him, he suppressed a chuckle. "Permit me to reword my invitation to the seaside. I should like to spend a day at the seaside with you so that I might unbind your hair and see for myself what the sunlight does when it bounces off your tresses. So I may judge for myself if your eyes truly are the color of the North Sea." He cocked his head to one side, narrowing his eyes. "Although I would probably have to wait for a stormy day to properly reflect the color I see there now."

"Y-you speak like a painter."

He smiled. "So, what say you to my invitation to the seashore?"

Her lips curled upward in an unwilling smile. "Perchance if I'm abducted once more."

He quirked an eyebrow upward. Was she jesting with him? Abduction. The idea was tempting. To be alone with her on the sand dunes along the coast. "Many know better than to challenge me, dear lady."

Instead of replying, she frowned. "I am relieved, mynheer, that you did believe my story all along. What I fail to understand is why you did not tell my guardian this."

"Do you?"

"From what Mynheer Jacob has said, you appear to be a gentleman of some means. You could have any bride in the city. Why should you wish to wed me?" She gave a small laugh. "I've heard the Bickers have a marriageable daughter, if it's a wife you seek. She is quite pretty by all accounts."

The significance of the name was not lost on Dirk, who knew the Bickers were one of the most important families in the city. "Why should I want someone else's money when I have my own?"

Her eyes widened. "That is a novel idea from a man of wealth and importance. Marriage in your class is meant to increase and consolidate your fortune."

He gave a grunt of amusement. "What class do you think I come from?"

She waved a hand. "Why, of Mynheer Jacob's, the Bickers..."

He decided to test her. "Everything I am I learned on the streets of Amsterdam or as a deckhand aboard ship." He rocked back on his heels, watching her reaction.

She smiled gently. "Nothing from your own mother or father?"

He turned away from her and looked at the pinpoints of sunlight bouncing off the canal below. Maidenly shock or a tactful change of subject, he had expected, but not that deceptively simple question. So simple it cut right to the heart.

He searched for words, not knowing how he would answer until he heard himself saying, "Unlike you, I had no loving father. My mother was ill for as long as I had her.

I'm the one who needed to look after her. I didn't do a very good job of it," he ended, picturing the gaunt, stringy-haired woman coughing up blood on her dirty pallet, as he knelt helpless beside her.

"I'm sorry."

He dismissed her softly-uttered sympathy with a shake of his head. "It happened a long time ago."

"Yet you carry it with you still."

Drawn by her soft words, he studied her profile as she stared at the murky canal below, and felt suspended between simple enjoyment of her beauty and the quiet echo her words wrought in him.

Beautiful, modest—and fiery only where her art was concerned, the woman before him aroused his curiosity and wonder.

What conceit had he to claim her? As he'd confessed, his origins were nothing. Yet his words had not shocked her at all. Did she pity him?

He didn't want her pity.

He wanted her passion. The passion he had glimpsed when she spoke of her art.

"Come," he said at last with deep sigh of regret that he couldn't prolong their time together. "I shall accompany you home."

Francesca opened her shutters and breathed in the early morning air. She could see by the still, gray, cloudless sky that it promised to be another glorious day of early summer.

Leaning over the sill, she let her eyes wander over the shadowy geometrical shapes of the garden below. The box hedge had been clipped in straight lines and curves, spheres and circles, and its white gravel paths shone starkly in the gray light. Enclosed within the neat borders of the hedge, Francesca could just discern the reds and pinks of the rosebushes.

She must not dawdle. There was too much to do before

the morning service. Although the Sabbath was a day of rest, any work frowned upon by the church, someone had to see to the family's needs. In Mynheer Jacob's household, this fell to Francesca and whichever maid did not have the day free.

Francesca turned to her washstand and poured cold water from her pitcher into a large porcelain washbowl. After a quick but thorough wash, she took clean linen from a cupboard and grabbed her black velvet overskirt and bodice from their hook. Quickly, she donned chemise, petticoats, and underskirt then laced up the dark bodice over her white chemise. Lastly, she put on the black skirt and selected a plain square collar from several starched and folded ones in the cupboard. Over everything she tied a large white apron.

She moved toward the glass to comb her hair. Her fingers unfurled the two long braids with the nimble ease of years' practice, and her comb glided through the unraveled locks. As she gathered them up into her customary knot, she paused an instant, Mynheer Dirk's words coming back to her.

He was right. She had never studied her face as an artist, preferring to look at those around her, especially at strangers, as she attempted to discern what lay beneath the surface and made them frown or smile or pout.

She stared now at the two solemn eyes reflected in the glass. Was it because she didn't want to probe behind her unsmiling face?

Mynheer Dirk had called her beautiful. The word sounded foreign to her. Her skin was pale, framed by a cloud of hair billowing out around her. She took some in her hand, feeling its springy softness, wondering what it would feel like to someone else. No, she corrected, what would it feel like in Mynheer Dirk's hand?

She felt again his fingertip upon her cheek. He seemed to touch her at every opportunity. Did he like the feel of her so much? Ever since she'd moved to the van Diemen household five years ago, she'd grown used to the lack of physical contact.

Both her father and mother had lavished much affection on their only daughter.

Not until Mynheer Dirk had come into her life, had she felt so...special. Why did she pull back, not trusting his affection?

What would it be like to allow the real Francesca to respond, instead of the unfeeling, waxen image molded by her years in Mynheer Jacob's household?

Was she afraid it would all prove to be an illusion?

She had not been jesting when she'd mentioned the Bickers' daughter to Dirk. She was the kind of young woman a man of his position would normally aim for.

She frowned, remembering Mynheer Dirk's words of his poor beginnings. They had shocked her of course, and she hoped she had successfully masked that. The words had made her see him in a different light.

Did he perhaps feel he wasn't worthy of a young lady like Juffrouw de Bicker?

But his past no longer mattered. If Mynheer Jacob had approved of him, then surely his wealth and demeanor were all any family would look for.

Was that why he chose her instead—impoverished orphan dependent on Mynheer Jacob? Did Mynheer Dirk feel more comfortable with a woman of her lowly position?

It explained his desire to have her for his wife more satisfactorily to her. But it didn't make her feel any better.

What would it be like to be loved for herself?

What if he discovered that, although penniless, she had been quite well-educated by her parents, both of whom had taught her to appreciate the finer thing in life? Her father had been every bit the equal of Mynheer Jacob in his day. If Mynheer Dirk knew this, would he feel uncomfortable with her? Would she have to dissemble and pretend to be less than she was...the way she was forced to do every day in her guardian's house?

Foolish creature to be wasting time on such nonsensical thoughts! With an impatient twist, Francesca gathered her hair away from her face in a tighter than usual knot. There, that should last her the day without coming loose, and the slight tug at her scalp would serve as a lesson to her vanity.

Beautiful were the women on a Rubens' canvas, golden-haired and voluptuous. In comparison, she looked like a child. About as close as she could come to a Rubens' canvas was to play Bacchus. Wood nymph. There, that was as romantic as she would ever be!

Tying her lace cap under her chin, she turned from the glass and headed down to the cellar kitchen.

Katryn was already slicing the loaf of bread. A platter of sliced ham and cheese lay beside it.

"There, Frannie, take your plate while you may."

Francesca obediently took a plate and cup from the older woman. She poured herself some buttermilk from the larder and spread a piece of bread with butter, topping it with a slice of cheese.

She didn't take the time to sit down, but between mouthfuls, poured hot water from the fireplace into the ewers, which stood on the tile hearth. With half her bread still left on her plate, she gathered up the two ewers, stuck her flint into an apron pocket and made her way back up the steep back stairs.

She knocked on her guardian's door and opened at his prompt. He was already in dressing gown, writing at his desk and didn't look up when she entered. She placed the pitcher on his dressing table and knelt at the fireplace to kindle a fire.

His words stopped her as she stood by the door ready to leave the room. "Francesca, make sure you behave yourself with Mynheer Dirk today. Engage him in conversation on topics he introduces. And for pity's sake, do not speak to him about art!"

She bit her lip. "Yes, mynheer." What would her guardian say if he knew of her visit to Pieter's atelier—and of Dirk's knowledge of it?

At Lisbet's door, Francesca did not bother for a summons after her knock but entered and strode to the windows, pulling back the brocade drapes. She did the same with the drapes around Lisbet's bed. The sunlight did nothing to disturb the girl's sound slumber. Stooping at the fireplace, Francesca made up the fire, then called over her shoulder, "Arise, Lisbet, you must start getting ready for church."

The only response was Lisbet's form turning away from her and burrowing deeper into the mound of her quilt.

Francesca continued her prompting while she cleared away the hearth, and as she laid out fresh towels and linen for Lisbet. When she had finished, she returned downstairs to collect the breakfast trays Katryn had prepared.

On her last trip upstairs she found Lisbet as she had left her. Francesca approached the bed and did what she always did when Lisbet had to be up and about early. With one swoop, she grabbed the bedclothes in two hands and pulled them back to the foot of the bed.

"Oh! Leave off! Do you want me to catch a chill?" Lisbet groaned from deep in her pillows. Francesca ignored her as she set the tray on the edge of her bed and grabbed first one pillow and then the other to beat them into shape and replace them behind Lisbet's back.

With a loud yawn, Lisbet sat up and rubbed her eyes. "For pity's sake, I'm up, I'm up! Now leave me in peace 'til I call for you to help me dress."

While the girl began listlessly picking at her bread and cheese, Francesca poured out the water into the bowl.

That done, Francesca went through the receiving rooms on both the ground and first floors, opening drapes and shutters, glancing about with a critical eye to see that everything was in order for any Sunday visitors.

No sooner had Francesca arrived back at the kitchen and taken another bite of her bread, than Lisbet's bell sounded. With a dusting off of crumbs from her apron, she turned and ascended the stairs.

She helped Lisbet into her bodice and underskirt of brocade ivory. Over it she wore another skirt of sky-blue satin. A scalloped lace collar covered the wide neck of her bodice.

"Oh, that's not right." Lisbet pushed Francesca's hand away and proceeded to pull the thin batiste of her chemise through the sleeve herself. Without a word, Francesca loosened Lisbet's golden braid and began combing her hair. As was the fashion, she pulled the back tresses into a knot and let the shorter side locks hang free about her face in rippled waves. Around her chignon, she looped a double strand of pearls, while Lisbet inserted a pair of pearl drop earrings in each lobe.

"I rue the day I ever persuaded you to go in my place to visit Tante Blankaart," she said giving Francesca a smile and shake of the head from her reflection in the mirror. "I would be abducted any day if it meant betrothal to a man who looks like a god, is as rich as a king, and seems as wicked as the devil himself."

Francesca frowned at the latter part. "Why do you say 'wicked'?"

"Didn't you hear the way he talked of making money on the *beurs*? I'll bet he's as ruthless as a slave trader."

"He certainly seems a knowledgeable man. That doesn't mean he's wicked." Francesca studied the clasp of Lisbet's pearl bracelet before unhooking it. She didn't like hearing Mynheer Dirk described that way. He had rescued her. He'd not dishonored her. If anything, he was doing his utmost to protect her virtue. However needless the cause, his intentions were good.

Lisbet smacked her lips while eyeing her reflection. "The wickedness makes him all the more alluring. His height and his build take my breath away, and that glint in his eye. Why, I felt as if he saw right into my innermost thoughts—and that he wouldn't hesitate to use them to get whatever he wanted." She shivered.

Francesca felt uncomfortable with Lisbet's description. They reminded her of Dirk's admission that he always went after what he wanted. It forced her to consider again why he wanted her with such determination. "What nonsense," she said with more firmness than she felt.

Lisbet gave her a pitying look. "My dear, Francesca, I realize you know next to nothing about men. But 'sooth, with the way he is rushing you to the altar, you'd better learn a few things before your wedding day—or night," she added, fiddling with the fringe of hair across her brow, unaware of Francesca, who stood paralyzed beside her.

Lisbet examined the effects of her hair in a hand mirror. "Of course, you haven't much time to learn. With a husband like Mynheer Dirk, I wouldn't advise any woman to go in unprepared. You have to know how to handle his sort."

The buttermilk Francesca had gulped down felt like a pot of paint in her stomach. She turned away from Lisbet's knowing reflection in the mirror to arranged the clutter on the dresser top. Attempting a tone of indifference, she asked, "And how do you 'handle' his sort?"

"Dear Francesca, you hardly expect me to explain it to you in a matter of minutes when you've been a hopeless student on the art of men and women up to now? It takes more than a few instructions to understand the subtle exchanges between a gentleman and lady, conversations that require no words. With a mere flurry of an eyelash, a hint of a smile, a woman can have a man at her feet."

Francesca turned away to collect the fallen articles of clothing around the room. She didn't need to listen to Lisbet's lecture on men. She'd heard that discourse countless times before. Francesca didn't even hear the words, only the cadence of sounds and an occasional laugh, as she folded garments and placed them in the cupboard.

She was about to leave the room with an armful of linens when Lisbet turned on her stool.

"There is one thing, my dear, that will never fail you with Mynheer Dirk."

Amused curiosity got the better of Francesca. "And what is that?"

"All men, no matter how tough the exterior, are vulnerable somewhere."

Francesca's smile faded. Mynheer Dirk was not someone who struck her as vulnerable. Quite the contrary. His strength was what had drawn her from the start. And yet, she remembered his words on the bridge about taking care of his mother. There was grief there from his boyhood. But he'd dismissed her words of sympathy almost indifferently.

"The art of controlling the situation," Lisbet continued, "is to find his weakness. Find it and guard your knowledge well." She tapped her comb against her jaw and nodded. "Someday, when your back is against the wall, you will have the ultimate weapon. The one that will bring that man, however powerful, to his knees."

Five

Dirk emerged from the church in no mood to make small talk with the van Diemen family. He had arrived at their door at the appointed hour that morning and accompanied them along the linden-tree-lined Prinsengracht to the Westerkerk.

He hadn't stepped inside a church in years. The only Christian churches he'd seen in the Indies were made up of corrupt and drunken sailors and merchants preaching to another corrupt lot of slaves and princes with their own set of gods.

He'd been ill-prepared for the strict moralist tone of the Reformist preaching. It didn't sit well with his intentions toward van Diemen. The last thing he needed at the moment was a twinge of conscious at this late date.

He was relieved that Mynheer Jacob and his daughter chose to walk ahead of him now, leaving Dirk with only Francesca at his side. Miss Lisbet was accompanied by a suitor. Jacob had suggested a stroll along the city walls a few blocks away from the church since it was a mild day.

The walls were built atop the wide, thick dike protecting the city from the surrounding water. Like stout guardsmen, windmills stood at intervals along the high wall, pumping water from the city's canal system into the canals bisecting the fields beyond as far as the eye could see.

Dirk's sigh of relief was cut off by Francesca's question. "How did you find the morning's sermon?"

He gave her a sharp look, but seeing only polite inquiry on her face, he shrugged. "The usual."

"I received the impression you were not too comfortable

with the dominee's message of forgiving one's neighbor."

"How did I give you that impression?"

"You seemed restless."

Who wouldn't be, forced to sit upon a hard pew for upwards of two hours? But all he said was, "Mayhap my mind was on a different matter."

She stuck to the subject like a determined little mouse nibbling at her piece of stolen cheese. "What do you think about forgiveness?"

"Pretty much what I think of all the twaddle pastors must fill up the hour preaching about."

Her eyes widened at his tone. "But the Bible commands us to forgive."

He gave her a measured look, the mockery erased for the moment. "When someone wrongs me, I will go to the ends of the earth after him. I shan't rest until he has repaid in full." He brushed aside the topic with a wave of his hand, it being the last thing he wanted to dwell on at the moment, preferring to focus on his bride-to-be. "Forgiveness is for fools."

Before she could dispute this, he smiled at her. "I'm glad it was only my attention to the sermon you were interested in. The way you were studying me in church, I was afraid I had grown two horns, and the church elders would throw me out at any moment."

Good. Now she was the one discomfited if the way she turned her face away and the soft color stole over her cheeks were any indication.

"I—I was only studying you as a...a subject."

"Ah yes, the artist studying her subject just as you were the other night while I slept. So, I begin to think I'm naught but an object for your canvas. I could as lief be a bowl of fruit."

A smile tugged at her lips. His own mood lightened. He found he enjoyed making her smile. It must be an all too infrequent occurrence in Jacob's household.

"You make it sound so arrogant. I simply like to draw

and paint." She spoke slowly, as if choosing her words with care, all the while keeping her gaze ahead of her. "Of course, I still require a great deal of training in these areas."

"Which you receive at the capable hands of Pieter the painter. In his private quarters."

She came to a halt, causing the pedestrians behind them to veer around them. "That remark, mynheer, is unworthy of you." Her pointed chin went up. "I thought you said you believed me to be chaste."

"Dirk," he corrected. "Before I am obliged to explain to your guardian why we have stopped on this promenade, let me offer you my excuses." He bowed from the waist, one boot forward, his plumed hat removed with a flourish.

She laughed at the exaggerated gesture of a courtier.

The cheerful sound lifted his own spirits.

He resumed walking, tucking her hand into the crook of his arm, thankful when she did not draw away.

Lisbet and her father stopped several paces ahead to chat with some acquaintances. Dirk took advantage of the opportunity to pause and regard the view beyond the city walls.

Neatly parceled fields stretched before them, deep green rectangles of land claimed from the sea, now divided by long, dark strips of canals. Windmills dotted the landscape, their arms turning constantly from the wind that blew across the flat land from the North Sea.

They listened to the rhythmic creak of the windmill blades. "So you were studying my face as an artist would. Tell me, is my countenance worthy of the canvas?"

Francesca took a few moments to answer, appearing to give his question serious consideration. "I find your face an interesting study."

He didn't know whether to be amused or insulted. Many women had called him handsome, the more so since he had gained wealth. "I confess my face has never been called merely 'interesting.'"

"For an"—she hesitated on the next word—"artist, every

face presents a challenge." At his questioning look, she said, "The aim of a portraitist is to convey on paper something of the subject's character through his countenance. Preferably something that is not revealed to everyone."

He mulled on her reply. "What do you find worth conveying from my face?"

"I'm not certain." She pursed her lips, as if puzzled by something. "There is strength and determination, certainly. But I am seeking something deeper." She shrugged and looked away as if embarrassed by the admission.

He listened, fascinated despite himself. "I shall strike a bargain with you."

Her velvety-gray eyes turned back to him.

"No more nursemaid sketches of me. I shall sit for you, so you'll make a proper likeness this time."

Her lips parted and she looked like a little girl who'd just been given a treat by Sint Nicolaas. "Would you really?"

It gave him an odd warm feeling that was so foreign to him it was painful to his chest. If they hadn't been surrounded by soberly-clad churchgoers, Dirk would have kissed her. As it was, he'd probably be chained to the pillory for such a forward gesture on a Sunday noon. And he had no intention of ever standing on the pillory again.

He cleared his throat. "Just name for me the time and the place and I shall bring this 'interesting study' to the appointment."

The look of enchantment faded from her face. A corresponding cold invaded his heart, when she moved away from him to face the fields again. "What makes you think my work will satisfy you? You said I had no talent the last time you viewed my sketches."

"I never said you lacked talent. Your sketches...astounded me, 'tis all." He chuckled wryly. "It was the first time a woman regarded me whilst I slept and was content to merely sit and sketch me."

He almost laughed aloud when he saw she was about to ask him to explain the remark, then abruptly shut her mouth, thinking better of it. He was looking forward more and more to getting better acquainted with this young lady.

"At any rate, I'm not sure painting a full portrait will be possible," she continued, all business again. "I haven't much experience for one thing. For another, Mynheer Jacob does not wish me to spend time painting or sketching."

He glanced down the wall toward van Diemen, who was still engaged in conversation. "I don't think he'll mind when he knows I have requested it."

She cocked her head at him. "He does seem to be most impressed by you."

He chuckled. "Don't I merit it?"

She shook her head. "'Tisn't a question of merit. 'Tis that he so seldom shows such interest in anyone."

"Too busy counting his coin?"

She frowned at him. "Mynheer Jacob works very hard. He takes little pleasure in anything outside his business. Perhaps that is what draws him to you. You seem to have common interests there."

"In a manner of speaking. Unfinished business and new business."

"You speak in riddles, mynheer."

"Dirk. My name is Dirk," he said softly, wanting badly to reach out his hand to touch her skin. Instead, he balled it into a fist. No woman had ever affected him this way. She had him almost telling her his darkest secrets.

If she heard his statement, she didn't acknowledge it. He could see something troubled her. He waited, hoping she would eventually reveal it to him. His patience was rewarded when a few seconds later, her question came out hesitantly. "You don't like Mynheer Jacob, do you?"

Dirk considered carefully how to answer. "Why do you say that? I treat him quite civilly."

She scanned his eyes. "I don't know. Forgive my impertinence. It's that I observe people's faces closely, too closely perhaps. To sketch them, you see. Perhaps I read too much into certain gestures, remarks. You and Mynheer

Jacob seem to be stalking one another, like two cats meeting for the first time."

He hid his surprise at the astuteness of her observation, she who had sat so quietly plying her needlework in the corner during his visit. "All you see, dear lady, is the way two men of business habitually confront one another. They take each other's measure."

She smiled, as if in relief. "Poor Mynheer Jacob, when you told him you had purchased a villa with the profits of that nutmeg transaction! He has wanted to buy a villa for ever so long."

He stroked his beard. "Has he now?"

She nodded. "Oh, yes. Especially since he began looking for a proper suitor for Lisbet. Of course, now that he is considering a betrothal between her and Bicker's younger son, it is probably no longer important."

He glanced ahead of them where Jacob and his daughter and her suitor were bidding farewell to the group. "Bicker's son? How did your guardian manage to attract him?"

Her chin went up. "Mynheer Jacob is an important man in the city."

"But he is not in Bicker's class."

"Perhaps not. But Lisbet's very fetching, is she not?"

"Lisbet can't hold a candle to you," he said in a caressing voice, his attention returning to Francesca.

"What nonsense you speak, mynheer! At any rate, I think a portrait of you would be difficult. I don't think—"

Dirk took her chin in his hand, forcing her to look at him again. "Methinks, dear lady, you can do anything you put that pretty little head of yours to."

※

The next afternoon, Francesca nearly dropped her needlework at the sound of someone clearing his throat. "I'm here for the masterpiece to begin."

In the doorway of her small sitting room stood Mynheer Dirk, feet planted apart, plumed hat in hand.

Her hand went to her cap. "How did you get in here?"

"Good day to you, Francesca. I've already spoken to the good woman, Katryn, who assures me you are not too busy at this hour of the day."

She smoothed down her apron. If she'd known he was coming, she would have put a clean one on. "I...see." Why did he look so incongruous in her room? She had the sense of a tawny lion stalking its prey.

Without waiting to be asked, he settled himself on one of the larger chairs. "So, when is it to begin?"

"I beg your pardon?" Her thoughts felt all muddled.

"My portrait." He sat back and waited, a small smile under his golden moustache.

"I explained to you that I didn't think—" At the lift of one golden eyebrow, she paused. She did so want to attempt her hand at painting him. How could she resist his splendid form as he sat reclined in deep brown doublet and knee breeches? But she was suddenly terrified.

"What's the matter? Don't you think you would be capable of capturing my likeness?"

She blinked at his ability to read her secret fears.

He waved a hand. "Come, how difficult can it be? A few strokes of paint on canvas." The glint in his eye told her he was deliberately provoking her.

She raised her chin. "Not so long ago you didn't think me capable at all."

"I want to be proved wrong." He leaned forward and took a saffron cake from a silver dish in front of him.

Francesca watched him, feeling both disturbed and challenged. She was not accustomed to having her carefully-hidden thoughts and feelings so clearly read—nor having anyone care enough to do so.

She bent to pick up her fallen needlepoint and folded it up.

Mynheer Dirk looked around the sitting room. "What must one do to get refreshment around here? By the way, my compliments to your cook. These cakes are excellent. Just the thing to whet a man's appetite."

She inclined her head. "I accept the compliment."

He looked at the slice of cake in his hand. "You baked this?"

"This morning."

"Woman, your talents are boundless. You have all the makings of a good wife. I'm fortunate you were not already spoken for when I happened along."

For some absurd reason, his comment pleased her. She struggled to maintain a serious demeanor. "As a good merchant, I trust you haven't already forgotten my penniless state?"

"A good merchant looks at more than just the monetary value when making an investment. He also measures the long-term value of an asset."

She didn't like being reminded that she was merely a commodity to be traded like the spices off his ship. It was her own fault for bringing up the comparison in the first place. "As I recall, my artistic talents needed proving, not my wifely abilities."

"So you've accepted my commission." He sat back with a look of satisfaction.

"To paint you? No, no, I could do nothing more than a sketch—" Too late she realized he had gotten her to agree to that much. What was it about him that imperiled her thinking?

"Nay, I shan't be satisfied with anything less than a fully-executed portrait."

Francesca went to the table where the decanters were set and filled a Venetian roemer with Rhenish wine. "I haven't as yet much experience with oils," she hedged, handing him the glass. "I—I've done a few small portraits—"

"Consider me a chance to practice your craft."

"My guardian—"

"I told you, I will handle him. You needn't concern yourself."

Francesca heard the finality in his tone and shook her head. "Yes, I believe you can, Myn—"

"Let this be the last time I remind you to call me by my given name." His voice was silky smooth, but the glint in his eyes told her he would brook no disobedience.

Francesca swallowed before pronouncing the simple word. "Dirk." The name took on two syllables with its rolled r.

He smiled. "Thank you."

She inclined her head. "I agree to paint your portrait on one condition."

He cocked an eyebrow at her. "Which is?"

"You agree not to view my work 'til it is completed."

To her surprise he conceded. "Very well, if you wish it."

"You are certain?" Most people were always wanting to see their likeness as it emerged on the canvas.

He shrugged. "After my first reaction to your sketches, I can hardly blame you for that stipulation."

She nodded, unable to fault his reasoning, though still doubtful that he would have no interest in the work in progress.

As another consideration occurred to her, she looked away uncertainly.

"What is it?"

She cleared her throat. "I shall need to...to purchase a canvas. It is quite dear."

"You needn't fret over cost. I intend to pay you for the work and materials."

She lifted her chin. "I'm not asking for payment. 'Tis only for the canvas." She could not explain that to purchase materials out of the housekeeping money her guardian gave her was out of the question.

"I shall not only pay you for materials but give you whatever a portrait would cost me anywhere else." He took a long draft of wine, then set the glass down carefully. Reaching into a pocket, he took out a few coins and set them on the table. "That should do for your canvas and paints. If you need more, let me know. Now, shouldn't you begin? I haven't the patience to sit still for long."

Francesca stifled the urge to argue further with him. That could wait for another occasion. "No, I'll vow you haven't."

With growing excitement she gathered pencil and sketch pad. She then directed Dirk to place his chair by the window.

She settled herself opposite him in the small hexagonal room. "Now, what kind of portrait do you wish? A bust, half-length? With arms, without?"

"What about a full-length? Isn't that the most expensive?"

She looked up to see the crinkles at the corners of his eyes. "Yes, but I prefer starting on a smaller scale if you don't mind. I am not a master painter."

"Yet. Very well, do whichever you prefer."

"I shall have to make several sketches first. I'll only do a few today. I shall endeavor not to overtax your patience."

"Never fear, you shan't be relieved of your task so easily." He settled back and placed one booted foot atop his knee. "Just worry about your sketching, and I'll let you know when I must move."

"Feel free to move about. I shall just be capturing rapid impressions for the moment." She took up her pencil and began what her fingers had been itching to do since she had first met him.

"Tell me about the East." Francesca thought to distract him so she would not encounter his deceptively lazy gaze each time she looked up. She was almost afraid he would be able to discern what she was putting on paper just by reading her face.

"What do you wish to know?"

"How did you decide to go there?" She began drawing rapid ovals and lines to get the overall outlines of his head and chest.

"A fourteen-year-old with no parents, who's been thrown in the Tughuis for thieving, hasn't much choice when it comes to his future. I was lucky I had an opportunity to go to sea."

"You were in the Tughuis?" She was unable to mask her shock. The Tughuis was a place that had been set up by the reform-minded to put criminals to work and re-establish them. But she knew all the horrible stories of how it was nothing more than a jail throwing together young delinquents with hardened criminals and working them at backbreaking tasks. Those who managed to leave its doors usually found themselves back in within a matter of months for repeated crimes.

Dirk shrugged. "Aye, I did a few stints there after I was caught stealing anything from a gentleman's purse to a piece of fruit off a market stall."

Just as the other day on the bridge, he was doing nothing to soften the truth. "You...stole?"

"I was hungry and so was my mother."

The simple words reverberated in the room. "H-how awful for you," she whispered. What had his childhood been like? "It must have been terrible for your mother to know that you were forced to steal."

"My mother was lying on a pallet in a broken-down warehouse at the time, racked with consumption. I doubt she knew much of what was going on around her by then." The offhand voice only confirmed to Francesca that Dirk was a man who hid his true feelings behind a mask of indifference and irony. Her pencil had stopped in midair, but now she began to sketch rapidly.

As she drew, she realized with amazement that any respectable person would not flaunt such beginnings once he'd attained the status of a gentleman. But not this man. He presented the facts of his past with the boldness of someone throwing down the gauntlet.

After a few moments of silent work she spoke again though she kept her eyes on her drawing. "Your mother died shortly after?"

"So I was told. I wasn't around at the time to witness it. I had been safely locked away in the Tughuis for the third time by then."

She bit her lip, her heart going out to the young boy. "What of your father? Could you not call upon him?"

He did not reply at once. Francesca wondered whether she should repeat the question or remain silent. All the while her gaze moved constantly from paper to man and back again.

"No," he answered at last, his tone flat.

"Were you an orphan?"

After a few seconds, he smiled at her. "Yes. I suppose we have that in common."

"What do you mean?" With her pencil, she tried to capture the bittersweet mockery in his eye.

"I mean that you had no family recourse either when your guardian took you in. Did you have much choice at that point about where you were to go?"

She looked down at her paper, her pencil stopping. "My case is different. When Mynheer Jacob took me in, it was he who had no choice." She swallowed, finding it painful to say the rest, but wanting to repay his honesty with her own. "My father had left him with...many debts. I had no family. Not in Holland at any rate."

"What of your Florentine relatives?"

"Mynheer Jacob tried to contact them, but they wanted nothing to do with me," she said in a low voice, not liking to recall that time.

"Why not?"

She lifted her chin at the sharp question. "They did not want an infidel among them. They were afraid my parents had corrupted me for good with the reformed religion." She did not tell him of her guardian's explosive reaction when he had received their rejection. The voices raised behind closed doors, however, were forever etched in Francesca's mind.

I'm saddled with Enrico's daughter because her own family is too miserable to take her back. An extra mouth to feed, when I need all my capital now for the business. Curse di Paolo's soul for leaving behind a penniless orphan!

And his wife's calmer voice reasoning with him. I need her around the house. She can help Katryn. 'Twill be cheaper than hiring another girl.

Dirk's voice penetrated her thoughts. "My face must be truly captivating."

"What!" Francesca's pencil slid across the surface of paper, marring the sketch. "I'm sorry, I didn't hear what you said."

"Never mind. 'Twasn't important." His intent look and quiet words made Francesca wonder whether he could read her dismay.

She brought her mind back to the present and worked in silence, finding it too difficult to keep up a conversation and draw at the same time. She worked on the contours of Dirk's face. Wavy locks framing a wide forehead...slight hollow of his cheek above the line of beard...narrow curve of his nostrils. But what fascinated her most were his eyes. Today she had captured several expressions: bitterness, amusement, contempt...genuine concern.

After several minutes, Francesca broke the silence, unable to resist asking him more about himself. She wanted to learn as much as possible of her subject while he was in a talkative mood. It would help her in painting him, she told herself.

"It must have been difficult for you, a lad of fourteen on a sailing vessel among grown men."

He shrugged, making her aware once again of his massive shoulders. She moved her pen downward, attempting to catch their breadth. "No more difficult than the Tughuis. I survived."

What did the stark words hide? "I would say you've done better than mere survival."

He answered her smile with the lazy one she was coming to recognize. It reminded her of a great, contented beast after a satisfying meal. "I worked hard. And now fortune has favored me. I was lucky in the Indies."

"I would say Divine Providence has aided you."

He shrugged. "I would not say God has looked upon me with any benevolence, except perhaps to spare my life."

She felt a twinge of sadness that he held bitterness in his heart toward the Lord. Francesca knew she would not have survived much of the last five years without God's grace.

Dirk stood and rubbed a shoulder with an apologetic smile. Francesca quickly sketched downward, forming limbs and torso.

"But as a young boy at sea, among a bunch of hardy sailors?"

He stood before the window, flexing his arms. "I was able to fit in with the company at sea. The crew is a family of sorts." He shrugged. "For those able to abide by its rules and tough enough to endure them, life is tolerable. I was big for my age, and had learned quite a few tricks of survival in the years beforehand."

Turning to her, he leaned against the sill, crossing his arms over his chest, his face in shadow. "I gained the crew's respect, wasn't afraid to use my fists if I had to, but knew enough not to go around picking fights." His voice became grim. "If I learned one hard lesson at the Tughuis, it was to control my temper and bide my time."

Before Francesca had done little more than begin to shape the twist of his lips, she jumped at her guardian's voice.

"What in thunder!" Mynheer Jacob strode across the room and snatched Francesca's paper from her hand. "I thought I made it clear I wanted no more time wasted on this foolishness. If Katryn hasn't given you enough to do, I am sure I shall find more useful occupations for your idleness. Furthermore, I distinctly recall telling you I wanted no household money to be used for purchasing these drawing materials."

"Mynheer Jacob, good afternoon." Dirk advanced towards him from the window, an unmistakable edge of steel to his voice. Although her guardian was tall, Dirk stood a fraction above him.

The other man started, then flushed in recognition. "Ah, Mynheer Dirk, I didn't see you there in the embrasure. Forgive me for my rudeness. Please, be seated. Would you care for some refreshment?"

"Thank you. Francesca has kept me well provided." He gestured to the platter. "She bakes an excellent cake, as I have already told her." He smiled disarmingly at Mynheer Jacob before reseating himself. "I fear if anyone deserves your censure, it must be I. If your ward is disobeying you, 'tis only because I commissioned her to paint my portrait. I requested something on a grand scale, which my posterity can look upon, and say, 'There he is, the one who began it all.'"

"I see." With a doubtful glance from Francesca to Dirk, the bluster went out of her guardian like a singing kettle being whisked off the flame. He looked down at the sheet of paper he had torn from her hand as if to verify Dirk's claim.

Dirk immediately engaged him in conversation about the trading of shares, and the moment of awkwardness passed. Her guardian settled in a chair by Dirk, his anger forgotten. Francesca marveled again at how deftly Dirk had been able to steer Mynheer Jacob's attention away from her and her sketches.

She did not listen to their talk, preferring to use the time to continue sketching. She was able to draw Dirk's face from several angles. She concentrated on it and his upper body, already having an idea of the pose she would use for his portrait.

Her eyes roamed over his features, free at last to study them at leisure. She shivered inwardly. From the breadth of his shoulders to the knuckles that curved around the crystal roemer, the man exuded movement and suppressed energy even when sitting still.

Dirk engaged her guardian in a lively discussion over the merits of different commodities. Mynheer Jacob appeared more animated than usual. She gave a slight shake of her head. Really, the two men were very much alike at the moment. Even their gestures were similar. If no one knew better, it could be said they were related, perhaps an uncle and nephew or something more distant. She studied them. Their coloring was certainly different, and their eyes nothing alike. No, it was more a matter of overall shape of face and expression. Perhaps all merchants got that same look in their eyes, when they talked of wealth, she mused.

Suddenly she caught their words.

"Yes, the wedding can take place in a fortnight. The villa should be ready to receive guests by the weekend. All of you can come out then. That should give you ample time to make any preparations beforehand.

Francesca's sketching pad fell to her lap. "But I—"
Dirk's gaze shifted to her. She found she couldn't speak. A thundering grew in her ears. Married in a fortnight—?

Six

Francesca returned home the next afternoon tired but satisfied from Pieter's studio. She had overheard Dirk arrange to take Mynheer Jacob to the stock exchange, so she had taken advantage of her guardian's absence to hurry to Pieter's.

Pieter had looked at her sketches and helped her select which one should be used for Dirk's portrait. She felt a quiver of excitement at the thought of beginning in oils.

Being in Pieter's company had helped allay her fears over her impending wedding. For an hour or two, at least, she could pretend to be in a world where only art existed.

"There you are, Frannie," Katryn greeted her as Francesca entered the back door into the kitchen. "Mynheer Jacob has returned and asked for you." She eyed Francesca worriedly. "I told him I'd sent you to fetch some more leeks and carrots for the hutspot."

Francesca gave the cook a grateful look. "Thank you. I didn't think I'd be so long."

Katryn took a ladle and stirred the stewing pot of meat on the fire as she spoke, then wiped at the spotless tiles around it with her immaculate apron before returning to her cutting board to chop some greens. "Lisbet's been plaguing me as well. She was making me so nervous I had to shoo her out my kitchen. She's jumping round like a candle flame."

Francesca set down her things. "I'll just see what mynheer wants, then come down to help you."

The housekeeper gave her a sharp look. "Best scurry up to your room and put those papers away first, whilst Lisbet's in the music room practicing on the harpsichord." She sniffed. "Mynheer wants her to play for de Heer Bicker next time he comes for a visit, so he sent her in to pound on the keyboard 'til she gets it right."

Francesca smiled before doing just as Katryn suggested. She trod lightly up the back stairs to her room and carefully placed her sketches in the rear of her heavy oaken armoire. She was none too soon. A few minutes later as she was changing her apron, there was a knock on her door.

Before she had a chance to utter "Come in," Lisbet entered. She closed the door behind her and leaned against it. "I just heard the news. I can hardly wait!"

"What news?" Francesca asked, her mind on what her guardian could want. Had he found out about her visit to Pieter?

"What news indeed! Your news! The villa. Oh, I can scarcely wait. A villa by the sea." Lisbet's eyes gleamed at Francesca. "Tucked in among all the best families of Holland. Think of the parties. I'm sure I can persuade that husband-to-be of yours to entertain lavishly. And once you are married, you will be a perfect chaperon for me."

Francesca stepped back, not wanting to be reminded of the upcoming week. Dirk had persuaded her guardian to come out and visit his new villa before the wedding. "I see. That should be very nice for you."

"A girl must do what she can until her wedding day." Lisbet advanced into the room. "I've been waiting an age for you." She frowned at her. "Where were you, anyway?"

Francesca turned back to the glass and pretended to fix her cap. "Katryn needed a few more things."

"So she said. It certainly took you long enough. Now then," she continued, her annoyance put aside for more pressing problems, "I need you to tell Papa that you shall be accompanying me to the kermis tomorrow."

"Kermis?" Francesca thought of the wild street festival with little enthusiasm. Normally, she would have enjoyed the carnival with its exotic parade of performers, but she knew chaperoning Lisbet was an effort in futility. "I had no plans to go."

"Of course not, but you can go somewhere for a few hours can you not?" She smiled slyly as a new thought hit her. "Or, you can ask that betrothed of yours to take us there together." She nodded. "That should satisfy Papa nicely. I will tell him that Mynheer Dirk will be accompanying us."

Francesca's heart sank. She hated subterfuge. Lisbet was always forcing her into schemes behind her father's back. Now that Francesca was betrothed, she had thought—hoped—Lisbet wouldn't require her assistance anymore in secret trysts. But it seemed Lisbet's reasoning was the opposite.

"Your father will wonder why Johan Bicker is not coming with us," she hedged.

Lisbet waved a hand airily. "Don't worry about that. I'll handle what I tell Papa about Johan. You just worry about Dirk, that he doesn't say anything to Papa."

The use of Dirk's name so familiarly on Lisbet's lips caused Francesca a twinge of displeasure. "Where will you be?"

Lisbet twirled a curl around her forefinger, looking suddenly very pleased. "Oh, I shall be at the kermis, never fear, and in very good company, I might add. So you needn't worry. And as long as no one's the wiser..." Her voice trailed off with a smile.

Francesca sighed inwardly. "Who is it this time, the butcher's son?"

Lisbet scowled, throwing her pretty features into the thin, hard lines of her father for an instant. The next second her features smoothed again and she laughed. "Why should I bother with pebbles when I can have pearls?" She gave Francesca a disparaging look. "'Tis a pity some of us cannot even manage to attract the likes of Jaap Janzoon," she laughed, referring to the butcher's son who had a club foot and whose hands were always red and raw-looking. "You should be on your knees daily thanking the Almighty for your abduction.

"No, I risk Papa's wrath on much finer fare. And what finer fare!" Lisbet ran her fingers over the long strand of pearls at her neck. "What think you of Carel van Milne? Isn't he worth a little risk?"

Francesca swallowed, her throat suddenly dry. The man was one of the richest in the city. He was also married. "He's meeting you at the kermis?" she whispered, genuinely shocked.

Lisbet walked back to Francesca's door. "He has graciously invited me." She shivered in anticipation. "What a god among men. Have you noticed the width of his shoulders? Why, they're twice the size of poor Johan's." Lisbet's laughter tinkled out at her betrothed's expense.

"Does he know you are to wed Bicker's son?"

"No, but that doesn't signify."

"Johan might not think so."

"Carel is after a good time as am I. Once I'm a married matron, the pleasure of his company can only increase. Why, Carel makes my poor Johan Bicker look like an ailing scarecrow."

"What if someone recognizes you?"

Lisbet shrugged with a laugh. "That is what masks are for."

Francesca shook her head at her guardian's daughter, wishing there was a way to persuade her to desist with such wicked activities. But ever since Francesca had moved into the van Diemen household, she'd discovered that Lisbet was determined to get her way in everything she set her mind to. Francesca pitied her at times, realizing how desperately she craved her father's attention. Even though he lavished every material luxury on his only child, he spent little time praising her.

Francesca made her way to the door. "Excuse me, I must go to your father, who asked for me earlier."

Lisbet grabbed Francesca's wrist as she passed her. "You'll tell Dirk about the kermis?" Her hold tightened until Francesca winced and finally nodded. "Remember, not a word about Carel. Although with the way you two were conversing on Sunday, Dirk will have eyes only for you." She laughed. "You must have learned something from me after all."

A moment later, Francesca entered her guardian's study hoping she wouldn't betray her concern over Lisbet's latest plan. She'd been aiding Lisbet for so long, mainly to try and protect the headstrong girl, that she could no longer extricate herself when Lisbet commanded her.

It had all begun when Lisbet had threatened to have their drawing lessons cancelled if Francesca didn't help her.

When Francesca had first been allowed to sit in on the lessons—only because Pieter, seeing her interest, had told Mynheer Jacob he would not charge for an additional student—Francesca had discovered a whole new world.

She'd always enjoyed drawing, and her father had engaged a drawing master for her.

But under Pieter's tutelage, she'd learned so much more technique, for here was a serious artist pursuing his craft, who'd allowed her a glimpse of the world of painters.

She hadn't been able to bear the thought of losing that link. So, she had submitted to Lisbet's threat and had been paying for her moment of selfish indulgence ever since.

Mynheer Jacob looked up when she entered his office. "Francesca," he said, sitting back and folding his hands atop his ledgers. "I am going to be direct with you. I want you to listen closely."

Knowing it was his way to come to the point, Francesca braced herself for a sound lecture on having spent too much on some household item or having neglected to give the proper amount to the church or to the almshouse.

"As you know, your father left you no marriage portion."

Francesca nodded, having supposed that was all settled between him and Mynheer Dirk.

"I have decided after careful consideration that I cannot extend anything more for you at this time."

"Yes, mynheer. I didn't expect you, too."

He continued speaking, hardly registering her reply. "I have taken care of you financially since your father and mother passed away. They left me with the moral obligation to look after their only offspring. I consider I have done my Christian duty." He pursed his thin lips. "In the years you've been under my roof, I've fed and clothed you and provided you with an education most young ladies would envy." Mynheer Jacob didn't look at her directly as he spoke but at an indeterminate point between her face and the ledgers on his desk.

"I can with a clear conscience declare I have fulfilled my duty. You've no dowry, your father having graced me with debts that ate up his half of the business partnership we enjoyed."

Uncomfortable as always whenever Mynheer Jacob reminded her of this fact, she shifted her own gaze to the engraving hanging above his desk. Her years of standing in this same position, hearing the same speech in different ways, had given her ample time to study the framed scene in all its detail. Francesca could close her eyes and picture the moralizing print.

Like many of his contemporaries, her guardian was fond of the stark contrast between duty and irresponsibility, vanity and modesty, earthly treasure weighed against the heavenly. This allegory depicted the folly of avarice in a series of scenes showing a young man embarking upon his fortune. The final scene showed him begging in the streets.

Francesca had always felt a little sorry for the young fellow. His life seemed predestined to end in ruin, almost as if he'd never had a chance to follow the straight and narrow, since the artist had etched his actions onto the parchment.

She thought of Dirk, the young boy who'd had no childhood. She must be grateful to her guardian and make allowances, she told herself sternly, for saving her from a similar fate. She repressed a shudder as she remembered the fate of Dirk's mother.

Her attention swung back to her guardian's words, catching the very name she'd been thinking. "I am very sorry you must present yourself to Dirk Vredeman in such an impoverished state."

"Yes, mynheer." No one was more aware of the financial disparity of their union than she.

"That is why I believe it imperative that you do everything to please your intended." His stern gaze met hers for the first time. "Opportunity like this will not strike twice." He swept her up and down with a swift, indifferent glance. "You have neither the looks nor temperament to make a man forget your penniless condition. Count yourself exceedingly fortunate to have found a man, who has spent so many years in the Indies that he has doubtless lost his sensibilities and is willing to marry you despite your lack of dowry and family name."

He cleared his throat. "I don't want you to try Mynheer Dirk's patience with your painting nonsense. As your suitor he is likely humoring you with this notion of having his portrait done. I don't want you to do anything to jeopardize this betrothal. Is that clear?"

Francesca stared at her guardian's remorseless gaze, her throat going dry at the thought of what would happen to her if Dirk hated the portrait and decided to withdraw his suit. What would Mynheer Jacob do? She could only nod. "Yes, mynheer."

"Very well." Her guardian shifted his attention back to his ledgers as if satisfied. "Mynheer Dirk strikes me as a knowledgeable merchant. He has generously offered to guide me in some transactions on the exchange."

She let out a breath. So that was why her guardian was so concerned about her behavior with Dirk. "Mynheer Jacob," she ventured, "If Mynheer Dirk's assistance is so important to you, 'twould it not be better to pursue your business affairs with him without the pretense of my betrothal?"

"Don't be impertinent, girl!"

"I beg your pardon, mynheer," she hastened. "I only meant, I don't want to do anything to hurt your business prospects with him—"

His dark eyes again looked into hers. "You dare to say such a thing after your scandalous conduct with him the night of your absence from this house?"

Francesca blinked at the fury in his tone and gaze. "I—we—did nothing—"

"You shameless girl. I only agreed to house you here before the wedding because that was the only condition Mynheer Dirk imposed on me. But after what he himself admitted concerning the two of you—"

"I give you my word, mynheer—"

Her guardian held up a long-fingered hand which stood pale against his black doublet. "I will not have you lie to me, girl. Not after Dirk himself admitted that he had lain with you."

Francesca gripped the edge of the desk, unable to believe what she heard.

"Don't play the innocent maiden with me, Francesca. The sooner you are wed, the better. I will have you bring no scandal to Lisbet. Nothing must impede my progress with the Bickers. Is that understood?" At Francesca's mute nod, Mynheer Jacob said in a calmer voice, "Good."

With a brisk movement of his hand, he turned his attention back to his ledgers. "That is all." He had regained his composure, and his tone gave no indication of the turmoil he had wreaked in Francesca. "Now, be off with you and help Katryn."

Trembling inwardly, Francesca staggered out.

What had Dirk done to her?

Dirk exited the newly established coffeehouse on the Kalverstraat, bidding goodbye to his companion, a trader he had spent an hour with.

Dirk lingered a moment outside the shop, watching the matrons pass him, their starched white apron fronts like armor plates, their reed baskets swinging in front of them like maces as they entered into good-natured battle with the merchants who sang out the merits of their goods as they walked by.

Dirk felt a nudge at his toe. Looking down, he saw a brown-spotted dog sniffing between the cracks in the cobblestones, seeking a bit of refuse from the never-ending traffic. He smiled and tossed the dog a crumb from his pocket.

A horse-drawn dray bearing a pyramid of flat yellow disks of cheese maneuvered the narrow street.

The neighborhood held a mixture of smells and noises from his childhood. Despite the hardships, there were pleasant memories as well, especially when he'd been younger, before his mother had fallen so ill.

During the torrid heat of a tropical night or with the crisp ocean breeze off a ship's deck brushing his forehead, he had closed his eyes and relived each sound and smell of his native city. The clip-clop of horses' hooves. The duller clump of wooden shoes. The pungent smell of vegetables just pulled from the earth.

Sweetest of all was the scent reaching him now as he crossed the street, his eyes drawn to the clamoring children clustered around the waffle man. The smell of melting butter and sugar proclaimed all that was most wholesome and unchanging in this land of farmers and merchants.

The lines around his mouth deepened in bitter recollection of the times he had stood as a child, the gnawing hunger at his belly never fully satisfied, and watched the burghers' children clamoring for waffles and sugar-dusted poffertjes, those puffed-up little pancakes the size of a large gold ducat.

He could still feel his breath blowing on his stiffened fingers as he hovered by the heat of the griddle, watching enviously as mamas obliged their chubby-cheeked angels with a treat.

With a shake of his head to dispel the images, Dirk now sauntered toward the waffle man. Before he reached the vendor, his eye caught sight of a familiar face exiting a shop a few doors down.

Francesca stepped onto the street, a roll of canvas under her arm. A second later Dirk's pleasure dimmed as he caught sight of Pieter following behind.

What the devil was she doing with that ill-fed, ill-dressed painter? What was the matter with her guardian, anyway? He had barred Francesca access to her own house, yet here he let her run around Amsterdam accompanied by that gangly apprentice!

Dirk swiveled away from his destination and directed his footsteps toward the pair, his heart pumping like the tom-tom drum of a heathen warrior preparing for a skirmish with an adversary.

Neither turned as he approached, too wrapped up in their conversation to be aware of his presence. At the corner they stopped. Francesca hugged the roll of canvas to her breast as she smiled up at Pieter. Her eyes sparkled and her cheeks shone with animation. All of a sudden she burst into lighthearted laughter.

She had a funny way of laughing. Her eyes flicked downward shyly, then back up again to Pieter's smiling face. It was as if she were afraid she'd be caught at it at any moment.

Pieter stepped back, waving an arm in farewell before turning down a narrow alley leading toward the Rokin. Francesca remained where she was, her smile disappearing gradually like the softly waning light of day, to be replaced by her more habitual expression, solemn and wistful.

Something twisted in Dirk's gut. A sharp, intense yearning, gone as quickly as it hit. He wanted to be the man that made Francesca di Paolo's face glow.

Bedeviled! He was becoming a sentimental sot. It must be his return to this damp bog called Holland that was more marsh than dry land. It was wreaking havoc with his humors. The sooner he finished his business and got out of this wretched land the better. That decided, he turned toward the waffle man.

Francesca looked after Pieter's disappearing figure, satisfied that soon she would be ready to begin her painting—her first real portrait in oils!

"A sweet for a lady."

She jumped at the object flourished under her nose. The buttery smell of the waffle reached her nostrils and her face softened. Before she could think she took the paper-wrapped confection, which was still warm from the griddle, smiling up at Dirk, who appeared before her. The low, potent timbre of his voice sent a quiver through her.

He doffed his wide-brimmed hat and sketched her a bow. "Good afternoon, fair maid."

She swallowed, overwhelmed by his height and breadth. The sun glinted off his tawny locks, turning them to burnished bronze.

Then she remembered her conversation with her guardian, and she felt sick inside. Without thinking she thrust the waffle back at him.

His smile evaporated. "What's the matter? Has my face all of a sudden become displeasing to you? 'Twas not so long ago you found something of interest in it." His mouth flattened. "Or were you expecting Pieter again?"

Francesca's emotions warred within her. Something in his tone tugged at her. He sounded almost defiant as if girding himself for her reply. She stared at him, trying to reconcile the attentive, almost uncertain, man before her with one who would slander her to her guardian.

Finally, she lifted her chin, having to know the truth first. "At least Pieter would never do anything dishonorable or immoral, and it isn't because he lacks strength."

His amber eyes regarded her steadily. "It takes more than physical brawn, dear lady, to go after what you want." All mockery had left his tone. It almost sounded weary.

"And what more than brawn is required to dishonor a woman?" she asked, distressed to find her voice trembling.

He narrowed his eyes, suddenly seeming very much on his guard. "Who is the dishonored woman we are speaking of?"

Francesca braced herself, determined not to let his soft tone mislead her. If Mynheer Jacob were to be believed—and she had no reason to doubt his word—then Mynheer Dirk had done an unpardonable thing. She had hardly slept since her interview with her guardian. How could she hold her head up as this man's betrothed, knowing he had claimed she'd lain with him? She swallowed, hardly able to repeat the words. "Mynheer Jacob said we...you..." She dropped her gaze. "That you'd dishonored me that night at the farmhouse," she ended in a whisper, her eyes fixed on the warm waffle she still held in her hand.

She waited for his denial, for an explanation, for some kind of recognition of the enormity of what she'd told him.

"Does it make that much difference? He already believed you to be dishonored."

Her gaze flew up. How could he sound so callous? "D-does that make any difference!"

"'Twouldn't you rather he believe it was your future husband than a band of ruffians?"

She could only gape at his matter-of-fact reasoning. "S-so you did tell him this?"

He nodded slowly, his eyes never leaving her face, as if he were puzzled by her reaction.

She shook her head, taking a step back from him. "You told him an untruth! He believes I am a fallen woman." She shuddered at the injustice of such an accusation. "How could you shame me so?"

His golden eyes met her gaze steadily. "Your guardian wouldn't believe the truth even if he'd been there that night. I thought it was better he should believe that your future husband had taken what would soon rightfully belong to him, than to have him believe a far worse fate had overtaken you, especially after you implied the betrothal was a figment of my imagination."

She looked down, remembering her own careless words spoken in exasperation. How could she have known they would have motivated Dirk to act in such a high-handed manner?

"Perhaps you'd care to sample the treat?"

She blinked at the waffle in her hand. "No, thank you, my appetite is quite gone."

"Pity. A bit of sweet might improve your frame of mind."

She let out a breath in asperity. "'Twould take more than food to improve my frame of mind this day."

Something in his golden eyes made her reconsider. He seemed almost like a little boy who'd had his gift rejected. While his explanation of his untruth hadn't satisfied her, it had shown her he'd meant it for her good. She lifted his gift to her lips and took a bite of the warm waffle. It was crispy on the outside and oozing with buttery syrup in the middle, and made her forget her anger for the moment.

"Thank you. It...it's delicious. I shall enjoy the rest later."

Without asking her leave, he took her by the arm and began to walk with her toward the canal at the end of the block.

She would have protested, but then she remembered Lisbet's command. She cleared her throat, her steps slowing. Her mood darkened even more at what she found herself forced to do now. "Are you...that is, would you like to attend the kermis tomorrow with me—with Lisbet and myself, that is?" she added quickly.

He inclined his head. "'Twould be my pleasure." A few seconds later, he said, "I suppose I should be grateful you are asking me, your betrothed, and not Pieter."

She glanced at him. "What a foolish idea. I'm only asking because—" She stopped, realizing what she would have blurted out. It was all Lisbet's fault for putting her in such a position!

As Dirk continued to look at her, she tried to smile. "I'm only asking you because...because we are betrothed, and I thought this was what a betrothed couple ought to be doing."

He lifted the corner of his mouth. "Yes, they ought, oughtn't they?"

Ignoring the gentle irony in his tone, she forged on, feeling more and more like a fraud herself the further she went. "I mean, we really know each other very little, do we not? This would be an opportunity to become better acquainted."

"An excellent suggestion."

She decided to take another bite of her waffle, to avoid saying anything.

"I used to dream of tasting those as a boy."

She glanced at him, remembering his history. "W-were you not able to indulge your desire?"

He gave a brief shake of his head. "Rarely."

On impulse she held the round, flat disk up to him. "Here, take a bite while it's still warm."

With almost a wary glance at her, he leaned forward and obliged. "Thank you," he said after he'd swallowed.

She took another bite, feeling his gaze on her, aware of touching the place he'd just bitten from.

They reached the Spui, a wide canal that crossed the Kalverstraat. "Are you on your way home?" he asked her.

"Yes."

"I shall accompany you then."

They crossed the bridge in silence, then turned left on the cobbled street adjoining the canal. "You don't mind if Lisbet accompanies us, do you? I mean, she will be practically family to you once we are...wed." It was still difficult for her to imagine that state.

"Ah yes, Lisbet. She shall be almost like a sister to me then, will she not?"

Francesca drew her eyebrows together, unsure how to read his tone. "Yes." She glanced over at him. "Is three o'clock agreeable with you?"

He nodded, regarding her sidelong. It made her feel as if it was now she who had done something dishonorable. It was not the same as what he had told her guardian, she argued to herself.

"Good, that's settled then." She let out a deep breath, realizing how tense she'd been. Noticing how tightly she was clutching both her new canvas and the waffle, she loosened her hold. "I shall see you on the morrow, then."

"And will we be honored with young Bicker's presence?"

His question threw her. "I beg your pardon?"

"Lisbet's suitor. You did say it was Bicker's son?"

Francesca nodded.

"Then we shall make up a foursome. I'm flattered that Mynheer Jacob considers me of sufficient social standing for his daughter and young Bicker."

"Of course he does. Mynheer Jacob has a high regard for you," she said quickly, attempting to throw the focus off Bicker and onto Dirk.

He made an unintelligible sound in his throat. "So, it is to be a foursome?"

Francesca paused at the next little bridge they were obliged to cross, realizing she could not lie to him. "No."

He cocked an eyebrow at her.

Her eyelids flickered downward. "'Tisn't to be a foursome. Mynheer Johan Bicker is...unable to accompany us." When he said nothing, she forced herself to continue.

"Lisbet has her heart set on attending the kermis. I offered to take her." She moistened her lips, still tasting the sweet syrup of the waffles. "That is, Lisbet asked me to take her."

He touched her cheek, bringing it around to face him. "Francesca, what is it?"

How to explain without implicating Lisbet? "She wanted so badly to go."

"Tell me, does she simply want to attend the carnival, or has she some particular reason for wanting to be there, that perhaps her father is not aware of?"

He was entirely too discerning. How did he know Lisbet so well? "I-I'm not entirely sure," she replied honestly. "Lisbet and I frequently attend things together. But I am worried. There are so many people at a kermis and de Heer Bicker is not accompanying her. If anything should happen to jeopardize their betrothal agreement—"

"Van Diemen expects you to watch his daughter, doesn't he?"

She nodded.

"Well, then, watch her we shall."

She couldn't help responding to the twinkle in his eyes with a small smile of her own. "Thank you, Dirk." It was the first time she had called him by his name of her own volition.

He replied with a slow smile of his own. "That's better." He took her elbow and they resumed walking. "Remember, you are a betrothed woman now. You might not appreciate how you entered into that state, but at least you have no need to fear your guardian anymore."

Although she didn't like to be reminded of her disgraced state in her guardian's eyes, she did feel a sudden comfort at having someone she could turn to. It had been so long since she'd had someone to defend her.

"Come, eat up your waffle before it gets cold."

When they reached her guardian's house, she was ready to go down the alleyway toward the back entrance, but Dirk escorted her up the front stoop.

"I shall fetch you and Lisbet at three o'clock," he said with a bow.

"Thank you," she answered, still grateful for his help.

The next moment he took her chin between his fingertips. She stood perfectly still, her heart pumping so loudly it deafened her to all street sounds. Gently, his palm closed over her jaw and he leaned forward until his lips touched hers, as light as goose down.

"Until tomorrow then," he said against her mouth, before straightening.

And then he was heading back down the steps, leaving her with the taste of him...and the yearning for more.

Seven

Lisbet pointed to the procession of animals being paraded down the crowded street. "Look at the elephants!"

Dirk turned in the direction of her finger. The pair of elephants lumbered by them, their wrinkled gray trunks swinging slowly back and forth. Atop each beast sat a young African boy clothed in voluminous, gilt-edged breeches, velvet cape and turban. Every so often they would strike the elephants with the long switch each held in his hand.

To Dirk, the elephants were merely two beasts of burden, taken out of their warm, sunny clime and transplanted to a damp, cold one for the pleasure of a strange, noisy crowd.

Dirk glanced over to Francesca who stood at his side, his frame of mind softening at her look of wonder. She had probably never seen such exotic creatures except in picture books. He nudged her elbow. "Look what's coming behind them."

She craned her neck. "Oh!" she marveled, clapping a hand over her mouth. A tall, black man led a lion on a chain. Despite the animal's bondage, his walk was regal. The rude, gawking mass of people could not rob him of his dignity and lazy grace.

The lion was followed by a group of monkeys dressed in braided costume.

"How adorable!" Lisbet exclaimed. "I wish I could have one for a pet," she said, batting her eyelashes at Dirk.

"They're not as adorable as they look now. They can be an accursed nuisance. I know, I had one for a pet for a while in Batavia."

"Really? Did you teach him any tricks?"

"A few. But he only performed when he felt like it. Impudent little fellow, always looking for a way to upset my household."

"I'm sure you kept him under very good control." Lisbet took hold of Dirk's arm in her two hands and urged him along.

He grasped Francesca's elbow on his other side and continued their slow promenade on the Dam, amazed anew at the impudence of Mynheer Jacob's daughter. They paused in the wide square in front of the town hall and watched the performances of tightrope walkers, acrobats, and jugglers.

"Look, a fortune teller!" Lisbet dashed over without asking them if they wished to stop by the woman's tent. Dirk followed more slowly with Francesca.

"Care to have your fortune told?"

Francesca shook her head, her attention on the tent flap, through which Lisbet had just disappeared. "I don't believe in such things."

"Probably some old crone just trying to make a living," he said quietly.

She glanced up at him, but said nothing more.

A few moments later, Lisbet emerged from the woman's tent with a smile on her lips.

"Fame and fortune in your future?" he asked as they continued their promenade.

She twirled the colorful sash she wore around her waist. "Indeed—and many more interesting things—mayhap even this evening!" She laughed and walked ahead of them.

He was beginning to understand the tension visible in Francesca's features.

Fulfilling his promise to Francesca, he had kept any eye on Lisbet all afternoon, bearing her antics with fortitude.

But the day was waning, and he wished he could return her home and enjoy the rest of the evening alone with Francesca.

But Lisbet flitted from entertainment to entertainment without the least sign of fatigue. She had even dressed the part, Dirk observed, eyeing her peasant garb and kerchief.

As twilight descended, he felt like a seaman on the first watch with a storm brewing on the horizon. Lisbet kept looking about the crowd as if in search of someone. He wondered if perhaps she was meeting Bicker on the sly.

As far as he was concerned, she could ruin herself, with his blessing, since it was little over a fortnight ago that he had planned to bring about the very thing—if not the reality, then the appearance of it.

Instead, he'd managed to compromise Francesca's future, offending her with his falsehood to Jacob van Diemen. Did she truly deplore their betrothal? Wasn't it better than her servitude at Jacob's?

He expelled a breath, turning his attention back to her. She smiled at the acrobats and once again, he felt a queer sensation in his chest, as if some unused, almost forgotten feeling were stirring in him, and its waking was painful and slow.

As soon as the performance was over, Lisbet turned to him. "I must have something to eat. After all, there is still the dancing. Come along, Dirk." She took his hand and pulled him toward the food vendors.

They ate currant-studded buns while stopping to view a Punch and Judy show. As the shadows lengthened he found them a seat under a linden tree, from where they could hear the strains of lute and mandolins drifting over the strolling crowd.

Paper lanterns were lit as dusk fell. Fiddlers tuned their instruments. When the music began in earnest, Lisbet stood up and brushed off her skirt. Then she pulled out a mask from a pocket and tied it on, effectively covering her eyes.

He stood. "Not wishing to be recognized?"

She tilted her head back and laughed. "It's more fun this way!" With those words, she disappeared into the dancing crowd.

He swore under his breath, unable to leave Francesca alone. Scanning the crowd, he finally spotted her weaving in and out among the dancers until she reached the other side.

"What does she intend?" he asked, his eyes never leaving Lisbet. She seemed to be searching for someone.

Francesca stood on her tiptoes, trying to see above the crowd.

Before she could reply, a man approached Lisbet. He, too, wore a half-mask, like many in the crowd, and was dressed as a pirate.

Lisbet and the stranger took their places among the dancers. It was evident she knew her partner, from the way she spoke to him.

Most likely, the meeting had been prearranged. What better place than the anonymity of a crowded dance in the twilight hours, amidst a pack of common folk?

He glanced at Francesca. "Is it Bicker?"

Francesca did not meet his eyes. Finally, she shook her head reluctantly. He waited, realizing how grave the situation was. "Carel van Milne."

He frowned, the name familiar to him. "Of the armament wealth?"

She nodded again, clearly reluctant to say more.

He whistled, then turned to watch Lisbet and her partner once more. He had heard of the family and now tried to recollect what he knew. His eyes narrowed. "He is married, is he not?"

"Yes."

"Lisbet's a fool if she thinks she can win Bicker's son."

Francesca gave him a worried look. "Do you think someone will recognize her?"

"'Twould serve her right."

"Does that mean you shan't do anything to help me protect her?"

Dirk cursed silently at the pleading look in her eyes. Lisbet's virtue had probably been lost long ago. But her reputation remained unsullied, probably due more to Francesca's diligence than anything. He suppressed a sigh, his annoyance tempered by understanding. If anything did happen to Lisbet, he knew whom Jacob would blame.

"Very well," he said at last, telling himself it was in his own self-interest to protect Lisbet's virtue. "But you must cooperate with me."

Francesca nodded.

"I shall cut into Lisbet's dance and remove her from Mynheer Carel's clutches," he said with a grim smile. "You step in her place with van Milne."

At her startled look, he touched her cheek. "You needn't fear. I'll protect you as closely as I guard Lisbet's reputation tonight."

Her eyelashes fluttered downward.

"Ready?"

She nodded.

He took her hand and plunged his way into the crowd of dancers. Leaning down, he said in Francesca's ear, "Try to keep your eyes on me. As soon as you see me leaving the dancers, excuse yourself from van Milne and rejoin us. I don't think you'll have any problem with van Milne. If you do, I'll come to your rescue. Understood?"

She nodded.

"Good." He gave her hand a squeeze.

When they reached the couple, Dirk let Francesca's hand go with a twinge of regret and tapped the masked pirate on the shoulder. "Excuse me," he shouted above the music. With a smile to the gentleman, he took Lisbet's hands, ignoring her cry of outrage, as he swung her away from her partner. With a nod to Francesca, he urged her forward.

Thankfully, she understood the importance of following his instructions. With only a second's hesitation, she stepped in front of van Milne with a hesitant smile. The man was forced to return her smile and offer his arms.

Dirk led Lisbet away in time to the music, feeling her trying to break loose. He merely smiled at her and tightened his hold.

He had to hold back laughter at her attempt to put on a good face as she realized who had claimed her. "What in heaven's name are you about?" she shouted above the music.

He inclined his head with a smile. "What think you, but dancing with the loveliest lady at the kermis? You expressed a desire to dance. I was certain by now you had tired of common folk. Would you give me the pleasure of your fair company?"

Lisbet smiled with visible effort. "Of course, but what of Francesca?"

He maneuvered Lisbet around so he was facing toward where he had left Francesca and breathed a sigh of relief to see her dancing still with van Milne. "I see she has found some lout to twirl her about."

"Very well. Just one dance, then—" She craned her neck, trying to spot her partner. Dirk immediately swung her the other way, deciding all of a sudden his mission would not be so burdensome after all. He would have some sport of it.

He smiled at her again. "'Sooth, what is your haste? Do you begrudge me some time with my future 'sister'? What a sore trial you plan to afflict upon the men of Amsterdam, when you are wed to Johan Bicker. They will surely go into mourning when you are no longer an available maiden." He looked her over at the last word.

Lisbet gave him an uncertain look, as if not sure whether he was paying her a compliment or jesting with her.

As the music continued, he smiled and uttered a few more flattering phrases. When there was finally a break in the music, he took her arm and guided her to the edge of the square. He gave one glance behind him, scanning the dancers. When he saw Francesca, he lifted one hand. She spotted him and nodded.

Good girl, he told her silently.

He led Lisbet to a little space between the onlookers, keeping her arm firmly in his grip.

Francesca wended her way slowly between the dancers.

Lisbet put a hand to her heaving chest. "That was most enjoyable, Dirk. As I'm not nearly fatigued, I will rejoin the dancers."

He only smiled and shook his head.

Francesco emerged from the crowd then. "Good, you didn't leave without me," she said, panting with exertion from the dance.

He winked at her. "Never." Then he turned back to Lisbet. "'Sooth, my dear sister, I thought it best if I escorted the two of you fair damsels home. The hour grows late and I wouldn't have your father fret."

Blue eyes narrowed through the slits of her mask, but Dirk only smiled as he took both ladies by the arm and turned their steps away from the kermis.

Perhaps his help tonight would bring Francesca closer to him and make her forget that painting master.

The brief taste of her lips had only left him wanting more. He yearned for their marriage day, but he would not have some frightened bride. He desired a woman as eager as he.

He had enjoyed being her ally this night. How would it feel to have a loyal mate, someone to champion him and trust him through thick and thin?

A niggling worry flickered through his mind. How would she react if she knew what he was planning for her guardian?

He shrugged aside the fear. If all went according to plan, she would never know who was responsible for van Diemen's downfall.

Vowing to continue his wooing of his bride-to-be, Dirk tightened his hold on her arm as he guided both ladies to a trekschuit.

Dirk shifted on the leather-bottomed chair before Mynheer Jacob's desk. He never felt comfortable in this man's sanctum. It reminded him too strongly of all the man had accumulated over the years, while condemning an innocent young woman to the streets.

Jacob leaned back in his chair behind the desk. "I wanted to thank you for the tip the other day." Dirk interpreted the slight tug of his lips as a smile.

Dirk made a gesture to forget it.

"Not at all," the older man insisted. "I must admit I made a tidy sum on that shipment of hardwood."

"A trifle."

"Come now, that was a most respectable profit."

Dirk shrugged. "I'm glad you are content with it. Those sums are easy enough to make on the beurs."

"It will go a long way in financing my daughter's wedding."

Dirk stretched out his legs in front of him. "Ah, yes, with de Heer Bicker's youngest?" He put just the slightest emphasis on the word.

The lines in the man's forehead deepened at the slight note of disdain. "Their oldest son is already married and the next eldest is betrothed to one of the Tripps."

"The youngest is, nevertheless, an accomplishment," Dirk returned in a soothing tone. He tipped his head. "My congratulations on the union."

"Of course, the negotiations are by no means finalized. They are but suitors." Jacob drummed the desktop with his fingers, his gaze not meeting Dirk's. "There are still questions concerning the marriage portion... It isn't cheap to maintain a residence of this sort in Amsterdam. Then there is the cost of the wedding, which must needs be an elaborate affair with half the population invited." His tone echoed his impatience at this last requirement.

"And then, of course, to maintain one's status there is the villa in the country," Dirk reminded him.

"Why, er, yes, of course." Jacob picked up a paper knife and rolled it between his palms. "You mentioned your villa the other day."

"Yes, I've just purchased it. The owner went bankrupt, leaving it half completed. I've had it finished. It's quite a pleasant locale by the dunes."

"Ah, an ocean villa. Whereabouts?"

"Zandvoort."

Jacob looked at him sharply under his dark eyebrows. "That's quite an accomplishment for one of your years. Your time in the Indies has paid off richly for you."

Dirk smoothed down his mustache to hide his smile at the grudging accolade. "I worked hard for what I earned there." Time to whet the man's greed some more. "Since returning to Amsterdam, I've been able to triple my original capital." A slight exaggeration, but close enough to the truth.

Jacob's eyebrows drew together sharply, forming a deep furrow between them. "Buying and selling on the exchange?"

Dirk nodded slowly, controlling his features.

Jacob swallowed, doubt and avarice wrestling across his features.

Dirk eased his weight in the chair, beginning to feel more comfortable at this meeting the man had requested. "I know what it's like to work hard and save coin by coin." He surveyed his enemy's office with its gold-framed paintings and porcelain curios. "Bit by bit the profits increase until one day you can call yourself well-to-do and begin to enjoy the fruits of your labor."

He watched Jacob's face under his brow. "An alliance with a powerful family is the crowning achievement."

Jacob nodded, his features easing. "Yes, you see how important that is."

Before the man could get too self-congratulatory, Dirk added, "The trick is maintaining your position amidst the Bickers. You must never become a mere pawn of theirs through a marriage contract."

A flicker of fear appeared in Jacob's dark eyes. "My wealth is not insignificant."

"I'm sure it is not." Dirk paused. "Still, people like the Bickers love nothing better than to swallow up those beneath them. Amalgamate the wealth, they call it. Build a dynasty. Where does that leave someone like you or me?"

Jacob's lean fingers once again toyed restlessly with the paper knife on his desk, making Dirk sure the thought had crossed the man's mind.

"The only defense, as I see it," Dirk continued, "is substantial wealth of one's own. That is, if you wish to move as an equal in their circles."

"Yes." Jacob's voice was soft, speculative.

"As they say 'money begets money.' It is only with accumulated capital that you can begin to increase it five-, ten- even twenty-fold."

Jacob's hooded eyes gleamed with the desire Dirk knew well. He had seen it countless times from the lowliest criminal to the most powerful merchant.

He sat back. Enough for one day. "Apropos, I had mentioned having you and your family come down to my villa until the wedding. The place still needs some final touches—the gardens, as well as some furnishings. I thought that Miss Francesca, with her artistic talent, and Miss Lisbet, with her refined taste, could aid me with their advice."

Jacob nodded his head, his thoughts elsewhere.

"What say you to Sunday after service? It gives me the opportunity to become better acquainted with my future wife. I don't believe Lisbet will be bored. There are quite a few neighboring villas. If I recall, the Bicker's country seat is only a short ride away."

Jacob's eyes lifted, his attention caught by the name, as his visitor knew it would be. "I believe we can make our preparations for Sunday."

His purpose accomplished, Dirk rose. At the door the two men bid each other farewell. As Dirk turned to leave, he felt the other man detain him with a touch on the arm, causing him to stiffen. But he managed a look of polite inquiry.

"I want to thank you again for your tip on the exchange. If you should hear of anything else in future—" Jacob cleared his throat. "Anything more—ahem—substantial."

Dirk nodded.

"I would be most interested."

"You will be the first to know."

⁂

Francesca dabbed a bit of paint on the canvas, attempting the tawny eyebrows that framed Dirk's eyes. She wasn't satisfied with the eyes she'd painted. They did not capture that blend of amusement, irony, and hint of vulnerability she had glimpsed upon occasion.

It was hard to focus on the painting the way she ought. She kept finding herself thinking of Dirk's lips on hers. When he'd bid them goodnight after the kermis, he'd kissed her lightly once again.

Francesca gave her head a small shake and studied the canvas before her. A quick glance at Dirk seated in her sitting room showed him still staring out the window. He seemed distracted today, so Francesca hoped he would not notice her own inattention.

After being closeted some time with her guardian, Dirk had marched into her sitting room, dropped into his chair and demanded she begin earning her wages.

He had made no reference to the kermis or to Lisbet. Grateful still for his help that evening, Francesca made no retort to his brusque greeting. She got out her oils instead. But now, after several minutes had gone by in silence,

Francesca craved the conversation she'd grown accustomed to with him.

She put down her brush and picked up another, swirling it into the flesh tone she had mixed earlier, and glanced at her subject.

She cleared her throat. When he seemed to awaken from his reverie, focusing on her, she said, "Could you please look forward a little?" She pointed her brush toward the wall at her side. "If you look at that painting it should give me the right angle." He complied without a word.

She dashed away her disappointment that he hardly seemed aware of her.

She concentrated on his features. His nose was strong and high-bridged, with nostrils that could flare in an instant. His narrowly bearded jaw tightened for a moment, emphasizing the ridges and planes of his cheeks. With a start, Francesca realized she was learning to read his face and could spot anger, impatience, and genuine amusement by the merest tensing or relaxing of his features. Had she read desire? Heat rose in her cheeks as she remembered the look in his eyes the moment before he'd kissed her.

Yet, for all her physical awareness of him, she knew very little of the man within, she conceded. For most often, he exhibited a tough exterior, one that very little could ruffle or discompose. But to paint him successfully, she must know what drove him—or hurt him.

Glancing at the canvas, Francesca exhaled in frustration. Without that insight the portrait would be nothing more than a passable likeness. The face that was emerging was the one Dirk turned on her every time he sat there. It was the face of cynical amusement. But she was missing something. She must be!

The sheer determination that had transformed the boy from the Tughuis into the wealthy gentleman now sitting before her in velvet finery. The vivid spark that made her aware of him the moment he entered the house. The man who rushed through her blood like the most potent wine as soon as he drew near, the mere touch of whose lips on hers created a storm in her, which haunted her very sleep.

Francesca cleared her throat again. Best to initiate some conversation before her emotions took complete control of her. "I showed Pieter the portrait. He...likes it thus far." Perhaps that would please him, at least restore some confidence in her abilities. It certainly had reassured her.

Dirk gave her a long look. "What does he have to do with my portrait?" Though he hadn't moved in the slightest, Francesca sensed he was ready to spring.

She bit her bottom lip, realizing she had said the wrong thing. In the tension-filled atmosphere, the ticking clock suddenly took on a disproportionately loud sound.

"He is a gifted artist who knows when a work is good. If this portrait turns out at all well, it will be thanks to his guidance."

In one quick motion Dirk was out of his chair and began to pace the small room. "Who gave you permission to show my portrait to that simpering parasite who doesn't even know what an honest day's labor is?"

Francesca put down her brush, grieved for her friend. "There is no harder worker than Pieter. He not only toils for another artist, but gives lessons as well, all the while trying to complete his own canvasses. There is no more deserving man I know. He is doing me a priceless favor by helping me in his precious little spare time—"

He turned to her so fast, she flinched. Quickly, she set down her brush before it could ruin her progress.

He gave a bark of laughter. "Painters? Deserving? Devil take the lot of them! What do they do all day but feed on the vanity of their rich patrons? They're slaves to a bunch of rich merchants like your guardian, who are only a generation or two removed from the boers. Crass men who don't care what price they pay for immortalization, as long as they have washed the smell of mud and manure from their boots and can pretend to some non-existent aristocratic blood."

Francesca stared at him, fascinated by the anger his words revealed. "As a rich merchant yourself, I suppose you would know all about that," she said, wondering if she would at last glean more about the man behind the mocking facade.

But his anger evaporated as quickly as it had arisen. His mouth quirked upward ruefully. "At least I'm honest about my origins."

She wiped her brush, sorry he had gained control so quickly.

"Forgive my outburst." He raked a hand through his hair. "I—have things on my mind today."

"Yes, I noticed."

Suddenly, he strode toward her and she braced herself, afraid he would look at her canvas.

But he stopped behind it. "I find I haven't the patience to sit for you today. Would you let me take you somewhere instead?"

Thankful he had not attempted to view her work, she only nodded in relief. "If you wish."

He held out his hand.

"Wait, my brushes—"

"Your brushes will still be here when we return. And if they're ruined, I'll buy you some new ones."

When they were halfway out the room, she asked, "Where are we going?"

A gleam shone in his amber eyes. "You shall see."

Her heart stepped up its beat. Wherever he was taking her, she had no doubt she would not be disappointed.

They stepped out of the trekschuit at the Damrak, the largest canal spilling into Amsterdam harbor. Dirk took her arm and led her to the edge of the harbor.

They could hardly see the water for the ships lining the quays.

Twin rows of pilings were strung from one end of the curved harbor to the other. The ships—perhaps a hundred, perhaps more—sat so closely moored their sides almost touched. Francesca listened to the creak of settling timbers and the gentle lap of water hitting the ships' sloping sides.

As far as they could see, flags of all colors flapped in the breeze from the thick forest of masts covering the horizon.

"They hail from every corner of the globe," he said.

Francesca looked behind her at the ancient Weeper's Tower, where for centuries women had waved farewell to their adventuring menfolk. "What did you wish to show me?"

Dirk smiled down at her, his mood lightened. "Allow me to give you a glimpse of my world this afternoon."

She caught the faraway look in his eye. Would she at last be privy to the man behind the mocking smile? Remembering his outburst, she couldn't help a small smile. "The one filled with rich merchants willing to pay the price of immortalization?"

His eyes twinkled. "Aye. The coin has created it, but only a man's sense of adventure and craving to surpass himself has sustained it. The greedy sit in their counting houses here in Amsterdam and watch their profits multiply, having nary a clue what these profits cost the men who bring them in."

As he stood immobile, breathing deeply of the salt-laden air, she could imagine him on prow of one of the ships before them.

"Smell that?" His head fell back a fraction, nostrils flared.

She took a tentative whiff. A jumble of scents greeted her, not all of them pleasant. There was the acrid, burning pitch stirred in a large iron cauldron at the water's edge, used to tar the ropes and seams of the ships. There was the sweet-acrid tobacco smoke from a clay pipe of a passing seaman. There was the stink of rotting fish, which seemed to have seeped into the very stones and planks of the dike at her feet.

Dirk chuckled at her gesture of distaste. "What you smell is risk. Man pitting himself against the elements and against his fellow man. You smell the hair-raising danger of our swift renegades capturing a Spanish prize right under the very noses of their mighty fortresses. You smell our daring when we outmaneuver the English on the Narrow Seas, which they call their own"—he chuckled deeply—"and we show them otherwise."

Francesca nodded in understanding, feeling as if she were standing on the deck of one of the mighty ships anchored in the harbor, just waiting to weigh anchor. The city at her back was her vessel, the life beckoning her, an unchartered ocean.

Dirk gestured to the harbor. "These East Indiamen elude the Spanish, the Portuguese, and the English to bring back untold riches from the Malay Archipelago and the China coast."

Looking into his glowing eyes, Francesca could almost picture those far-off lands.

He took her hand once more. "Come along. This is an area you must see on foot."

They walked along the quay beside the Ij, the arm of the Zuiderzee which washed Amsterdam's shores. "Stick close beside me. Today, you will be seeing a seamier side of the city than your Prinsengracht address.

"It's the world that begat me. 'Tis a world of sailors and harlots of every stripe and race. A world the immaculate housewives of our city wash from their front stoops every morning, guarding their neighborhoods vigilantly against the filth and sin they are afraid might infiltrate from the wrong quarters."

With a fearful yet curious look around her, she drew closer to Dirk, as if she'd see the vice he spoke about reaching out its tentacles toward her.

He pointed out the timber- and grain-laden ships from the Baltic. "Those are bound for the fair land of your father. And those over there hail from the Scandinavian ports of Bergen and Copenhagen. They bring their tar, iron, and copper to feed our thriving munitions industry. Your Lisbet shall enjoy the profits that fill the Bickers' coffers—if she manages to retain her virtue until the betrothal documents are signed."

Francesca was too distracted by the sights and sounds around her to spare more than a passing thought to Lisbet.

Sailors rolling casks of wine from Nantes shouted good-naturedly to one another in a babble of languages. Black-skinned men piled hempen bags of Javanese rice one atop the other. Copper-skinned Indians and turbaned Arabs threw bolts of Chinese silk and bales of Madras cotton into the warehouses fronting the harbor.

Dirk led her across New Bridge, lined with its bookshops, stationers, and ships' chandlers and continued to the next quay. As they passed a narrow alley, Francesca recoiled at the sight of a haggard woman eyeing them.

"A harlot too wretched to ply her trade in a tavern," Dirk said in her ear.

Instead of drawing Francesca away from the pale, pathetic form with pock-marked face and scarlet lips, her tangled hair the color of crushed, dirty straw, he veered towards her. "Good day, to you. Not much trade this hour, I'll warrant?"

"Nay, mynheer."

She put out a grimy hand when Dirk reached into his pocket. The clink of coins changed hands. "God be with you, mynheer." She smiled widely, revealing toothless gums.

As they walked away, Francesca studied Dirk's face. "You know her?"

"I make it my business to know them." At her dismay, he frowned. "'Tisn't because I use their services. I just know the life they lead. When they get too disease-ridden, they must leave the taverns and ply their trade in the alleys."

Francesca shuddered.

"How old do you think she is?"

She shook her head, at a loss. The woman seemed old, yet ageless, as if she'd never known youth. "Forty?" she ventured, naming a number that sounded indeterminate.

He gave a grunt of laughter. "Seven-and-twenty is her age."

"I can scarcely credit it." She looked to see if he were teasing her but there was no humor in his eyes. Only a sadness she'd never seen in them.

"Yes, only a little older than yourself. Not so long ago, she was still a girl, not so different from you or Lisbet. Probably just beginning to work as a serving girl. Then, perhaps used by her master and thrown out on the street when she became with child, she was left to fend for herself. A tale told countless times on these streets. If she was lucky, she'll have lost the babe," he added bitterly.

She began to look more closely at the faces around her. She'd been brought up to fear the docks as a place of filth and vice. Those elements were present, to be sure, but now she began to glimpse the rich and exotic elements making up the tapestry of harbor life.

They turned a corner and once more were by the sea. Two different worlds existed next to each other, one filled with the bright promise of the future, the other with the despair of the past.

Dirk's sudden stop jerked her out of her sobering discovery. Francesca glanced up at him, wondering what he had seen to halt him in mid-stride. She followed his line of sight and frowned in confusion at the open doors of a warehouse.

"An East India pakhuis," he explained, leading her inside the cavernous interior.

Francesca drew in a breath as she stepped across the threshold of the gray stone building. She stopped short, a smile of wonder creasing her lips. If she had ever imagined a Far Eastern sultan's lair, she need go no further. Spread before her was a treasure trove of wealth as far as she could see. Bolts of gold-threaded silk spilled from copper-plated chests. Others held raw silks and grosgrains, while still farther inside, Chinese Blue Ming ware vied with Japanese and Korean porcelain for attention.

"The latest cargo is on display for those buying and selling on the exchange," he said.

Francesca was overwhelmed by more rich merchandise than she had ever seen. Her fingertips followed Dirk's, caressing the black, polished surface of a lacquer-work cabinet with a silvery-white, inlaid mother-of-pearl design. He showed her the ships' list and she read with growing astonishment the hundreds of thousands of pounds' worth of spices, jewels, wood, furniture, and indigo aboard the fleet.

Down one aisle the scene conjured up a Mideastern bazaar with its jute bags overflowing with a myriad of colored spices.

Dirk took up a handful of brown nuts covered by spidery red husks. He brought them up to Francesca's nostrils, and she inhaled their woody, slightly lemony scent. "Nutmeg and mace from the Banda Islands," he identified for her.

Francesca felt like a child as she followed his lead, going from bag to bag, touching and sniffing the contents. Black, wrinkled peppercorns from Sumatra. The hard brown swirls of cinnamon bark from Ceylon and the sugary bits of preserved ginger from Japan. But the scent she loved best was the most mysterious and aromatic of all.

Dirk thrust his hand into the burlap sack and held out the small black, spiked orbs in his palm for her to sniff. "The very essence of the Indies—the cloves of Amboina." He smiled. Gone was the sadness and bitterness of before. In its place a boyish sort of pride. "This is where my fortune began."

Francesca closed her eyes and breathed in the spicy aroma.

"No self-respecting Holland's kitchen is without it. It's

at the heart of our country's wealth."

By the time she stepped back outside, her senses were reeling.

"Seen enough?"

She blinked in the sunlight. Could there possibly be more to see? The challenge in his amber eyes compelled her to shake her head. If he had more to show her of his world, she wanted to see it.

"Very well. I shall show you the inside of a musico."

Francesca gasped, looking up at Dirk to see if he was teasing her.

To enter a tavern patronized by sailors, prostitutes, and every other unsavory character. Was this what he meant by his world?

Eight

Francesca hesitated in the doorway of the drinking and gaming den, reluctant to enter the smoke-filled room. She knew no woman of good repute ever went inside such establishments.

"Frightened you'll be recognized by an acquaintance?" Dirk's soft voice taunted in her ear.

She remembered that if she wished to know the man whose likeness she strove to capture, she mustn't lose heart now. She gathered her skirts, preparing to enter the lion's den. "Of course not."

He held her back an instant. "Not so fast. Come this way." He led her along the edge of the crowded, noisy room. "We scarcely need throw your whole reputation out the window a second time. Look what drastic measures it took me the first time around."

She stumbled at the reminder of that fateful night of her abduction before realizing he was making sport.

"Easy there." His hold tightened as he guided her along the sawdust and sand-strewn floor. Through the hazy, smoke-filled interior, Francesca's eyes widened at the sight of the women around her. They were as loud and raucous as the men. Many sat upon their companions' laps, their generous bosoms barely concealed, as they laughed and sang bawdy ditties.

Dirk greeted several patrons along the way. They glanced up from their games of cards or dice, hailing him with evident pleasure.

He didn't stop until they arrived at an inconspicuous corner where he offered Francesca a bench at a sturdy, wood-planked table.

A tall, serving maid, with arms as brawny as a sailor's, came over. "Haven't seen you for an age, Dirk," she said with a smile and wink. Her blond hair fell in stringy wisps from the edges of her wilted cap.

"Hello, Gert," he drawled. As he chatted with her, she eyed Francesca with a speculative look.

Francesca realized she must appear a strange sight in her dark, sober gown, sitting across the table from a man so handsome and commanding. Today, he wore a dark green doublet embroidered in gold. She felt like a dowdy peahen alongside a colorful bird of plumage.

And, yet, for all his fine gentlemanly garb, he seemed as at home in these surroundings as he did in her receiving room.

When it was clear Dirk was not going to introduce her to the waitress, the woman took his order and sauntered off with a shrug, her hips swaying from side to side, reminding Francesca of the broad ships at anchor.

As the woman disappeared between the smoky, boisterous tables, Francesca's attention was caught by one couple, the woman seated atop the man's lap. With a start, she realized the man's hand was up the woman's skirt.

She hastily looked away only to find Dirk observing her. Fighting the blush flaming her cheeks, she clasped her hands atop the table, trying to appear composed.

"What do you think thus far?"

She moistened her lips, unsure what to say. "I-it's very different."

He gave a short laugh. "About as far removed from your guardian's as the South Seas."

When the Gert returned and placed a jug of wine and a quart flagon of ale before them, Francesca eyed the drinks warily.

"Don't fret, they're not spiked."

Francesca's glance shot up to his. "Spiked?"

He chuckled at her look. "Black henbane seed,

belladonna, thorn apple—those are the usual agents used to drug an unsuspecting innocent." He poured her a cup of wine and lifted the golden liquid to eye level. "But I know the owner—Klaus—and he serves his patrons unadulterated beverages." He handed her the glass.

Francesca held the goblet in her hand, wondering if she were equal to the challenge she read in his gaze.

When she still hesitated, he lifted his tankard in a toast. "To your artistic education."

Taking up her goblet, she took a tentative swallow, surprised to find the sweet wine palatable.

"'Tis not what you drink at Jacob's, but it won't kill you."

As they sipped their drinks and Dirk engaged a sailor behind her in conversation, Francesca continued observing the patrons. Despite her shocked sensibilities, the more she watched, the more fascinated she grew. If Dirk had intended to pique her artistic interest, he'd reasoned accurately. Her fingers itched to sketch the faces around her.

Before they left the tavern, Dirk introduced her to its owner. Klaus was a large man with a shock of white hair, matched by a tuft of beard at his chin and lush mustache hiding his upper lip. Looking at him, Francesca found it difficult to believe he owned this den of iniquity. His fatherly air belied his rough trade and customers. It was another example, she realized, where the surface hid a person's true qualities.

"How has Dirk enticed you into this slop joint?" he asked with a wry chuckle, the shrewd look in his eyes telling her there was little in his establishment he didn't see.

"She's a painter," Dirk explained. "And as my future wife, she ought to see a slice of Amsterdam life that doesn't usually find itself on the canvas or along the banks of the Herengracht, don't you think?"

"Future wife, eh?" Klaus looked her up and down with more interest. "Well, well, this is a tale I must hear. And a painter, too!" He waved a hand around the tavern. "What think you of this scene before you?"

Francesca opened her mouth, unsure what to say.

Dirk grinned. "As you can see, my friend, Miss Francesca is rendered speechless by the specimens of humanity you have on display."

The two men's banter gave way to talk of the ships that had come into port, captains they both knew, and cargos to be sold. Francesca was content to listen, all the while watching the tavern keeper's face. His knowledge of the goings-on about the wharf astonished her. Why, it even sounded as if he did some buying and selling on the beurs himself.

When they finally left the harbor area, Francesca heard the carillons of the Nieuwe Kerk ringing, reminding her how late it was. She sighed with something akin to regret, realizing only now how much she had enjoyed the unorthodox afternoon.

Like the barge being pulled by the heavy draft horse along the nearby canal, her thoughts were tugged against her will back to her quarter of the world. "I must go. Katryn will worry, and I must help her with supper."

Dirk nodded. "I'll take you on a trekschuit, and you'll be home in a thrice."

As they sat in the barge together, neither spoke much. Francesca gazed at the rows of brick houses she passed, her mind picturing again all the strange sights and individuals she'd seen in Dirk's company. Even though she'd been born and bred in Amsterdam, she had never been privy to the kinds of people Dirk had shown her.

She sneaked a peek at his profile, realizing it was the company he'd grown up with. How far he'd come from those people, and yet how at home he still seemed among them.

As soon as she arrived home—no, she amended hastily—as soon as all the evening chores were finished and she could retire to her room, she would sketch some of the sights she'd seen. The people, particularly, interested her.

When they arrived at the large townhouse on the Prinsengracht, Dirk helped her alight from the barge. At her front door, she turned to him, her mind full of all she'd experienced in the last few hours. "Thank you for—" At a loss for words, she ended lamely, "Showing me your world."

His eyes looked into hers and in them she thought she read a question. But then it was gone, and his amber eyes were filled with their usual mix of irony and mirth. "Now that you have seen it, think you it so far removed from your own world here on the Prinsengracht?"

She opened her mouth to reply in the affirmative, when she stopped, unsure how to answer. Barely a mile apart, the differences seemed vast. Yet, were they so very different? Her painter's eye longed to reach the privacy of her room and begin to work out the answer with pen and ink.

The following Sunday, Dirk stood under the portico of his rose-pink brick Palladian villa, surveying the drive for the dozenth time that afternoon.

He glowered at the heavy sky. Not a cloud in the dratted sky until now, the day Francesca was arriving for her stay. The rain poured down as if the very heavens had opened their dikes and let the torrents gush forth.

With a muttered oath, he turned on his heel and stepped back inside. His sharp gaze searched for any detail out of place or left undone. Of course, the vase of flowers to welcome them in the entry was missing. The maid had fallen short of her duty again. He gritted his teeth, then strode to the back of the house to call her. What was the woman's name?

Dirk raked a hand through his hair, racking his brain for the name of one of the village girls he'd hired that week. Why weren't these Holland's maids like his Indies' slaves who walked about on silent bare feet, anticipating his needs before he could voice them?

Then he remembered. "Ada!" he roared, and he tensed at the clumsy sound of wooden shoes hitting the polished marble tiles. She should know better than to wear those indoors.

A flaxen-haired girl, tall and large-boned, appeared from a side corridor. "Yes, mynheer?"

He motioned impatiently toward a table along one wall. "Where are the flowers that go there?"

The girl blushed. "Oh, pardon, mynheer, I forgot." One look at his face, and she was curtsying out the room. "I'll fetch some."

He rubbed the back of his neck, wishing once again that his business with Jacob were over and done with. The man had taken the bait with such alacrity that it made Dirk almost ashamed. He could have been dealing with a child. Within a few months, Jacob would sell the very clothes off his back for a chance at buying and selling some choice cargo.

No, that business was not the problem. The aggravations came from other quarters. The way Jacob insisted on confiding things to him, for one thing. The last thing he wanted was to have the man's friendship.

But the more he saw of him, the more Dirk was forced to see the lonely, embittered man lurking behind the cold facade. Jacob would corner Dirk after transacting their business and insist he take a drink with him, smoke a pipe, and then tell him of his struggle to build his business. It was after a few such conversations that Dirk realized the man had no one else to talk to. He was suspicious of all his business associates. His daughter only approached him when she needed some material article. No personal acquaintances ever came to call except for Lisbet's friends and suitors.

Dismissing these thoughts, Dirk went back out on the portico to watch for his guests. He removed a handkerchief from a pocket and wiped his damp palms, his thoughts straying to Francesca.

In a short while he would wed her.

Wed her and bed her. He couldn't help the immediate direction of his thoughts.

Every time he was in her company, his desire for her grew. But it was more than that, he was coming to see.

He thought of their outing to the harbor. He'd taken her there on a whim. In retrospect, he realized he'd wanted to shake aside the qualms he'd been feeling after being closeted with Jacob for an hour. Perhaps in some way he wanted to justify his actions to Francesca—show her where he came from and in some way, make her his ally—even though she would remain ignorant of his true intentions toward her guardian.

But in the course of their afternoon along the quays and later in the musico, she had astounded him with her unabashed curiosity. She had been equal to every new and strange experience he'd shown her. He could almost see the painter's eye expanding its vision, and he'd felt like a fairy godfather opening new worlds to her.

He couldn't help a grin now, remembering her initial shock and discomfort in the bawdy house. But she had risen to the occasion, and by the end, it had seemed as if she had been reluctant to leave.

His thoughts strayed to their upcoming wedding night. Would she be as open and willing for him to show her new experiences in that realm?

He shook aside the question. Time enough for that. In the coming days, he intended to continue wooing her, behaving as courtly as any fine gentleman of Amsterdam.

In the meantime, he needed to remain cool and in control until all was put into place. It was no time to have a long-dormant conscience begin to rear its head. He had maneuvered his enemy right where he wanted him.

He heard the baying of his pack of hounds.

"Saskia! Druifje! Bloemtje!" His shout did little to slow the hounds' race to the arched gateway at the end of the long drive. Once there, they ran alongside the carriage that turned into the drive.

Dirk tensed, recognizing Jacob's ornate coach. Clearing his mind of all thoughts but those of being a welcoming host, he watched the carriage approach his villa.

His villa. There he stood, lord of the manor, in a position he had only dreamed of in those long-ago nights locked in the Tughuis, the only thought keeping him alive his desire for revenge.

He pasted a smile on his face as the carriage came to a stop under the portico. A village lad he had hired ran to open the carriage door and lower the step. Dirk stepped forward to greet his visitors. The first to emerge was Jacob. His smile, like his gestures, was stiff. Dirk suppressed a grim sigh of satisfaction, noticing the man's quick, sharp glance around the villa and grounds as if assessing the worth of every brick and stone.

"Dirk!" Lisbet rushed forward and extended her hand to be kissed. "What a charming country place." Apparently, he had been forgiven for having ruined her tryst the other night at the kermis.

He bent over her hand with his most charming smile. "I am sorry the weather is so bad you cannot see it to advantage. Perhaps tomorrow." He let her hand go and turned to the coach, seeking Francesca, who was the last to descend.

Her air of quiet elegance and self-possession left him feeling suddenly large and clumsy, his sordid origins gaping open like an ugly wound.

But the feeling passed when she gave him a smile of genuine pleasure. For the first time, he felt real enthusiasm about showing somebody his residence, the evidence of his success. He covered her fingers with his hand, lightly rubbing his thumb across the ridges of her cold knuckles.

"Did you have a pleasant journey?"

"Yes, thank you," she said. "Less eventful than the last one, thankfully."

He blinked in surprise, then threw his head back in laughter, glad to see she was finally recovering from that ill-fated abduction. Perhaps it meant that she was beginning to accept her betrothal to him.

He kept her hand in his. "Yes, thankfully. I wouldn't guarantee the life of anyone who would dare to abduct you again, my dear."

Her gray eyes widened. "I didn't mean you had to—oh, no—"

He smiled at her genuine shock. "You need have no fear. Anyone who dares bother you will have to answer to me."

With a last squeeze of her hand, he took Francesca lightly by the elbow and stepped over to Jacob. His guest stood staring up at the crest emblazoned above the open double wooden doors.

"My congratulations," Jacob said, a trace of surprise and irritation in his tone. "As owner of your own villa, I suppose I must address you as de heer now."

"You may call me anything you like. The title comes with the property, just as the crest." Dirk gave the older man an ironic smile. "In Holland nobility is measured by the weight of one's pocketbook. You will have a title as easily when you purchase your own villa."

Jacob's smile thawed a fraction, as if mollified by Dirk's downplaying of his achievement. He continued his perusal of the villa's facade. "It's lovely. Who was your architect?"

"It was begun by van Campen. When I purchased it half-finished, he was gracious enough to complete it, even though he is much sought-after and had several commissions at the time."

Jacob nodded, his eyes closely examining the Corinthian pilasters gracing the wide entryway.

"Come in, come in." Dirk gestured them toward the interior. Ada, he noticed with satisfaction, had placed the bowl of flowers on the table and now stood at attention with a tray of refreshments on the ebony buffet.

Jacob walked the perimeters of the room, inspecting and appraising everything in sight, while he sipped from an etched Venetian roemer.

Dirk walked beside him, studying the man's face for the merest hint of his reaction to all that he was seeing.

Jacob stopped before the long tapestries covering one wall. "Gobelins?"

"Nay, Flemish," he corrected.

The older man moved to the rear of the airy salon, where long windows overlooked the formal park. "'Tis well-laid out," he acknowledged.

Dirk nodded at the landscaped gardens and dark, rain-soaked forest beyond. "As you can see, we've begun planting the fruit trees. Unfortunately, there won't be much before next year."

"What beautiful porcelain," Lisbet exclaimed, looking at the vases lining a cupboard.

"Korean," Dirk replied. Turning, he caught a glimpse of Francesca's troubled face. His good humor at Jacob's reaction evaporated. In its place, Dirk suddenly felt nothing but self-loathing at his eager display of wealth. Who was he fooling? He was nothing but a bastard from the gutter aping a high-born nobleman. No amount of finery would hide the fact that he had once begged for bread.

"Ada, show our guests to their rooms." He inclined his head toward Jacob. "If you will excuse me, I must attend to a few matters. Please make yourselves at home. If any of you have need of anything, let one of the servants know." With no further words for the company, he pivoted on his heel and exited the foyer. At that moment, he no longer cared what his guests thought about his acquisitions.

The next afternoon Francesca strolled the gravel paths of the gardens at the rear of the villa. It felt wonderful to finally walk outside in the sunshine and be away from Lisbet for a spell. For the past hour, since Lisbet had finally emerged from her room, she'd done nothing but talk of the villa's grandeur and her anticipation at visiting the Bickers to compare it in size and value.

Francesca had not yet seen Dirk that day even though she had been up early.

The previous afternoon, he had disappeared so abruptly, she had wondered what had happened to suddenly change his sunny mood.

At dinner, however, his spirits had seemed restored, as he played the attentive host. He had a knack for drawing out her dour guardian, even making him laugh at his description of the various important men of business in the city. For someone who had only recently returned to the city, Dirk amazed Francesca by his thorough knowledge of its goings on.

With Lisbet, Dirk praised her in a way that had her glowing. Only Francesca seemed to sense an underlying irony to his compliments, but it was so subtle, she told herself she was imagining it.

He divided his attention equally among the three of them, making Francesca feel special each time his golden eyes met hers and he addressed some word to her. A part of her wondered how sincere his flattery was, if it flowed from his tongue so smoothly. She tried to tell herself she was being unfair, but she couldn't help the niggle of doubt.

She frowned, thinking back to their arrival at the villa. Dirk had overshadowed her guardian, like a boy showing off his bigger, more costly toys. It hadn't been anything he'd said or done. Francesca didn't even think it was deliberate. But the contrast had been painful for her to watch—Dirk, hale and hearty and powerful while Mynheer Jacob seemed to diminish with each step around the villa. Francesca had been filled with a strange, inexplicable foreboding.

The only comfort she'd felt at entering into a marriage with someone so superior in situation had been the belief that her future husband might actually need her. The more she got to know him, the more she sensed that behind his brash manner lurked the boy from the streets, who still hurt over the sufferings and deprivations he'd endured.

Francesca pondered these things as she walked around the well-laid garden paths. "Almost you convince me, Dirk Vredeman, that you don't need anything, not even a wife," she said to the vegetation and birds around her.

She reached the end of the park where a forest surrounded the villa's grounds. A narrow riding path beckoned her. She knew from Dirk that beyond it lay the sea. She could hear the faint lap of waves.

With barely a moment's hesitation, she took the dirt path. She smiled and tipped her face upwards. The cool forest felt good after the bright sunlight.

She continued walking until the house was no longer visible, welcoming the solitude where she could think undisturbed about all the changes that had come upon her life in scarcely more than a fortnight.

The land was softly undulating, as it led upward to the dunes.

Francesca was lost in thought when the sound of hoofbeats muffled against the leaf-strewn path brought her awareness of her surroundings once again. She glanced about, annoyed at first that her solitary walk was about to be disrupted, then suddenly fearful as she noticed the secluded area. Flashes of her terrifying ride upon a horse, bound and blindfolded, came back to her in a rush.

As the rider came around a bend, she sagged in relief at the sight of Dirk astride a chestnut stallion. Her heart began to hammer in another kind of anticipation.

He left her no time to react further. In a few seconds, he was almost upon her. She drew back from the path, suddenly afraid he wasn't going to stop. She brought her hands to her mouth to stifle a scream. As the horse drew abreast of her, Dirk slowed the beast. Without bringing it to a complete halt, he bent down and with one strong arm, grasped Francesca around the waist and lifted her atop his steed. She screamed, screwing her eyes shut, and clung to Dirk's arm as he urged the horse on again.

"Is this what you had in mind?" His deep voice rumbled in her ear as he kept his arm firmly around her waist.

"Are you mad?" She gripped his muscled forearm with rigid fingers, her lips stiff with fear.

"You challenged me, and I rarely turn down a challenge."

She shook her head, her eyes shut tight, hardly hearing what he said.

"You told me once I would have to abduct you in order to show you the sea."

She could scarcely breathe, let alone remember her silly words.

He chuckled. "You thought I'd forgotten. You must know, there is little I forget, especially when it concerns my bride. You needn't fear. I shall have you safely home by sundown."

His hold tightened on her a fraction. "Watch out for the branch," he warned, at the same moment ducking over her.

"W-wouldn't it be better to slow down a trifle?" She risked opening her eyes and the tall trees flew by her, their branches forming a canopy above her head. Francesca looked downward and saw twisted roots across the path. Before she could take in enough air for another scream, horse and rider had maneuvered around another bend.

"Scared?"

"You s-seem a capable rider," she stuttered. "'T-tis... 'tis just, I don't fancy riding."

He tightened his hold around her waist. "Don't worry, we shan't have any mishaps."

To her intense relief, the ride lasted only a few minutes more. When they emerged from the trees, they faced the grassy, undulating sand dunes, the only natural barrier between land and sea along the coast.

Dirk dismounted, then reached up for her. His two hands spanned her waist and lowered her to the ground. She tried to hide her reaction to the ride, but her hands were shaking too badly. She concentrated on the solid land beneath her, and heard Dirk's voice as if from a distance. "Isn't this day magnificent? The sky is clear blue. A perfect midsummer's day to spend at the seashore. Smell the salt-laden air." He took in a deep breath as if to illustrate.

She busied herself with smoothing her skirt until she trusted her hands not to betray her.

She almost screamed again when Dirk's thumb hooked her chin, forcing her gaze upward.

She read real concern in his eyes. "'Sooth, I did frighten you."

She pulled her chin loose and focused away from him. "Nay. You merely took me unawares."

"'Twas the horse ride, wasn't it?"

"No! It was the...way you appeared...so suddenly."

He didn't pursue the topic but turned to unstrap a saddlebag and blanket from his horse. He left the animal grazing amid the tall grass and slung the bag over his shoulder.

Francesca began climbing up the side of the dune, lifting her skirts above the tufts of long, dry grass.

She gasped when Dirk grasped her arm, bringing her to a halt. "You don't like sitting atop a horse."

Francesca tried to meet his gaze without wavering, but his look told her he would not be satisfied until he knew the truth.

"Much less a moving one," she muttered, her glance sliding away from his.

He laughed. "You poke fun at yourself when I least expect it."

"As do you."

He raised an eyebrow. "Do I?"

"One moment you're a rich, powerful, arrogant—"

"Don't forget boastful."

She stared at him a second before nodding. "Boastful man. And the next, it seems you are laughing at yourself as much as at the rest of us."

At the sight of his eyes crinkling at the corners, the bright sun bringing out the honey-gold highlights of his irises, Francesca's belly did a queer flip-flop. She shivered, wondering what it was going to be like joined in marriage to this man.

The two stood looking at each other a moment, until Francesca thought he was going to bend down and kiss her. She held her breath, her heart thudding.

But instead, his mouth broke into a grin and he took her hand. "Come on, we haven't a moment to waste."

As they trudged up the sandy slope, his boyish mood was contagious. Francesca forgot her fear as well as her earlier introspections. She inhaled the sweet fragrance of wild pink roses growing between the high grass and spotted tiny yellow wildflowers interspersed through it.

The ocean wasn't yet visible, but already she smelled its tang and heard the surf's steady pounding.

She soon found it hard to keep up with Dirk's long stride. His high boots were not inhibited by the sand which became looser and finer the higher they climbed. Her own feet sank into its soft dry depths, and her slippers were quickly filled with the warm, powdery grit.

"You can't walk in those."

Throwing aside the saddlebag, Dirk stooped down and grasped one of her ankles, lifting her leg. She was forced to clutch his shoulder to keep from losing her balance. Without asking her leave, he placed her foot upon his thigh.

Quickly, he doffed one of her slippers and proceeded with the other.

"Your stockings," he ordered, glancing up at her.

She stared at him, then fearing he would do the honors himself, she turned without a word. With her back to him, she reached below her petticoats to undo her garters. When she turned to face him again, ready to continue their walk,

Dirk took her ankle again before she could take a step. He slid his hand around her bare foot and up her calf.

Obliged once again to hold onto his shoulders for support, her thoughts scattered at the feel of his palm against her skin. "W-what are you doing?" No man had ever touched her there.

He smiled up at her, his hand caressing her heel and arch. "Admiring God's handiwork,"

"I'll wager you've seen many a woman's foot before." Her attempt at asperity came out a breathless whisper.

"Aye, but never such a fine specimen," he replied. "Nor one as delicately shaped, nor as soft as this one," he added as if discovering each new quality the longer his hand traveled over each contour. He grinned up at her. "What's the matter? Not accustomed to hearing the praises of your foot sung? You are turning as red as one of the plums I've brought for our meal."

"You seem to enjoy discomfiting me."

"I must admit I've never enjoyed seeing someone blush, and so prettily."

"Thank you for the fine compliments, but I…I think I can manage on my own now." She removed her foot from his hand and shook out her skirts with an effort. Once again, her hands were trembling, but this time not from fear. Now, it was a strange, new sensation.

"You enjoy managing alone, do you not?"

Saying nothing, she turned from his discerning eyes. Alone? No, she thought to herself, but there had been no one since her parents died and she'd grown used to thinking there never would be.

They reached the top of the dunes. From their height they could look down at the wide swath of beach below.

"Ah!" Dirk patted his chest with his two hands. Meeting her glance, he smiled. "Clears out the rubbish up here," he said, pointing to his head. Before she could fathom his meaning, he picked up the blanket and saddlebag and slung them back over his shoulder. "Come on," he said, taking her hand once again.

He led her down a sandy path worn through the tall grass. Once on the damp, hard-packed sand of the beach, he threw down the satchel and spread out the blanket. Then he proceeded to remove his own boots and stockings. Francesca sat down gingerly on one corner of the blanket, trying not to look. When he began shedding his doublet, she turned away and stared straight ahead at the sea.

It was a rich, deep blue and extended as far as she could see. The waves were mild, with only small white caps breaking the surf.

A moment later, her view was blocked. Dirk stood in front of her in just his knee breeches and billowing white shirt. Before she could evade him, he pulled her to her feet and steered her to the water's edge.

"What are you doing?" she cried when he showed no signs of stopping.

"Teaching you how to get your feet wet."

"Stop, my hem's getting soaked," she yelped, jerking back from his hold.

"Hike up your skirts, woman. I want you to feel the water swirling 'round your ankles and feel the sand oozing between your toes." He stopped and eyed her with that challenging look she was coming to know. It made her very blood tingle through her.

"Maybe it'll distract you enough to stop mooning over some callow art instructor not worth your attention and show you what painting is really about—"

A burst of resentment shattered her pleasure. With a final tug, she pulled away from his grasp. "What do you know about painting? Or about a person's sentiments? Sentiments that may be pure and noble. You've marched into my life and taken it over, forcing me into a betrothal, planning my wedding without so much as a thought to how I might feel about it." She shook her head in frustration, suddenly overwhelmed by all that was taking place around her.

"One moment you seem to read my very mind, the next you are as unfeeling and autocratic as an—" She threw her hands out. "Oh, what's the use?" She spun around, kicking up a spray of water, and gathering up her skirts, she began to run.

She had not felt so free since her parents had died.

Since then, she'd had to play a role.

And now...and now—what role would she be forced to play? In a few days she would be wed. Panic filled her. Dear God, she prayed, what am I to do?

Nine

Winded, Francesca finally stopped running. She forced herself not to look back to see if Dirk had followed her.

Allowing her breathing to subside to normal, she stared out to sea. The water lapped around her ankles, and she reluctantly admitted Dirk had been right. Wet sand did feel good between her toes. When had been the last time she'd experienced it? A vague memory teased her, of being a child and clinging to her mother's and father's hands on either side. She remembered being lifted over the water by them and giggling as they let her down into the surf again.

Finally, when it was clear Dirk had not come after her, she shaded her eyes against the sun and turned to look back, unsure whether she felt relief or disappointment that he hadn't followed her.

He stood far down the beach, where she had left him, a few feet into the water, throwing something to the sea gulls, which swooped down to catch it in their beaks.

Her own distress evaporated at the sight of him, and she regretted her rash words, remembering again the little lost boy she sometimes glimpsed in him. Why had she reacted so violently? She realized whenever he said something about her painting, she lashed out. It was where she was most vulnerable, perhaps because it was all she had.

Her outburst hadn't even affected him, it was clear. She frowned. Why then had he taunted her about her friendship with Pieter? She shook her head, at a loss. If only he realized how different her feelings for him were from her feelings for Pieter.

Pieter was a friend and teacher—a man she looked up to and whose counsel she sought. But he didn't awaken the confusion, the longings, the absolute mayhem Dirk did in her. He didn't cause her to question her artistic ability.

She took a deep breath of the bracing air, knowing she must turn back and face the lion who was soon to be her husband. Slowly, she began walking toward Dirk. He had been right, it was a glorious day, and even if she did not have all the answers as yet, she would not waste this day. Perhaps she could capture it afterward on canvas.

When she arrived where Dirk stood, his glance flickered to her and back to the gulls. "Have you ever seen such greedy, indiscriminate birds? Good company for me."

She blinked. Had her words hurt him? But she saw only good-natured irony in his expression. He tore off another crust of bread and flung it skyward, only to have it immediately caught in a hungry beak. Francesca felt oddly deflated. She'd walked back ready to ask his pardon but his tone implied he didn't need any consoling words from her. Doubtless he'd been his master so long he didn't need anyone's apology.

Feeling the gulf between them, she waited quietly until all the bread disappeared.

As if by silent accord, the two walked back to the blanket. She helped lay out their lunch, surprised to see he had brought a bottle of Rhenish wine. She had expected to find only a jug of ale. The man was a mass of contradictions, rough waterfront sailor one moment, suave merchant the next.

When everything sat upon the cloth, she bowed her head to say a blessing and he followed suit.

"Doesn't this food taste about as fine as anything you've ever eaten?" he asked when they'd each taken a few bites from the sausage-stuffed rolls.

"Yes, I would have to agree that it does." She savored the finely spiced meat, stealing a glance at him. He appeared to have forgotten her outburst. Did it mean so little to him?

"I must have been hungrier than I thought."

He lay on his side, propping himself on an elbow, and examined his roll. "Hunger, yes, that's the first element. But the taste wouldn't be the same without the sound of the waves and the feel of the breeze and the warmth of the sun to accompany it."

She stared at him. It was as if he was the one with a painter's heart, knowing it was more than the mere object that had to be captured.

Closing her eyes, she tried to feel what he described. It astonished her how magnified the elements became against her closed lids and cheeks. She dug her toes into the sun-warmed sand at the blanket's edge and felt it cascade between her toes like granules through an hourglass. Could she have had half as much pleasure from her simple repast away from the seaside? Or without her companion?

Slowly, almost reluctantly, she opened her eyes and looked at him. He had sat up and was peeling a peach with a china-handled knife. She watched as he deftly wound it around the peach, removing the skin in one long swirling tail, barely scraping the surface of the fruit. When he finished, he speared it upon his knife and held it out to her with a smile.

She scarcely noticed the proffered fruit, her eyes drawn to the curve of his lip and his white teeth. Her gaze lifted to his golden eyes. What lay behind them? She read no mockery. Did he feel as shaky and uncertain inside as she did at this very moment?

She reached out and took the knife by its handle, her fingers grazing his. She brought the peach to her mouth and bit into its juicy flesh, watching him all the while.

If she could but capture with paint and brush the intensity she read in his eyes.

With a gentleness which surprised her, he brought a linen napkin to her chin and dabbed at the juice. Their eyes met and locked. "I know a more effective way of removing it," he whispered, "but I fear you wouldn't approve."

Warmth suffused her cheeks and spread to her limbs, as she remembered the taste of his finger when he had popped the strawberry into her mouth. At the memory of his fingertip against her tongue, her eyes dropped to his lips. For one instant, she admitted to herself she wanted to feel his lips pressed against hers again, not softly this time, but hard and consuming. Her lips parted at the thought.

She bit into her peach, desperately hoping its cool juice would quench her scalding thoughts—thoughts which couldn't be her own.

When she finished the peach, Dirk reached up towards her lace cap. "Today I must be satisfied in this regard." He firmly grasped her hands, which she had raised, and placed them in her lap. "Stay, my lady. You will not fight me on this. I am autocratic, as you pointed out."

She flushed at his reference to her outburst and let her hands lie still.

After untying and discarding her cap, he removed her hair pins one by one until her knot fell in a loose roll down her back.

His fingers ran through it, unraveling it, and spread the filmy mass upon her shoulders. She tried to move away, but his hand curved around her nape, stilling her movements. "I could only imagine how it would glint it the sun. But now I know. 'Tis rich indeed."

Dirk contemplated Francesca's glorious mane almost reverently, hardly daring to touch it. Its dark brown waves fell in airiest ripples down her back. Its feel was soft and springy, its scent an elusive flowery fragrance. He wound a silky strand around his finger and held it up against the light. Its coppery sheen was the perfect complement to her creamy skin and silvery eyes. Would such rich coloring not go along with a fiery nature? Her show of temper at the sea's edge had hinted at it.

At that moment, he no longer remembered nor cared

what his original motives for marrying her had been. All he knew was he wanted her as he had never wanted any other woman.

He was no longer satisfied with just possessing her body. No, he must possess her soul. That devotion she reserved for the likes of those unworthy souls like her guardian and that painter must be for him. He scowled, conceding that she'd not denied her affection for Pieter. For a few seconds he allowed himself to covet her love and loyalty with the simple longing of a child.

He clenched his hand around a handful of her hair. It was only by a supreme effort of will that he held back from burying his face in those coppery-tinted tresses and absorbing its very essence.

Rather than tempt himself too far, Dirk inhaled deeply, then with a deliberate motion, removed his hand and leaned back on his elbows. His body stretched out before him, his leg touching the material of Francesca's black skirt.

Momentary retreat, he decided. He mustn't scare her away. She'd accused him of not caring about her sentiments. Well, he would show her he could be as gentle and courtly as that anemic painter.

He couldn't—wouldn't—admit to himself his own fear. If she were to reject his advances in favor of that painter— he swallowed, refusing to consider what he would do.

"Why were you so frightened on the horse today?" he asked instead, remembering her reaction to the ride. No, fright was too mild a word. Stark terror had filled her eyes.

"I fell off a horse once."

"And you never got over that fall?"

"No."

He paused at her abrupt response.

"Tell me about it," he asked, making his voice as soothing as the soft lap of the waves. If he ever wanted to learn her secrets he would have to probe her skillfully.

She smoothed her skirt over her knees. "I had just come to live with Mynheer Jacob and Lisbet. That was five years ago. Lisbet was an accomplished rider, but I'd never ridden. M-Mynheer Jacob wanted me to learn, to be able to accompany her." Francesca's tone remained deceptively calm. "Lisbet wanted—needed—me to ride with her one afternoon before...before I felt ready." She gave a hollow laugh. "She took off before I had my horse under control. It threw me when we had to jump a low hedgerow."

Dirk pictured the scene. Francesca's tense fingers dug into the sand. He shifted onto his side and laid a comforting hand upon her shoulder. "Your horse was probably the wrong mount for you, a beginner. Lisbet shouldn't have taken you out so soon."

"Yes. At any rate, I sprained an ankle and broke my collarbone. I didn't mind the pain since it gave me an excuse not to go riding for some time." She paused. "I haven't been atop a horse since."

"How did Lisbet manage without your companionship?" he asked curiously.

She didn't reply right away. Finally, he heard her slow words. "It was...only one more tool she used...to make me... comply with her...schemes."

His eyes narrowed. "You mean accompanying her to the kermis so she could keep her assignation?"

She nodded, as if the revelation were painful. "I know it was wrong, but I couldn't bear the thought of ever mounting a horse again."

He shook his head. "You needn't berate yourself. It was perfectly natural not to want to ride again." He remembered what else she'd said. "You said it was only one more tool Lisbet used. What else did she have in her arsenal against you?"

She gave a twisted smile. "My drawing lessons."

His frown deepened. "How so?"

"Mynheer Jacob would have canceled them for me, but I...I promised Lisbet to help her if I could only continue receiving lessons. It worked for a time." She pressed her lips together and shook her head. "I regret ever making that rash promise."

"Somehow I doubt you came up with the scheme yourself. Tell me," he said, lifting her chin with a fingertip, "wasn't it Lisbet who figured how much you enjoyed the lessons and held it out as bait to get you to go along with her schemes?"

She looked at him, wonder in her eyes. It hadn't been too difficult to figure out. Didn't she realize he knew her enough to know she didn't have that kind of guile in her? "Yes," she finally whispered.

"I wouldn't worry too much about your complicity with Lisbet. She is the kind of resourceful girl who would have found a way to defy her father, whether you had been around or not."

Dirk withdrew his hand from her chin and lay down on the blanket, closing his eyes against the sun. To distract her thoughts, he told her, "I've arranged to drive your guardian and Lisbet over to the Bickers tomorrow."

"Oh?"

Even with his eyes closed, Dirk felt her surprised look resting on him. "Yes. I hope you don't mind not going along. 'Tis not that you are not welcome." He paused. "I thought perhaps you would prefer to stay here and work on the portrait, now that the light is better."

"Yes, of course," she said. "That was very thoughtful of you." She didn't sound as enthusiastic as he'd imagined she'd be to have time to paint to her heart's content. Neither did he detect any nervousness in her tone at the thought of being left alone with him. Mayhap she thought he was being autocratic again, when all he'd wanted was some time alone with her.

"You needn't worry about your reputation," he added. "Jacob's sister will arrive tomorrow to see that propriety is kept. She will stay at the villa a few days during his absence."

"Tante Blankaart?" Francesca's tone sounded vague, then on a sharper note, she added, "You mean they'll be gone more than an afternoon?"

"Mmm." The sun felt good upon his chest. He parted his shirt wider to receive its rays.

Silence ensued as he imagined she mulled over that bit of information. "Wh-what shall you occupy yourself with?" she asked after a while.

"As a matter of fact, I thought you could help me with the wedding arrangements." In truth, he had planned to handle the preparations himself, but after her accusations, he realized she was right. It was as much her wedding as his, and she had every right to plan the special day.

"I...see."

His lips twitched at her tone, as if she perhaps felt a bit nonplussed. "That should still give us ample time to continue our acquaintance. I shall be free to devote my attention to my future bride." He smiled, enjoying carrying on a conversation without seeing her face. Her tone, by merest inflection, conveyed so much.

"You are a most incomprehensible man." She sounded annoyed.

He chuckled. "I try to be when it suits me." Again, he felt her gaze leveled on him, studying him. Then suddenly he heard the rustle of her petticoats.

"Go ahead and take a nap. I shall tidy up while you rest."

Dirk knew in that moment she had withdrawn back into the protective shell of the prim, efficient Juffrouw Francesca, and he regretted teasing her.

Hoping to discover something more about her feelings for Pieter, he asked her softly, "Do you and Lisbet confide in each other?" At her silence he cracked open an eye. Her look was one of bewilderment as she knelt before the picnic basket. "I can't imagine Lisbet keeping everything to herself," he commented.

"She tells me...certain things. You should know that as you saw from the kermis. I try to be a wise counselor, although she listens to me but infrequently."

"Do you return her confidences?"

"I haven't anything to confide."

"Come, come, you must have all manner of things to confide. The manner in which you should dress your hair. The color of ribbon for your gown. The way a certain unmentionable young man glanced at you during your painting lessons."

"You seem to fancy yourself an expert on young ladies."

"I know something of women, though precious little of young ladies."

Francesca brushed off her skirts, as if the topic were at an end. "Whatever I would have to confide would be of no interest to Lisbet. So I hold my thoughts in private."

"What would you confide that I have not already mentioned?"

Her silvery eyes chided him in turn. "You should know better than most."

He hesitated, fearing the answer was Pieter. "Your painting?"

She smiled and he felt like a lad rewarded. "Yes."

Dirk heard the depth of her feeling in that one syllable. "And when does Juffrouw Francesca play?"

At the sound of her laughter, he gazed fascinated at the light-hearted girl kneeling before him. Her eyes sparkled like the sun-dappled water behind her. But it was her lush mane of hair that held him rapt. It looked like copper fire in the afternoon sun. She had an ephemeral yet eternal quality that defied age. He suddenly understood what she felt when she wanted to capture someone on canvas.

When her laughter subsided, she said with genuine pleasure, "My painting is my play."

"One must have play that is distinct from work," he insisted.

"Sometimes one derives all one's pleasure from one's work."

He shook his head at her. His smile held an ageless wisdom of its own. "Nay, there are other things."

Francesca awoke to see pale blue sky above her and hear the steady ripple of calm seas against the sand.

She lay motionless a moment longer, reveling in the peace she felt. Recollection of where she was, and with whom, came to her as gently as the incoming tide. Dirk had suggested a nap after their picnic, and to her surprise, she had fallen asleep to the sound of the waves.

Suddenly, the sky was shut out and she was staring up at Dirk and into eyes as warm as melting honey.

"You're awake." He was so close to her she could see her reflection in his pupils. That couldn't be she, that maiden who looked so untamed, with tresses fanned against the blanket and eyes wide. Involuntarily, her hand came up to her hair, but his hand cupped hers against the blanket.

The temptation to give in to his superior strength drained her of all will to move. Her eyes dropped to the well of his collar bone. She knew without looking farther that his shirt was wide open, exposing a generous portion of broad golden chest.

"I must have fallen asleep," she whispered, while keeping her eyes on the sculpted curve of his lips, afraid he could all too easily read her thoughts. Observing his unsmiling lips, she raised her eyes in question and then couldn't gaze away. As she lost herself in his amber eyes, she no longer heard the lap of the waves. When his eyes flickered downward, she knew they rested on her lips. She waited for the tidal wave of emotion that would hit the moment his lips met hers. But the cataclysm never came.

Dirk stayed poised above her a second longer, then moved away. Francesca felt the blood ebb from her. Weak and incapable of rising, she listened to the erratic rhythm of her heartbeat until it finally regained the even cadence of the waves.

When she could manage it, she sat up and brought her knees up to her chin, wrapping her arms around them, the sense of disappointment almost unbearable.

Dirk bent to pick up the picnic basket. "Although I hate to bring an end to our afternoon, I fear 'tis getting late. The others will wonder where we've disappeared to."

With a start, she stood and helped him fold the blanket she had lain on.

Thankfully, he did not oblige her to remount the stallion. Instead he led the horse back and walked beside her through the woodland path.

Upon returning to the villa, Francesca had no time to dwell on her disappointment. As soon as she entered the doorway, she was accosted by Lisbet.

"Where on earth have you been?"

Dirk answered for her. "She has been with me. Why do you ask?"

The bluster went out of Lisbet. "I...I needed her help in packing my bags for our visit to the Bickers. She always helps me." Her lip jutted out.

Out of habit, Francesca stepped forward. "It's all right. Let me help her."

She could tell Dirk wanted to dispute, but finally with a sharp nod, he said nothing more and excused himself.

Francesca watched him walk away, his absence leaving an immediate void in her. Part of her wanted to run after him, but her common sense told her she needed to be away from him to regain her equilibrium.

This afternoon, he'd thrown her off balance more than once. It scared her. She felt like a puppet on a string where he was concerned. One moment she felt he wanted her, the next he acted as indifferently as he did towards Lisbet.

How was she ever to trust him with her own feelings? And how did she know what they were?

Tante Blankaart, Jacob's older sister, arrived in her coach the following afternoon.

Dirk stood with the others under the portico to welcome her.

"Jacob, what a fuss you put me to, sending me word to pack my bags and come to Zandvoort without delay." The frail-looking lady dressed in a rich silk gown of deep burgundy remonstrated as her brother helped her descend. "Such a rush and bother. You know I need to have time to plan things. What are you doing here, anyway? I didn't know you had any acquaintances in Zandvoort. Or is it Lisbet's latest suitor?" Mevrouw Blankaart fumbled in her beaded reticule. "Francesca, my spectacles—"

Dirk frowned as Francesca rushed forward, taking the drawstring purse from the lady's arm and searching for the missing glasses. As soon as she'd located them, the old lady put them on and glanced up. "Is this your villa, Jacob? Have you finally purchased what you've hankered after? Very lovely," she concluded, looking the building up and down.

"No, Grietje—" Jacob began.

"My handkerchief, Francesca. These dusty roads..." As she took the item, she continued. "Then we are guests, are we not?" She finally noticed Dirk, when he stepped forward. She smiled, her wrinkled face framed by a lacy white cap. "And to whom do I have the pleasure? Are you Lisbet's intended?"

"Dirk Vredeman, at your service." He bowed over the dry, powdery-pink hand held out to him and brought it briefly to his lips. "Welcome, Mevrouw Blankaart. No, I am not Lisbet's suitor, but Francesca's."

"A pity for Lisbet," she commented, giving him a thorough going over. "And, please, 'tis Tante Blankaart to all."

He bowed. "Very well. As long as you call me Dirk."

"I shall be delighted. Now then, Francesca, can you please see to Minionne? The poor dear must be parched. You know how she dislikes traveling."

Before Dirk could put a stop to Francesca's fetching and carrying, a volley of barking erupted from Dirk's hounds, which had been circling the carriage. Above their bellow, he heard a shrill yap-yap at the coach's window and spied a small white head and pink nose of what he assumed to be Minionne.

"Francesca, do something!" Tante Blankaart's hands fluttered toward the coach. Sensing Francesca's move, Dirk clamped his hand on her shoulder.

"Saskia! Druifje! Bloemtje!" he rapped out. Immediately, the hounds looked at him, but the next second, they resumed their barking, their necks craning forward. He shouted at them again. Then he leaned into the coach. The miniscule lapdog gave him a startled glance before growling. As he reached out for her, she snapped her sharp little teeth. With a muffled oath, he grabbed her under the belly.

When he reemerged with the pink, white pooch squirming in the crook of his arm, he met Francesca's glance. She was biting her lip and her eyes were twinkling. His annoyance turned to amusement.

He handed Tante Blankaart her pet with a flourish. "The hounds won't hurt her. They just know how to make a lot of noise."

"Oh, thank you, dear man. There, there," she crooned, bringing the dog's face close to her own. "Mama's here. No one's going to hurt you."

When she looked up again, he said, "I can provide you with a personal maid, if you did not bring your own."

She blinked her blue eyes at him through her spectacles. "That is kind of you, mynheer, but Francesca knows my habits."

"Francesca will be very busy in the coming days with her wedding preparations."

The old lady looked crestfallen as she glanced between Francesca and him. "Oh, well, I daresay I can spare her, but if you please, sir, for this afternoon, she knows just how to make me comfortable."

He suppressed a sigh. "Very well, for this afternoon."

※

Once her guardian and Lisbet had been waved off in their carriage and Tante Blankaart settled in her room for a nap with her poodle, Francesca descended the stairs to a house that seemed quiet and empty.

Before she had reached the bottom step, Dirk stepped into the entry hall from another room.

"Is Tante Blankaart settled?"

"Yes," she answered and looked away. It was the first time they had been together unaccompanied since their outing to the beach. There was no sign of a servant anywhere. She shivered, feeling as if the two of them were the only ones in the vast house.

"I expected no less under your ministrations." When she did not reply to his teasing tone, he asked, "Tell me, does she ever stop?"

"Who?"

"Tante Blankaart. Since the moment she arrived, she has been needing something or someone."

She could only smile ruefully at his dry tone. "Only in her sleep, I think."

He shook his head, clearly not amused. "Since we're not sure how long this silence will last, I say we make good use of it. If she awakes and needs something, there are ample servants to attend to her."

She eyed him, guarding herself against any more surprises. "What did you have in mind?"

"Come along and I shall show you." He held out his arm.

Curiosity got the better of her. Resting her hand in the crook of his arm, she accompanied him outside and down a gravel path. It led beyond the gardens and down a tree-lined lane.

"Where are we going?" she asked when they neared some outbuildings.

"There's someone I'd like you to meet," was all he said.

Her pace slowed when they reached the stables.

"Here we are," he announced, propelling her toward a paddock.

He greeted the man who stood beside a pair of horses. "Good, I'm glad you have them saddled, Willem."

Francesca looked at the two animals before her, recognizing Dirk's sleek stallion. She backed away a pace from the mammoth animal, only to bump into Dirk behind her.

"Easy there," his soft voice murmured.

Suddenly, all she wanted was to turn and hide herself against him. But she straightened and pretended to examine the horses. Tentatively, she reached up and patted the smaller horse's neck. "She is very pretty."

The groom's tone dismissed the bay. "She's nothing but an old nag—"

"Willem. That's enough. Be about your chores."

Francesca glanced from the servant to Dirk. She'd never heard him use that tone of voice. With a quick bow, the man retreated.

"I chose this mount especially for you." Dirk's normal tone drew Francesca's attention back to the horses. "She's a gentle old mare who, I'm told, has never thrown anyone in her life."

"You mean, she's nothing but an old nag," she mimicked the stable hand's words.

"I mean," he said, steering her hand towards the horse's nose, "I thought you might start off on a gentle mount before progressing to a more spirited one."

She moistened dry lips. "I see." Guided by Dirk's much larger hand, Francesca stroked the horse's soft coat.

When Dirk said nothing more, she realized he was leaving the choice up to her. If she chose not to ride, he would not force her atop that horse. Gone was the autocratic suitor. In his place stood a discerning, sensitive man.

On the heels of that realization came the desire to please her future husband. She wanted to overcome her fear. By God's grace, she would overcome her fear. "Very well."

Dirk smiled at her. She felt his tension melt, leaving a young, devastatingly handsome man standing beside her. "Good girl. You won't regret it."

For some reason, she believed him.

He leaned toward her and Francesca sucked in her breath, her fear of the horse momentarily forgotten. But Dirk only helped her onto the mounting block.

She found that while the decision to overcome her fear was simple, carrying out her intentions required strength of mind. Once atop the mare, she fought a queasy stomach. If only she weren't so far above the ground!

Instead of mounting his own horse, Dirk guided her mare around the paddock, his capable hand covering hers as it gripped the pommel. He told her how he had learned to ride, as a grown man in the Indies. She listened to all the mistakes he had made, the falls he had taken. He described his plantation there.

Every once in a while he interjected a word about her riding, a word of advice, a compliment on her technique or a cautious warning. His fingers echoed the intent of his words with their varied pressure.

Once he was confident of her ability to stay in her seat, he mounted his horse and they rode a short ways over the hilly dunes.

By the end of the lesson, Francesca thought she would feel nothing but relief to be back on solid ground. She never thought a part of her would be sorry the ride was over.

When they returned to the villa, she was further surprised when Dirk showed her a little room tucked off to one side of the main salon. "You can use this if you'd like as a studio while you are here."

She looked around the room in amazement, her gaze finally coming to rest on him.

Taking her silence for a refusal, he coughed. "Perhaps it isn't suitable. We can always find something else—"

"No—it's perfect." She walked toward the windows lining the back wall. "There's sufficient light, which is the only requirement. I...I brought my canvas—your portrait," she said, then hesitated. "I didn't know if perhaps you'd have time to continue sitting for me."

He inclined his head. "I can do so right now, if you wish."

She nodded before he changed his mind. "That would be perfect. Let me get my things."

He helped her set up her easel, and she spent the rest of the afternoon at it, even after she had dismissed him, sensing his restlessness.

Supper was a comfortable affair, with them both amused by Tante Blankaart's whims.

Later that night, from the safety of her room, Francesca relived her riding lesson, marveling anew at how patient Dirk had been with her. And how accommodating with her painting. She rose from her bed and approached the open window, listening to the distant sound of the sea.

What did Dirk Vredeman see in her, she asked herself yet again? Why did he seem so attentive one moment, looking at her in a way that made her think he wanted her? Yet, when he was alone with her, he made no attempt to take any liberties. Was that the way it should be? She had no experience with suitors. She did not possess Lisbet's easy ability to flirt with a man.

She had been so certain Dirk would kiss her at the seashore. Why hadn't he? Had she displeased him in some way? She balled the lacy curtain in her fist.

Before she could puzzle any further, Tante Blankaart's little silver bell tinkled in the still night air. Grabbing her wrap from the foot of her bed, Francesca stumbled down the dark corridor.

She entered the stuffy room. The older woman greeted her in a pathetic voice. "Francesca, thank goodness you're here. Can you refill my water pitcher? And one of my pillows has fallen to the floor. You know how hard it is for me to sleep in a strange bed. Where are my spectacles? I left them right here beside me purposely." She patted the side of the bed. "Oh, I knew this would happen," she fretted. "Help me, child. Do you see them anywhere?"

Francesca jumped at the sound of a knock on the half-open door behind her.

Tante Blankaart looked up in alarm. "Who is it?"

Dirk's tousled head appeared around the door. With a quick nod in Francesca's direction, he entered the bedroom. He was still dressed, though only in shirt and breeches. "Is there anything amiss?"

"I apologize, dear man, if I have disturbed you. Francesca is used to my insomnia. Why, ever since my husband passed away..." She leaned her lacy cap against the headboard in preparation for a lengthy chat.

Dirk cut into her monologue in a soft, but clear tone. "I'm sorry to hear that sleep eludes you. Since it is a habitual condition, I shall hire a village girl for you tomorrow to attend to your nightly requirements. That way you shan't need to interrupt Francesca's sleep."

Tante Blankaart blinked at the man standing over the foot of her bed. A second later her voice returned. "That's very kind of you. Now, if I might bother Francesca for a wee bit of water for my pitcher and to see if my spectacles have fallen to the floor, I shall be fine."

At Dirk's brief nod to her, Francesca hurried to Tante Blankaart's bedside table and located the spectacles amidst the clutter of books and pills and potions. She set her cup upright and took the empty pitcher away.

"Good night, Dirk," Tante Blankaart called to his retreating back after he had bowed to her. "And thank you so much for your thoughtfulness."

As Dirk and Francesca exited the room, Dirk took the pitcher from Francesca. "Wait here."

Some minutes later, he returned with full pitcher in hand and presented it to her.

Francesca took it in to Tante Blankaart and poured her a cup. She picked up her fallen pillow and fluffed it up, placing it behind her back. Before leaving, she checked on Minionne in her basket and after assuring Tante Blankaart that her pet slept, she smoothed the bed linens over Tante Blankaart.

Assuring herself the older lady rested comfortably, Francesca left the room, securing the door softly behind her.

"What did you do in there, tell her a bedtime story and sing her a lullaby?"

Francesca jumped at the low voice coming to her from across the corridor.

Dirk straightened from the wall and approached her. Before she could say anything, he took her by the elbow and began guiding her back to her own door.

Once there, instead of opening it, he stopped in front of her, still holding her. She held her breath, afraid he could read what she'd been thinking earlier. When he reached out a hand, she drew back instinctively, but all he did was take a lock of hair that had escaped her braid.

He drew his hand closer to her face and touched her lower lip with his thumb, stroking it. With each stroke, her head fell back a little more, each petal-soft touch weakening her a bit more.

She resisted the urge to part her lips even when everything in her wanted to move toward him. But she was afraid if she did so, he would stop.

Before she could give in to her desires, he drew his thumb downward, along the contours of her chin and down the expanse of her arched neck. When he reached the neckline of her nightgown, she couldn't help a sigh escaping her throat.

His eyes scanned her shadowed face. "When you are wed to me, you shall fetch and carry for no one. No one will treat what belongs to me like a servant."

Belongs to me. The words sent a chill over her flesh. Her earlier fears returned. Was that all she was to him, a possession?

With a sigh, he dropped his hand. "Why do you bewitch me, woman?" Before she could puzzle his words, he strode away from her.

She gazed after him, no longer needing to disguise the longing she felt.

Once he reached the safety of his room, Dirk stepped out onto the balcony overlooking the back gardens and wood and gripped the marble balustrade between his fingers. He'd had to escape from Francesca while he was still strong enough to resist her.

He would take no innocent out of wedlock.

He longed for the ceremony that would finally make her his.

He'd never felt so sure of himself and so unsure at the same time.

He looked down at his white knuckles in the moonlight. He knew what was wrong with him since the fouled-up abduction. Francesca and those soulful gray eyes of hers. They made a man want to be strong and noble.

What would she think if she knew he was not good and pure the way she was? He'd tried to be honest about his beginnings. But he knew he could never reveal his greatest secret. If she knew of his role in her abduction, what would she think of him then?

He'd had a moment of worry at the stables, afraid she'd recognize Willem. But he needn't have feared. All her attention had been upon the horses. He'd warned Willem later to stay out of her sight whenever she came to the stables.

He turned away from the window, telling himself his fears were groundless. Once they were married, she'd be too overwhelmed by the passion he would show her, by her privileged position as his wife, by her freedom to paint as many pictures as she wanted to ever think back to that cursed abduction.

Ten

On the morning of her wedding, Francesca stood at her window, hardly believing the day had arrived.

She thought over the past week at Dirk's villa with the absence of her guardian and Lisbet. It had been a magical time, like nothing she'd ever known since losing her parents. Dirk seemed to have placed himself at her disposal. In the mornings they rode along the grounds. In the afternoons when the light was best, she worked on his portrait, and in the cool of the evenings after a festive dinner with Tante Blankaart, they sat in the gardens listening to the tinkle of the fountain. They talked of his childhood and hers, of his travels and of her love of art.

Since her parents had passed away, she'd not opened up to anyone so much, not even her beloved Katryn, who'd stood as a mother to her.

Francesca had tried to keep her feelings in check, but every day Dirk whittled at her reserve and she felt powerless against falling in love with him.

It made her realize how much she longed for a union of love and trust with her future husband.

Her guardian and Lisbet had only returned from their visit to the Bickers on the eve of Francesca's wedding. She wondered if Dirk had arranged that as well, giving her a sense of freedom she had not experienced since coming to live with her guardian.

Now the day of her wedding was here. She pushed aside the lace curtain, happy to see the clear sky. Taking it as a blessing of things to come, she allowed Katryn and Marta, who had both arrived from Amsterdam a couple of days before, to help her dress.

"I've never seen such a beautiful gown," Katryn said, fussing with Francesca's veil.

Francesca glanced down at her wedding dress. "It was a gift from Dirk."

Her first, he'd said, in a whole wardrobe he was having made for her. "No more black for you. I want to attire you in every hue of the rainbow."

"What a fine gentleman he is, to be sure," Katryn said.

Her wedding dress was the prettiest gown Francesca had ever owned, she conceded, brocaded silk in a pale shade of peach with silver thread running through it. She stroked the velvet edgings of the outer skirt. It must have cost him very dear. She had no idea when he'd had it made, but it must have been in this last week, since he'd said the seamstress had used one of her gowns for measurements.

She hadn't anything to give him, she thought with a sigh. Except the portrait. That would be her wedding gift. The thought lifted her spirits. She had completed it yesterday but had not had a chance to show him yet. He had been so considerate, never taking a peek at it. She smiled, wondering when to unveil it for him.

In truth she was pleased with it. It was her best work so far. How she wished Pieter could see it. She'd sent him a note, inviting him to the festivities. Perhaps she'd have a moment to show him although she wanted nothing to mar this day, neither Dirk's displeasure if he saw her with Pieter, nor any less-than-enthusiastic response on Pieter's part to her painting. The showing could wait, she decided.

At the moment she had too many other things occupying her mind, not least of which was the moment when she would finally be alone as wife with her new husband.

The entire village was invited to the wedding ceremony, which took place in the Church of Saints Agatha and Adrianus in the village. Afterward, the company filled the square, where trestle tables were laden with food. The festivities were to last for at least two days.

By late afternoon, Francesca, who had been up since dawn, sat down at a table, exhausted from greeting so many guests. From the rich and powerful of Amsterdam to the villagers of Zandvoort, Francesca smiled and accepted well wishes from one and all. There had even been some folks from the tavern, including Klaus himself, who had enveloped her in a hug, smacking her cheek with a kiss. "What a fine thing it is for Dirk to finally take a wife, and such a pretty one at that."

Her new husband seemed to know everyone. She glanced at him now, as he stood over her guardian, who sat at a table full of wealthy burghers from Amsterdam. Whatever Dirk had said made them all burst into laughter, even Mynheer Jacob.

Apart from his official role in the wedding ceremony, her guardian had not approached her all day. What would Papà have thought, seeing her today? She knew none of the pomp or lavish wealth displayed would have meant anything to him if he knew his daughter was unhappy.

He and Francesca's mother had had a union of love, and Papà had never tired of telling her how important this was to a marriage. And how a marriage was a partnership of sharing.

She sighed, deciding he would have liked Dirk and been happy to see her married to a man she could love and honor.

She turned her attention to the table before her. She'd barely had a chance to swallow more than a few mouthfuls of the rich and delectable dishes offered to her, which had been prepared by specially hired cooks. Fat capons stuffed with apricots, a splendid peacock arrayed on a vast platter with all its colorful feathers spread around it, thick slices of eel, broiled, stewed and stuffed, a whole roasted oxen and several pigs, trenchers of sweet and savory pies, pink sides of smoked hams and deep red sausages, herring pickled in brine. Dirk must have spent a fortune on the repast alone.

Poor Mynheer Jacob, he'd be forced to top Dirk's extravagant endeavor when it came time for his daughter's wedding, since Francesca doubted Lisbet would be satisfied with anything less.

Before she could decide what she would sample, she heard loud chanting around her. Dirk came towards her, the goblet of traditional hippocras in his hand. Time to drink the toast, she realized. With an enigmatic smile, he brought the spicy goblet of Rhine wine to her lips and she took a tentative sip of the sweet mixture overlaid with the flavors of cloves and ginger. The guests cheered the bride and groom.

Afterwards the musicians began to play.

"Ah, Dirk," Tante Blankaart exclaimed, coming up to them, her hands extended. "I don't know when I've had more fun. I wouldn't have enjoyed it nearly so much if it hadn't been for that dear girl you found for me in the village. Why, Minionne took to her right away. What a treasure she's been. I have half a mind to take her back home with me when I leave."

Dirk gave Francesca a wink over Tante Blankaart's head. "You can't call it a day without some dancing," he told the older lady.

"Dancing, me? Bless you! I haven't danced since I was Francesca's age. No, thank you, my dear man. I'd keel over in a faint I'm sure."

"Nonsense! A twirl about the yard will do you good. What say you, mevrouw?" Dirk took her hand, bowing over it formally.

Tante Blankaart giggled like a girl. "You make me feel quite spry again."

Dirk gave Francesca a quick smile as he took Tante Blankaart's arm, whispering, "I shall be back in a thrice. Don't disappear."

He maneuvered Tante Blankaart through the merry couples dancing to the sound of fiddles and accordions. Francesca was reminded of a mighty warrior leading a fragile fairy princess through a stampeding horde. Not a bump or jostle harmed his charge. Francesca felt a shiver of anticipation, looking forward to the moment when she would feel his strong arms swinging her around in a country jig.

She felt a tap on her arm and turned to find Pieter smiling at her. She returned the smile, feeling as if he and Katryn were her only real guests at her wedding. Katryn had been overjoyed with her good fortune, wiping her eyes with her handkerchief earlier, saying, "Thank the good Lord for blessing you with such a fine man."

Pieter bowed. "May I have the honor of dancing with the new bride?"

She curtsied. "The honor would be mine, mynheer."

Pieter took her in his arms and twirled her around the crowded square. "I begin to think you shall do very well with your new husband," he shouted to her above the loud music.

"Do you?" Pieter's approval would mean a lot to her.

He nodded. "I wasn't sure what to think when I first met him. I didn't want you to go from one form of servitude into another. Despite his powerful manner, Mynheer Dirk seems smitten." He smiled. "I think you will have no trouble taming the beast."

She shook her head at his nonsense. How little Pieter knew Dirk if he thought she would have that kind of sway with him.

A moment later, Klaus cut in and whisked her away.

Midway through the next tune, she found herself with another partner. He ducked his head in greeting, and she recognized the stable hand. Willem, she remembered.

"My felicitations, Mevrouw Francesca."

Unused to the matronly title, she stammered her thanks. He took her in a strong, if clumsy, grip. She looked once more at his face, thinking there was something familiar about him but couldn't determine what. Probably just the fact that she had seen him that day at the stables, she decided. Strange she had not seen him on any of her subsequent visits.

Francesca had no time to worry about missing steps or following his lead. His brawny arms swung her up and around before she could think what to do. Sweaty bodies bumped and jostled her, and if she trod on anyone's foot, her own felt just as bruised.

Before the tune ended, she was beginning to feel at ease in the crowd and enjoying herself for the first time that day. The stress of the wedding preparations was over, the gravity of the ceremony behind her, and all around her people who knew Dirk had been telling her she would make him an exceptional wife. She was almost beginning to believe it.

Breathless and feeling the perspiration dampen her neck, Francesca was nevertheless prepared to continue dancing. Just as she looked up to nod at Willem, he let her go, his gaze fixed over her shoulder.

She turned to find Dirk standing behind her. With a nod, he dismissed Willem and held out his arms to her.

It was as if she had waited all day for this moment. As the strains of the melody flowed through the twilit air, Francesca took a step toward him and accepted his hand. Her heart began a familiar pounding which had nothing to do with her exertions.

His face was unsmiling. "Not winded yet, are you?"

Francesca shook her head as they began to move with the music. "Willem's not in trouble for dancing with me, is he?"

"Of course not." But he remained serious as he took her in his arms.

She felt safe within their circle. Safe and protected and...cherished. Francesca breathed in the scent of him when he drew her close to avoid an overzealous couple behind her. He smelled of leather and soap and spicy wine.

When the tune ended, someone tried to cut in, but Dirk pushed him away. "She's mine now!"

As dusk deepened to night, a chain formed, and Francesca was grasped by either hand and pulled along. Laughing and singing, the human chain snaked its way through the lamp-lit village streets and strolling crowds.

Yet for all her gaiety, Francesca could not help thinking of the coming night. Would she please her new husband? Would he frighten her? But she shoved aside her fears, throwing herself into the music.

When she could no longer stand on her feet, Dirk seemed to sense it, for he took her arm and made a way through the dancing throng. She clung to him as he steered them away from the crowd and down a quiet alley.

In one swift motion, he lifted her by the waist onto a low brick wall. "Wait here."

She sat fanning herself with a handkerchief, glad for the respite.

By the time Dirk returned, Francesca's breathing was back to normal and the cool night air had dried her skin.

"Here you go." He handed her a tankard of ale and a sausage tucked into a warm roll, taking the same for himself. Lifting his tankard, he toasted. "To our union."

She drank deeply of the bitter brew, watching him do the same over the rim of her cup. With her immediate thirst quenched, she turned her attention to the meat, her appetite awakened.

The first bite of succulent sausage confirmed how ravenous she was. Neither spoke until after they had finished eating, and she realized Dirk had probably had as little chance as she to partake of the banquet.

She licked the last traces of food from her lips. She caught Dirk's smile and smiled in return, feeling suddenly very warm and good inside.

"I didn't think it was possible," he murmured.

"What?"

"That your hair should ever come loose of its own accord from that knot you've got it in. It looked tighter than the best sailor's knot." He brought a hand forward and touched a tendril.

"Oh." Francesca put a hand to her head and attempted to adjust the pins.

"Leave it. It becomes you."

"What did you do with Tante Blankaart?" she asked after a short silence.

"A servant has seen her home. I told her she had better get a good night's rest since the feasting and dancing will continue on the morrow." He took up his tankard once more.

"You worked wonders with her. I think that's the first time I've ever seen her dance."

"Is it the first time you've ever danced?" he asked.

Francesca met his teasing gaze, her heart stepping up its rhythm. "These country dances, yes."

"I didn't think you'd know them."

Some imp in her prompted her to reply, "Did I surprise you?"

"'Tis not the first time."

"I imagined by now you knew all about me." Francesca didn't know whether it was the ale or the recent exhilaration of the dancing, but she felt like Lisbet, a woman adept at verbal sparring with a man like Dirk.

He chuckled. "I believe you have many surprises left for me this night."

At the knowing look in his eyes, her cheeks suffused with warmth. Tracing the rim of her tankard, she asked, "Can you tell if a woman's never been kissed?"

Instead of laughing as she half expected, he remained silent until she was forced to look at him once more.

"Is that an invitation?"

She looked away from him. "You did once before without awaiting one."

Her breath hitched at the clink of his tankard against the brick. The next instant his fingertips edged her face up to his. She kept her eyes downcast, losing all boldness. Her earlier fears returned, tightening her throat so she could hardly breathe. What if she disappointed him?

She prepared herself for the moment of encounter, keeping her lips pursed. She wouldn't be caught unawares this time, or worse, feel spurned, if he chose not to follow through again.

The shock of his lips touching hers made her jerk the tankard she still held. To her dismay he withdrew.

His eyes twinkled as he rocked back on his heels. Francesca waited, fear and dismay curdling the food in her stomach.

"If that's any sign, I would wager you hadn't."

"Hadn't what?" she asked, hating the defensive note in her tone.

"Ever been kissed before." Before she could ask how he knew that, he murmured, "Mayhap we should try once more."

Without giving her a chance to disagree, he took the tankard from her hand and set it down on the wall alongside his own. "Now, I want you to pretend you are just as you were the first time I kissed you."

His forefinger touched her chin and his mouth met hers once more. His lips felt warm as they brushed against hers, tantalizing her with their hairsbreadth proximity. A flush of heat stole over her neck and face. Involuntarily her body swayed forward, her lips instinctively wanting to join with his.

When his lips began nuzzling hers apart, Francesca responded as if they spoke the same language. She felt the tip of his tongue touch hers, tentatively at first, then growing bolder. Instead of shock or disgust, a flame sparked in her veins, gaining intensity the deeper he explored. Her head fell back. Her bones seemed turned to jelly, making it impossible for her to remain upright.

As her body leaned into his, his hands spanned her waist, bringing her closer. Their bodies melted into each other, soft and hard, small and large, curved and flat. Her arms, as of their own volition, wrapped around his neck, her fingers entwining in the locks of hair brushing his shoulders.

She lost all awareness of the music in the background, of the shouts of laughter in the distance, of his earlier teasing. Time ceased.

She thought she heard him breathe her name against her mouth, but she couldn't be sure. Like a sculptress, she had to explore his face with her fingertips. Hard planes, hollow curves. With wonderment she realized his beard wasn't rough at all but silky soft. His neck, on the other hand, was rope-like muscle, unyielding to her fingertips.

Again, he breathed her name against her mouth and pushed his broad hands against her back, pressing her to him. The next moment his hands came up to her hair, pulling it down. With a shock she caught herself wishing her body could be released from its confinement as easily as her hair from its pins.

She had no time for further thought. Dirk pulled away from her, his breath coming in quick, jerky gusts. His eyes scanned her face, all levity gone. She wondered whether her eyes looked as wild as his, or her lips as bruised.

"Come with me." His voice was husky. To Francesca, the words seemed torn from his lips as if he, too, felt a measure of desperation. She nodded, touching her fingertips to his damp lips.

He kissed them, then wrapped his arm around her, bringing her close to his side.

Before she knew it they had left the crowds behind and he was helping her atop his horse. During the ride through the dim country road, Francesca was unaware of anything save the feel of his arms around her, like the haven of a harbor during a storm. Fleetingly she wondered at the absence of fear atop the cantering stallion. But her mind was too full of the new and strange sensations assaulting her and the overwhelming need for some kind of fulfillment that night.

Her head was tucked beneath his chin. From time to time she could feel his lips nuzzling the top of her head, his whisper urging her not to be afraid, that the ride would be over soon. In response Francesca covered his hands with her own, reveling in the hard contours of his knuckles.

They arrived at the villa where Dirk gave her a quick, searing kiss, instructing her to wait for him in his room.

Francesca reached it in a daze. The moonlit chamber was a mere extension of the unreality of the evening. By now the exhilaration of the dance and ale had worn off. She was left with questions and wonderment. Was this Francesca, entering her husband's room on their wedding night? She was no Lisbet, expert on the ways of men.

Her ignorance be cursed. Tonight she would feel fully alive—desired and loved. And she knew, as surely as she knew the moon's ivory orb glowed in the night sky, that Dirk would make her feel so.

When Dirk entered his room, his eyes searched for Francesca. As soon as she heard him, she turned from where she'd been standing by the window and came toward him.

For a long moment they stood facing each other. He fought the urge to draw her to him, preferring instead to savor the agony of anticipation.

During the ride home, all he could think of was how much he wanted her.

Was she as unsure as he? Since her passionate response earlier to his kiss, he had felt like a puppet, with Francesca in control of the strings. He wondered if she was even conscious of her power over him. He'd not let someone rule him since he'd made his fortune.

But now, here in his bedroom, the scales were tipped. Tonight, Dirk intended to show her who was master.

Francesca's lips curved into a tremulous smile, and Dirk knew all efforts at restraint were in vain. His hands snaked through her windblown hair, pulling her to his chest. His thumbs touched her cheeks, his palms enveloping her jaws, before his lips came downward.

Her skin felt finer than the finest China silk beneath the roughened pads of his thumb. Her lips were a dew-sprinkled rosebud beneath the hard slant of his mouth. He deepened the kiss.

The pictures he'd rehearsed in his mind of this seduction fled in the intensity of the reality. Instead of the skillful, controlled lover he knew himself to be, he felt like a bull crashing around his pen in blinding fury.

How he wanted her! Before he could act like a callow youth, he swept her up in his arms and carried her to the bed.

She was his now, finally and completely his, was his last rational thought.

Francesca became gradually aware of full sunlight against her closed lids. With a deep sigh, she opened them to find herself lying in a strange bed, the linens twisted around her.

Her bare limbs brought it all back. Had she been dreaming?

The night had been a revelation to her. The physical closeness of their union was something she had never dreamed of. Dirk had made her feel as desirable and beautiful as any woman could wish to feel. He had been gentle, thoughtful, and ardent all at once.

She sighed in contentment, bringing the covers up to her chin. Surely, now she would be blessed with the kind of marriage she had so fervently desired, a spiritual joining following the physical.

She turned as quietly as possible to look at her new husband. He slept on his stomach, his face turned toward her. His golden body was so strong, she marveled, forgetting her concerns as she looked at his muscular arms and shoulders. Then she drew in her breath at the scars crisscrossing his back.

Lashes. When had he endured such whippings? In the Tughuis?

Though she would have dearly loved to stroke that evidence of his past, she didn't dare, not wishing to wake him.

But she couldn't help reaching out with a fingertip to push aside a fallen lock of his hair from his forehead. Though she barely touched him, it was enough to rouse him. Like a child caught in a forbidden act, she drew back her hand when she saw his eyelids lift. Tawny eyes stared at her across the pillows. He had beautiful eyelashes, she thought, the color of toasted almonds.

"Good morning." His voice sounded rich and low, as if he'd had a good sleep.

Feeling her skin tingle, she struggled to maintain eye contact. "Good morning." Her prim tone sounded ludicrous. Her fingers tensed on the bed sheet, as she waited for his mocking reply, sure that he would laugh at her modesty.

Instead, he reached out, covering her cheek and side of her neck with his hand. She swallowed, already beginning to crave his touch once more. She must maintain her decorum, she told herself sternly, glad she had drawn the covers up around herself. Now, if he would only rise first to take care of his needs, she could retrieve her garments in privacy. She was certain, once dressed, her body would forget its traitorous yearnings.

Instead his hand began an exploratory journey along her shoulder, moving aside the modest covering in its wake. Francesca resisted the urge to move the sheet back into place. Instead, she lay stock-still, hoping he would go no farther down.

"I trust you slept well."

She nodded, no longer looking at him directly, but down at his neck.

"Moonlight is very flattering, but I myself prefer the warm light of morning." Before she could stop him, he'd drawn the covers all the way down to her hip. She couldn't help curling into a ball, ashamed of her state.

She heard him sigh. Peeking up at him, certain she'd displeased him, all she saw was a slight smile playing across his features. "I thought you'd gotten over any shyness last night."

"That was last night." Her face burned at the matter-of-fact way they were carrying on this topic of conversation.

He sat up on an elbow and began to touch her. She could hardly breathe, much less think.

"You were beautiful last night. And you are still beautiful in the light."

She dared glance at him, but found no teasing in his eyes. "Am I?" she whispered.

As if she'd uttered some magical phrase, in one swift movement he was on top of her, framing her face with his hands, covering her nakedness with his own. His eyes held no mirth. "You are the most beautiful woman I've ever seen."

She swallowed. "Have you...seen many?"

He didn't laugh at her question. "I've seen many, but I haven't lain with all I've seen, if that is what is worrying you."

"Were...were they all like me?" She moistened her lips. "I mean...did they—do they all behave—" She could no longer meet his eyes, no matter how gentle they were.

His hands brought her chin upward. His two thumbs rubbed her lower lip. "You are very passionate, sweet Francesca. I always suspected as much." He sighed. "Not all women can boast such. Some are cold as ice. Others feign passion just to please a man. But some, like you, respond with all their being. And when a man finds such a one, he's found wealth indeed."

She stared at him, mesmerized by his look and words. How she wanted to believe him. Before she could make any response, he grinned down at her with a roguish glint in his eye. "You pleased me greatly, wench, and I trust you found some pleasure as well."

She flinched at the words, not yet ready to be teased about their lovemaking, much less her response. He began nibbling on her earlobe, murmuring, "I hope at last you've discovered there is pleasure in play." He raised himself on his elbows, smiling down at her. "Not all enjoyment is to be found at the tip of your paintbrush. Have I at last helped you discover a rival to your paints? Have you finally gotten over your anger when those abductors tore apart your sketches? You showed your passion even then with your small clenched fists. Let no one touch your sacred art, they said."

Before she could take in the meaning of his words, Dirk claimed her once again. In his assault all else was forgotten but the feel of him.

Francesca sank further down into the tub, her head resting along its rim. The steamy water felt good. Dirk had thoughtfully ordered the tub brought to her own room so that she could bathe in privacy.

The scent of the perfumed oils rose to her nostrils. She inhaled deeply, reveling in her senses, the way Dirk had taught her. Even as she blushed, she smiled, remembering all the things he'd said to her. Even his teasing words had been used to help her overcome her modesty.

As she rubbed vigorously at her arms with a sponge, she couldn't help once again going over everything of the evening and morning. She was not the same person, she realized. For that she must thank her new husband. He had taught her much about herself and revealed so many new things to her.

She smiled, thinking of his remarks about showing her something besides painting. He need never worry about her painting. Nothing could ever rival him in her affections.

Francesca brought the heavily laden sponge up to her raised arm and squeezed the water out of it. She watched the streams of water course down her arm.

Suddenly her whole body stilled.

Have you at last gotten over your anger when those abductors tore apart your sketches? You showed your passion even then with your small clenched fists. Dirk's words reverberated in the silent room. A silence broken only by the last drops of water falling off her arm into the cooling water. *Plop. Plop.*

Eleven

How had Dirk known about her abductors' treatment of her sketches?

Francesca tried to dismiss his words. Obviously, he'd used his imagination, picturing how she had reacted that evening.

She frowned, struggling to remember that evening she'd blotted from her memory. When Dirk had found her bound and blindfolded, had she told him about her sketches? She must have. But she didn't remember doing so. She never revealed to strangers her love of drawing.

She'd been overwhelmed by her rescuer and had wanted nothing more than to forget about the previous hours. She'd basked in the warmth of the fire Dirk had built up and enjoyed the wholesomeness of the food he'd set before her.

So, how had Dirk known? Her suspicions clung to the air like the droplets of moisture to her skin.

Dirk had appeared at the farmhouse shortly after her abductors had left. Who would ever have found her in that forsaken place if he hadn't happened along? Memories from that night tumbled through her mind—being held at gunpoint, blindfolded, bound, taken atop that galloping horse, roughly handled by those awful men. She shuddered.

She remembered the moment she'd heard those abusive men empty her satchel. She couldn't see a thing, but she'd heard the crumple of her papers. She'd heard their sneers as they tore through her things. The leader had dismissed her pleas without a word of acknowledgement. He'd torn the sketches from her hand when she'd groped for them.

Then Dirk had arrived, so thoughtful and strong, cutting

her bonds, wrapping her in his cloak, dispelling the nightmare.

What could it mean? The questions pummeled her. Did Dirk know about her abductors? Francesca had no answers. All she had was a deep uneasiness. What had Dirk meant by those words?

Francesca shivered, suddenly realizing how cold the bathwater had become.

With a decisive movement, she lifted herself out of the tub, ignoring the splash of water over the rim. She concentrated on drying herself off, then dressing, as if these were the only things that concerned her.

Just as she was tying her cap under her chin, she remembered something else. Willem. She must see him. Must see for herself that he was someone else. She didn't know him. Had never seen him before in her life. He merely reminded her of someone or something.

Francesca hurried down the stairs, glad for the absence of people, since most had returned to the feasting and reveling still going on in the village. Dirk expected her there as well, as soon as she had finished dressing. She would check the stables first, she decided, then go to the village.

The stables were deserted. Francesca felt relief. She took one more look around. Just as she was about to leave, she noticed a shadow in the darkened interior. She peered toward it.

"Afternoon, juffrouw—beg pardon, mevrouw. Like me to take you to the festivities?"

At the sound of his voice, Francesca almost turned to flee. She recognized that voice. Without seeing his face, it was just as it had been that afternoon when she'd been blindfolded and terrified. How could she have missed it before?

"Excuse me, mevrouw, is something the matter? Would you like me to fetch Mynheer Dirk for you?"

Francesca shook her head. "No, no thank you, Willem." She straightened, telling herself she had nothing to fear.

Willem wouldn't hurt her, would he? She didn't want to think about that right now.

"Could you come out a moment, please, Willem?" Her voice sounded strained.

"Certainly, mevrouw." Willem's dark form let the harness he'd been cleaning drop to the floor. He stood up, brushing his hands off, then approached the stable door. Francesca backed up into the sunlight.

"What can I do for you, mevrouw?" he asked with a diffident smile, the same smile he had worn the evening before when he had asked her to dance. Only now, instead of seeming shy, it looked sinister, like that of a sheep in wolf's clothing.

"You were one of my abductors."

She could see his discomfiture immediately. "Beg pardon, juff—mevrouw? Abduction?"

"Yes, I recognize your voice, your accent," she continued, her own voice growing firmer with conviction.

Willem shook his head vehemently. "Nay, mevrouw, I don't know what you be talking of." When he backed away from her, Francesca's fears disappeared, replaced by growing anger.

"Why did you do it? On whose orders?" Willem just continued shaking his head at her. "Answer me, Willem," she ordered sharply, not used to taking that tone with anyone, but knowing instinctively it would bring her results.

"Mevrouw, I—we—didn't mean no harm. I swear it! I know we frightened you terribly, but you were never in any danger, not after we knew you weren't the one. It was all a mistake, see, but we couldn't know, not 'til it were too late. I swear it, juffrouw, beg pardon—mevrouw." He touched a forelock, not meeting her eyes any longer.

"I want to know why I was abducted. What do you mean it was a mistake?" For a brief moment, Francesca felt overwhelming relief, after the horror of a moment ago, when Willem had first admitted his guilt.

"'Twasn't supposed to have been you in that trekschuit,

was it?" he asked as if she should have understood it all. Francesca's momentary relief evaporated, replaced by a new horror.

"Lisbet van Diemen was to have been in that barge," she whispered, staring at Willem's face, willing him to say something else, anything but what she feared he would say.

"That's right, mevrouw. But when we discovered it was you, everything changed. We had to leave you there, see. We had to make as if we was going to rob ye, but 'tweren't so at all. We never intended ye no harm."

"What did you intend had it been Miss Lisbet?"

His jaw moved, but his lips remained silent.

"Answer me, Willem. I shall find out the truth one way or the other."

"I'm sorry, ju—mevrouw, but I can't. You'll have to ask mynheer. He'll have me flogged, surely, if not worse, for all I've said already."

Francesca didn't hear his last words. The ugly truth had been spoken and couldn't be unsaid. Dirk had been involved. He'd been behind her abduction. Not until the words had been uttered did she realize how greatly she had feared hearing them.

Without another word, she spun away from Willem and ran.

She felt like laughing and crying at the same time when she heard Willem calling after her, "I hope you'll forgive us for abducting you so cruelly—"

⁂

Dirk strode back outside, his alarm growing. It was midafternoon and his bride had been missing since midmorning. He'd searched the house and nearly the entire grounds.

He'd waited for her at the village. At first when she hadn't shown up, he'd thought nothing of it, knowing how tired she must be. He gave a grim snort, thinking of all the ribald comments he'd had to endure from the villagers.

"Ye've tired out your new bride!" "You ought to space things out a bit better." "Save some for tonight!"

He'd borne it all with good grace at first. It was all in fun . . . and not far from the truth. But when she didn't appear, things had begun to get awkward, and he'd begun to grow worried.

Just as he was ready to head back to the villa, Willem had appeared and given him the news.

He'd hurried back to the villa. But she was nowhere to be found. He'd torn through every room, only to find them empty. He'd stopped in their bedroom, seeing the disarray since every servant was at the village. He'd bent down to pick up Francesca's wedding gown, where it still lay in a crumpled heap where he had let it drop. He'd breathed in the fragrance of his wife, worry gnawing at the pit of his stomach.

No matter how much he'd cursed Willem, deep down he knew he had no one to blame but himself.

It was he who had let slip that careless remark about her sketches. It always came back to her sketches!

Damn and blast him! He'd been so caught up in his desire for her, he hadn't been able to keep his tongue still.

He let the gown fall, going to the next chamber. The tub of water stood there, now stone cold.

Where had she gone! He'd questioned the few servants in the house but no one had seen her since mid-morn.

Willem said she'd run off—

He pulled at his beard. Dear God, where was she?

With a half-oath, half-prayer, he left the room and ran back down the stairs.

He reached the end of the gardens and looked down the forest bridle path. The sea. Could she have—?

When he emerged once more into the sunlight, he continued up the grassy dunes without a break in his long stride. At the crest he stood a moment, remembering the last time he'd been there. Had it been scarcely over a week?

Then he hadn't even dared touch Francesca, afraid to scare her. His fists tightened. He wouldn't lose her. He couldn't lose her.

Turning to scan the horizon, he spotted her.

She stood far below him by the water's edge, her arms crossed about her. He couldn't help a smile, noting her submerged feet. He remembered her hesitation the first time he had dragged her into the surf.

Dirk descended the dunes, a single purpose in mind. Angry or hurt, she had to be made to see.

She gave no sign that she heard his approach.

"It's not often a bride is absent from her own celebrations."

She finally turned, her hair in its customary knot, her gown one of her old black ones, by no sign revealing the passionate woman she'd been the night before.

"I've been looking for you," he said quietly, unsure of himself.

"Have you?"

Her tone, like her expression, was cold and remote. Her eyes, he noticed at last, were red-rimmed, as if she'd spent these past hours crying. They smote him.

He reached out a hand.

She stepped back unmindful of the surf and glared at him. "Don't touch me."

He curled his hand at his side.

"Tell me, dear husband, how long did you think you could keep me in ignorance? Did you think by lust alone to blind me for a lifetime? Or were you planning something much shorter? Was I to be your wife only until you obtained whatever it is you wanted?"

His mind went over what he could say, but discarded every possible reply.

She let out a brief, bitter laugh. "There you go, calculating. Always calculating. What does she know? What does she suspect? What do I tell her?" She looked at him with contempt. "How about the truth for once, or is that concept too foreign?"

Dirk reached out again but she jumped away from him. "I told you not to touch me."

He wasn't prepared for her tone, filled with repugnance, wiping out all the passion the two of them had shared the night before. "As I recall, last night you didn't find my touch displeasing."

She flinched. "What we did was a lie, and I will never cease to regret it!"

The words were like a dagger in his gut. "What we did was what a husband and wife have been doing since time began."

She stamped her bare foot in the water, her hands knotted at her sides. "Not when a man has been deceiving his wife since the day—since the very hour—he met her." She took a step toward him. "Tell me the truth, Dirk! Tell me why you married me!"

For a second all he felt was relief to see that rather than cold and unapproachable, Francesca was on the edge of hysteria.

"Why do you think I married you?" he countered in a quiet voice, hoping to gain time to convince her, to give her a believable answer. Because he could never tell her the truth.

Not when he didn't know what the truth was himself.

"I don't know!" she shouted back at him. "I didn't know until this very day. But I always knew you wouldn't marry a pauper without some good reason." She gave a strangled laugh. "You didn't want me at all! You only wanted to get at my guardian. You saw me for the gullible, grateful little fool that I was. Lisbet was right. You are dangerous. Not only dangerous, but despicable!"

So, she thought she knew everything. Everything but why. But could he trust her with the reasons? "And so because of some tale of Willem's, you think you know all." At all costs he must remain calm.

"I didn't have to listen to anyone's tales. I only had to use my eyes and ears. What happened, Dirk? You're so cunning, didn't you foresee the possibility that I would recognize your men about this place?" She waved an arm.

"You had your henchmen do your dirty work for you, then you showed up to 'rescue' me." She gave a strangled laugh. "You were waiting in the wings until I was good and scared, so I would cling to you in gratitude." Suddenly, her eyes widened in horror, as if a new thought occurred to her. "Or, were you with the band of abductors, too?" Her hand went to her mouth, her words a whisper. "No. . .no, you weren't. . .you weren't—" She shook her head in denial. "Their leader? The one who gave the orders? Who let them rip apart my things? Who told them to abandon me there?"

Dirk's mind raced, thinking of a way to salvage the situation. Perhaps it was time to try something else. The truth, or enough to convince her. Could he convince her or would he lose her?

"What's yer name, wench?" he growled in the coarse accent he had assumed that night.

She looked at him, startled for an instant, as if she hadn't been prepared for him to admit anything. Then she stepped back as if he had wounded her physically. "How could you?" she whispered.

He looked at her squarely. "As you said, I was planning to get to Jacob."

She shook her head as if not wanting to believe.

He turned away from her, no longer able to bear the disenchantment and accusation in her eyes. "He wronged me...long ago." Would that be enough? Would she want to know the how and why? Would she take his side over her guardian, or would she turn from him for good?

"What could he possibly have done that would justify ruining his daughter?"

There was no sympathy in her tone, only accusation.

When he made no reply, she said, "You are the devil himself!"

Without another word, she spun away from him and began to run.

"Francesca!"

She only increased her stride.

Since the day he'd met her, he'd not been calculating with his usual acumen. She'd enthralled him from the moment he'd uncovered her blindfold and looked into her eyes.

His assessment of the situation did nothing, however, to ease the bitter taste in his mouth. Francesca had judged and condemned him without bothering to know the why of his actions. She talked about the truth. The truth! That was the last thing she wanted to hear.

If she had shown the least inclination to get at the truth...to trust him. What then? Would he have trusted her with the truth?

It had been too long since he had trusted anyone fully that he didn't know if he was capable of it.

This afternoon had shown him how dangerous it was to trust. He'd been very careless up to now, letting his feelings cloud his judgment. This was a warning.

He would deal with Francesca later. After she'd had a chance to cool off and after he'd repaired any damage she might have caused. He would not permit her to get under his skin a second time, he promised himself. She'd caused enough trouble already, since she'd switched places with Lisbet in that confounded barge.

His resolutions made, Dirk still didn't move. He had to use every ounce of self control to keep from running after Francesca's diminishing figure. To keep from grabbing her slim shoulders and shaking her until her denunciations were flung out to sea. Then kiss her until he erased that look of abhorrence in her eyes and made her forget his role in her abduction.

He cursed, kicking at the sand with his boot. How could one woman have him so devilishly angry, so devilishly ablaze, so devilishly remorseful all at one time?

Francesca ran from Dirk, his confession pursuing her like a lash. Her hem, heavy with salt water, dragged about her ankles. With an angry moan, she clutched her skirts and swerved above the waterline.

The sand beneath her feet was cold and unyielding. She welcomed its hard slap against her soles. Anything to take away the harsh sting of the truth.

How could one man at the same time be so loving and tender, so vile and contemptible?

Who had she thought she was, letting herself be caught by Dirk's skillful charm? He had known exactly how to stroke her vanity, pretending an interest in her artistic talent!

She coiled her fingers around her damp skirts, her body shrinking in shame from her eager response to Dirk's ploys. Painting his portrait! What a stupid little fool she'd been to think a man as experienced as he would want what she had to give. To think she had decided to present the portrait to him as a wedding gift. What conceited pride!

A sob escaped Francesca's lips, and she brought her arm up to her mouth, wanting to wipe away all memory of Dirk's scorching kisses from her lips. She shuddered, feeling soiled and used. And betrayed. She was worse than Lisbet. She was the same as one of those harlots in the street, selling her body for a few flattering words of a man's.

Dirk had seen nothing but an unloved and unlovely woman, whom it would be amusing to seduce while he carried out his plans. A lighthearted sport for one whose palate had likely become jaded.

She wouldn't cry. So help her, she wouldn't cry anymore, she vowed, struggling up the dry sandy dune before her. Her feet slipped down the powdery sand, creating furrows that quickly vanished as more sand slithered down.

Cursed be the day she had ever made Dirk's acquaintance! Much better had she never seen his face than let him use her. Blackguard! Her hands clutched at the stalks of dry grass to pull herself onto the dunes.

What would she do now?

She must go to Mynheer Jacob. She must tell him. Francesca stood up straight when she reached the top of the dunes at last. She looked down the length of the beach, then turned quickly away when she saw Dirk's figure in the far distance. She struggled to don her shoes, then raced back to the villa. She knew Mynheer Jacob intended to return to Amsterdam soon. She must reach him in time.

Another thought came to her as she ran. She must return with her guardian. She couldn't stay another moment in this place full of lies and deceit. A sob escaped her lips as a picture of last night rose in her mind. A dozen scenes came to her...memories of Dirk's wooing her.

She was hot and winded, with a stitch in her side, by the time she entered the villa. To her relief, the entrance hall was deserted, and she passed only one servant as she ran up the stairs. She went immediately to her guardian's room, praying he had returned from the village by now.

"Come in!" She almost collapsed in relief at his peremptory tone.

She stood at his threshold a few seconds, trying to calm her breathing.

"Where in heaven's name have you been all day?" Mynheer Jacob demanded as soon as he saw her, then frowned. "You look a fright. Whatever is the matter?"

"Mynheer Jacob—" Francesca gulped air. "Thank goodness—you're still here." She paused to take a breath, then shook her head to clear her thoughts. What was she to tell him? "You mustn't—mustn't—"

"What is it, girl?" Her guardian asked, approaching her. "I can't understand you."

"'Tis Dirk."

Mynheer Jacob became instantly alarmed. "What's the matter with him? Has something happened to him?"

"No!" Francesca shook her head, at the same trying to calm her breathing. "You—you mustn't trust him. He's not to be trusted," she repeated, this time more calmly. "He's lied to me."

He looked immediately relieved. "What foolish things are you saying, girl? Lied to you?" When he saw her agitation increase, he gave an impatient sigh. Seeing her shake her head and attempt to speak again, he patted her arm awkwardly. "Now, now, you're only trying to settle into marriage. Every bride goes through it. Just because a man promises you something before your wedding, doesn't mean he'll do it afterward. You'll adjust to your husband in time."

He turned away from her, clearly ill at ease with the turn of the conversation. "You must talk with Tante Blankaart or to Katryn. They'll advise you better than I how to submit to your husband."

"Mynheer Jacob, I must leave him. He's the one who abducted me—"

He didn't even turn around. "Enough hysterics, Francesca. You've always been an overly imaginative child. Now, go to your room and wash your face."

"Mynheer, Dirk is deceitful. He wishes you harm." She enunciated each word clearly to show him she was in her right mind.

He looked around once more, his expression full of annoyance. "How could a man, who has given me more than any other business associate I know, wish to harm me? How can someone as respected by the community be deceitful? You saw his guests yesterday. He had the most important families flock here to his wedding to a nobody!"

She fell back at the word. For all the attention she had received the day before, in her guardian's eyes, she was still a charity case he had taken on sufferance.

"Now, I want you to stop all this foolish talk this instant. Go back to your new husband and apologize. I warned you to behave with him. I have much to gain from my friendship with Dirk, and much to lose, if that friendship is ruined because of you."

"Mynheer Jacob, I don't know what he intends, but don't listen to him, whatever he asks of you. Take me back to Amsterdam. I can't stay here any longer."

"Silence, Francesca! I will hear none of this. You are married to the man. You will go nowhere. And you will not jeopardize my friendship with him." He thrust his forefinger under her nose. "Do you hear me?"

She stared at her guardian, not hearing his words anymore, feeling only the anger radiating against her.

She recoiled, knowing she would find no succor with him—nor did she want to.

In that instant, she knew she had nowhere to go, but leave she must.

Without a word, she turned from him.

Once in her room, with trembling fingers, she collected a drawstring bag and stuffed a few toiletries in it and the little money she had left from Dirk's advance on the portrait. She wished she could leave the money, but she would need it to take a trekschuit back to Amsterdam.

She would take nothing else with her, she decided, looking with sudden revulsion at her wedding gown. The gown that had appeared so beautiful to her only a day ago was now a mocking reminder of her wedding night.

A wave of despair engulfed her. How could she have been so happy one day...and have it all turned to dust in the space of a morning?

Dear Lord, help me! Show me what to do, where to go!

Downstairs she paused, debating for a moment, before turning toward the small alcove Dirk had given her for a studio. Along one side, the late afternoon sun streamed in from a row of windows. Francesca's gaze fell upon the leather-backed chair where Dirk had sat, teasing her during those quiet hours. She turned away from its mocking emptiness and packed her painting supplies. She stopped before the portrait of Dirk, her fingers straying over the thick brush strokes of the dried paint. Her first full portrait. She should leave it, she thought with a surge of bitterness, as token payment for his services.

Suddenly she grabbed up the canvas stretched on its frame. Pieter had told her the sketches of Dirk were her best work. What would he think of the finished product? Mayhap she could sell it. Perhaps Dirk Vredeman had been good for something after all, she decided with a determined nod at the mocking face staring back at her.

Francesca grabbed up a hammer from her work table nearby. Biting her bottom lip in effort, she pried off each nail around the wooden frame. Once the canvas was free, she rolled it up carefully.

When she marched out of the villa, Francesca was no longer the ward of Jacob van Diemen, his unpaid servant and companion to his daughter to pay off her father's debt. Nor was she Francesca Vredeman, wife, a title she had borne but a day.

She was now Francesca di Paolo, a woman alone and on her own.

Twelve

Dirk stuffed a few articles of clothing into a bag in preparation for his return to Amsterdam. Behind him, the rain fell against the window panes. It had started to rain at twilight. He prayed it wouldn't get any heavier as night fell, thinking of Francesca somewhere out there alone.

At the loud knock on the door, he swiveled around, hoping for some word. "Come in."

But it was only Jacob. Dirk's shoulders slumped a fraction, and he returned to his packing. He had little interest in dealing with Francesca's guardian and wished he'd returned to Amsterdam by now.

"No news?"

Dirk shook his head. "No one's seen a sign of Francesca since this afternoon. A servant said she saw her heading towards her room around four o'clock." Although his voice was calm, inside fear gnawed at him, but he would show none of this to Jacob.

Dirk had possessed her body and soul the night before, and now she had left him without a word. Where had she gone?

He hoped back to Jacob's residence. Thank goodness Katryn had returned this noon.

Jacob came to stand alongside him. "She's clearly abused your good intentions."

Dirk flicked a glance at the older man, feeling no desire to explain to him what had transpired between Francesca and himself.

He let out a breath, knowing he must say something. He wondered if Francesca had revealed things to her guardian.

It certainly didn't appear so. "Francesca and I had a . . . disagreement."

Jacob seemed to accept that.

Dirk continued. "I think she has left me."

Jacob tut-tutted. "She has gotten under your skin, hasn't she?" he asked in a voice of quiet sympathy.

Dirk rubbed his bearded jaw in an impatient gesture and turned away. He didn't want this man's pity or understanding. "I married her," he answered shortly, knowing in that instant that nothing and no one would separate them. He wouldn't permit it. She might think she could run away from him but he would hunt her down. He would make her see how much she needed him, how much she felt for him. He would make her forget her former loyalties.

"I suppose I was the last person to talk to her."

Dirk turned, every fiber alert. "What did she tell you?" he asked in a neutral tone.

Jacob shrugged without interest. "A lot of female nonsense." He waved a hand in annoyance. "Typical of a lover's tiff. I told her she'd have to accustom herself to being a wife."

The tension in Dirk's shoulders eased a fraction. "Yes, I'm afraid I offended my bride," he said at last, turning to close his bag.

"Offended her? What nonsense. She's your wife now. She must learn to submit. Why, you should have sent her to me. I would have set her straight."

"I suppose I...underestimated her sensibilities."

He could feel Jacob's sharp eyes on him. "She said I wasn't to trust you," he said with a short laugh.

So, she had said something to her guardian. Dirk let out his breath and met Jacob's gaze squarely. "I think Francesca is afraid of the easy wealth to be made on the beurs." Best to use the truth as far as he could. He shrugged. "She has been brought up differently. I can't blame her. The risks are not for everyone."

Jacob snorted. "That gives her no right to lecture you." Dirk nodded absently as the other man spoke, but his thoughts were elsewhere. In the ensuing silence all he could hear were Francesca's icy words, ordering him not to touch her. He pictured her running away from him as if the farthest corner of the earth would not put enough distance between the two of them.

"Just give her a few days," Jacob continued. "Let her see for herself just how far she can manage on her own. She'll soon be running back."

Dirk sighed. "I'm sure you're right. I would wager she's gone back to Amsterdam, since Tante Blankaart is still here. She's probably sitting at home with Katryn. Francesca hasn't anywhere else to go, has she?" He raised an eyebrow at Jacob.

If he detected the irony in Dirk's tone, he didn't show it. His lips pursed downwards, Jacob shook his head slowly from side to side. "Nay, she has only Lisbet and myself, and she'll not be hiding behind our skirts, I made that clear enough to her this afternoon."

"What do you mean?"

"I forbade her accompanying us back. I told her she must stay here."

Dirk could not detect the slightest interest or concern in Jacob's tone. Only annoyance. Dirk stared at van Diemen a moment longer, struggling not to show the revulsion he felt for this man. He had thought that he could feel no deeper loathing for him.

He swallowed his distaste and merely nodded. He mustn't waste his time on futile emotions when Francesca was alone somewhere, friendless. He turned away from Jacob and headed for the door. "I'm going after her."

―――

Francesca stood her ground, trying not to show the fear she was feeling. Pieter's landlady eyed her up and down. Francesca was well aware the hour was unseemly for a young woman to be paying a call upon a man.

Francesca's shoulders slumped in relief when the woman recognized her from her previous visits and finally motioned her up the stairs.

Night had fallen by the time Francesca reached Amsterdam. It had also begun to rain during her long journey, reminding her too closely of the night of her abduction. She had not traveled alone outside the city since then.

She had had to fight her fears, looking suspiciously at every man who came near her, and praying all the while for the Lord's protection.

She had no idea what she would do once she reached the city. After her guardian's reaction, she dared not go to his residence, not even to seek Katryn's help. As she'd stood uncertainly by the city's gates, with darkness descending, Francesca had felt the full weight of her situation. Bereft and forlorn, she felt like a lost little girl who was ready to sit down and cry. What a pitiful figure she must present, she thought, squaring her shoulders wearily and considering where to go.

She'd prayed for direction, and like a bright beacon in darkness, Pieter's name beckoned her.

Her friend. Her one true and only friend, she thought. She wasn't so alone after all.

Now, as she climbed the stairs to his garret, Francesca thought with deep, bitter regret of her faithlessness to her art. If she had kept her dedication to her painting pure and untainted as Pieter did, she never would have been fooled by Dirk's snake-like charm and sweet words.

She shuddered in recollection of his caresses, before ascending the last steps.

"Francesca!" Pieter jumped up from the couch, dropping a volume of engravings he had been leafing through in the candlelight. "What in the world are you doing here?" He took Francesca by the arms and peered at her in the circle of light. "What's happened? You look pale." His face turned grim. "Is it your new husband? What has he done to you?"

Francesca shook her head, her throat too constricted to speak. The genuine caring visible in Pieter's eyes was suddenly too much. She had sworn since she had left Zandvoort she would not cry anymore. She would not break down now.

Before she knew it, Pieter gathered her up against his wiry frame, and the tears coursed freely down her face. Once again, the self-recriminations began.

When she hiccupped for the last time and tried to pull away, Pieter held her fast and led her to the couch. He kept his arm tightly around her shoulders after they were seated.

"I'm sorry, Pieter. I didn't want to burden you with my troubles. I'm all right, really I am."

"Tell me what it's all about."

Francesca wiped her face with a handkerchief. "I've been so foolish," she began. "I can't go back to him."

"Mynheer Dirk? What has he done?"

Her lips trembled, threatening to leave her incoherent once again. Pieter said nothing, waiting patiently. "I can't live under his roof anymore. Not now," she said in a whisper.

"You speak in mysteries," Pieter chided softly. "What has your new husband done that's so terrible?"

"He lied to me about everything. I should have known, of course. Why else would he want me? It makes no sense otherwise." She gave Pieter a bittersweet smile. "Why should a gentleman who has everything go after someone like me to wife?" She shook her head, ignoring Pieter's attempt to speak.

"No, it's all clear now. He saw his advantage and took it. Shrewdly and methodically, he courted me, all the while paying his courtesy calls upon Mynheer Jacob, to further his entry there. The entry I provided." Francesca gave a bitter laugh. "He has my guardian enthralled now. Dirk can do no wrong in his eyes."

Pieter's dark brows drew together, his dark eyes troubled. "Perhaps you've misunderstood. Perhaps if you spoke to your husband about your misgivings—"

"What's the matter? Don't you trust my judgment either? Do you think me just a foolish bride unable to face the demands of the marriage bed?"

Pieter looked at her searchingly before speaking. "Of course not," he said, rubbing away a tear from her cheek with his knuckle. "If you say you had good reason to leave your husband, I believe you. Just let me know how I can help you."

"Oh, Pieter." Her eyes softened. "I'm sorry I accused you. It's just that Mynheer Jacob dismissed my warnings as foolishness."

Pieter frowned. "What kind of warnings?"

Francesca shook her head. "I myself scarcely know. Perhaps that is why Mynheer Jacob thought me only a hysterical female. All I know is that Dirk means him some harm. He's intent on some revenge, the purpose of which I don't know. Enough that he used me to get to my guardian." She gave him a twisted smile. "'Sooth, I was a foolish woman. I let myself be deluded, against my better judgment, thinking Dirk might want to marry me for some...some romantic notion. How silly of me."

"Francesca," he whispered, his voice full of compassion. "I'm sure Mynheer Dirk saw something that was good and fine in you and desired you for his wife."

She looked away from him, afraid of being undone. "Don't try to comfort me with vain imaginings. I can stand anything but more lies."

"Of course not. I just wish I could take away your pain."

Francesca straightened, then wiped her face one last time. "I shall survive it. It's just—I don't know where to go at present."

"Well, you came to the right place." Pieter gathered her once more against him.

"I won't stay long," she hastened to assure him. "But I ran away so quickly this afternoon. Mynheer Jacob has forbidden my returning to the house. Mayhap when I can manage to see Katryn, she'll...she'll know of something. Perhaps I can stay with family of hers until I can find a situation."

"Shh. You did well to come to me. And you are not going into service. You will stay as long as you need to here. We'll sort things out together," Pieter promised, smoothing her hair.

Francesca raised her head a moment later. "I don't want to go back to him. I don't—can't—face Dirk again. You mustn't let anyone know I'm here. Mynheer Jacob, if he knows, might force me to go back. I won't have to, will I?" she asked, suddenly afraid of Dirk's legal rights over her.

"Of course not." He thought a moment. "You could stay with a friend of mine. She's an apprentice at Vondel's studio."

"I don't know. . .I wouldn't want to put her to any trouble."

"She wouldn't be bothered at all. She's a very nice and generous-hearted woman. I'll take you there now."

Francesca sat up. "Now?"

"Your husband is probably looking for you already. If the way he eyed me at the wedding is any indication, I wouldn't be surprised if he came looking for you here tonight." Pieter grinned at her. "With a dagger in his hand for me."

Dirk hastened down the stairs from the street to the service entrance of van Diemen's residence. He had arrived in Amsterdam, and though the hour was late, headed straight to see Katryn. The front of the house was dark, except for a light he could just discern at the back. He hoped it meant the woman was still up.

After pounding repeatedly on the door, he heard a bolt being pulled back, then the top half of the door opened. The plump, red-cheeked woman came into view, wiping her hands on a cloth.

"Mynheer Dirk!" Her shocked face broke into a smile. "What are you doing here?" Hastily, she opened the rest of the door, motioning him to enter. "Come in, come in. You should have come by the front door, but you did well to come here since the house is empty. It would take me an age to make my way upstairs."

At her insistence, he sank into a chair she indicated by the scrubbed wooden table. Suddenly he felt the full weariness of the trip back to Amsterdam overtake him.

"You caught me still up. I'm in the midst of preparing the dough for tomorrow's bread. I had expected Mynheer and Lisbet this evening, but they appear to have been unable to tear themselves away from the festivities." She chuckled, patting some flour on her hands to continue kneading the dough. "But of course, you must know that. Tell me now, is there something Francesca needs, to have you come back at so late an hour? The wedding was beautiful, by the way. I was so happy to see my Frannie married so well. She truly deserves it."

He cut into her friendly chatter. "Did my wife come here at all this afternoon?"

Katryn stopped her kneading. "Francesca? What's this? What would she be doing back here without you?" Katryn's cheery face reflected alarm.

"So she didn't come here?" he asked more to himself than to her. He had been so sure she'd go to Katryn first. No, he just had not wanted to consider the other possibility. "Are you sure? Have you checked her room?" he asked sharply.

"Her room? No, of course not. But I shall do so right now." Katryn was already wiping her hands, the bread forgotten.

It was clear when they stood surveying Francesca's neat room that no one had been there. The room had a still, undisturbed look and airless smell.

"Now, what did you mean, mynheer, has Frannie been here?"

Dirk's shoulders slumped. "She ran away from the villa this afternoon." He couldn't bring himself to say from him. "Jacob and Lisbet are still there. That's the reason they didn't return today, in case she shows up there."

"Francesca run away? What nonsense is this?" She wrung her hands as the meaning sank in. "Oh, my poor dear. What did Jacob do to her?"

He let out a breath and looked at Katryn's fierce countenance. "Her guardian did nothing. Not this time." All of a sudden he felt a deep gratitude that someone was ready to defend Francesca against all threats. "Francesca ran away from me, dear lady."

"You, mynheer?" Her face began to clear. "Oh, no, there must be some mistake! A simple lovers' spat. With some sweet words and perhaps a gift, all can be made up in a thrice."

Dirk gave a grunt and looked away. "I'm afraid 'tis not as simple as that with Francesca."

Katryn gave an understanding nod. "Aye, she's had a lot to bear in her young life. You can't blame her if she resists those who would try to come close to her." She frowned as a new thought occurred to her. "You didn't say a word of criticism about mynheer or Lisbet? You know she won't hear a word against them, no matter how they treat her. She feels keenly the debt she owes them for taking her in when her parents died."

"I see." That would help explain her anger in part.

Katryn tut-tutted. "Ah, mynheer, she won't easily forgive you then. She's very loyal."

"I'm her husband now. She must learn to transfer her loyalties to me." His tone was sharper than he intended, but

Katryn's words, rather than console him, had only increased his worry and doubt.

Katryn shook her head at him sadly. "You must try to understand, mynheer. I know it is difficult, but give her time—"

"Time is what I don't have," he threw over his shoulder, heading toward the bedroom door. "Right now she might be alone in this city. I must find her." He paused at the threshold. "You have no idea where she could have gone? Mayhap to a friend's or to a relative of yours?"

"No." Katryn frowned. "She might be at my sister's, but I can't imagine her having gone there without coming to me first. Oh, Mynheer Dirk, you must find her. She might be out in the streets for all we know. I can't imagine where she could be." Her forehead creased in worry.

"Don't worry, good lady, I shall find her." If it's the last thing I do, he added grimly to himself. "If she comes here, I would be grateful if you could notify me immediately."

"Of course, of course. Oh, dear me, where can she be?" she murmured, following Dirk out of the room. "I'll tell her how distraught she's made you. How I've wished for a good man like you to come and take her away from her servitude, and now she goes and disappears. You mustn't be too angry with her when you do find her."

At least one person appreciated his deeds.

※

Dirk had no qualms about pounding on the door to Pieter de Brune's lodgings, despite the time. After what seemed an interminable wait, the door opened a crack.

"I need to speak to Pieter de Brune."

A man scowled at him from the crack. "Have you any idea how late the hour?"

"I beg you to excuse this inconvenience. But 'tis a matter of some urgency." He jingled some coins.

The man eyed his hand, opening the door wider. Dirk took advantage of the moment to insert his boot into the space. "Fear not, I shan't be but a moment." He entered into the dark corridor and handed the man the coins. With a nod of his head Dirk indicated the staircase. "This way?"

The man nodded. "Top floor. It's the only room."

When Dirk reached the top, he banged on the trap door with his stick.

A few minutes later, a sleepy-eyed Pieter, his black hair tousled, lifted the door with one hand, the other holding a candle. "Yes?"

He tried to gauge his tone—he sounded more wary than surprised at seeing him. "May I come up?" he asked, barely able to keep his tone civil.

"Now?"

Dirk took a deep breath, reining in his anger. "Yes, now."

Pieter nodded slowly. "Very well."

As soon as Pieter moved out of the way to secure the trap door, Dirk climbed the last steps.

When he stood in the garret, he planted his booted feet apart, his hand on his sword hilt, and eyed the man as a foe. He had never liked the underfed painter, but now his dislike intensified with the suspicion that Francesca might have turned to him. Since his bride had not sought succor with Katryn, who was like a mother to her, could she have come here? Venom laced through his veins at the mere thought.

If Francesca had come here, by now the painter probably knew everything. Dirk felt at a distinct disadvantage and he didn't like it. So help him, when he got his hands on his wife, she would never speak to this man again.

With a supreme effort, Dirk kept his growing anger under control. "I've come to inquire whether you've seen my wife today."

"Francesca?" Pieter raised his eyebrows in surprise, too exaggerated to be genuine. "Why no, I haven't seen her since your wedding yesterday. I returned this morning from there."

Dirk glowered at him, barely holding onto his frazzled temper. "She left my villa this afternoon, causing her family and me great worry. She hasn't been back to her house." Dirk's eyes challenged Pieter. "The housemaid, Katryn, knows of nowhere else she'd go." He took a step closer, towering over the painter. "That leaves only here. Where is she, de Brune?"

Dirk had to admire the man's bravado. Pieter returned his look steadily. To Dirk's extreme annoyance, he thought he detected a trace of amusement in the man's dark eyes. He recalled the first time Francesca had introduced Pieter to him. She had fairly glowed around the painter.

"I'm sorry, but I don't know where Francesca is. This is the first I've heard she was missing."

Dirk reached out, ready to grab him by the throat, but before he could do anything, Pieter dodged out of his way and gestured about the garret. "You can see for yourself she's not here."

After a quick glance around the shadowy interior, Dirk turned his attention back to the painter. "You're lying if you say you don't know her whereabouts. I don't intend to leave here without knowing where my wife is."

The man had the temerity to continue studying him as if he were considering him for a portrait. A comical portrait. Dirk had had enough of portraits. He ground his teeth when Pieter gave a casual shrug. "Well, it looks as if you will be hanging around here some time then."

A throbbing pulse began to beat at Dirk's temple. He grabbed the slighter man by the shirt front and hauled him upward. "You bloody fool. You can't take care of her. She could be with child!" he hissed between his clenched teeth.

He'd finally succeeded in shocking the painter.

His fingers tightened on Pieter's shirt. The throb in Dirk's temples had grown to a pounding. He gave an angry laugh. "Yes, those things happen when a man and woman lie together. Curse you, de Brune, you'd better not be lying to me. I intend to find Francesca, and when I do, you can be sure I won't let her within a mile of you ever again."

The artist seemed to hesitate, as if he might actually sympathize with him. But then he gave a slight shake of his head and even managed a small smile in Dirk's grip. "Then let us hope you do find her. But as I said, I can't help you. She hasn't been here."

Dirk let Pieter drop with a thud. While the painter was righting himself, Dirk was already thinking of what steps to take next. It wasn't worth knocking the man flat. De Brune wasn't a coward, he'd give him that. He could probably get more information out of him eventually by other means.

He took a long look around the cavernous garret. Somewhere, deep down, he felt a profound relief that Francesca was not there. Whether she had been there was another question. But it was clear she was not spending the evening with the painter.

He turned to Pieter. "So help me, de Brune, if she comes to you, I shall know about it. She can't hide from me forever."

Pieter made a gesture of resignation. "I can't stop you from looking for her."

Before stepping back onto the stairs, Dirk paused, a thought occurring to him. Without allowing himself to consider further, he took out his purse. The next instant he flung it toward Pieter, who was forced to catch it in midair. When he felt its weight and heard the jingling of coins, he began to shake his head and extend it back towards Dirk. "She won't—I can't take—"

Dirk ignored his words, knowing in that instant that Pieter had seen her. "There are a few hundred guilders in there, if Francesca should need it. Let me know if she needs more." If he let himself dwell on the possibility of Francesca with child—his child—and nowhere to go, he would go mad. As it was, he already felt his sanity slipping dangerously.

With an effort, he softened his tone. "I don't take lightly the notion of spawning a child with a naïve, young innocent who has no one to turn to, and hasn't an inkling of how hard it is to survive out there." He made a motion with his chin toward the streets.

Pieter held the money uncertainly, and finally gave a clipped nod. "If she comes here, I'll see that she gets it."

Thirteen

Francesca jumped at the sound behind her, then seeing it was only Katryn, she let out her breath in relief. She had waited until she had seen both Mynheer Jacob and Lisbet depart by the main entrance before entering the house to fetch some of her things.

"Just when were you going to tell me you were here, Frannie?" Katryn stood in the doorway of Francesca's bedroom, her arms folded across her bosom.

"I...I was just coming down to the kitchen as soon as I finished here." She continued folding the petticoat in her hand and nervously pushed it into the satchel on her bed.

"Well, I certainly hope so. If you think you can keep things from me, you should know better by now."

"I wasn't intending to keep anything from you," Francesca hastened to assure her. "I just knew there wasn't much time." She flushed. "I mean, before Mynheer Jacob returns."

Katryn nodded in comprehension. "Your husband has already been here," she said with a significant look. "Yester eve."

Francesca's hand went to her chest. "Dirk has been here? What did he want?" she added in a more belligerent tone.

"He told me all about your misunderstanding." At Francesca's look of surprise, she continued with a smile of sympathetic understanding. "He said he'd offended you. I understand he must have criticized Mynheer Jacob in some form." Katryn shook her head, advancing toward Francesca.

"You didn't have to run away from your husband for such a thing," she said, clucking her tongue. "Come here, child." Katryn took Francesca's unresisting body into an embrace. "It will be all right. Mynheer Dirk will see that everything's set straight. Now, you just come down to the kitchen and tell me what possessed you to run away like a thief in the night. You've caused us all a lot of worry and grief."

Once downstairs, Katryn scurried about getting together a light repast for Francesca. "Doesn't look as if you've eaten anything since the wedding," she observed, setting raisin and currant buns spread liberally with butter before Francesca. She poured them each a glass of fresh buttermilk before seating herself across from Francesca. "Eat up, Frannie. I just baked the krentenbollen this morning."

"Thank you, Katryn, but I'm fine." In truth, she hadn't eaten since she'd left the villa, hadn't wanted to. But to please Katryn, she picked up the thick bun and bit into it, then began to cough as it went down the wrong way.

"There, there, I didn't say you had to wolf it down." Katryn hurried over and patted her on the back. "Take a sip of buttermilk and you'll be all right."

When she'd resumed her seat, silence descended between the two of them. Katryn cleared her throat, her hands folded on the table. "Mynheer Dirk is very concerned about you."

Francesca was about to take another bite, but the tasty bun lost its appeal. She lowered it to her plate. "Yes, I'm sure he is." Concerned about how to explain her disappearance to Mynheer Jacob and all his acquaintances.

Katryn peered at her. "What makes you so disbelieving, child? The poor man was distraught when he came here last night. He was out looking for you all night." She reached across the tabletop and covered one of Francesca's hands. "He was by again at first light to see if you'd come by. It was clear he hadn't been to bed."

Francesca stood, not wanting to believe Dirk did it out of concern for her. "I mustn't linger."

Katryn stood and pushed her back down. "There now,

child. He means well by you. If he said something to displease you, he'll make it up to you. You'll see. Give him time. Men's sensibilities are ofttimes rougher than a woman's. They take a bit of getting used to."

"How do I get used to the fact that he merely used me to get closer to Mynheer Jacob?"

Katryn looked shocked. "What makes you think he used you?"

The concern in the older woman's eyes almost undid her again. Francesca looked down at her raisin bun, the image before her blurring. "He admitted it himself, Katryn," she said quietly, when she could trust herself to speak again.

Katryn sighed. "I don't know what he may have said to you, or how you may have understood what he said. What I do know is that the man who came here last night and again at daybreak was not a cold-hearted man hunting down his wife like some piece of property. He was a man worried sick over his wife's well-being and safety."

"Dirk has a very smooth way with words. Unfortunately, I've learned his words can mean very little."

"He is a most charming man, to be sure. But the man who pounded on my door last night was not delivering a fancy speech or trying to mislead me. He was a man whose speech was direct and not always pleasing. What is clear is that he appeared most determined to find you." Katryn sat back as if she had said all that needed to be said.

Francesca's mouth hardened to a straight line. Well, Dirk could search from one end of the city to the other. She was one quarry who would not be found. She would never make the same mistake twice. "Yes, Dirk can be most determined when it suits him."

"Frannie, Dirk is your husband. He deserves your loyalty. Besides, he doesn't seem the kind of man to carry out an injustice against anyone."

Francesca looked at Katryn sadly. It was clear Dirk had fooled the older woman as easily as he had once fooled her.

Katryn added carefully, "A man like your guardian is bound to have enemies." When Francesca said nothing, she asked, "What can I tell Mynheer Dirk when he comes back?"

Francesca looked away. "Tell him...tell him you don't know."

"Oh, Frannie, where are you? How can I know you are all right, all alone out there?"

Francesca felt a twinge of helplessness at the loving concern she saw in Katryn's eyes. She came around the table and bent over the woman who had been like a mother to her since she'd lost her own. "I'm fine, I promise you. Don't fret about me. I've found someone to stay with. A friend," she added, meeting Katryn's disbelieving gaze and doing her utmost to convince her. "I'm starting a new life, something I've always wanted."

"You're...you're not with your old painting master, are you?"

Francesca shook her head, suddenly glad for Pieter's caution. "Of course not. Please, Katryn, don't say anything to Mynheer Jacob that you saw me. He forbade me to come here."

"You needn't worry. I shan't say anything to him," she said with a sniff. "But you must go back to your husband."

Francesca refused to answer Katryn's plea. "Promise me something else."

"Of course, dear."

"Promise to let me know if you discover anything about Dirk's dealings with Mynheer Jacob. You can send a message to Pieter. He'll...he'll know where to find me. I tell you, Katryn, Dirk means him harm."

When Francesca stopped to see Pieter to let him know that she had settled in with his apprentice friend, the first words he said to her were, "Your husband paid me a call."

Her heart began to beat with the quickened rhythm of the hunted. "Today?"

Pieter cracked a wry smile. "In the wee hours of last night."

"Oh!" Her hand went to her throat. She hadn't expected him to look for her at Pieter's so soon. Despite Katryn's words, she hadn't expected Dirk to come looking for her at all. "What did he say?"

"He accused me of knowing your whereabouts."

Her fear grew. "Wh-what did you say?"

"Oh, never fear, I told him nothing." Pieter smiled. "Though he was most adamant, as if I could conjure you up out of thin air that very instant." He rubbed his chest. "The man can be very convincing."

Her eyes widened in alarm. "He didn't hurt you?"

He laughed, shaking his head. "Never fear, I'm in one piece as you can see." His voice sobered. "But he's not a stupid man. My poor lies didn't fool him." He paused. "He said he would be back, that you couldn't hide from him forever."

"That's what he thinks." Righteous anger came to her aid again. The gall of the man! When he couldn't get his way with deceitful words, he turned to brute force.

"A man of his caliber won't be dissuaded once he's plotted a course."

No one was more aware of that than she. Francesca glanced at Pieter with worried eyes. "You don't think he can find me where I am, do you? If so, I must leave. I—I can't face him again."

Pieter went to her. "Don't worry, Francesca. We'll move you as often as we have to. We'll lead your ferocious lion a merry chase throughout Amsterdam if need be." Laughter erupted from his throat. "The mouse will prove elusive prey indeed."

"It's not funny! You don't know Dirk. I didn't myself until now." She turned from Pieter's comforting arm. "I trusted my instincts and look how wrong I was."

"Are you sure your instincts weren't right?"

"Instincts!" She shook her head vehemently, tears once more threatening. "Not when one is hoping for someone to be something he is not."

Dirk was breathing fire when he stomped up Pieter de Brune's stairs for the second time that week. That lying devil's spawn was going to tell him the truth if it was the last thing he ever did.

Dirk had spent the intervening days scouring every employment agency for domestic servants in the entire city. His men had been to every wealthy burgher's house inquiring at the service entrances for someone recently hired who fit Francesca's description. Dirk had expended a good sum in bribes and tips, but had come up with nothing.

Gone without a trace. She had even disdained to take any possessions with her from the villa, including her new dress.

Nothing. Not a clue to either Miss Francesca di Paolo's or Mevrouw Francesca Vredeman's whereabouts. Mynheer Jacob was worthless in the search. The man knew nothing and cared even less what happened to his ward. These days Jacob cared little about anything save buying and selling on the beurs. After those few, gradually increasing killings Dirk had carefully orchestrated for him, van Diemen seemed possessed by the idea of sudden, vast wealth to rival the Bickers. He pestered Dirk every chance he got for more information on incoming ships and their cargo.

Dirk wanted nothing better than to tell the man to go to perdition. If Jacob was obsessed by profits to be gained on the exchange, Dirk's obsession, he discovered, had become finding Francesca. Ironically enough, it seemed the more Dirk's indifference to profits, the greater grew Jacob's desire for a tip on the stock exchange.

Dirk's only ally in the search so far proved to be Katryn. But even she hadn't been able to tell him much, except what he already suspected. It was obvious Francesca didn't want to see him. He had also known she'd go running to Pieter the first chance she got. Dirk cursed the painter's soul, imagining even now Francesca sharing the man's bed now that she'd had a taste of what passion could be. Dirk saw a blinding rush of red before him and swore to kill the painter if he had so much as touched her.

He entered Pieter's garret. A quick glance toward the sunlit window revealed the painter sitting at his easel. Striding toward him, Dirk caught sight of a dark-haired, naked woman reclining on a couch in front of Pieter's easel.

It wasn't Francesca. Relief coursed through him in such waves, he almost staggered.

He examined the woman critically. Although she, too, had long, wavy, dark locks, her build was larger, more voluptuous than Francesca's. She also looked used. She met his gaze head on, with no hint of shame for her state of undress. Dirk was accustomed to that lack of modesty in women. It was what made Francesca's modesty all the more appealing.

He bowed low toward the woman, saying sardonically, "Excuse me for interrupting your work. I won't be but a moment." His smile disappeared as soon as he turned away from the model to face Pieter.

"I thought your specialty was landscapes, de Brune, but I see you enjoy all kinds of vistas."

Pieter looked at him warily. "I'm in the middle of working."

"As I said, I won't be long." In one smooth motion, he grabbed Pieter by his jerkin and pulled him to his feet.

"Hey!" he yelped, looking at the streak of paint his brush had made on the canvas. "That represents hours of work."

"Don't worry, I'll let you get back to your play in a moment," Dirk said softly, dragging Pieter across the room to a shadowy corner. Pinning his gaze on the painter's face, he said in a silky voice, "I want some answers and I want them now. Francesca came here and I know you know where she is. And you are going to tell me where that is. Understood?"

"Why don't you let me loose?" he said with difficulty. "We can discuss this civilly."

"As soon as I have the truth. I'm through discussing things civilly with you, de Brune. And you know why?" Dirk narrowed his eyes at the painter. "Because you're nothing but a lying blackguard."

Pieter swallowed visibly. "That's funny, because she said the same thing about you."

The two of them stared at each other for what seemed an eternity. Abruptly, Dirk let him go. "Francesca is my wife," he said, running a hand wearily through his hair.

"Francesca is her own person."

"She married me." She belonged to him as much as he belonged to her.

As if taking a decision, Pieter finally said. "'Tis true, Francesca was here."

Dirk's hands went slack at his sides, the tension draining from his whole body.

She was alive! was his first thought. Since the moment Francesca had left the villa, he hadn't dared voice the other possibility, but it had been there, haunting the edges of his mind, terrorizing his dreams.

Pieter plunged on, as if having decided to confess the truth, he was willing to tell him everything. "She made me promise not to tell anyone she was here. And now she's left. In fact, she only stayed a few moments."

Dirk's gaze never left Pieter's, gauging if the man were telling the truth. "Where is she now?"

"I'm her friend. She trusts me. I—I can't tell you."

He clenched his fists, feeling his hackles rising once more. "Devil take it, de Brune, I'm fast losing patience with you. You'll tell me now, or I shall dog your every footstep 'til I know the truth."

Seconds ticked by as the painter seemed to measure him.

"She's...she's—" Pieter's gaze faltered momentarily. "She's gone to Florence!"

"What nonsense is this?" Dirk growled, certain the man was lying.

He met Dirk's gaze head-on, as if daring him to refute the statement. "She left on yesterday's tide. At first she lodged with an apprentice friend of mine—a woman," Pieter hastened to add as Dirk's hands came up once more. "I took her there myself. I assure you she was safe. Then yester morn, she told me she'd decided to go to seek her father's family. They come from Florence. She's gone to them.

"As an artist, it's the only place to study seriously," he explained. "She's hoping her family will house her so that she can pursue her painting studies." He stepped away from Dirk and began to pace the room. "Why, can you imagine it? Florence!" The painter's eyes seemed to light up. "'Tis every painter's dream of paradise. Just imagine, the opportunity to study in the land that produced the Renaissance. To see first-hand the works of Leonardo, Michelangelo, Raphael..."

His speech quickened. "To study the perspective of Uccello, the sculptures of Verrocchio, the ceramics of della Robbia, the frescoes of Giotto! Why, she could never hope to learn a fraction of what she'll learn there if she stayed here in Holland."

Dirk rocked back on his heels, stroking his beard, considering, and trying to mask the uncertainty he felt.

He remembered the look in Francesca's eyes the day on the beach when she spoke of her art being all for her. Pieter had that same look when he spoke of studying in Florence.

"How in all that's holy did she have the coin for such a journey?"

Pieter stopped his pacing in mid-stride. He looked around him as if searching for the answer in his garret. Then he met Dirk's gaze with one of embarrassment. "I—I gave her your money."

Dirk took a deep breath. His words when they finally came were quiet. "I see." For another moment, the two men were silent, Dirk weighing Pieter's words. "She runs away from me, yet is not averse to using my coin to pursue her art."

"That's not the way of it at all! You know she would be too proud to take your money." Pieter shuffled his feet, not meeting Dirk's gaze. "The truth is, well, I didn't tell her the money came from you." As if fearing Dirk's reaction, he said quickly, "I know 'twas wrong of me, but I knew of no other way to give her the money. I thought it would be good for her to get away. It was an opportunity of a lifetime. The only reason she even considered going was because she has family there. It was a chance to discover something of them as well."

Dirk rubbed the back of his neck in frustration, forced to admit the truth of de Brune's assertions. Francesca was hungry for family, for belonging somewhere, whether she knew it or not herself.

It didn't make the tale any easier to accept. His shy little sparrow had bested him at every step. Now she had succeeded in flying away with his money. Not that he begrudged her the money. She could have had it all.

But, to have run away from him like that? Never giving him the chance to explain?

Without another look at Pieter or his model, Dirk turned on his heel and strode from the room.

※

That evening when Francesca came to visit Pieter, they sat down to a simple meal of bread and salted herring.

"I don't think you need fret about your husband anymore," Pieter said after swallowing a mouthful of herring.

Francesca tore off a piece of bread. "I wish you wouldn't call him that. He is no husband of mine."

Pieter cleared his throat, looking down at his plate. "He...he implied your marriage had been consummated."

She felt the blood rush to the roots of her hair. "He what?"

"He was afraid you might be with—ahem—child."

Francesca had not thought of that. In the stillness, her hand reached down to her belly. A child. A whole new world opened up for her. The next second reality crashed around her. What would she do if she found herself with child? Dirk's child? Stark fear filled her. Dear Lord, she prayed, what am I to do?

Pieter reached across and took her hand. "He was frantic with worry, I would say."

She swallowed with effort. "What if I am?"

He shrugged. "We shall face that eventuality if it happens. At any rate, I do believe you've seen the last of Dirk for a while."

Distracted from the thought of a child, she asked, "Why is that?"

"I told him you had gone to Florence."

Her mouth fell open. "You what?"

He laughed. "It's not so unreasonable. I told him you wished to search for your father's family and to study painting."

She shook her head, dazed. "Whatever possessed you to say such an outrageous thing?"

"My neck, for one thing." He grinned, rubbing his collar with a hand. "Your husband—beg pardon—Mynheer Dirk is a man who holds his temper in check with an effort. I had to think of something." He leaned forward, like a fellow conspirator. "But think about it. Is it really so outrageous? Dirk didn't seem to think so when he finally left."

Pieter continued. "Mayhap it was the part about seeking your family that convinced him...or studying under the finest masters in the world...or seeing firsthand the work of the Renaissance masters. Believe me, I got so wrapped up in the opportunities beckoning you, I began to believe the tale myself." Pieter smiled at her, as if proud of his embroidery.

Francesca couldn't help returning his smile, knowing it had been his dream for so long to study in Florence.

"'Tis good to see you smile again, Francesca, even if it is a trifle bittersweet—'tis a smile nevertheless."

She shook her head "I still don't see how you convinced him. He's a very shrewd man." She remembered Dirk's uncanny ability to read her very thoughts.

Pieter pursed his lips, looking up at the ceiling rafters. "I believe fear gave my words conviction. Ah, you should have seen him. At first I don't know who was the angrier of us. He came stomping in here and nearly ruined one of my paintings."

Her eyes widened in horror. "No!"

Pieter nodded. "He grabbed me so fast while I was sitting at the easel that I left a whole steak of paint on the study I've been doing of Maria."

"Oh, Pieter, I'm sorry."

Pieter laughed. "Don't look so distraught. There was no real harm done. Believe me, I almost felt sorry for the man. I could see his torment was real."

For a moment, she felt an acute sense of longing to go to Dirk.

"I can understand why you wanted to paint him. He's a fascinating study. Today he was like wounded beast, who would attack anyone who stood in his path. I had to admire his persistence. He cares for you a great deal."

"He is single-minded where his ambitions are concerned. I admired that in him, too." She thought of Dirk's rise from the Tughuis to a plantation in the Indies. Before Pieter could try to convince her any further of Dirk's devotion, she came back to the original topic. "I still can scarce believe you convinced him I had gone to Florence."

Pieter gave her a knowing smile. "Actually I think what finally did it was the fact that you had the means to do it."

At her questioning look, he explained, "I told him I had given you the money to make the voyage."

"Oh." She didn't know how she felt about the news. All of a sudden everything seemed so final.

"Come on, eat up," he urged her with a light touch to the back of her hand. "I have some even better news for you. It's clear we can't keep up this fiction of your whereabouts. Although Dirk seemed to accept my story about Italy, he could very well show up here again."

"I know." Francesca sighed. "What am I to do? I can't stay with your friend indefinitely. I have no money. There must be some work I could do."

"Sh. I told you, I have some good news." He paused, awaiting her full attention. "I took the liberty of showing your portfolio to Bartholomeus van der Helst."

"Van der Helst?" Her eyes widened in disbelief. "He's the leading portraitist in the city. I can't believe you allowed him to view my paltry efforts." She crumpled her napkin in her hand in embarrassment.

Pieter grinned broadly. "It's too late now, Francesca. He has not only seen your efforts, but he's agreed to take you on as an apprentice."

Francesca forgot everything else for a moment. "Pieter, I can't believe you!"

"Believe it, 'tis the truth. He's ready to have you start immediately."

The next moment her face fell. "'Twill be impossible. Even if true, I could never get the money for his fees."

Pieter's eyes lit with amusement. "I knew I would eventually find a good use for this." He walked over to the other end of the room and rummaged through an old bucket filled with dry brushes. When he returned to the table, he had a leather drawstring bag in his hand. Without a word, he opened it and poured out its contents. Gold and silver coins fell upon each other like a fountain of water.

"I've been saving this for just the right occasion. It should cover your first year fees under van der Helst."

Francesca looked at the mound of coins in amazement. "Where did you get all this money?"

"Let's just say a windfall I received not too long ago. I stashed it away for an emergency. Well, I believe we have found just the right emergency."

Even before he finished, Francesca was already shaking her head. "No, absolutely not."

Pieter nodded his head just as adamantly. "Have some faith in your abilities. Van der Helst's fees are usually a hundred guilders a year. Soon you'll be making that yourself in commissions."

"'Tis a veritable fortune, Pieter. I could never make such a sum. It takes years."

"Nonsense. You have more talent than the average apprentice. Besides, I want you to accept this from me as your friend. I don't need this money right now. Someday, if I ever need anything, I know I can come to you. That's what friends are for."

Francesca looked at him, her heart overflowing with gratitude. Friendship. The truth lay there. She might have no family. Her husband might have proven false. But she had a true friend.

※

Dirk stopped by to see Katryn before heading upstairs to his appointment with Jacob. The good woman immediately insisted on fixing him a snack.

He couldn't remember when his last meal had been. He watched Katryn reach up to take a joint of ham from the rafters. More and more he felt at ease in this kitchen. In some strange way it brought him closer to Francesca. He watched Katryn and pictured Francesca going through the same motions. Cutting through the round ball of cumin-studded cheese. Loping thick slices of pink ham off the joint. Slathering fresh-churned butter on a piece of just-baked brown bread.

"There you go, mynheer. Eat hearty." Katryn pushed the plate toward him. "I'll just pour us both some ale." She walked to the larder. In a few minutes she returned with a pewter tankard.

"So, you think our Frannie's gone off to foreign lands?" Katryn shook her head with a sigh, considering the news. "'Twouldn't surprise me, you know. She's never talked about her family there, since they made it clear they didn't want her, but I know, deep down, she's always wanted to know something of her father's people."

Dirk frowned, taking up the open-faced sandwich. "How could they not want her?"

Katryn shrugged. "Who's to know the minds of these foreigners? Different religion, different ways. But I tremble to think of her on a ship all alone. Will she be safe?"

Dirk closed his mind to all the perils he knew firsthand and sought to reassure Katryn, realizing it did no good to worry. "Pieter has told me since that she went accompanied by a fellow painter, who was going to pursue a course of study for a year. It seems de Brune has arranged everything quite handily," he added dryly. "I didn't think he had such capabilities."

Katryn smiled. "I know how difficult this must be for you. Let us be grateful she didn't go alone."

Dirk finished his meal in silence. When he had drained the last of his ale, he stood. "I'll see myself up. Thank you, good woman, for the refreshment."

"Not at all. Please come down to see me whenever you stop by."

Dirk had just reached the door when he stopped. He had gone around and around it in his mind, and still he couldn't understand it. "Why is it, Katryn, that Francesca finds it so difficult to switch her loyalties from Jacob to me?"

He looked at the older woman, hoping to read an answer in her face. "I thought I treated her well enough. I did everything I know to make her feel"—he searched for words—"differently from what I saw she underwent in this household. I mean no offense to you, for I can see you have cared for her as a mother would, but for the rest..."

He gestured, a feeling of helplessness overcoming him. "By heaven, Katryn, van Diemen wasn't going to admit her into his house after her abduction! What kind of treatment is that to merit such unswerving loyalty? And yet she cannot forgive the fact I have some ancient feud with her guardian, a business that involves only him and me, and has nothing to do with her." He gave a hollow laugh. "She should be overjoyed. I would gladly take up her cause and right all the wrongs Jacob has done her all these years."

Katryn nodded sympathetically. "Aye, mynheer, I believe you. But 'tisn't Mynheer Jacob at all she's protecting. Haven't you seen that by now?"

Dirk frowned at her, not understanding her meaning.

"'Tis her sense of duty and loyalty to her own father."

"You speak in riddles."

"When Francesca's father died, he left her penniless—not only that, but saddled with debts. 'Twas Mynheer Jacob who took her in and settled all the debts. 'Tis true she was made little better than a serving maid here, but Francesca would have had it no other way. It's her way of earning her keep and paying off her father's debts."

Dirk continued to frown. A man befriending a penniless orphan. It didn't sound at all like the Jacob he knew. Could he perhaps be wrong about the man?

He shook his head, doubting it. It was certainly something that required looking into, however.

A few moments later, Dirk entered Jacob's office and eased himself into the leather seat facing his desk.

After talking business matters for a while, enough to satisfy the man's appetite for wealth, Dirk approached his real reason for the visit.

"I've discovered Francesca might have gone to Florence to seek her father's family."

Jacob frowned. "I doubt they'll receive her, even if she does manage to locate them."

"Why wouldn't they welcome her?"

He shrugged. "Her father became a member of the Reformed Church, anathema to his Catholic family. The family has never been in contact with Francesca since his death."

"And before that? Did Francesca's father keep any ties with his native land?"

Jacob sat up and made a motion to straighten a ledger on his desk. "He handled some of our business with Italy. But I don't know how much contact he had with his family."

"You said you had notified them after her father's death, to see if they would take her in. Where do they reside?"

Jacob made a vague motion with his hands. "It was so long ago, I hardly recall."

"I think you had mentioned Florence," he persisted. Jacob's replies didn't satisfy him. "It shouldn't be too difficult to locate a family called di Paolo in the city. I have some business acquaintances there as well. I think I shall make some inquiries. Do you know what line of business the family was in?"

He shook his head, not meeting Dirk's gaze. "I really can't say."

Can't or won't, he thought, wondering at Jacob's reticence. "Tell me," he asked softly, "why didn't you continue your partner's business dealings with Florence after he died?"

Jacob flicked a look at him before glancing back down at his papers. "There was no profit in it. Besides, di Paolo left a mass of personal debts when he died. It took me months to straighten everything out." Jacob rose from his chair. "I told you before, the man was a financial disaster. For years I have taken care of the daughter because my conscience would allow me to do no less."

Dirk stood to bid him farewell, in that moment making up his mind for certain on his next course of action. It had been plaguing at him all along, but Jacob's hedging had settled it.

Dirk was taking the next ship to Florence.

Fourteen

May 1642

Francesca stood looking up at the imposing facade of the della Torre mansion fronting the Herengracht. Pieter had instructed her to meet him there at three o'clock, saying he had a surprise for her.

She had no idea what it could be, but knew Pieter would not summon her from van der Helst's atelier without good reason.

"Let's just say, I have something that will mark the beginning of your career as a true painter," he'd said, toasting her with a pint of ale.

She'd laughed ruefully. "Isn't that what I am now?"

"You're still but an apprentice."

"But I've been there almost a year. Does that count for nothing?"

Pieter chuckled. "We all know the first several months are spent doing nothing but such menial tasks as cleaning brushes, stitching together and stretching canvasses onto wood frames, cleaning the presses and copper plates for engravings."

Yes, she remembered those dreary months of autumn and winter when mornings had begun pitch black in her icy chamber. With stiff fingers she would don her clothes, eat a piece of day-old bread, and hurry outside to make her way through the windy streets towards van der Helst's atelier.

It had surprised her that with all the tasks to fill up her hours, time had not moved more quickly for her. For the first time in her life painting did not provide a lifeline of escape. In her free hours, Francesca had to force herself to sketch. Anything to keep from thinking of her former life. Even now, almost a year later, she dreaded being alone with her thoughts. For in those hours before dawn, she relived Dirk's passion and tenderness. They were infinitely harder to bear than the memory of his treachery.

But little by little, she was learning to live with the hollow ache, she told herself.

Months after beginning her apprenticeship, when Francesca had started exercises in oils at the atelier, a carelessly uttered word of criticism from the master himself would send her into a deep depression for days.

One day however, in the dead of winter, a gruff compliment from van der Helst had penetrated Francesca's darkness. Strange how that one word of praise had given her the courage to stay the course and continue with renewed determination. And slowly, her desire to paint had re-emerged, and its healing power commenced to work in her.

"So," she had said to Pieter, intrigued by his assertion that she had yet to begin her real career, "even my painting at the wharf has not made me a real painter?"

"Not until you receive a bona fide commission are you a real painter." He squeezed her hand. "I think your sketches and paintings from the tavern are truly wonderful, but you have received nothing from them."

She laughed. "What about the cup of soup or warm jug of ale Klaus would give me?"

"Just to keep you coming to his establishment."

She hadn't needed that enticement. With her reawakened desire to paint, her thoughts turned to the wretched harlots Dirk had shown her by the wharf that summer day. If Pieter had not found her the position in van der Helst's atelier, who was to say she would not have joined the ranks of some tavern wench, serving the rough sailors their ale, then leading them up to some flea-ridden pallet for a few minutes of degradation?

She shuddered, realizing there would have been few

avenues open to her. Girls who had started down that road began early. By the time they reached thirty, most were disease-ridden or locked in the Spinhuis for theft.

With her first free moments from her apprenticeship, during the lengthening days of spring, Francesca went back to the wharves. Intimidated by that world, which she knew almost nothing about, she hesitated at its border. Almost by accident she found the tavern where Dirk had taken her. The Bruin Biertje.

Emotions she'd succeeded in burying deep enough to live with day by day choked her as she entered its doors. Snatches of her conversation with Dirk on that long-ago afternoon came back to her. She could see the varying expressions in Dirk's amber eyes as he had looked at her—teasing mockery, skepticism, and even...tenderness. No! Lying, deceitful eyes, she corrected herself. But the conviction was no longer there.

Francesca was tempted to turn and run, abandoning her resolve to paint the personalities by the wharf. But instead, she straightened her shoulders and marched in. Even that gesture brought the memory of Dirk's touch on her sleeve. She started, glancing downward. She could have sworn she had actually felt his hand.

Jerking her gaze from her sleeve, Francesca looked up and locked eyes with the tavern keeper's. And like a shipwreck victim seeing an island, she headed toward him, hoping he would remember her.

"Well, well, who have we here?" Klaus said with a chuckle, taking her two hands in his and looking her up and down with evident pleasure. "Finally deigned to visit us from your fancy address?"

She started, before realizing he thought she was living at Dirk's canal home. A home she had never yet seen.

She did nothing to contradict him. "I'm sorry to have taken so long to visit you." She went on to explain her purpose in wanting to sketch his patrons.

After that he asked her little about herself. Before long

Francesca understood the ways of the port, where a person's background was as shadowy as a ship's hold.

But as Klaus sat for his own portrait, he began to reminisce about Dirk.

Francesca sighed, feeling wistful. "You sound as if you've known Dirk a long time."

Klaus smiled fondly. "'Twas I who gave him his first chance at sea. Oh, yes," he answered Francesca's look of surprise. "He had just been released, for the third time, from a spell in the Tughuis, and would no doubt have landed back in there shortly, if he hadn't put to sea."

Klaus refilled some tankards, which Gert had brought to him, with ale from a keg behind the bar. As the woman walked away with her loaded tray, he continued his story. "I knew Dirk's mother slightly. Ye get to know most of the women doing business in this quarter. I felt sorry for her little lad, having to learn the ways of the street at such a tender age. But his story was not unique. I had seen many such a boy."

Klaus pursed his lips, shaking his head. "I don't know what it was that caught my eye, 'specially about this tyke. Mayhap 'twas his fierce devotion to his mother. Most urchins learn to steal out of necessity, but then become cunning little foxes with a stealthy look in their eyes, completely incapable of any reform, even if the chance were to present itself.

"With Dirk it was different. You could see he detested the life but would do anything to ease his mother's burden. Most of all, I could see Dirk hated what his mother was forced to do for a living."

As she listened riveted, her pencil fell to her lap.

"Aye, and soon enough he learned the meaning of the name 'bastard.'" Klaus shook his white head. "Little Dirk suffered many a black eye over that stamp.

"Each time I saw him, after he'd been in the Tughuis, I marveled that he hadn't turned into some hardened criminal. 'Tis a brutal place from the stories I hear. Imagine a place where they throw in men and boys, thieves alongside mere loafers and beggars. You have to be tough to survive. Dirk was tough, all right. Yet, instead of turning him into a criminal, it made him all the more determined to survive. And, it didn't touch him in here." Klaus tapped his chest at the place of his heart. "He still knew how to treat his friends. He had a sort of inborn honor that nothing could rob him of."

Francesca wanted to weep. What had happened to that young boy?

"I was first mate on a ship in those days." He nodded proudly. "When I came into port that last time and chanced to see young Dirk, I said to meself, this city's no place for the lad. Let him go somewhere, where he can begin afresh and have a fighting chance. I took him on as part of the crew." Klaus chuckled. "His time in the Rasphuis stood him in good stead. No one could bully him! Nor was he afraid of hard work. And he had plenty of that, aye, that he did.

"But now you see, 'twas all he needed, a chance. He's become as rich as Croesus, lived like a pasha out there in the Indies. He set me up in this place, don't ye know, after I got too old to sail."

Francesca's breath caught. "He bought you this tavern?"

"Aye. He saw the life on the sea was getting too hard for me." He sighed in satisfaction. "A good friend and a good man is Dirk Vredeman."

Francesca glanced down at her bare finger. She'd removed her wedding band, when she'd begun her apprenticeship, but she wore it on her mother's chain around her neck. For safekeeping, she told herself. Yet the feel of the metal between her breasts brought a sense of possession...and possessed.

Francesca had discovered something while sketching the tavern's clients. Deny it though she would, once she had opened her heart a crack, no matter how despicably used, she could never again close it. She found it impossible to suppress its clamoring for love. It was the desire she had denied herself ever since her parents had been taken from her.

Instead of openly satisfying the longings of her heart, however, Francesca found herself searching each face she painted or sketched for that same yearning. From brassy harlot to crusty sailor, from Klaus's paternal features to the slack jaw of a dozing drunk, Francesca sought that one trace that showed her their hunger for love.

She had a whole portfolio full of those yearning faces. For in them, Francesca forged her bond to other human souls without any risk of rejection or disappointment.

"Francesca!"

She jumped at the shout, her thoughts yanked back to the present.

Pieter was hurrying down the street along the canal. She waved a hand, then awaited his approach.

After greeting her, he led her up the steps to the della Torre mansion. It was the first time she had entered one of the residences along the Herengracht, where the wealthiest merchants and noblemen of the city lived. She wondered if this was where Dirk's home was located.

Once inside, her first impression was of sunlight filtering into the many long windows lining one wall of a long salon—a room so much brighter and airier than her guardian's canal house.

Crystal chandeliers glinted from the ceiling, rich carpets covered a marble floor, and ornately carved wooden wall panels and armoires provided an appropriate backdrop to the many bright paintings on the wall.

Pieter clasped hands with a richly dressed, rotund man, whose florid features were turned to her. "Don Lorenzo, may I present a compatriot. Though she was born in Holland, her father was Florentine. Juffrouw Francesca di Paolo."

Francesca had reverted to her maiden name, preferring to erase any physical evidence of a marriage she still told herself had been a sham.

"Francesca, this is Don Lorenzo della Torre, a patron of the arts."

"Delighted," Don Lorenzo murmured in Italian, bowing low over her hand. When he looked back up at her, he smiled slowly. "You cannot be the artist Pieter has been telling me about. You must be the subject, for who could deny such beauty to the canvas?"

Francesca appraised the man with curiosity. Despite the friendliness in his dark, thickly-fringed eyes, she did not miss the shrewdness in them. The man was of middling height and stocky, with a substantial girth about the waist. Nevertheless, he was a man women would look at twice, she guessed. In spite of his flattering words, his eyes exuded a subtle charm.

Don Lorenzo led her across the room, continuing to praise her. "Come, sit beside me, Francesca. May I be so bold to call you that? I feel that as compatriots we can dispense with some of the formalities and proceed to friendship." His smile began in his black eyes and flowed to his rosy lips.

"Of course," she murmured. To escape the man's frankly admiring perusal, she looked about the room again. Her eye was immediately caught by the paintings lining the walls. No Dutch scenes of somber, everyday life, she noted. Colorful, larger-than-life Biblical and mythological characters in bright reds, blues, and pinks. Billowing, sunlit clouds surrounded dimpled cherubim. Mighty male nudes and sublime Madonnas faced each other across the walls.

"I see your eyes are drawn to my Italian masters." She noticed how his voice was as mellow as rich tobacco.

"You have a beautiful collection," she said in frank admiration.

"'Scusi, but no Dutch masters grace my walls as yet. I brought my most favored paintings from home." He shrugged with a deprecating smile. "But wait a few weeks. I have already begun my collection. That is my primary reason for coming to the Lowlands for a season, to expand my collection to include the northern masters." He rose and went over to a finely carved cabinet. Francesca noticed his small, slim feet and the graceful way he moved for one of his girth. He reminded her of a dancer. She would like to paint him, she decided.

From a flat, narrow drawer Don Lorenzo removed an unframed canvas. Discarding the cloth that covered it, he handed it to Francesca.

She drew in her breath when she saw it. It was small, but she recognized it almost immediately as one of Master Rembrandt's. Dark shadows surrounded the lone figure in the center, whose face radiated holy light.

"It's exquisite," she said quietly, when she had finished studying it. "Just as everything of Master Rembrandt's."

Don Lorenzo bowed his head slightly as if she had complimented him directly. "I see you are as discerning as you are beautiful." He returned to the cabinet, saying over his shoulder. "Pieter has told me something of your work and offered to show me some of your portraits."

Francesca looked quickly to Pieter, who smiled in reassurance.

"I'm only just beginning to learn my trade," she said in a careful voice, not sure if she was ready to have a stranger—a collector—view her efforts.

"Nevertheless," Don Lorenzo said with a smile, seating himself beside a beautiful nutwood table by the windows, "I am intrigued. It is not often one meets a female painter. And to have her works praised by someone whose opinion I highly respect." His glance encompassed Pieter.

Pieter hurried forward, bringing with him the large portfolio he had carried with him, and which she'd assumed was his own.

"What—?" The rest of her question died on her lips as Pieter explained in an easy voice, "I took the liberty of bringing some samples of your work, Francesca, since I knew you would be coming straight from the atelier."

"If you will permit me," Don Lorenzo said, taking the portfolio and laying it upon the table before him. Francesca backed away to another part of the long room. No matter how much her work at the atelier had been under the scrutiny of other artists' expert eyes, she was still hesitant to show it to anyone outside her immediate sphere of work, except for Pieter.

But she couldn't help glancing over to Don Lorenzo. He took his time over each sketch and painting. Sometimes his eyes narrowed, at others, his lips spread in a faint smile. Francesca could feel her palms grow damp. She tried to turn her back and study the Italian paintings, but her mind refused to concentrate. She told herself she had no reason to become nervous. This man was not her master. No criticism of his should have the power to affect her. Dear Lord, she prayed, please guide how he views my work.

"Bellissima," Don Lorenzo sighed at the last sketch, one of a young woman.

Francesca returned to his side. What would he think if he knew the subject was the youngest harlot at the tavern?

"On the edge of innocence, yet already soiled by worldly knowledge," Don Lorenzo commented, meeting Francesca's startled gaze with one of amusement.

"Yes," she said, unable to keep the surprise from her tone.

Don Lorenzo chuckled. "You didn't think I would perceive it? That's quite all right. 'Tis clear you haven't the same advantage Pieter gave me in telling me a little about you. I knew today I would be glimpsing a rare new talent. Perhaps Pieter did not tell you how fond I am of art. Alas, I have no talent with the brush, but my heart"—he pointed to his brocaded chest, giving a deep sigh—"my heart feels what you painters and sculptors feel. My eyes see what you see." He shook his head with a small smile. "If God had given me an ounce of this talent"—he gestured toward Francesca's paintings—"what my soul could express."

Instead of continuing in this sentimental vein, he surprised Francesca again with a lighthearted laugh. "But no matter, the good Lord has given me something almost as good. All the money I should wish to be able to surround myself with beautiful works."

He turned back to her canvasses, rubbing his hands. "Francesca, mia cara, I think we shall get along famously. You have an eye for the soul. It shines through each portrait you've done, even the quickest sketch. I particularly liked this one and this one..." He began extracting some of the sketches from the stack.

When he removed one that was larger than the rest, Francesca reached forward to stop him. Pieter's hand held her arm back. "I took the liberty of adding that one," he explained in an undertone. "It's one of your best."

Francesca could only stare at the portrait of Dirk she had brought back with her from the villa and had not been able to bear looking at again since arriving at Pieter's doorstep. She swallowed, finally finding her voice. "That one was done long before I began at van der Helst's atelier. I've done so much better since then. It's much too crude."

"Not at all. That's its essence. You've captured the vigor and intensity of the subject. Why, the man fair leaps from the canvas, bold as brass. It makes me think I'd like him for a protector but would fear for my life if he were an enemy."

"I can certainly attest to the truth of your observation," Pieter said wryly, rubbing his neck in remembered pain.

Don Lorenzo raised an eyebrow. "There lurks a tale behind those words, I'd vow, that would surely keep me spellbound. You must relate it to me over a glass of wine."

Pieter smiled. "Ask Francesca to tell it to you sometime."

Don Lorenzo nodded thoughtfully, his gaze straying to her. "Indeed I shall. At any rate, 'tis wonderfully executed. Just what I was seeking."

Throughout this dialogue Francesca had kept her mouth clamped shut, feeling an indescribable terror invade her. Did the man want to purchase the portrait? And if so, what would she say? That had been her original intention when she'd taken the canvas with her, but now every instinct cried out to clasp the canvas to her breast.

Don Lorenzo tapped the stack he had extracted from the rest and smiled at Pieter. "I must thank you once again, Pietro, for bringing this young lady's work to my attention. I have searched everywhere for a portraitist. I have seen the work of the best, and yet I have not been"—he sucked in his breath, rubbing two fingers together as if searching for some mysterious ingredient—"wholly satisfied that it's been quite what I wanted. But this! This is it. I wanted freshness, and you have found it for me, Pietro. I wanted insight, attention to just the right detail in a person's physiognomy, and here I have beheld it." He tapped the stack once more.

At another time, Don Lorenzo's words would have held Francesca riveted. Now she could hardly focus on them. Her mind was numbed by the fear of losing Dirk's portrait.

"Did I tell you how I made Pietro's acquaintance?" he asked Francesca with a smile.

"Er—no," she managed. She tried to follow his monologue of going to Pieter's atelier to purchase some works. Pieter had been put in charge of showing him a selection.

"I was so pleased with his recommendations that I requested his help in all my purchases here in Amsterdam. I've also commissioned him to do a few landscapes for me of this wonderful flat countryside and its waterways. In a sense, Pietro is on loan to me from Vondel during my stay in Holland." Don Lorenzo chuckled richly. "Although at a price. A rather steep price, but worth every penny."

Francesca gave Pieter a faint smile, momentarily distracted by the news of her friend's good fortune. "That's wonderful. You could have no more talented painter than Pieter."

"No, indeed. He is surely one of Holland's rising young talents." Don Lorenzo looked at her significantly. "As are you."

"Thank you," she replied with an uncertain smile.

Just then a young boy ran into the room, trailed by a younger girl.

"Papi!" He flung himself against Don Lorenzo's thigh and began a breathless tale in Italian. Don Lorenzo scooped him up in his arms with a hearty laugh and held his other arm out for the little girl.

After a few soothing words to straighten out the problem that had arisen between the two siblings, Don Lorenzo glanced over their heads to his guests. "My two bambinos. Please excuse their unruly behavior. Ever since their mama passed away, I am afraid they have become shamelessly spoiled.

"Niccòlo, Angela, you must greet our guests, Signorina Francesca and Signor Pietro." The two children, dressed like miniature adults, advanced towards Pieter and Francesca. Niccòlo gave a solemn bow to each while his sister curtsied.

"As a matter of fact, Francesca, I am glad you have the opportunity to make their acquaintance today." Don Lorenzo sat back in his chair and motioned them to be seated. The children excused themselves, and Don Lorenzo faced Francesca with a serious countenance. "I would like to commission you to do a series of family portraits. A group portrait of myself and my two children, a painting of each child, and a couple of them both. These last can be less formal, as your style is wont to be."

Francesca stared openmouthed at the man, then turned to Pieter, who was smiling at her. Was this what he had meant by his "surprise"?

Her attention went back to Don Lorenzo. "I—I don't know what to say. I haven't much experience—"

"Accomplish what you have accomplished here." He waved toward her portfolio. "And I shall be satisfied."

He went on to discuss details and terms in a very business-like way that showed Francesca that beneath his flowery exterior, Don Lorenzo was a practical merchant. Before she knew it, she was committed to beginning a series of works immediately, which would take her several weeks to complete.

"I shall have to obtain special permission from Master van der Helst," she said, when the reality of it began to sink in.

"I'll take care of that myself. Have no fear, mia cara, I am developing a reputation here in the city as a collector, and I haven't yet met a painter who isn't eager to please me."

When Francesca thought to ask Don Lorenzo when he wanted her to set up her easel, he surprised her again. "I think everything can be arranged within a week's time. I don't want the portraits done here. No, no," he replied to her questioning look. "I want these to be open air, country scenes, with my villa in the background, the children frolicking in bucolic merriment." He came back down to business. "I have rented a villa for the summer in Zandvoort. It's a lovely location, pastures and forest, gardens and the sea."

But Francesca heard no more after the name of the village. Would she ever be strong enough to face that place again?

Fifteen

Dirk gave some last instructions to the crew unloading the cargo from the heavily-laden fleet that had just sailed into Amsterdam harbor from a dozen Mediterranean and Levantine ports. Then he turned on his heel and headed for a well-known alley. He was tired to death of the taste of salt upon his tongue. What he needed most was some good Holland's ale to wash away the memory of his long voyage. He needed to feel the solid ground of a tavern beneath his feet before he figured out what he was to do now that he was back in Holland.

Dirk pushed open the door of the Bruin Biertje. Its dim interior welcomed him as if he'd never been away. He marched straight to his accustomed table, relieved to find it empty. He kicked his chair back with the toe of his boot and sat down.

"Dirk! Well, well, look what the tide's dragged in!" Gert stood at his table, her hands on her hips.

"Get me a tankard of ale and be quick about it, wench." But his words lacked their usual gusto.

"Humph! What think ye now, that ye're captain of this fleet? Yer ale'll be coming as soon as Gertie has a mind to ignore yer uncivil tongue."

"Get me that swill you call ale around here before you feel the back of my hand against that lazy carcass of yours."

Gert sniffed again and turned away from him with a swish of her broad hips.

He sat back, staring at the noisy company about him. Nothing had changed in his absence. Yet, he felt as if he was not the same man who had started from this harbor almost a year ago.

If Francesca had wanted to pay him back for his deception during the abduction, Dirk now considered the debt cancelled in full, indeed with usury. She and that painting master of hers had certainly taken him for a fool.

But he was long past the anger that had first filled him when he'd arrived in Florence and found nary a trace of his wife. What he had found instead had made up for Pieter's lie.

He stroked his beard, ignoring the noise and smoke around him, still figuring how he was going to approach Francesca with his news, when at last he found her.

He wondered what she had been doing all these months on her own. Somehow, he trusted that she was safe, for Pieter would have told him if it had been otherwise. He had to believe that.

Had she left Amsterdam, or was she still somewhere in its crowded rows of brick houses?

He would soon know—he had to—even if he had to search every house in the city.

Dirk lifted the tankard of ale Gert thumped down in front of him and drank long and deep, mulling over the news he brought back to Francesca.

It had been easy enough to locate the di Paolo family once he had docked in Livorno. He had made the overland journey to Florence and stayed only a few days. Once there, finding no sign of Francesca, he had learned enough interesting facts from the di Paolo family to make his trip worthwhile.

Dirk had stopped in again on the fleet's return from the Levantine. The di Paolo family still had received no word from the elusive Francesca. They hadn't heard anything concerning the di Paolos in Holland since Francesca's father had passed away.

He drained the tankard and wiped his mouth. Hanging around here would be of no use, he decided, throwing a coin on the table and standing. Just then he spotted a white-haired man with matching white apron tied around his middle. Dirk headed toward the open hearth.

"Still employing surly maids and cheating the customers blind with inferior ale, I see," he greeted Klaus.

Klaus broke into a wide grin and threw his brawny arms around Dirk. "Well, as I live and breathe, 'tis an age since last I saw your ugly mug around my alehouse. Back at last from your voyage?"

Dirk pulled a chair over and straddled it, leaning his arms along its back. "My journey took longer than planned, since I was forced to make a detour, but the profits it will yield will be worth my time."

Klaus shook his head. "Thought you'd grown tired of my ale and had started frequenting Jan Luik's place. Now there's a vermin-infested hole if ever there was one." Klaus gestured with his clay pipe to emphasize his point. "Here I suffer you to curse my Gert, when all you get at Jan's place are slatterns, who'd as lief piss in your ale as greet you with a smile."

Before Klaus could work himself up any further or take out Dirk's eye with his swinging pipe, Dirk interrupted, "I knew 'twould be too much to ask you to keep a civil tongue in your head for more than two words. Before you tar and feather me, let me tell you where I hail from. As far as the Levantine, with many a Mediterranean port in between."

Klaus's eyes widened with interest at the news. "It must have been worth your while to leave behind such a lovely new bride. That was as fine a wedding you put on as I've ever attended. I haven't eaten so many fancy victuals since then." Klaus patted his stomach. "You should be grateful—"

"You'll be wanting to hear about the cargo before it's made public." Dirk cut into Klaus's speech, preferring to speak of anything but his ill-fated wedding day.

Klaus was immediately attentive, nodding sagely at the description of satins and damasks, Turkish carpets, nutwood furniture, and majolica earthenware that would be going on the market over the next few days.

"Heard tell of an East Indies' convoy that has rounded the Cape. Should be clear sailing the rest of the way," Klaus told him when he'd finished.

Dirk nodded and stood up. "Aye. I received word while in Naples. There's a wealth of cargo on that fleet. The trading in blanco will be fierce. I'm going to go 'round now and see what information I can glean."

"Let me know if there's anything worthwhile." Klaus bent over and knocked the ash from his cold pipe onto the stone hearth before sitting back and addressing Dirk again. "I'm glad you had a profitable trip. Cesca'll certainly be happy to see you back hale and hearty."

Dirk stopped in his tracks, thinking he'd not heard a right. Slowly he turned back to Klaus. "Cesca?"

"'Twouldn't blame her, though, for getting angry at you for being away so long, then stopping by a tavern for a pint of beer 'fore going home to her." He chuckled. "I bet she started coming here just to ease her loneliness. Little did I imagine when you brought her here the first time..." He shook his head.

But Dirk didn't hear the rest. The pounding in his temples drowned out all else. Klaus continued talking oblivious to Dirk's stare.

"Egad, but it's a fine thing you introduced her to me. If it hadn't been for my protection," Klaus's chest swelled with pride, "she would have been pawed at by every lout in this den." He made a disgusted gesture toward the men seated at the various tables before turning back to give Dirk a wink. "But trust old Klaus. I took her under my wing, right enough, and after no time at all, every scoundrel in this place thought it a mark of honor to have a painter in their midst." Klaus chuckled, still unaware of Dirk's white knuckles gripping the back of his chair. "Even the crustiest old salt wanted his portrait painted."

Klaus waved toward the shadowed wall behind the bar. Dirk noticed for the first time the sketches tacked carelessly among the various other objects hanging from the wall and rafters above. Like a sleepwalker, he walked past Klaus, who continued talking.

Dirk stood for several minutes, studying each sketch. Though executed in charcoal with a minimum of quick, bold strokes, each face had a distinct personality. He recognized immediately Gert's lusty bravado. Many of the sailors and farmers were also familiar to him. And there stood Klaus himself, his fatherly smile not masking the shrewd glint in his eye.

Klaus had come up behind him and now pointed to his own portrait. "Naturally, as tavern keeper, I was her first 'study.'"

With an effort, Dirk tore his gaze from the sketches. "'Study'?"

"Well"—Klaus shrugged unabashed—"you pick up the lingo around these painters."

The only emotion Dirk felt at that moment was a sense of overwhelming, stunned disbelief. Although understanding the words, he felt that Klaus was speaking a foreign tongue. The only reality he could grasp was the evidence hanging on the wall before him. He would know the artist of those sketches anywhere. "You called her 'Cesca'?" he said at last.

Klaus winked. "Catchy isn't it? I thought it easier on the tongue than 'Francesca,'" he boasted, as if proud that he had coined the nickname himself. "Everyone calls Mevrouw Francesca Cesca around here now."

Now there could be doubt of the woman's identity. But there had been no doubt for Dirk as soon as he had seen the sketches. "Do...do you expect her in today?" he managed, his voice unsteady.

"Nay, it must be nigh on a month now that she's been gone. We sure do miss her. Brought a real touch of gentility to these surroundings." He shook his head. "There were quite a few tears shed when she bid us goodbye. Even Gertie, who was jealous of Cesca when she first came. But your wife won her over."

"Where did she go from here?" At Klaus's look of surprise, Dirk hastened to add, "I mean did she have some other commission to paint?"

Klaus nodded importantly. "Oh, yes. I heard she received a big commission from some wealthy patron. But we gave Cesca a proper send-off. This place hasn't seen such a festivity in many an age, nor will again for some time, I'll be bound!"

Dirk felt he couldn't take much more of Klaus's artistic talk. "Where is she now?"

"Cesca?" Klaus's underlip puckered out. "Why I haven't a clue."

Dirk felt as if his gut had been ripped open, sewn together, and now ripped apart again before it scarce had had a chance to heal. He pressed the bridge of his nose between his thumb and forefinger. "She must have mentioned something."

Klaus rubbed his whiskered chin. "She's not in Amsterdam, methinks. She told me she'd be working at the gentleman's villa."

"Gentleman's villa?" He sounded like an echo, but he could not seem to get his wits about him. Abruptly, he wheeled away from Klaus with a muttered farewell and staggered toward the exit.

※

He spent the next few hours visiting several coffeehouses on the Kalverstraat, gathering what information he could about the incoming East India fleet from the punters and couriers, and sundry other individuals willing to provide information. He scanned the courants for the latest political and military intelligence that could affect the convoy. His own couriers, which he had left along the various ports en route on his way back to Amsterdam, were not due in for some weeks.

He kept his emotions ruthlessly in check. Since leaving the Bruin Biertje, he had not allowed himself to think about

Francesca. He was not going to let her rule him any longer. First, he must set in motion the plans that had been delayed far too long. Later, he would deal with his wife's whereabouts.

The exchange had already closed for the day, so he decided to go there on the morrow. Next, he paid a visit to Jacob van Diemen and told him about the incoming cargo.

"This is your chance, Jacob, to buy up as much East India stock as you can get your hands on," Dirk urged him. He asked him how he had his assets tied up.

Jacob motioned around him. "In this house, as well as in cash, jewels, an annuity, some municipal bonds, and the bills of exchange from my business."

"Is the house mortgaged?"

"No."

"You should liquidate as many of your assets as possible and borrow against your property. That should bring you a sufficient sum."

Jacob's brow furrowed. "I don't know..."

Dirk rose to go as if the whole subject were of little interest to him. "'Tis up to you. Any sum less will be too paltry to scarce make it worth your while. There won't be such a risk-free shipment like this for many a month. The fleet has already rounded the Cape. The rest is clear sailing to Amsterdam."

As the older man pondered his words, Dirk wandered over to the globe in the corner of Jacob's office. He gave it a twirl with his forefinger. "How are the wedding plans going?"

A look of annoyance crossed Jacob's features. "The Bickers won't be satisfied with anything less than a full week's celebration. I've practically had to mortgage this place to meet all the expenses."

Dirk pursed his lips, eyeing him. "You can submit yourself to punishing rates of interest and spend the rest of your days paying it off, or you can make it all in one go on the exchange."

Jacob looked troubled when Dirk left him. But the allure of a promised fortune would be hard to pass up, Dirk knew. Jacob needed an inflow of money badly.

Now was the test, Dirk thought grimly.

He spent the afternoon in the type of maneuvering he was accustomed to, in order to make the most reasonable decision about the eventual price of a commodity before it reached port. This was the way he had multiplied his own wealth, which he'd built up in the Indies from the sweat of his toil.

On this day, however, when he had concluded his business he felt no satisfaction. Inside himself, a raging lion waited to be unleashed. It had waited patiently, but resolutely. Every once in a while it had reminded Dirk it was still there. By a sudden jab in the gut or twist of the spleen, Dirk remembered his wasted months of searching.

And all along, his wife had been making her way as a painter in Amsterdam, needing nothing from him. It was clear she had forgotten his existence.

While remorse and regret had been eating at his insides, she had rid herself of him as surely as she had promised that day in Zandvoort.

When the sun had set, Dirk returned to his house. After dismissing the servants for the evening, he made his way up to his bed chamber, a bottle of arrack clutched by its neck.

His movements deliberate, he removed his boots and doublet. Then in breeches and shirtsleeves, he raised the bottle to his mouth and took a long pull of the fiery liquid.

Dirk went about his inebriation as methodically as he had Jacob's downfall. No ale or wine would do. Only the potent East Indian brew of distilled rice and molasses could deaden the rage and pain that rumbled just below the surface of his rational mind.

He could take pride in his steadiness of purpose that day. Not once during the afternoon had he wavered.

Accustomed to scheme for a profit most of his life, he'd never planned someone's total ruin. Never until today had he worked so calmly and systematically to bring about a man's downfall. His enemies had always been those he could face down man-to-man in physical combat or in the openly admitted combat of commerce, where everyone understood the rules of survival. Those who couldn't measure up got out early in the game.

But Jacob van Diemen was different. It was time to settle that old score. The day of reckoning had at last arrived. And now, Dirk was doing it not only for himself, but for Francesca. Ever since he'd learned of Jacob's perfidy regarding her family in Italy, his anger toward the man had grown.

Dirk took another long swig. Was he drinking the arrack to cleanse himself from that sense of filth, or was he drinking to rid himself of the emotions caused by one slip of a woman?

He gave a grunt of laughter. Good, the arrack must already be working to dull his ability to reason.

He should be congratulated today. Pity there was no one around to oblige. He had succeeded in keeping all feelings under control from the moment he'd first heard Francesca's name on Klaus's lips. "Cesca." He uttered the name with a snort of disgust.

Initial disbelief had quickly given way to overwhelming relief. After months of not knowing whether Francesca was dead or alive, he could finally be certain that she was not only alive but well. At one point, he'd had to stop beside a canal and clutch the trunk of a linden tree, his relief had been so intense.

So many nights he'd woken up in a sweat, his heart pounding, with visions of Francesca looking as gaunt as his mother, her body sold to a nameless, faceless parade of men.

He needn't have feared. The little minx had been living in Amsterdam. No doubt that painter had helped set her up in the art world. At what price?

He gulped down more arrack, almost choking on it, but it was the only way to bear the thought of Pieter enjoying

Francesca's charms. All these months the two had probably enjoyed a good chuckle or two thinking of Dirk's fruitless voyage. A voyage made in the dangerous winter months of sailing.

In the stillness of the night, Dirk could let loose the lion within him. Anger, bitterness, pain could have their expression. The arrack gave him the fortitude to face them.

He examined each emotion in turn with the objectivity of a surgeon dissecting a cadaver. Except the body was his own.

Never had he gotten drunk over a woman. He stifled bitter laughter. He'd thought he'd been immune to that sort of behavior. Love was a costly emotion with little return on investment. He'd watched the fate of his mother and countless of her companions, all because of their infatuation for some worthless man. Pain, degradation, and, finally, blessed numbness was all their reward.

But tonight, Dirk, like countless men he'd witnessed in countless taverns in nameless ports, intended to seek the oblivion found in the bottle and not stop until he had obliterated all feeling for Francesca.

After the months of searching, of sailing around the continent and back, of worrying himself sick in the dead of night—his wife had been here all along.

The irony was too much. He brought the bottle to his lips and drank long and deep. Not only had Francesca been in Amsterdam, but in his very own quarter. The one he had shown her.

His world. Not the polished world of some powerful burgher that she was accustomed to, taking care of his children or polishing his silverware, but amidst the vice and squalor of the harbor.

Francesca, who had wrinkled her nose at the smells of the wharf, had sat day in and day out in the dark ale- and tobacco-drenched room in the very tavern he had introduced her to, sketching to her heart's content. Making a name for herself, if what Klaus had told him of a rich patron was true.

Almighty heaven! The woman would surely drive him mad. He clutched his head, the images refusing to go away.

He took another swallow, then another until the bottle was almost empty. Surely it would soon blot out the images.

He snorted. The fact that Francesca had been sitting in his tavern all along wasn't the worst. No, the worst was that she, like a hummingbird, had managed to escape him yet again. Just before he had arrived upon the scene, she had flitted away, leaving behind the teasing remnants of her presence, those damnable portraits of hers.

But had Francesca left behind his portrait when she'd run away from him? Nay. Every drunken sot in Klaus's tavern deserved his sketch. But Dirk Vredeman wasn't good enough. He had never even seen it, respecting Francesca's feelings at the time too much to look at it without her permission. Permission that she had never granted him.

With an angry roar, he threw aside the empty bottle and watched it crash against the brick fireplace, leaving a multitude of broken shards over the hearth.

※

Dirk rolled out of bed toward noon the next day. The throbbing in his head, the ache behind his eyes, and the sour taste in his mouth only served to harden his resolution. After washing and dressing, he dismissed his intention to go to the exchange first thing that day and headed instead toward Nieuwmarkt.

His first attempt was thwarted since no one was home.

He tried again later that afternoon, his humor in no way improved. This time, he found Pieter sitting at his easel.

Stifling his first urge to strangle the man, he cleared his throat.

Pieter looked up and started, his dark eyes widening in momentary fear. Under other circumstances, Dirk might have found it amusing.

Without waiting for an invitation, Dirk walked over to sit on the couch opposite Pieter. He leaned back as if he had all the time in the world. "No naked companions today, de Brune?"

Pieter looked away from him and carefully wiped his brush before laying it upon the palette. This time Dirk smiled a fraction. "Afraid I'll ruin another of your masterpieces?"

"Hello, Dirk." Pieter sat back from his canvas and gave Dirk his full attention.

"Damn your soul, Pieter," Dirk answered quietly, suddenly feeling too weary to do more than shake his head slowly from side to side, ignoring the dull throb each movement brought.

"You didn't find Francesca."

"You know good and well I didn't find Francesca, because Francesca was here all along."

"I was trying to help her." When Dirk made no reply, Pieter continued. "I was afraid you would come around again and eventually find her." The painter gave him a pleading look. "She would have run away from here if she thought I'd betrayed her. She didn't have any place else to go."

Dirk was determined to remain unmoved.

"I wanted to give her time. She's my friend, and I had to trust her when she said she didn't want to see you. I didn't know what you felt for her. I thought you'd just give up once you thought she'd gone to Italy."

"I just came back from Florence." The only sounds following Dirk's pronouncement were the muted street noises through the opened window from four stories below.

Pieter had the grace to look ashamed. "I—I never really expected you to go all the way there, when I made that story up."

Dirk snorted. "What did you expect me to do? Let my wife run off to some foreign land on her own? After all, you made it sound quite practicable when you reminded me of the money I'd left her."

Pieter flushed. "The story just popped into my head. I was desperate that day. You looked as if you would kill me. Believe me, Francesca knew nothing of my intention."

All of a sudden, the painter stood with a jerky movement and walked to a corner of the room. Dirk watched him impassively, strangely feeling little curiosity about the man's actions.

When he returned, Pieter held out a leather drawstring pouch that Dirk recognized as his own. "This is the remainder of your money. More than half is still there." When Dirk made no move to take it, Pieter held onto it uncertainly for a few seconds longer and finally laid it on the seat beside Dirk.

At his silence Pieter continued. "I used what's missing for Francesca—to pay for a painter's apprenticeship for her. She doesn't know it came from you," he added quietly.

Dirk raised an eyebrow at him and asked, "What does she think, that you found it lying around somewhere?"

Pieter took a step back, running a hand through his dark, uncombed hair. "She believed me when I said the money was mine. An inheritance."

Meeting Dirk's disbelieving eye, he added, "Is it so unreasonable a notion that it would never occur to Francesca that you would give her money? After all, she's grown up in a household where no one has ever given her so much as a stuiver without asking her to account for it."

Dirk looked away, rubbing his face, wishing he could rub away the confusion as easily.

Pieter began to pace the room. "She was hap—" Pieter sighed before continuing. "She was content at the atelier. She has really been given a chance to develop her gift.

"Francesca has worked very hard over the last months. You gave her the opportunity she needed. Her work has improved tremendously. 'Twould all have been impossible without you. She's very talented."

"I know she's talented!"

Pieter studied him a moment in silence. Then as if on impulse, he asked, "Would you like to see some of her work? She keeps it here," he explained quickly.

He almost refused. The idea galled him that Pieter was the one she trusted most in the world. What he wouldn't give to have that trust. But he'd lost it. Perhaps he'd never had it.

"Very well," he surprised himself by saying.

Pieter smiled as if in relief and led him to a sunny spot near the window and cleared off a space on his work table. One by one he laid each canvas before Dirk. "Of course, she has sold some of her best works. She's beginning to develop a reputation."

Dirk merely grunted, studying the blowzy harlot on the painting before him. Her skirt was pushed up, revealing stockings half rolled down. Her large hand playfully swatted at her companion's hairy paw. She was sitting on his lap as his lustful eyes devoured her half-bared bosom. She merely laughed knowingly at the viewer.

Dirk drew in his breath sharply at the next portrait. This time the girl sitting in the tavern looked like an innocent. He could easily picture her in a burgher's salon dressed in satins and fur. Even the background was dark and indistinct, making the setting unclear. But Dirk recognized the telltale signs: the girl's open décolleté, the mule half slipped off her delectable foot, and the open oyster shells scattered on the plate before her. Most significant of all was the presence of the man behind her, a soldier by the looks of his cuirass and the baldric draped across his chest.

The man had a fatherly look about him, but Dirk knew the picture told another story. Before the night was through, the soldier would have the maiden's chastity and the coins in his waist pocket would grace her fair palm.

The picture disturbed Dirk more than he cared to admit. Once his own mother had looked as fresh and unused as the girl smiling shyly up at him. He was unaware of the muscle working in his jaw, but when he glanced up he noticed Pieter studying his profile.

Dirk thought of his own iron-clad rule of never taking a woman's maidenhead. The only one he'd had that way had been within the sanctity of marriage. And she had run away from him as if he'd been poxed.

Dirk shoved the painting away from him. He'd had enough of regrets and recriminations the night before. His aching body and pounding head attested to that.

He didn't even notice the next few canvasses put in front of him until one made him stop dead. Pieter's voice came softly to his ear. "I've always told Francesca this is her finest work. I know she's had offers for it, but she always laughs them off, saying the portrait was done before she had any serious training. She says it's too raw to be displayed." Pieter paused, then resumed after a moment when Dirk did not react visibly. "I disagree with Francesca. I tell her its rawness is its very essence."

Dirk stared at the image of himself. A sardonic tilt of his mouth taunted him with some hidden knowledge. Bitterness peered through the cynicism in those tawny irises gazing back at him lazily. But there was something more flickering in those eyes. Vulnerability? Dirk rubbed his mouth, not caring to analyze it further.

The painting was executed in thick strokes, giving it a sense of movement. His mouth seemed on the verge of addressing him. His hand would move beyond the confines of the canvas at any moment. His lips would part in issuing some challenge.

Dirk had never glimpsed the portrait until that moment. Francesca's talent had been evident in the sketches he had seen. But here before him was the irrefutable truth of it. Only he could know to the full extent how well Francesca had read his soul and put it down in a handful of colors for all the world to see.

"I want to buy it." The words were terse. One way or the other he would leave with the portrait in his possession.

Pieter seemed to sense the conviction in his tone. "She won't approve of my selling it to you. The other day she received a very generous offering for it and wouldn't part with it."

The answer surprised him until he remembered Pieter's words. Obviously, she was ashamed of it.

Dirk kept his eyes fixed steadily on Pieter until the latter cleared his throat and named a sum.

It was more than he'd ever paid for a work of art. Was Pieter merely trying to put him off?

Without a word, Dirk pulled out a purse and laid it on the table. "There. That's double that. Will it pay for this one as well?" He indicated the portrait of the young harlot.

Pieter nodded, not touching the money. Instead he looked for paper and twine in which to wrap the canvasses.

When Dirk took up the packages, prepared to leave, he turned one last time to Pieter. "Where is she?"

The painter hesitated. Dirk pressed his advantage in the charged silence. "You know I shall find her eventually. You can congratulate yourself on having made it infinitely more time consuming for me already."

Pieter sighed audibly. "She's found herself a Maecenas, you know."

Dirk's fingers tapped impatiently on the package. "What is that?"

"A wealthy patron. He likes her work and will help her advance."

"What are you saying?" Dirk's tone was sharp, imagining a lover.

Pieter cleared his throat. "It won't be easy...if you want her back. He—Don Lorenzo—can offer her anything. In no time at all, her name will be one to be reckoned with in the art world."

The one place he could not compete. He kept his features impassive. "Where is she?"

"She's been at his villa for the last month. In Zandvoort."

Dirk almost laughed out loud. Clearly someone up above was having a bellyful of mirth at his expense. For the past month, it would seem, Miss Francesca had been his neighbor.

Well, the trail had come to an end. He would wrap things up with Jacob and by tomorrow evening, he would set out for his villa.

Sixteen

Dirk paused at the tall, wrought-iron gates of Don Lorenzo's villa. It had not been difficult to inform himself in the small village of Zandvoort of the location of a villa that had been let for the summer to a foreigner.

After discovering Francesca's location, Dirk had not high-tailed it to the coast.

No, after speaking with Pieter, he realized a few things. Foremost was that his wife had made a new life for herself. She had no need of him anymore to rescue her from the life she'd led under her guardian's roof.

Moreover, Dirk knew how deeply he'd destroyed any trust she'd had in him. What he wouldn't give to regain the admiration he used to read in those silvery-gray eyes.

Lastly, he was no longer certain he could do anything to win her back—and if he didn't, he didn't know how he would go on. During his long journey to the East and back, he'd survived only because he had been driven to find his wife, and on the return journey, to tell her what he'd discovered about her family.

He gave a grunt at the gates of the Italian's villa. He'd thought that his good news regarding her family would somehow appease Francesca and bring her to forget his past misdemeanor.

Only now, as he stared at the beautifully-proportioned villa, did he acknowledge that in her eyes it was no misdemeanor he'd committed.

He drew in a long breath and urged his stallion through the open gates.

The villa was just visible at the end of a long alley of slim, straight trees whose boughs met overhead. He rode at a leisurely pace through the parkland, taking time to study his surroundings.

Beyond the sentry-like trees were grassy fields where he spotted a few sheep grazing. He crossed a narrow bridge over a trickling brook that meandered through the fields.

His eyes narrowed a second on a grove in the distance, bisected by the brook. He spotted the running figure of a child. From behind a thick, gnarled tree ran a taller figure.

With a sharp jolt, he recognized that billowing cloud of hair. It was unmistakable although he had only seen it loose a pair of times. His fingers could still feel its silky texture when he'd buried his hands in it as it lay spread upon his pillow. Damp tendrils had clung to Francesca's cheeks then.

His jaw clamped down, as if that action could stop his memory or slow the wave of desire rising within him. Deciding to continue his trek on foot, he dismounted and let the horse free to graze. The faint sound of a child's laughing voice reached his ears.

Now that the moment had finally arrived, he had no idea what to say to his wife. None of the strategies he'd gone over in his mind over the last few days and none of the words of explanation seemed adequate.

Francesca did not see his arrival. She was standing with her back to him at the foot of a tree. Her head was tilted upward towards its leafy branches, her hair cascading down her back. Dirk drew in an involuntary breath at the sight of her splendid mane. Her hair was fine textured but thick, falling in ripples down to her waist. The light caught its coppery highlights amidst the deeper mahogany. Only two thin strands had been caught from each side of her face and twisted together down her back.

"Niccolò, come down this instant." The stern words did not mask the laughter behind them. The little boy answered in a string of Italian too rapid for Dirk to follow. The elusive boy appeared to be about ten years old, Dirk judged, from what he could glimpse among the leaves.

"Catch me if you can, Cesca!" came the giggling challenge.

"Oh ho, you won't like it if I catch you!" The sound of her exuberant laughter sent a sharp stab of yearning through Dirk. Before the boy could throw down another challenge, Francesca hiked up her skirts and flinging them over one arm, grabbed the lowest branch and lifted a leg high.

Dirk swallowed, his mouth tasting like parchment. The woman before him seemed a stranger, with her careless coiffure and lighthearted laughter. It was the way he had always imagined her to be behind her sober demeanor. The sight of her legs, however, was not unfamiliar. The view of their stockinged length to the knee and the portion of bare flesh between them and her upraised skirts brought an immediate primitive response to his body.

A movement at his left caught his attention. Dragging his gaze from the climbing woman, he spied a ginger-colored cat bounding in front of him. Behind it ran a little girl. "Cosmo!" she called in a plaintive voice to the now-departed feline.

"I'm afraid your entreaties will do no good." Dirk spoke to her in slow Dutch, wondering if she'd understand. "He'll come around when it's dinnertime."

The little girl, who appeared to be about six or seven years old regarded him with large brown eyes. "You scared him," she responded in Italian.

"Most likely," he answered in her language.

She nodded in agreement, her neck craned upward. "You are a big man."

He was surprised Francesca had still not noticed his arrival. From the sounds of her and the boy's laughter, the two were too busy chasing each other up the tree to pay heed to what was going on below.

"Who are you?" The little girl addressed him with a watchful look in her thickly fringed eyes.

"Dirk."

"Dirk." She pronounced the word slowly. "Do you know Cesca?"

Dirk turned toward the sound of tinkling laughter before eyeing the little girl once more. "Yes," he answered, a ghost of a smile crossing his features.

"My name is Angela."

"I'm very pleased to meet you, Signorina Angela." Dirk bowed over her small hand and saw her toothless smile when he straightened. "Shall we await Francesca?"

"Sì." She put her hand trustingly in his and marched alongside him until they reached the base of the tree.

It didn't take long before, first, the youngster, and then Francesca jumped down from the lowest leafy boughs. Francesca's face was flushed, her eyes twinkling until the moment she saw Dirk.

Her laughter died. Her hand clutched her throat, letting her skirt fall back around her ankles. Dirk forgot everything else, his gaze riveted to her face.

All humor left her eyes.

In the tense silence that followed, Dirk watched her grapple with her shock. She seemed to have grown more beautiful in the time he had been away. Her hair was parted in the middle and gave her the look more than ever of a fragile Madonna like the ones he had seen in the many churches of Tuscany.

Yes, he smiled sardonically to himself, he had viewed the artwork there in the hopes of better understanding his bride.

Her gown was no longer black, but a pinkish shade, like the flesh of a salmon, that enhanced her coloring. There was something different about the gown as well. No longer did a starched collar hide her neck and shoulders. Instead a sheer linen cape collar draped her shoulders loosely, leaving much of her creamy neck visible.

"What are you doing here?" The words were a sharp whisper.

He took a deep breath. "I've come for you."

For a few seconds Francesca could only stare at her husband, thinking him an apparition.

But his austere words were all too real. Their simplicity shook her out of her stupor. Renewed anger came to her rescue and she straightened her shoulders. "As autocratic as always—"

"Careful, there are little ears present," he cautioned, his words sounding as smooth as molasses. As usual he seemed to be ever watchful, no doubt considering every facet of the situation.

"Angela, Niccolò," she reverted to Italian in the desire to exclude Dirk. "This is Signor Dirk. He...he is an acquaintance of mine."

"'Sooth, signora, is that how you term your husband?"

Francesca sucked in her breath, realizing too late that he understood the language. What did he intend? She must show him no fear, no sign of discomposure.

When she made no answer, he continued speaking as if his dropping by were the most natural thing that morning. "I've already had the pleasure of greeting Signorina Angela, but I haven't yet met this big lad. How do you do?" Dirk bent down to the boy's level and held out his hand, greeting him in Italian.

The boy took his hand. "You are from Holland?"

"Aye, but I've just returned from a sailing voyage, to your native land, in fact."

"You were sailing?" Niccolò's Italian quickened in his excitement. "Can you sail a ship?"

To Francesca's surprise, Dirk continued speaking to him in his native tongue, albeit more slowly. "It takes many men to sail a ship."

"I have a ship. See?" The boy beckoned Dirk to the edge of the brook. Dirk glanced at Francesca, but she made no sign, either to encourage or discourage him, too stunned still to see him there.

She watched now as if in a dream Dirk follow Niccolò to the nearby brook with Angela tagging close behind. When Dirk noticed the little girl, he held out his hand to her. Francesca's throat suddenly constricted, remembering the fear she'd had of being with his child.

Scared and unsure of herself those first few weeks of her apprenticeship among so many experienced painters, she'd hardly been able to keep any food down. Pieter's words that she might be with child had haunted her.

What would she do? What would become of that poor soul? How would she take care of it? All these concerns had overwhelmed any joy she might feel at carrying a child formed of her union with Dirk.

But the sickness had passed, and Francesca attributed it to nerves at starting her new venture. Any disappointment she experienced had been buried along with the other disappointments in her life.

She shook away the bittersweet memories and observed the children and Dirk squatted down by the water's edge. "See my boat, signor?" Niccolò pointed to the wooden sailboat amidst the reeds.

"I see it's caught in the shoals. We'll soon remedy that." Dirk disentangled the line as he spoke. "There." With that, he shoved the boat free, launching it into the deeper part of the brook.

Watching him teach Niccolò a few nautical terms in a mix of Italian and Dutch, she wondered where he had learned Italian. In simple phrases and gestures, he recounted a little of his journey on the seas. Once he glanced back at her, but she looked away as soon as his eyes met hers.

But she could not resist the charming scene in front of her. No matter how much she wanted to harden her heart, she was forced to notice Dirk's easy manner with children. It made her go a step farther and reason what a good father he would make...would have made.

No! It was all a lie!

"Children, it's time to go inside," she called out, unable to bear it any longer. "Your father is awaiting you." At the sound of their father, both children hurried to her side.

"Miss Francesca and I are going to talk for a few minutes," Dirk told them, coming up behind them. Though he addressed the children, he looked at her. She recognized the challenge in those golden eyes all too well. It dared her to refuse.

He bent over the boy. "Niccolò, you are a big boy. Can you accompany your sister to the house?"

Niccolò's thin shoulders straightened. "But of course, signor."

"Wait—" Francesca knew she must assert herself before it was too late.

"If I do not speak to you here, I shall do so at the villa." Dirk spoke the words swiftly in Dutch, jutting his bearded chin toward Don Lorenzo's estate.

She shut her mouth, knowing he'd won the first round, but preferring to concede a minor skirmish rather than lose the whole battle. She couldn't go back to him—wouldn't go back. She had fashioned a new life for herself.

With renewed determination, she turned away from him to watch the two children race toward the villa. Only when satisfied they had reached the garden, did she face her husband again, bracing herself to meet his gaze.

She flinched when she found him standing so close to her. He smiled a fraction, as if aware of her discomfort. She lowered her eyes, only to find herself confronting his broad chest. Memories suffused her mind—caressing his golden skin, kissing it...

She stepped back, hardly able to breathe, and folded her arms in front of her.

"You have come up quite a ways in the world, Cesca."

She blinked at his use of the nickname. So, he knew. "I am where I am from merit, not from any man's favor."

He quirked an eyebrow upward. "I've heard you have an art patron eating out of your pretty hand."

She drew in her breath at the insinuation. "Where have you heard such things?" She needed her anger. It was her only protection against his overwhelming presence.

"I make it my business to know all about my wife."

"I am no longer your wife."

He raised a tawny eyebrow. "Do you deny that we were wed in the sight of God?"

Standing so close to him, she found it difficult to think straight, let alone maintain the resolve formed over months. "We may have been wed, but it was all a lie."

"You shouldn't have run away from me." He was no longer looking at her directly, but lower, at her mouth. Francesca felt a flush of heat invade her cheeks and knew at that moment they were both thinking the same thing—kisses, passionate kisses that led to other intimacies. She had difficulty swallowing. If he tried to kiss her now she knew she would be powerless to resist him.

She stepped away from him, afraid no longer of him, but of herself. "I will run as far as I must to get away from you."

"You'll never run far enough."

"Please...Dirk...leave me." The words came out strangled. "You had what you wanted from me. Are you not satisfied?"

He shook his head slowly. "Not by half. Are you?" He stepped forward. With his forefinger, he lifted her chin, forcing her to face him.

Her breath came in short, rapid gusts, betraying the emotion his mere touch incited.

"Does your passion still scare you so much, Francesca?" His voice was as soft and seductive as the fingertip which stroked her jaw. "You seem to have embraced it in your painting."

She caught her breath. When had he seen her work?

"Who has taught you to run free as a child, to let down your tresses...to venture into the taverns and paint with an abandon that only a woman who has known something of life can achieve?"

With each word, he moved closer to her until his mouth was only a hairsbreadth from hers. Without thinking, she brought her hands up to his chest.

His lips brushed hers, and her mouth parted, whether to protest or taste of him, she no longer cared.

It seemed to be all the invitation he needed. His eyelids lowered, their tawny lashes brushing his cheeks, the hair as fine as a camel's hair brush. The image of a little boy, vulnerable and alone, came to her in a rush. It was her undoing. Dirk's lips pressed their advantage, his tongue invading her, his moustache and beard tickling her sensitive skin. Her fingers clenched the cloth of his doublet. How she'd longed for—dreamed of—this moment. During those autumn and winter months of unrelenting rain, sleet, and snow, days upon days of leaden-gray clouds that mirrored the heaviness of her heart.

"Did the passion I awaken in you scare you so much," he murmured, nuzzling her lips with his, "that you had to run away?"

His words broke through the haze clouding her rational thoughts. Was it only about physical passion? She drew back enough to stare into his eyes. Didn't he realize it was about so much more?

Nothing had changed between them.

A sadness so profound filled her, it made the intervening months but a shadow of the pain that crushed her heart now.

She drew away from him though his arms still held her. "I'm no longer the innocent you charmed."

"Is that all you think it was?"

She swallowed, trying to discern what she saw in his eyes. How was she to trust him again? With a gentle push against his chest, she loosened his hold and stepped back.

"What more could it have been?" She smiled sadly. "You swept into my life, larger than life, with your tales of the Orient, knowing just what words to use on an impoverished orphan—a spinster—with no one to defend her. And they were all lies from beginning to end.

"Yes, you may congratulate yourself. You did awaken me to passion. You awakened me to the sights and sounds and smells around me and showed me if I truly wanted to become a painter, I mustn't shut myself away to experiences."

"Is that why you preferred running away to Pieter?" he asked with a sardonic twist of his lips. "Did you prefer a poor imitation of what we enjoyed?"

"Pieter can give me what you never can," she said quietly.

Something flickered in his eyes, and she wondered if her words had had any power to hurt him—the way he had hurt her.

But then his expression seemed to harden and his tone was cold. "Just be sure of this. No one takes what is mine, not without paying dearly for the privilege."

Taking a deep breath, she moved away from him still more. "And you may be sure of this. I have made a new life for myself here. I am no longer yours."

He said, as if she had not spoken, "From the moment you became my wife, you became mine."

That's all she was to him—a commodity like the bales of silk in the East India pakhuis.

"I ceased being yours when you betrayed my trust." Before he could do or say anything to tear down her defenses by his sheer physical presence, she turned from him and ran back to the villa.

As she reached the formal gardens, two figures exited from the house. Don Lorenzo and Pieter waved to her. She stopped, knotting her shaking hands in the folds of her skirt and attempting to still her panting breath, hoping she showed no signs of having been kissed.

"Ah, Francesca, look who's here," Don Lorenzo called with a smile.

"Hello, Pieter." She smiled with genuine relief at her friend.

"Hello, Francesca." Pieter gave her a light kiss on the cheek. "You look winded. Have Don Lorenzo's children been chasing you all over the garden?"

Niccolò raced up to them. "No! Cesca's husband came to see her."

Don Lorenzo raised an eyebrow. "Ah, so it is not signorina but signora?"

Pieter's gaze shot to her, his tone low. "Dirk found you?"

Francesca smiled, trying to make light of it. "Yes, h-he was here." Then she looked at Pieter more closely. "You don't sound surprised."

Pieter made no reply but for a shake of his head.

"Who might this Dirk be? Do I know him?" Don Lorenzo asked.

Thankfully, Pieter replied for her, giving a grateful Francesca time to compose herself. "I think not. Dirk Vredeman is an Amsterdam shipper and merchant. He has conducted business with Francesca's former guardian, Jacob van Diemen. Dirk and Francesca were but scarce married, when he was forced to go on a sea voyage."

He paused a second before adding carefully, "He's the one you saw in the portrait Francesca did. He commissioned it from her. Her first major work."

"Ah." The one syllable spoke more than Francesca would have liked. She found Don Lorenzo's discerning eyes focused on her. After a moment's silence he continued. "You promised me that tale someday, Pieter. I confess, I would love to hear more about the affair."

"Excuse me, I feel a bit faint." Francesca curtsied quickly in Don Lorenzo's direction. "I'm afraid I crossed the garden too rapidly in this heat. I shall just lie down a bit." She would leave Pieter to tell as little or as much as he cared to. She knew that Don Lorenzo would fill in the rest with his own assumptions. As long as she did not have to talk about it herself, she would be all right, she told herself.

She just needed to collect her thoughts and she would be all right. There would be no repeat of this afternoon.

After dinner, Francesca found Pieter standing beside the main fountain in the garden. Ever since her encounter with Dirk, she'd needed the solace of Pieter's quiet presence. She also wanted to talk to him alone, but had not had an opportunity until now. Thankfully, Don Lorenzo had made no mention of Dirk during the meal.

"I'm glad you came today," she said, coming up to him softly.

"I had to deliver some paintings to Don Lorenzo. I shall remain until tomorrow."

They stood silent, listening to the splash of water. "Wh- what did you tell Don Lorenzo about Dirk's appearance today?"

Pieter shrugged. "I told him only what I know myself, that he courted you for a few weeks during his dealings with your guardian—that the two of you had a lavish wedding, and then some disagreement that had caused you to leave him and him to go off on a sea voyage." Pieter smiled in the twilight. "It only intrigued Don Lorenzo, being a romantic at heart, but he is too refined to ask anything more."

She breathed a sigh of relief, allowing the tinkle of the fountain to soothe her. "You've been such a good friend to me, Pieter. I don't know what I would have done without you."

He waved away her gratitude. "Nothing any good friend wouldn't do for another."

She smiled. "Yes, any good friend, which you have proved yourself time and again with me, with very little in return."

"How can you say that?"

She shook her head, hoping that someday she would be able to help him the way he had her—not that she wished him the kind of heartache she'd endured, and continued to endure. "At any rate, please allow me to thank you for everything you've done for me this past year."

"Very well, I consider myself well thanked."

She couldn't help laughing. After a moment Francesca spoke, knowing Pieter was too sensitive to bring the subject up unless she did so herself.

"You were not surprised by Dirk's visit here. Why is that?"

He met her gaze. "I told him where to find you."

Francesca fell silent at this startling bit of information. Shock quickly gave way to puzzlement. She trusted Pieter. He must have had a good reason. "Why, when it was you who finally prevented his finding me last summer?"

Pieter ran a hand through his hair, looking away from her. "Perhaps it was a twinge of conscience." He paused, then met her gaze once more. "Perhaps it was the knowledge that those beautiful gray eyes of yours, which should be filled with laughter, are most often tinged with melancholy."

She swallowed with difficulty, feeling the tears very near the surface.

Pieter continued. "He took me by surprise. I think he'd only just arrived in port. He looked like death, by the way."

Francesca couldn't speak, too hungry to know more.

"And he was in no good humor, believe me. As I stood there expecting him to break every bone in my body, I found myself wondering what would compel a man to travel so far in pursuit of a woman. A sea voyage to Italy—" He shook his head as if in amazement.

Francesca's heart skipped a beat. "He's been to Italy?" Suddenly, Dirk's words to young Niccolò of visiting his native land began to sink in.

Pieter nodded slowly as if to prepare her for what he would say next. "After I told him you'd gone there."

She grappled with what he was saying to her. "I know you did. But he went to the Levant..."

"By way of the Mediterranean. His ship could easily have stopped in Italy."

She shook her head. "No, no! I can't believe it."

"Yes, Cesca, he went after you."

She paced before the fountain, unable to accept that as the reason. "It can't be true. He must have had some other reason—trading at those ports—"

Pieter laid a hand on her, stopping her in mid-stride. "Is it so impossible? I had convinced him you had sufficient funds to undertake the voyage. Between your having family there and the opportunity to study art, he swallowed my story. He has ships going all the time. All he had to do was hop on one and see for himself."

Francesca pounced on that. "Don't you see? He had an opportunity to combine it with his business interests." She nodded vigorously. "Yes, that must be it."

"Come, Francesca, might it not have been the other way around? He came straight to me upon his return, demanding to know where you were."

Francesca sucked in a breath, remembering Pieter's earlier words. "You said he was angry with you. Did he hurt you?"

Pieter looked bemused. "No, strangely enough. I thought he would surely murder me with his bare hands. But he was very calm. More determined than ever to find you." He scratched his head. "In a deadly quiet sort of way."

Francesca shivered. Well, he had found her and she had felt his absolute power over her once again. She looked away from Pieter's sympathetic eyes and gazed at the fountain.

"I know you wanted me to protect your whereabouts, Francesca. But I think this time Dirk would have found you, with or without my help. I can tell you one thing—"

She glanced at him, her heart beating faster, not sure she could withstand any more revelations.

But all he said was, "I felt ashamed almost that I had sent him on such a journey for nothing."

She stared at her friend. It seemed Dirk had even succeeded in winning Pieter over. What chance did she stand?

Pieter smiled. "I'm sorry, Francesca."

She returned his smile, unable to be upset with her friend. "You could have at least warned me."

Pieter cupped his hand over her shoulder. "Was it that bad? Did he hurt you? You looked most upset this afternoon."

She brought her fingertips to her lips, remembering the shock of Dirk's lips on hers. "It...it was just...I had not expected to see him again, ever."

"He's a very persistent man, when he is after something he wants."

"Yes." Her shoulders slumped. Even Pieter understood. Dirk just wanted her because he believed she belonged to him and to no other. She turned away from the fountain. "Well, he shan't have me."

Her emphatic words hid the niggling thought that perhaps he already did.

―※―

Sleep eluded her that night. The air was still and unseasonably hot.

Francesca kicked off her covers, her gown sticking to her. Finally, she turned on her back, allowing herself to relive Dirk's kiss.

Once again, she touched her lips, remembering the soft feel of his on hers and the desperate hunger he'd reawakened in her.

It terrified her to think that after all these months, after the truth she knew about him, after all he'd done to her, he still had the power to make her alive as no else could.

Who was the real Dirk Vredeman? In the stillness of the night, the images of the afternoon played across her mind. She pictured Dirk squatting down beside Niccolò at the water's edge.

With no thought to water or mud upon his fine clothes, he spun out a line and maneuvered the boat to the middle of the stream. Both his and Niccolò's profiles were animated as they watched the boat sail downstream. He had charmed the little boy just as quickly as he had once charmed her.

How she wished her portrait of him had been idealized, that the real man were a mere shadow of his image in oils.

But no, the living man at the base of the tree this afternoon outshone her portrait. Tall and straight with perfectly proportioned limbs, he'd stood before her in all the resplendent glory of an ancient god of mythology. The artist in her had gazed at him in awe. The woman in her with longing.

Although his assertion that she belonged to him had infuriated her, she could not deny to the silent shadows in her room that a secret part of her was thrilled at the words. It was as if all these months she had been sleepwalking through life, participating in all its functions, but not quite alive.

And in had marched Dirk Vredeman, shaking her awake, showing her she belonged to someone.

Nay! She pounded her pillow. She would not be lied to again.

But the images were stubborn. She had thought she was free. For ten months she had fought to forget him, to purge his very memory from her existence. A few minutes in his presence mocked all her efforts.

It would not be easy to fight his power. The look in his eyes had been too knowing. Even his words had told her he could see past her bravado to all the lonely and sleepless nights when she had not been able to silence her longings. And his kiss had proven it.

Seventeen

Don Lorenzo paused beside Francesca the next day as she was putting the finishing touches on one of the portraits of his children.

"Bellissimo," he murmured. After a few moments of silence, he sat down on a satin-covered couch facing her. "I hope you slept well, tesorina."

Francesca concentrated on a spot of gilt furniture in the painting. "Why, yes, of course." If dream-filled sleep in which it became harder and harder to distinguish the dream from the reality each time she awoke could be called restful.

"Ah, that is good. I was afraid the visit from your husband would have unsettled you."

"My husband?" She lifted her brush in the nick of time before she could mar the painting. The term "husband" still filled her with surprise. It seemed too alien for a man she'd resided with scarcely a day. She glanced around the easel to meet Don Lorenzo's eyes, knowing it would be difficult to fool him.

"No," she answered carefully. "Not at all. I was surprised by his visit, that is all, because it was so unexpected."

"I understand." Don Lorenzo walked over to straighten one of his newly acquired Dutch paintings on the wall. "Pieter told me a little of your...ah...estrangement from your new husband. I am sorry."

"Do not be. It is all over now."

Don Lorenzo studied her. Francesca steeled herself for more personal probing, but all he said was, "I am glad you have recovered from your surprise yesterday." He studied his beringed fingers. "A proposito, cara, I am planning a house party—a small gathering of artists and collectors—for a week hence. Pieter will carry my invitations back to Amsterdam. You wouldn't mind if I invited your husband, would you? I believe we might have some business interests in common."

Francesca looked down at the tip of her paintbrush, considering her reply. If she refused, it would give lie to all she'd said. But if she accepted, her new resolve would soon be put to the test.

Well, if she must brave the lion, it was best she do so here, on her own territory.

She lifted her head. "No, of course not. I wouldn't mind, Don Lorenzo, if you asked Dirk."

Don Lorenzo's guests began arriving on a Friday afternoon. Francesca only recognized a few—Pieter and his painting master, her own master—Bartolomeus van der Helst—and some collectors who had visited Don Lorenzo previously. The rest were painters and poets, as well as several wealthy merchants.

Francesca accompanied the children out to the garden, hesitant to venture alone into the crowded salons, and unwilling to seek out Pieter, who was accompanying Master Vondel.

Don Lorenzo proved an excellent host, structuring enough activity and entertainment, yet leaving his guests free to do as much or as little as they desired.

Francesca had just begun to participate in a conversation with some fellow painters at the edge of the gardens, when she felt a tingling up her spine. She was being watched. Turning slowly, she sensed even before she saw him that it was Dirk. He was the only person who had the ability to make her fear and yearn at the same time.

He walked onto the terrace, standing out among the guests like a mighty warship among a flotilla of flat barges.

She drew in a breath, already feeling her heartbeat accelerate merely at his appearance. He was dressed in black silk, edged in golden braid. The somber color did nothing to rob him of his physical attributes. He still commanded the attention of the people around him.

Neither did the reversal of their costumes escape her. Where once she had worn black, now it was he. Her own gown was pearl-gray brocaded satin with petticoats of cream-colored satin visible beneath. Don Lorenzo had had a few gowns ordered for her. He had made it a stipulation of her employment, insisting her beauty must be attired in like material.

Before she could find refuge somewhere, flee to Pieter's side, locate the children—anything—Don Lorenzo approached Dirk with a smile and spoke a few words of welcome. Francesca stood rooted, too curious to see the two men's reaction to each other.

Dirk looked to be sizing up Francesca's patron. It reminded her of the way he had first eyed Pieter.

Too late, she became the object of their attention. Before she could make her feet obey, the two men began walking toward her.

"Francesca, cara, here is your charming husband." He turned back to Dirk. "I am sorry I was not able to make your acquaintance sooner. I hope we can make up for lost time. I want to hear more of your journey to my country." Her patron gave them both a warm smile that began in his dark eyes and ended in his sensuous lips.

Francesca bowed her head, making no reply. She knew behind that smile lay the craftiness of a fox. What was he intending?

"Cara, why not show Signor Dirk the maze? It is quite intriguing," Don Lorenzo said to Dirk.

"Very well." The sooner she was away from Don Lorenzo's scrutiny, the better. She would walk Dirk around the gardens instead of taking him through the secluded maze. Being alone with him a second time would not be wise, not when her pulse had already accelerated an alarming degree.

Francesca and Dirk walked together in silence, past a few fountains and box-edged gardens. He had not attempted to touch her in any way, and she felt the absence of his hand on her arm acutely.

"Where is this maze?" he asked.

"Over there." She motioned vaguely, making no move to turn her footsteps in that direction. "This is the pear orchard," she explained, pointing out the espaliered trees along a brick wall.

"Perhaps we should see the maze. Unless, of course, you don't trust yourself alone with me."

Her gaze shot to his, only to find amusement in his eyes. "Your vanity has not altered any, I see."

He only chuckled.

With an exasperated flick of her skirts, she veered toward the precisely-trimmed yews. Would nothing ruffle the man? "Very well, you shall see the maze."

"Interesting," was his only comment once they entered the high shrubbery walls. "Can you be lost in here?"

"Not for too long. If you keep one hand upon the side at all times, you shall eventually find your way out."

The paths underfoot were velvety grass, so the two of them made no sound. Francesca was surprised that Dirk seemed disinclined to break the silence. She would have expected more challenges. Above the walls of the maze they began to hear the lyrical sounds of a flute. Nothing but green corridors and cul-de-sacs met them.

When they finally arrived at the center of the maze with its curved stone benches and miniature fountain, Francesca stopped short at the entrance. A pair of lovers were locked in an embrace.

Quickly, she backed out of the entrance, bumping into Dirk. She turned, seeking a way past him. He took her arm lightly and led her away from the area.

She didn't pay attention to the direction she was taking, too confused by his touch and the sight she had just witnessed.

"I suppose there are no other secluded benches in this labyrinth," Dirk muttered under his breath when they were well away from the pair of lovers. Francesca could find no reply, thinking how only yesterday she and Dirk had been wrapped in a similar embrace.

They turned a corner and came upon a crescent-shaped bench in a corner of one of the cul-de-sacs.

"Sit down," he ordered in a quiet command.

"I must be getting back. Don Lorenzo's childr—"

"Are none of your concern."

She was about to offer a retort, when he sighed, indicating the bench once again. "Please."

She hesitated a second longer, then did as he bade. He took the place beside her. With an effort, she resisted the urge to scoot away from him on the bench.

"You can't run away from the fact that you are my wife." He raised a hand before she could contradict him again. "The fact is we are wed, in the eyes of the law and in the eyes of God. I could force you home if I chose and be within my rights."

She raised her chin. "You couldn't hold me there."

One side of his mouth slanted upwards. "Which is precisely why I haven't taken you over my shoulder and marched you home."

Again he was seducing her with his charm. She determined to resist. "The sooner you accept that I am not going anywhere with you, the easier it will be to come to a solution to end this marriage."

He reached out and stroked her cheek. "I understand your anger at my initial deception. But is it so hard for you to believe that I saw in you a beautiful, passionate woman under all that severe black, and that I wished to have her for my own? If you are not convinced by now, look around you."

Her eyes widened and he chuckled. "I saw how the gentlemen ogled you in the garden. My only fear is your head will be turned by all the attention."

Trying to ignore the feel of his finger along her cheek, she said, "I am not interested in men's flattery."

"But you are not immune to all admiration." He looked pointedly at her garment. "Your dress is most becoming. You took none of the finery I gave you at our wedding. Tell me, how did come you by such lovely gowns? Don Lorenzo?"

She nodded, too aware of his light touch and caressing gaze to think of an evasion.

His jaw knotted. "In return for what?"

She should have known what conclusions his mind would draw. "In return for my services," she replied with a lift of her chin.

She could see her answer goaded him, and that gave her a perverse satisfaction. Let him know how it felt to be manipulated. Francesca almost smiled to see him struggle to maintain his civility, she who so well knew his temper.

"Have a care, his price might be too high," he cautioned softly.

She moved away from his hand. "And if it is, 'tis no concern of yours."

His gaze burned into her, as if by its very intensity he could make her yield to his will. "It ill becomes you to play the coquette."

"You are a fine one to instruct me. You, who well know how to flatter a maiden."

He passed a weary hand across his brow. "I never flattered you. I only spoke the truth." He took Francesca's chin in his calloused hand, forcing her to listen to his next words. "My courting you had nothing to do with my business with your guardian."

She broke away from his touch. "It had everything to do with Mynheer Jacob. If you hadn't wanted access to him, you would never have bothered with me at all." She shuddered. "You never would have questioned me the way you did at the farmhouse, pretending such sympathy when you had brought about my very abduction."

Dirk brushed aside her accusations like a few insignificant crumbs upon a tablecloth. "Your being in the barge that day was a mere accident of fate. If I had not met you that day, under those circumstances, I would have met you eventually when I found another way to approach Jacob. Did you ever consider that?"

His soft tone mesmerized her even as his thumb rubbed across her lower lip. "I would have found you just as fetching, just as enchanting. My interest in you would not have had anything to do with your guardian." His gaze locked onto hers. "I swear to you, marrying you had nothing to do with him. I had no intention until the day I stood at your front door of entering into a betrothal with you."

He ran a hand through his hair as if in frustration. "To become better acquainted with you, yes, perhaps to court you. You intrigued me that night at the farmhouse. But when I witnessed how cruelly Jacob treated you, assuming the worst about you—" His jaw hardened, and she shivered, realizing how dangerous it would be to be this man's enemy.

But his gaze softened, becoming almost pleading, as he said, "He forbade you access! You would have been left in the streets. I took my decision then, and it had nothing to do with my personal affair with Jacob!"

Everything in her yearned to believe him. She tried to draw her gaze from his, believing if she did not look into those honey-hued eyes, his words would have no power to convince her.

Dirk forced her face back to his. The lines around his mouth were creased in bitterness. "Are you still so blind that you persist in protecting that lying, cheating blackguard you call guardian? Or will you know the truth about what he did to your father's assets when he died?"

She gasped. He would stop at nothing to convince her! In a swift motion, she loosened herself from his hold and stood. "Mynheer Jacob guarded my father's good name, when he took care of the debts my father left."

"The question is, do you trust a man of van Diemen's avarice to have told you the truth of your father's estate?"

"What are you saying?" she whispered, feeling suddenly faint at the implication of Dirk's words.

"I was very angry with you and your Pieter, sending me on a vain journey to Italy and back. But not so angry as I might have been, had my voyage proved fruitless. I learned some interesting things from your father's family there."

At the mention of the people who had rejected her father and her, Francesca took another step away from him. "Now I know you lie!"

Dirk's fist hit his thigh with suppressed violence. "Why should I lie about your Florentine family? Do you honestly believe I would do such a thing?"

All the contradictions he represented formed a chaotic jumble in her mind until she remembered his conduct. She balled her hands into fists. "All I know is you would stoop to abducting an innocent female for your own dastardly ends. What did you plan for Lisbet that day in the barge—" Her eyes grew round with horror. "Would you have dishonored her? Oh, what kind of vile man are you—"

She could form no more words. With the lively strains of music wafting in the air like dust motes in the sun, the setting should have been one of peace and happiness, instead of the searing pain ripping apart any illusions she had about the man seated before her.

Stifling a sob, she ran from him, seeking refuge in the maze, not caring if Dirk were lost in its tricky corridors for all time.

Dirk vowed he wouldn't go near Francesca again. By the time he found his way out of that confounded maze, she had long since disappeared. Which was a good thing. In the mood he was in, he would have had plenty to say to her. Things better dealt with when he was in a calmer frame of mind. He had rarely won a battle when he went into one in hot anger. Only cold self control defeated the enemy, he'd learned long ago.

If Francesca wanted to deny the truth as if it were nothing but flotsam edging Amsterdam harbor, so be it.

He ground his teeth in frustration. The little fool!

She'd repudiated him as much as she'd repudiated the truth.

Dirk had felt dirty and worthless before. All his life he'd fought to overcome his dishonorable beginnings, but he'd never hidden what he was or what he'd had to do to get where he was. Only one other person had made him feel as shamed as Francesca had.

Jacob van Diemen.

No, he didn't plan on seeing Francesca anytime soon. Let her take her food and clothing from that wealthy Italian while she repudiated her own husband.

Dirk was well rid of her, he told himself.

For a week he told himself that.

Until he found himself knocking on the door of Don Lorenzo's townhouse in Amsterdam.

Returning to his own vomit, it seemed, as the Good Book said.

He told himself it was because of the message he carried, but he knew the real reason. He wanted another look at his wife. One more look at those soft lips, those delicately-flushed cheeks, that slim waist he longed to span with his hands.

He checked the direction of his thoughts, turning his attention to his host.

Don Lorenzo extended a hand. "Signor, welcome to my home. I am sorry you had to leave so quickly from my villa. I trust you had an agreeable time at the festivities?"

He bowed. "You were most hospitable. Unfortunately, business called me back to Amsterdam." Blast, why was his voice so stilted? Because he was deucedly uncomfortable in this man's sitting room, as if he had to ask permission to see his own wife.

There she stood by Lorenzo's side, like the man's mistress. The man held her possessively by the elbow, and his lecherous gaze on her was anything but fatherly. Francesca had as good as admitted she'd given herself to him. Dirk put a finger inside his collar, feeling it choking him.

"A glass of wine?" At Dirk's nod, Don Lorenzo waved him to a seat and gave instructions to a serving maid. "Francesca tells me you were the first to take a professional interest in her painting."

Dirk blinked in surprise, his glance going from Francesca back to his host.

"Your portrait," Lorenzo explained. "It was her first commission."

"It was as good an excuse as any," he muttered, bothered that Francesca should have been discussing it with this stranger and wondering if she had shown it to him.

"Oh?" Don Lorenzo smiled. "Excuse for what?"

The man's humor irked Dirk, as if he were toying with Dirk. And there sat Francesca, looking as delectable as an apricot in a gown that looked identical to the one he'd given her, but which she'd disdained to take with her.

Instead, she accepted everything from a man who looked old enough to be her father and acted like her lover.

Dirk sat forward. "An excuse to court Francesca." Like a lion baring his teeth, he smiled at Lorenzo. "She was a trifle shy then."

He watched with satisfaction as the telltale blush stole over Francesca's porcelain cheeks. But his triumph was short-lived. The next instant, Don Lorenzo reached over and covered Francesca's knee with his hand. "Did you hear that, mia cara?" The endearment caused Dirk's fingers to curl over the ends of the chair's arms. "It looks as if you have come quite a way since then."

She smiled demurely. "Yes."

Dirk's nails dug into the hard oak. Was it his imagination, or was she sending him a subtle threat? If so, Dirk would show her who was in control of the situation. "Aye, Francesca has come a long way from those days. I always told her she had it in her to go far."

Turning from Dirk, Francesca addressed her patron exclusively. "Dirk fancies himself quite the expert with the fair sex."

Don Lorenzo chuckled. "Ah, that is our greatest failing, is it not? No sooner do you think you have one figured out than she does the complete unexpected." He shook his head. "Many has been the time when I thought my strategy infallible, then presto!" He snapped his fingers. "She has me flat on my back, unsure from whence the blow fell." Don Lorenzo got up chuckling.

"I shall leave the two of you to your reminiscences. I'm certain that a husband and wife must have much to talk about after such a long separation." He bent and caressed Francesca's cheek with his plump, beringed fingers, causing Dirk to clench the chair arms to keep from lunging at the man and hauling him away from his wife.

"Ciao, tesorina."

Fortunately for his host's well-being, a maid entered and began serving them wine and almond cakes.

After Don Lorenzo left the room, Dirk drummed his fingers, waiting for the maid to depart.

When the two of them were finally alone, he ignored the refreshment set before him. "What is your precise relationship with Don Lorenzo?"

Francesca tossed her head. "What concern is that of yours?"

Dirk swallowed back a sarcastic retort. Careful, he cautioned himself. He shifted in his chair. "I brought a letter back for you from your grandmother."

For an instant he saw longing in Francesca's gray eyes.

He pressed his advantage. "Would you like to read it?"

She shrugged, looking away from him.

Dirk held out the sealed parchment. Francesca stared at it for a few seconds until he thought she would refuse it, but then stretched out her hand. He met her halfway.

"Why didn't you give it to me before?" she whispered, as if she didn't remember how their last conversation had ended. He realized she probably didn't at the moment. Her thoughts must be far away indeed.

He shrugged. "The time did not seem opportune. Read it." He picked up the wine set before him and took a sip, looking away, pretending an indifference he was far from feeling.

Francesca walked over to a window. She broke the seal then unrolled the paper as if it was very ancient and fragile.

The note was short, he knew, for he had watched it being written. But Francesca stayed at the window a long time. When she at last turned around, Dirk was surprised when she approached him. "I—" She looked away a second as if to regain control of her speech.

When she met his gaze once more, her voice was firm. "Dirk, if you meant anything at all of what you said to me—anything at all—if there was even a grain of truth in how you said you felt about me, I beg you, tell me if this letter was truly written by my grandmother." Her gray eyes were shiny. "You d-didn't pay someone to write it for you, did you?"

He couldn't answer for a few seconds. Did she believe he would lie to her about this? Didn't she realize he understood how important this was to her? His jaw clamped down. Or, was it because she knew this? Did she truly think he would use such knowledge against her? Did she think him such a scoundrel?

He drew in a deep breath. "Do you really think so little of me?"

She moved away from him then, as if ashamed of her question.

After a stillness which reverberated with so many unspoken things, she whispered, "I don't know what to think of you anymore."

Dirk let out a breath slowly. It was not much, but it was a beginning. He maintained a neutral tone. "Would you like to send your grandmother a reply?"

The look in her eyes told him she hadn't thought that far ahead. "W-would it be possible?"

"Why wouldn't it?"

"I know sufficient Italian to read, but writing might be a trifle more difficult. Do you think if I wrote in Dutch, she could get someone to translate it for her?"

"Possibly. Better yet, why not find someone here to help you compose it in Italian?" The next words almost choked him, but too much was at stake to keep them back. "Don Lorenzo?"

"Oh, no, I couldn't disturb him. He has too much to do."

"I know many foreigners here. Do you want me to send someone 'round you could interview?" He spoke gruffly, suddenly afraid she would turn his offer down.

Her face lit up, and Dirk felt something deep within him begin to ease. "Yes, that would be perfect." She added, "If it is no trouble for you."

"None at all." His relief was all out of proportion to the simple favor, he thought, running a hand across his beard, feeling as awkward and clumsy as a schoolboy.

He rose to leave, his commission carried out. Then he hesitated, sensing it was too soon but encouraged nevertheless by what had just transpired. Before he could change his mind, he took a little box from his pocket and handed it to her. "I brought you a gift from Florence."

Francesca hesitated, then extended her hand. She examined the box a moment, as if afraid of what it held. It was a rich brown wood, inlaid with creamy ivory. Finally she undid the clasp. As soon as she flipped it open, she drew in her breath.

The box contained a pair of sapphire earrings in filigreed gold. Dirk knew they were exquisite for he'd chosen the best. Their deep blue would dangle from her earlobes, catching and reflecting the light like the twinkling stars in the midnight sky.

Before he could say anything to her about the gift, tell her how he'd brought the stones with him from the Indies, with what intention he hadn't known back then, perhaps the wish to find someone, some day, to give them to, and how he'd found that individual where he'd least expected it—

Before he could tell her how he'd taken the stones to Tuscany with him, how he'd had them set by a Florentine goldsmith recommended by Francesca's grandmother, how the old woman had taken almost as much pleasure in the commission as he himself when she knew his purpose—

Before he could say any of these things, Francesca closed the box with a click. Without a word, she handed it back to him.

Dirk took his gift almost unaware of his action, so stunned was he by her change from a moment before. After all the gifts she had clearly accepted from Lorenzo, not to mention the money she'd thought had come from Pieter, Dirk could not believe she was refusing his one small token.

"Thank you, but I can take no gifts from someone I cannot trust with all my heart. It would not be honest."

The words silenced him. A blessed numbness filled him. It must be true the heart developed a thick shell the more snubs were inflicted upon it. "As you wish." Instead of pocketing the box, he set it on a small table, struggling to regain his composure. "But it is yours, I have no wish for it."

She made no move. After a moment he came to a decision. "If it is trust you require, I shall give you mine," he said quietly. "And I ask nothing in return."

When she continued looking at him, he took a deep breath, preparing himself for something he had not done since he'd lost his mother. "My feud with your guardian began when he ill-used someone I loved."

"You...you have never expressed such a sentiment before."

He realized she meant the word "love." He had never used it with her. The word scared him too much. It would give her too much power over him. He swallowed, still feeling his way. "Mayhap I have not felt it since then."

When she made no answer, he continued. "Do you remember the harlot I showed you in the alley?"

She nodded slowly as if having difficulty following what he was saying. He took another deep breath, finding it harder than he'd anticipated to continue. "My own mother looked much worse before she was through. And all because of your honorable, upright Mynheer Jacob."

Eighteen

Francesca sat in Katryn's kitchen, hardly listening to the conversation between Marta and Katryn. She had come here needing to talk to someone, someone whose wisdom she trusted.

For a day and a night now, her thoughts had been going around in circles. And still she didn't know what to believe.

All Dirk had told her was that her guardian—a man always known to be upright and moral, no matter how austere—had dishonored Dirk's mother. She could not get over the fact and could still scarcely believe it. Except for the look in Dirk's eyes as he had told her.

Katryn bustled about the kitchen. "Marta, take this tray up to Mynheer. Then bring down that gown of Lisbet's that needs mending, while she's away. Thank goodness mynheer has sent her off to visit Tante Blankaart before her wedding."

When Marta left the kitchen, Katryn turned to Francesca. "How good it is to see you, my dear. 'Tisn't often enough, indeed, these days. You've grown so important." The old woman's smile softened her words.

"Oh, Katryn, I miss you so. You don't know how much. I wish you and I could live together somewhere, just the two of us, away from everything. I would spend my days painting and you'd bake your bread and tend your garden."

Katryn's chuckle dispelled the image. "You don't wish any such thing. You wish what every woman wishes for, a home of your own with a good man to warm your bed, a family to cherish, and some time for your painting. Now, if you'd take me along to live with you there, I would be happy indeed to go along and make myself useful."

Francesca could not respond with the laughter Katryn expected. The picture was too close to what she might have had. Very likely Katryn didn't expect her to laugh at all, because she, too, knew what Francesca had lost.

"What is it, Frannie?" she asked, taking a seat across from her. "I haven't seen you so uncertain since those few weeks when your dear papa and mama passed away and you first came here."

Francesca's eyes watered as she met Katryn's loving gaze. "I don't know whether to believe him or not."

She didn't have to say anything more. Katryn leaned back in her chair with a sigh. "Mynheer Dirk has found you at last?"

Francesca nodded.

"A man must care a great deal about a woman to search so long and far for her."

Francesca said nothing. She had been over and over everything so much, nothing made sense anymore. If what Dirk said about her guardian were true, it would mean her whole existence here had been for naught.

"What does your heart tell you, child?"

Francesca swallowed back a sob. "That's the trouble. My heart is so confused. I don't know what to believe."

"Have you prayed?"

She nodded. "But I hear nothing clearly. Papà entreated me to honor Mynheer Jacob for all he'd done for him. I thought I was doing what was right." She turned anguished eyes to Katryn. "But what if what Dirk said is true, that my guardian is not who he pretends to be?" She shook her head. It couldn't be so. She'd always believed him to be a righteous man. He attended the kerk faithfully and tithed regularly. How could he be the man Dirk claimed?

"I know you've been trying to repay your poor dear papa's debts by all your service here. I think you've paid in full, myself. But no matter. No one could have done more than you.

"But your papa's gone. Nothing will change his love, whatever you do now." The older woman tapped her blunt finger on the tabletop. "But Mynheer Dirk is a man hale and hearty. A man who needs a woman's love, if ever I saw one. And mayhap a woman to help steer him a right."

Francesca left the kitchen feeling better but still with no clear idea what she was to do. Dirk's words haunted her. Was the hatred he felt for Mynheer Jacob justified?

If what Dirk had told her was true, then Mynheer Jacob had ill-used his mother indeed. But if Dirk's mother was already a...a prostitute—she found it difficult to utter the word, despite the time she'd spent at the tavern—then how responsible was her guardian for her fate?

The Lord commanded them to forgive, but clearly Dirk bore the desire for revenge in his heart. How could she live with a man eaten up by hate?

With slow footsteps she headed up the stairs. A stairs she hadn't climbed in many months. She no longer walked it with a rein of tight control around her feelings, she realized, but as a free woman.

She sent a silent word of thanks to Pieter and Don Lorenzo, who were responsible for her new independence.

She walked down the corridor to her guardian's office door. It was time to face this ghost as well, she had decided the previous night. Perhaps she'd learn something of her own past by coming face to face with him now.

"Come in," called the familiar impatient voice. Francesca paused in wonder that it no longer frightened her.

He half-stood from his desk chair. "Francesca! What in the world are you doing here?" He hadn't seen her since her disappearance. No hint of welcome eased his frown.

The next instant his eyes narrowed in suspicion. "Does Dirk know where you are?"

Francesca moistened her lips. She must remain calm if she was to accomplish anything. The hysterical woman who had pleaded with him almost a year ago must not be seen again. "Dirk knows where to find me if that is what you mean."

"And you've returned to him, the way you ought?"

"Not. . .yet." She breathed the last word, surprised to hear herself utter it. It sounded too full of promise.

He frowned at her. "Be careful he won't get tired of waiting for you."

"Please, mynheer, may I sit down?"

He jutted his chin toward an empty chair. "Tell me what it is, girl. You see I'm busy." He gestured towards his ledgers.

"Dirk tells me he...he met my grandmother in Florence."

Mynheer Jacob looked up sharply. "Yes, and—?"

"Nothing." She tried to hide her disappointment, having hoped for more. "She wrote me a letter, which Dirk brought me. She seems eager to hear from me."

"Humph. She's certainly changed her tune from when your father died. She didn't want to know a thing about you then."

Francesca bit her lip. It still pained her to think of that. "Perhaps you misunderstood her."

"Don't be impertinent! If I'd been a less God-fearing man, I'd have sent you there anyway. It was their duty to take you in. But what did I instead? I fed and clothed you. I housed and educated you—as well as my own daughter. I paid your father's debts. What thanks do I get for it? A woman who runs away from her husband. Disgraceful behavior. Ach!" He turned back to his documents.

She clenched her fists in her lap to keep from running from the room. "I'm sorry, Mynheer Jacob, I didn't mean to imply anything on your part. You did so much for me and I am truly grateful."

The only reply she got was the scratching of his quill upon a parchment.

It was no use. She shouldn't have come. The past was finished, and she'd never fully know what had happened to keep her apart from her Florentine relatives.

To change the subject and put her guardian in a better frame of mind, she asked, "Has Dirk been to see you?"

Mynheer Jacob relaxed visibly, setting down his quill. "Yes, yes, of course. He returned from Italy none too soon, I tell you. I was never more glad to see anyone. What with Lisbet's wedding, I have been strained to the limit. I honestly didn't know how I was going to manage."

"And Dirk has helped you?" Francesca felt a familiar foreboding.

"You wouldn't begin to understand how much." His features lightened. "He and I are putting our money on a cargo that's en route to Holland now. It's a sure thing with almost no risk involved. The most difficult sailing is behind it."

"Are you putting much money on this cargo?" she asked faintly.

Her guardian's features tightened for a second. "Nothing that will not be repaid many times over. Lisbet will have wealth beyond measure. The Bickers will be my equals. No one will dare snub me."

"Mynheer Jacob, have a care. Have you discussed this with anyone?" Inwardly, Francesca fought with herself. She saw Dirk's eyes as he told her of his mother. She heard her father's voice telling her to honor her guardian and give him her loyalty.

"Francesca, that is enough. I will have no interference from you. You came to me once with some foolish tale against your husband. I will have no more of that! He has already enabled me to multiply my investments several times. You shan't be hindering me anymore!" He stood to dismiss her. "Now, I am expecting someone very important. You'll have to excuse me."

She decided to go to Dirk himself. Maybe he would listen to her. Maybe he meant no real harm to Mynheer Jacob, merely intended to teach him a lesson. Perhaps she could help him overcome his resentments against her guardian.

As she leaned her fingers against the edge of the desk, in preparation to standing, she noticed the documents upon its polished surface. She was familiar enough with them since she had ofttimes helped her guardian with his accounts.

"I thought you had already negotiated Lisbet's marriage portion," she said, gesturing toward the annuities. She frowned. "What are you doing with the deed to the house?"

Her guardian looked uncomfortable for a second before waving an impatient hand. "Whatever I please, girl. Now, run along with you. One must raise capital to finance ventures," he added in a mollified tone when she did as he bade.

Francesca stopped in her tracks. "But with your property? Surely you are not thinking of mortgaging your house?" She stared at him in growing disbelief, seeing the truth even before he spoke. "Are you?"

"That's none—"

"Mynheer Jacob, has Dirk asked you to do this?"

"Dirk and I are men of business. You know nothing of these matters. At any rate, your interference comes too late."

Francesca stared at him. "It is already done, is it not?"

Her guardian cleared his throat. "I really have no time for this nonsense."

She must remain calm. "How much were you able to raise with the property?"

"That is none of your concern!" he shouted, becoming more agitated. "Now, for the last time, be off with you!"

Francesca turned, not trusting herself to speak. She mustn't make the same mistake she had the last time. No, this time she would make no more mistakes.

Francesca left her guardian. She went to his solicitor on the pretext that she had been sent by Mynheer Jacob. He did not find it strange to hear her questions since she had accompanied her guardian in the past.

He told her everything he knew of her guardian's latest venture, expressing his concern over the wisdom of putting everything into one transaction.

Francesca was desperate by the time she headed back toward the Prinsengracht. If Mynheer Jacob wouldn't listen to her, there must be someone she could talk to. How she wished Lisbet were there, so she could make her understand the gravity of the situation.

She was running up the stairs, ready to begin the ascent to the next floor when she heard Dirk's familiar voice. Marta was just closing the door after having shown him into Mynheer Jacob's office.

"Mevrouw Francesca! Did you forget something?" Marta began.

"No, Marta—" She pushed past the maid. "Excuse me, I must go in—" She didn't wait for a reply but rushed for the door.

After he left Francesca, Dirk spent a night of rare introspection. If he ever hoped to have Francesca back—to earn her love and respect—he must give up his thirst for justice. It was clear she hadn't yet accepted what he'd attempted to tell her of his mother and her guardian. He'd found himself unable to go further with the story.

He could not yet bring himself to acknowledge van Diemen as his father.

But in the stillness of the night, listening to the watchman call out the hour at regular intervals, he weighed his thirst for revenge with his need to win his wife back—his desire to avenge his mother's honor with his need to prove his love for Francesca.

It was not an easy choice. He gripped the edge of his open window, feeling again the frustrated anger of a boy not yet old enough or strong enough to defend his mother.

As dawn tinged the horizon over the slate rooftops in the city, Dirk bowed his head, finally relinquishing his quest of decades. "Thy will be done, Lord," he prayed, his throat thick, unshed tears filling his eyes.

A peace he'd never felt filled him.

Then, like the gentle lapping of a calm tide, he felt a new urging.

His fingers clenched the window sill anew, his mind recoiling from the thought. But try as he might, he couldn't banish it.

He banged the sill with his fist. He would desist with his carefully constructed plan of revenge. Wasn't that enough?

Must he also ensure Jacob van Diemen made the killing his greedy heart desired?

Dirk sucked in the cool morning air, his fists unclenching. Mayhap then—and only then—would Francesca believe his intentions for good and not for evil.

As the conviction took hold, he bowed his head again, this time the tears unleashed. "I'm sorry, Mother, so very...sorry." he whispered to the dawn.

※

Everything was going according to schedule, thought Dirk as he exited the stock exchange. As of that day, Jacob Van Diemen was owner of a large volume of the incoming cargo on the latest East India convoy.

Pausing on the marble steps, Dirk let the reality of this sink in. Funny how he felt nothing. Neither regret nor satisfaction, only a sense of relief.

Suddenly, a man rushed up past him, almost shoving Dirk aside in his haste.

"Whoa, what's this? Can't you look where you're going?"

The man hardly gave him a glance. "Beg pardon, mynheer—" The man was already gone.

Dirk meandered along the canal streets, his thoughts absorbed by the finality of things. He did not notice the passage of time, as he stopped on a bridge to gaze at the water below.

When he heard a church tower chime the hour, he realized it was the appointed hour to meet Jacob. Slowly, he turned toward the Prinsengracht residence, thinking it pointless to postpone the interview. But he wanted it over, so he could focus his attention once more on Francesca.

Once his errand was accomplished, he wanted nothing more to do with van Diemen. He had known nothing but pain at the man's hands.

"Ah, Dirk, come in." Jacob gave him a smile of welcome, when he entered the man's office, a smile which Dirk could not return. Rubbing his hands together, he motioned Dirk to a seat. "So, everything is all set?"

"Yes." Dirk handed him a sheaf of papers. "You are now owner of the cargo listed here. We will hold onto it as long as possible. You will see the price rise steadily over the coming weeks. Whatever happens, just hold onto it. I will let you know when the moment is right to sell."

Before Jacob could answer him, another voice spoke up behind Dirk. "Oh, yes, he'll let you know all right." Francesca's voice was crisp and firm, with no hint of the uncertainty of the day before.

Dirk turned to look at her. Without waiting for an invitation, she walked into the room. Her step, like her countenance, was resolute. "Tell him, Dirk, exactly when will that be?"

"Francesca, what are you doing here again?" Jacob asked. "Have you come back to pester me more about my affairs? I will not have it, do you hear me!"

Dirk looked from Jacob to Francesca. "Has my wife been here earlier?"

"Francesca came here this noon, and had the audacity to try to tell me not to move my assets as I saw fit. Well, it was too late then, as it is now. I have the papers here." With a triumphant look Francesca's way he tapped the sheaf Dirk had handed him.

Francesca turned to Dirk. "I congratulate you. You have what you wanted. And you have my reply as well," she added softly, as if to herself.

"Francesca—" he began, but didn't know how to finish. If only she would trust him over her guardian. Vain, foolish thought.

"It's all right, Dirk. I think I understand. You have your loyalties. Well, I have mine as well." As if getting back to her task after an interruption, she turned her attention to her guardian. "Ask Dirk when exactly he will tell you to unload your shares. Will it be after he's orchestrated a panic, when everyone is rushing around to sell worthless stock?"

Dirk felt his stomach muscles ease, as if the blow he'd long expected had finally found its target. After all, Francesca had never led him to believe she would act otherwise than unswerving loyalty to her guardian. Except for one brief moment—and that perhaps only in his imagination—her course hadn't wavered.

She looked at him. "Mynheer Jacob and I don't really understand how these things work, so you will have to tell us exactly how it's done. Surely you don't rely on natural disasters at sea? That would be too uncertain. Perhaps you've heard a rumor of war? That must be it." She nodded sagely. "Yes, the convoy will be attacked, and the cargo will be lost." Francesca smiled with no real humor in her face. "You see, I've learned a little more about your world since you've been away. Don Lorenzo has instructed me on certain things."

Jacob came around his desk. "That's enough, Francesca."

"Yes it is. I shall say no more, except"—she glanced at Dirk before addressing Jacob—"to repeat that Dirk bears you a grudge. A grudge that goes back some years.

"Tell me, Mynheer Jacob, do you remember Dirk's mother? He says you and she were once acquainted."

The first hint of uncertainty began to cloud Jacob's eyes. Had Francesca's ill-timed words finally jogged his memory? Dirk watched his face closely. Odd, after all this time, he felt nothing but curiosity.

Before Jacob could speak, the door burst open.

"Mynheer, I'm sorry, but this man—" Marta could say no more. A messenger from the exchange shoved her aside to enter the room.

"The East Indies' convoy—sunk...all sunk."

"What! How?" Everyone spoke at once.

The man gulped in air. "Storm...off...coast of Portugal. The Portuguese didn't even have...to fire a shot. They must be laughing with glee at the victory."

Dirk hardly heard the last words. It must have been some bizarre act of fate. It could not possibly be true. Not with the same cargo he'd built Jacob's financial future upon.

But here was his broker's messenger, reporting the latest information received by the East India's convoy itself.

Things had been taken out of his hands. Jacob's loss was now irrevocable. He was indeed ruined. His grandiose plans for amassing a great fortune were in ashes. His ambition to ally himself and be an equal to one of the greatest families in Amsterdam through his daughter's betrothal were finished.

Without another look at the rest of the company, Dirk headed toward the beurs to ascertain the truth.

By the time he entered the large hall of the stock exchange, a silence reigned, made all the more deathly by its contrast to the usual pandemonium that went on during the buying and selling hours. It had been kept open that day beyond its closing time because of the disaster at sea. Dirk gathered what information he could before heading back to van Diemen's.

Marta seemed nervous and unaccustomedly serious when she opened the door to him. "Oh, 'tis you, mynheer," she said with a sigh of relief. "You had best go straight up to him. He has admitted no one since that terrible news."

Dirk took the steps up to van Diemen's office slowly, dreading to have to deal with a weak, frightened shadow of a man. Preferable would be rage. He found neither.

Jacob was standing beside the window overlooking the hedged garden below. Dirk cleared his throat, stepping just inside the doorway.

"Ah, Dirk, come in. I was hoping you might stop by before too long."

Dirk glanced at him sharply. He could detect no irony in the man's tone. Jacob's greeting was uttered in an unnaturally calm voice. Most unusual, thought Dirk, for one who always seemed a bit on edge, as if his time were too valuable to be taken up with whomever he happened to be addressing.

"I was at the beurs to see what information I could glean," Dirk said, walking toward him. At Jacob's look of inquiry, he shook his head. "I didn't learn much more than what the messenger told us. There's a lot of panic right now."

Jacob gave a glimmer of a smile. "Yes, I suppose so. Rotten luck for us." It was then Dirk noticed the small dagger Jacob was toying with in his hands.

"How great is your loss?" Dirk asked quietly, knowing very well the reply. But for once he had no words. He had never seen this side of Jacob, so calm and fatalistic.

The older man gave a slight shrug. "Bankruptcy. I've lost everything, you know." He sighed. "I am sorry about Lisbet, though. I did so want to insure her future. I don't know what will become of her now."

Dirk rubbed his beard and heard himself speaking words that would have seemed impossible only a moment before. "I can take care of her...find her a suitable husband...provide her with a dowry." What in heaven's name was he saying?

The first flicker of emotion passed through Jacob's eyes as he met Dirk's gaze. "Thank you. I...I..." His voice threatened to break. "I did not want to ask. But somehow, I—" He cleared his throat. "I knew I could count on you." He looked back toward the window with a dry laugh. "Bicker has already sent a message canceling all further negotiations between us. Not that I am surprised, I expected as much. 'Tis only odd how quickly news travels."

"Yes." All at once the room felt airless. Dirk wanted to escape.

He had waited for this moment through most of his boyhood and manhood. And now all he wanted was to run from the sight of his enemy's total defeat. Why couldn't he gloat? Why the shame still—shame he'd lived with all his life?

Jacob resumed speaking and Dirk tried to concentrate on the words. "Everything will have to be auctioned." He motioned to the contents in the room. "There might possibly be a little something left over for Lisbet. You can take charge of it until you find her a husband."

The meaning started to penetrate Dirk. "What exactly are you planning?"

Jacob gave him a sideways smile. "I should think 'twould be obvious. Please, I do not mean to indulge in theatrics. It is just that you...you are the only one I can confide these last details to. Despite Francesca's accusations, I trust you." He gave a dry cough. "I know you could not possibly have orchestrated the disaster that struck the convoy."

No, not even he with all the thought and planning he'd put into Jacob's ruin could have accomplished this.

Jacob cleared his throat. "Lisbet will be better off without the shame of her father's failure." He stared down at the dagger again. Dirk realized how sharp it was when the tip pushed against the tip of Jacob's forefinger drew a dark red drop of blood.

"Please"—Jacob's eyes pleaded with him, his whisper hoarse—"try to explain things to Lisbet. Tell her it was best this way."

Suddenly Jacob began to pace the floor, assuming the restless behavior Dirk was accustomed to. "There is so much to say yet. I just do not know how to begin." He gave a bark of laughter. "I have spent most of my life running from any regrets, indeed, from any sort of contemplation, and now that it draws to a close, I find there isn't enough time to indulge in confessions. I can hardly collect my thoughts."

He ran a hand through his hair. "There's Francesca, for one thing. I know I have treated her shabbily, but her very presence always filled me with ire. Every time I laid eyes on her, I saw her father. Enrico, my partner, my nemesis!

"I thought it would prove so easy after his death. Fate had smiled upon me to have taken him so conveniently. Just when I needed a fresh infusion of capital to expand my business. 'Twas child's play to appropriate all that was his after his death."

Jacob swiveled around. "Curse him! Why did he have to make it so easy? He trusted me like a child. Left everything in my care, including his conscience," he said with a bitter laugh. "Yes!"

Jacob stopped before Dirk once again. "Francesca, with her solemn gray eyes that accused me every time I looked upon her. I could not be rid of her. First, my wife needed her. Then afterward, I knew 'twas hopeless. Those eyes would haunt me no matter how far away I banished her. I have found out the truth of that in these last months since she left."

Dirk knew well what the man meant. Hadn't her eyes haunted him to the Levant and back?

Jacob's voice softened. "I hope you and she can overcome your misunderstanding. She deserves a good man like you, a little happiness after all these years she endured with me."

He was quiet again for a long time. Just as Dirk thought Jacob had finished unburdening himself, he began to speak again. This time the words came out more slowly, as if they were more difficult.

"The funny thing is, my little gray-eyed conscience did not help me with my other regret. A regret far deeper, and one which I can do little about at this late date."

Jacob stared down at the knife in his hands, as if seeing something else. "Francesca knew nothing about that one. She had not even been born." Once more, Jacob faced out the window, as if seeing into the past. "'Tis only when one stares at death that everything becomes crystal clear. Why is it only then that everything else is swept aside? Knowledge I spent so many years covering up is the only thing I care about in my last moments."

Dirk swallowed, his throat dry. Would he finally hear what he had longed to hear?

"You probably think me an astute, successful merchant, when in truth I am nothing but a coward. All courage deserted me when I was called upon to stand and be a man of honor."

Dirk's heart began to thud, a dull pounding increasing in volume near his eardrums.

Jacob gave a shuddering sigh. "I could give you all kinds of excuses. I was so very young. Success beckoned me. It stood so close to me, all I needed to do was reach out and grasp it. You see, my father had just signed a betrothal for me with my future wife. One of four daughters of a wealthy merchant, she was getting past her prime. She was a few years older than I."

Time stood still for Dirk in the carpeted office. Like Francesca, he suddenly didn't want to hear justifications for a vile act. Did this man think he could absolve himself with weak explanations?

Jacob ran a hand through his hair. "Although her family had money, they had difficulty finding a husband for her because of a slight physical impediment. A childhood accident had left her with a limp. Since she was the eldest, they needed to marry her off in order to give her sisters a chance to wed.

"My father had only modest means, but he managed to convince my future father-in-law of my prospects. I had already been working in a linen firm in Haarlem and enjoyed a good reputation. The marriage contract was sealed, with the understanding that I would begin to work in my father-in-law's business, with a chance at succession, if I proved myself.

Dirk stood rooted, not wanting to hear anymore, yet drawn into the tale all the same.

"Imagine, for someone in my position, it was the opportunity of a lifetime, the thing I had dreamed of. All it required was that I make a tolerable husband for a pampered woman. I did not balk. I knew I would spend my days busily at work learning my father-in-law's business. I would be attentive to my new wife in the evenings. Soon she would bear my children and keep herself occupied. We would not lack any material goods."

Jacob turned the dagger over so that its blade caught the light. "I did not reckon upon one sweet-faced maid employed at my future bride's residence." He shook his head. "This very house. The house that I inherited upon my father-in-law's death."

Dirk waited, his breath caught. He could tell Jacob who that maid was.

"I noticed their young maid because it was she who used to open the door for me. I began spending most of my free time at my bride's. It was another world from my family's dark little house. Soon, cheerful Anna would greet me by name and ask me how I was. I was entranced by her tawny hair and laughing eyes.

"'Twould have gone no further than a few pleasantries if she had not one day come running after me. I had left a sheaf of papers from my work, and she was worried I might get in trouble for carelessness. I was so touched by the maid's concern."

A tender, faraway look came into the older man's eyes. "By the time she caught up with me, she was all out of breath. Her cheeks were tinged a pretty red. Her hair had begun to come loose of her kerchief. It had begun to rain, so I insisted on buying her a glass of ale until the rain stopped."

His dark eyes stared into Dirk's, as if he could make him see into the past. "It was a revelation that afternoon. We must have been together a few hours. I was late to work, but for the first time in my life I did not care."

Wonder tinged his tone. "I had never known what it was to have fun. My whole life had been one driving ambition to succeed. To make money and own a canal house. To rub shoulders with the wealthy burgers of Amsterdam. I had never joined in the pranks of schoolboys. In fact, I disdained most companions my age altogether and always sought the company of my betters. Yet, here I was, talking nonsense and laughing at anything and everything, forgetting the time, with a mere serving maid. But she was intelligent and lively...and innocent. She was fresh from the country. Everything around her filled her with delight and enthusiasm.

"After that afternoon, I doubled my efforts to visit my betrothed, but it was no longer for her, but for a glimpse of Anna and a few brief words. I took to leaving by the servants' entrance, where I could spend a few more minutes with Anna.

"She was barely more than a child. Seventeen, with no knowledge of the wiles of men. She trusted me completely." A strangled sound came from his throat. "And I took advantage of that trust." His eyes pleaded with Dirk's. "I could not help myself. May God forgive me! I thought I knew what being single-minded was about. But I knew nothing about wanting someone so badly, I was willing to risk everything I had worked so hard to achieve.

"I was on the brink of success, and suddenly I was blinded by a pair of mischievous eyes that seemed to read my innermost thoughts. Entranced by lips that begged to be kissed, a bosom as creamy as sweet butter, ankles that twirled away from me, teasing me.

"My betrothed appeared more and more distasteful to me. I did not know how I could ever face the marriage bed." Jacob's face turned the same ugly red of one of the Chinese porcelain bowls on the table beside him. "I had never...you see, I had never been with a woman. I had disdained such a pastime as a frivolity others could waste their time and money on.

"Now I knew I could not shackle myself to a lifetime of duty without ever tasting what real passion—love—was all about."

Jacob's narrative had the inevitability of the incoming tide. Dirk wanted to retain his anger, his loathing, his disgust. Instead, he stood mute, riveted by the other man's words.

"I did not intend to hurt Anna. My sweet Anna." Jacob's pain-filled eyes appealed to him, as if he was talking with the serving maid herself. "I fought my baser urges as long as I could. My conscience fought mercilessly with me, but I was blind and deaf to it when I was with Anna. All I wanted was her sweet mouth against mine, her soft body yielded to mine."

Jacob leaned forward, clutching the window sill, without letting go of his knife. "You can imagine what happened. It became a nightmare. From a few short moments of perfect bliss I was caught in a web I could see no way out of, except to hurt the one I held most dear." Jacob bowed his head, swallowing with difficulty. "You see, Anna became with child. She had no money, nowhere to go. She refused to go back to her parents. She never reproached me." His voice broke. "Never asked me for anything. Just looked at me with those large, tawny eyes, now filled with such sadness. Eyes that saw too much. I was terrified that my future father-in-law would discover the truth. In my panic, I raged at Anna, at poor defenseless Anna. She never said a word, just turned and walked away."

Jacob's eyes screwed shut, but they could not stop the bitter tears that escaped and dropped onto his white-knuckled hands. "I never saw her again," his voice rasped. "May God have mercy on me." His shoulders shook silently.

Dirk's heart felt hollow. For years his hatred for this man had fueled his every action, his every ambition. Now all he saw was a man who had never known pleasure but for a few stolen moments long ago. Moments that had ended in tragedy.

Was that all he himself would ever know?

The future stared at him in the shell of the man bowed before him.

Van Diemen remained silent, contemplating the dagger in his hands, as if he had emptied himself of everything burdening him since his youth.

Dirk spoke up softly, hardly recognizing his own voice. "I can finish the tale for you."

Jacob raised his head, looking at him, hesitation in his eyes. "What Francesca said earlier—"

"Anna bore a son."

Nineteen

Jacob turned eyes that teetered between hope and disbelief upon Dirk.

For so many years Dirk had pictured this scene. But now that he was living it, he felt more like an outsider, watching it unfold.

"Anna bore a son prematurely after scrubbing floors on her hands and knees for several months in a brothel."

Jacob staggered back as if Dirk had struck him. Ignoring the growing fear in the older man's eyes, Dirk hammered on. "Yes, that was the only place that opened its doors to her. She had tried the almshouses, but since she had no residency papers for Amsterdam, they refused her entry. The procuress of the whorehouse only took her in on the condition that she pay her way once the babe was born." He barked out a laugh. "She must have seen a future in Anna, because she was a young, healthy girl. What she had not reckoned upon was the frailty that comes with heartache."

Jacob's features had grown rigid.

"Anna appeared to do all right at first. After all, she had the joy of a child, though he was born small and sickly. She tried to do the work required of her. She took any client forced upon her—burly sailor, unwashed farmer, cooper, carter, fishmonger." He paused, wanting Jacob to absorb the full meaning of the words.

The color drained from his face until Dirk thought the man would faint.

"No, the proprietress was not particular with her clientele," Dirk continued in a dry tone. "She owned one of the meaner houses on the waterfront. She could not afford to turn anyone away. She worked Anna especially hard because she reckoned Anna owed her for several months' room and board during her confinement."

Jacob's Adam's apple worked silently up and down as if he wanted to speak but could not form the words.

Dirk raised his eyebrows. "You wonder how I know her history?" He folded his arms across his chest. "I know it very well, for you see, I was born in that slop house. I was the result of the seed you spilled so carelessly into Anna."

Dirk instinctively recoiled from Jacob's outstretched hand.

"By the time I was old enough to remember, I knew my mother was not well. She was diseased." Deliberately stressing the word, he had the satisfaction of seeing the older man flinch. "But I didn't understand how until a few years later. By then, she was also consumptive. When it got so bad she could no longer ply her trade, the owner threw her onto the streets. I would not allow her to 'work' anymore."

As the horror rose in the other man's eyes and a moan escaped his lips, Dirk gave a harsh laugh. "Oh, she could have. She could have become a back alley sister, diseased and all. But I preferred to steal to keep us alive.

"I joined a band of boys who taught me how to pick pockets and snatch food from the market stalls. I became fluent in peddler's French and knew the names all the thieves and whores in my neighborhood went by. Hendrika the Wafflewife, Mary the Lacemaker, Leentje the Starcher. Ironic, is it not, that their nicknames all represented the trades they could not make a sufficient living from? Only their bodies could bring in enough money to live on, until their bodies gave out, and they didn't have enough to bribe the schoutsmen with. So, into the Spinhuis they were hauled for a spell or made to stand on the pillory with a placard proclaiming their shame.

"I was not around when that happened to my mother. Because I myself was caught lifting some spoons from a street vendor. I was flogged on the pillory." He nodded toward Jacob. "Yes, I have the 'Spanish pox' on my back to prove it. The scars are not the result of one whipping, but the several I experienced over the next few years.

"From then on I was in and out of the Tughuis, or as we insiders christened it, the Rasphuis, for we spent our days powdering brazilwood for the dye works. Shifts that sometimes lasted to fourteen hours, pushing a saw back and forth to create a pile of sawdust. By the time I was released for the last time, and found a place on a ship, I was not surprised to find that my mother had died. On the street. Alone."

Dirk continued in a softer tone. "When I left Holland, bound for the Indies, I took on a new name. I wanted to put as much distance between you and me as possible." Dirk's mouth twisted in bitter amusement. "Ironic, isn't it, that I should choose your initials in reverse?

"You know what kept me going, Jacob?" Seeing the older man's attention riveted on his words, Dirk paused a second. "Not love of money and position, as you. No. My motive was more pure and enduring. Hatred. Hatred of the man who'd fathered me and destroyed my mother." Dirk's gaze allowed his sire no avenue of escape. "I dreamed of destroying you, just as you had my mother."

"Francesca was right," Jacob breathed. "But the sinking of the fleet. You could not know..."

Dirk shook his head. "No. That was pure luck. I had planned on setting a rumor afloat that would have brought the price of your cargo down to the floor in a matter of hours. For 'twas I who convinced you to invest the bulk of your assets on that cargo, remember?"

Jacob staggered toward a chair. He sat down, his head in his hands, the dagger at his feet momentarily forgotten.

"My God, my God, what have I done? My moment of happiness has destroyed the lives of two people. My son, my son..." he sobbed into his hands.

Dirk realized with an unpleasant jolt that it was not the

revelation of his plan for his father's ruin that caused the man's torment. Jacob's dry, racking sobs tore at Dirk, like the straight, sharp lacerations of the whip upon his back.

Jacob was not giving a thought to his lost riches or position. Like an animal having watched its young snatched from her, he was keening over the loss of the woman he had loved and the son he had never known.

The next instant Jacob grabbed his dagger up off the floor and thrust it towards himself. Without thinking, Dirk lunged at him. The two toppled to the ground. Dirk groped for Jacob's wrists and latched around them like manacles, but the other man's strength was born of determination and regret. For a few long moments, they struggled until with an oath, Dirk wrested the knife from his father. But it was too late. Dirk felt warm, sticky blood on his hands.

With frenzied desperation he fumbled at the older man's clothing. He was not going to die now, not now!

When he located the slash in the material, Dirk used the dagger to finish ripping open Jacob's doublet and shirt. Its blade had skimmed the surface of his belly, leaving a deep, ugly gash, but not penetrating far enough to harm his organs.

Dirk felt, rather than saw, someone kneeling at his side. He looked up, surprised to find Francesca's pale face beside his.

"Is he—?" she began.

"He's alive," he answered tersely. "I need something to staunch the blood.

"Here," she answered, yanking off her apron and handing it to him. He bunched it up and held it against Jacob's wound.

When the man lifted a hand as if to push him away, Dirk held his wrist back, addressing Francesca without looking at her. "Get me some brandy, will you?"

Her skirts rustled as she hurried away. A moment later she was back at his side, goblet and decanter in her hand.

Dirk lifted Jacob's head a little, then poured a bit of the liquor through his parted lips.

After sputtering on the first swallow, Jacob looked at Dirk. "You...shouldn't be...helping me. Leave me...to end it in my own way."

"And leave Lisbet to face the music herself?"

Jacob gave him a ghost of a smile. "You are a strong man, Dirk. A fine...fine son—man," he finished apologetically. "I am nothing but a coward. Always." His words were labored, and Dirk told him to hush.

"Let me get you up to your room to see to this cut properly." Before Jacob, who had closed his eyes, could protest, Dirk lifted him into his arms. He was no small man, but Dirk felt a strength born of determination.

He motioned to Francesca to precede him. "Show me to his room."

She led him down the hall and opened a door. She hurried to the bed and turned down the covers. With deft fingers, she removed her guardian's shoes, while Dirk attended to the removal of his shirt.

"I'll get some water and clean linen," she said softly before leaving the room.

At least she did not faint or go into hysterics at the sight of blood. For some perverse reason, Dirk wished he could fault her with something. But she was quick and efficient. He had discovered that since the day he'd first met her, he reminded himself. His mistake had been to think she had a heart of any sort beneath that prim and efficient exterior.

He took the things from Francesca when she returned and soon had the wound washed and bound. Together, he and Francesca pulled the covers up about Jacob's shoulders.

"Rest now, and no more thoughts of doing away with yourself, or I will think you are a coward," Dirk said to Jacob's closed eyes.

At his words, Jacob moved his hand over the bedclothes. Standing still, Dirk allowed his hand to be found. Jacob's grasp was surprisingly firm. "There's no hope."

"Be quiet." Dirk gave a cynical laugh. "There's always hope when you talk of money. Now, get some sleep and don't trouble yourself about anything else. The creditors will have to face me."

Jacob released his hand. "You have Anna's eyes and coloring, you know. . .don't know how I didn't notice that before. . ."

Francesca had drawn the curtains and now stood uncertainly at the door.

"Sh," Dirk ordered Jacob one last time before exiting the room with Francesca. When they were in the corridor with the door closed, he turned to her. "Tell Katryn what has happened. Where is Lisbet?"

"At Tante Blankaart's."

"That's something at least. Make sure Katryn allows no dangerous instruments near Jacob's reach. Does he have any firearms in his room?"

Francesca shook her head.

"He shall need watching. I shall bring my things and stay the night. That is, if you can spare the time away from Don Lorenzo to remain here until I get back," he added with an edge to his voice.

He saw the flash of anger in her eyes, but she answered him quietly. "Of course."

Francesca returned to the van Diemen residence as soon as she had explained to Don Lorenzo that she was needed there for a family emergency. He told her to take all the time she needed.

After Dirk came to relieve her at Mynheer Jacob's bedside, she spent the remainder of the afternoon down in the kitchen with Katryn, grateful that the shock of her guardian's action distracted Katryn from Francesca's situation.

"I'm glad that Mynheer Dirk is here. He shall see to things. Have no fear of that. He's a good man." The older woman sighed as if eased of a great burden. "And thank the good Lord Lisbet was away, when all this disaster struck. She would have been in hysterics and no help at all to her poor papa."

Francesca nodded, thankful, too.

She told Katryn nothing about Dirk's part in her guardian's ruin, but she did reveal that Dirk was his natural son.

"Oh, my heavens," Katryn kept clucking throughout Francesca's explanation.

"I always knew Mynheer wanted a son," she said when Francesca fell silent. "And what a fine one he has now. Sometimes, what starts out as a tragedy can turn into a blessing."

Francesca wished she could share Katryn's optimism. Having arrived and stood outside the door, she had overheard most of her guardian's confession, as well as Dirk's own story. She could only marvel at all Dirk had been through since the time of his birth. That he was not a hard, embittered man filled her with awe.

She was forced to examine her own hard shell, when she compared her childhood hardships to Dirk's. He had succeeded in overcoming so much more than she. He had become a man with a zest for life. He wasn't afraid of reaching for what he wanted. No, not as she was, she acknowledged to herself.

He could be as gentle and compassionate as he could be ruthless. Francesca knew that now. She had seen it in the way Dirk had fought to save his father's life. But deep down, she had known it earlier, by his treatment of her. She began to concede the possibility that he had never deliberately hurt her.

Maybe, just maybe, she considered, if she hadn't been so concerned with maintaining the protective shell she'd wrapped so tightly around herself since her parents had died, she would have sought Dirk out immediately for the truth.

Francesca flushed as she remembered her repudiation of his gift. No one had ever given her such a beautiful gift. He had brought those earrings all the way from Florence...he had traveled so far in search of her. Did he, could he, have cared a little for her?

But it was over now. She had destroyed any feelings he might have had for her.

Since returning to the house, she had stayed out of his way. The few words he'd directed at her were curt and aloof. She felt as if the very sight of her vexed him.

She ate her meal quickly below stairs with Katryn, hardly tasting the food. She sent Marta up with a tray for Dirk in Mynheer Jacob's room. The only comfort she felt was by Katryn's side. It reminded her of her childhood days.

When the bell sounded in the upstairs chamber, Francesca rose from her chair by the hearth with dread. What could Dirk want with her now? Mayhap Lisbet had returned, she thought with a sinking feeling. She did not know if Dirk had yet sent word to fetch her.

But Dirk sat alone by the fire. His words were brusque. "You're not expected to resume your role of servitude here. If Katryn needs help, I'll hire an additional kitchen maid."

The words were so unexpected Francesca flinched. He spoke without even a glance at her. The firelight deepened the lines around his mouth.

Only now could she see what she had striven so hard to see. She smiled to herself bitterly. Knowledge always came too late. She now understood his arrogance air, his tough demeanor, his mocking tone. They were all a defense.

She cringed, thinking once again how much she must have wounded his pride when she rejected his gift, when she'd rejected every overture he'd made since his return. How many people had Dirk Vredeman ever humbled himself to?

"I stayed down with Katryn because I didn't want to disturb you," she answered quietly.

The fire crackled in the grate and a clock above the mantel ticked a placid beat.

Francesca was on the point of leaving the room, unable to bear the silence any longer, when Dirk spoke again. His voice was controlled, but the coldness that had been there all afternoon was gone. Only weariness remained.

"How much did you overhear this afternoon?"

She cleared her throat. "Most everything, I think. I didn't mean to eavesdrop, but you had left the door ajar. I—I heard Mynheer Jacob speaking and just stood rooted."

Dirk made an impatient gesture, dismissing her apology.

He rested his head against the chair back and rubbed the bridge of his nose. "You heard about your father?"

"Yes." The shock had not been as great as might have been, since Dirk had already prepared her for her guardian's treachery. "I heard about...about your mother, too."

Dirk gave a grunt, which held both humor and cynicism. "I suppose I should be grateful. It saves a lot of explanation, which I really would be in no mood to go into at present."

"You don't owe me any explanations."

Dirk made a shrugging motion with his hand and let it drop onto the chair arm. "I don't suppose I do. They'd hardly serve any purpose now, would they?"

Francesca backed away a step. His words only confirmed what her conscience already had. Things had gone beyond a point of repair between them. Knowing this didn't make it any easier to bear.

"No, I don't suppose it does," she echoed softly, following his gaze to the fire. He had barely looked at her since she had made her presence known this afternoon, and when he did, the aloofness of his gaze was like a lash to her heart.

She hesitated before speaking. "You—you are going to help your father after all he has done to you?" It was as much a statement as a question.

"Don't call him that."

The harsh command made her want to weep more than anything she'd heard the entire afternoon. It made her want to run her hand across his forehead and sooth his brow and do anything to take away all painful memories.

But his countenance asked for no pity or sympathy. Francesca was afraid to offer comfort. She didn't know if she could bear his rejection. She, who had lived with rejection for so many years, wasn't sure she could survive an abrupt dismissal by Dirk now. No matter how deserved.

She had lost the thread of the conversation, when Dirk spoke again. "I find the taste of revenge not so sweet perhaps."

"Did you expect to?"

He gave her a sweeping look before turning back to his contemplation of the fire. "I suppose I never took the time to think about it. I was always too preoccupied with the means, not the end. All I could picture after destroying Jacob was the sight of him groveling at my feet, begging my forgiveness. Those are the feverish dreams that keep a young man going, struggling against whatever odds face him. To consume his enemy." He gave another grunt. "They are far removed from the reality of attainment.

"Whatever happened today, whatever Jacob did or did not say, cannot change the past. The past that is finished for good," he uttered with quiet finality. "The past which I've overcome in my own way."

They had fallen silent some moments, when he spoke again. "You want to know what is strangest?"

She nodded her head, wanting more than anything to linger, to hear whatever he wanted to tell her.

"I had decided last night that I could not go through with it."

Francesca drew in a quick breath.

If he noticed, he made no sign, too intent with his thoughts. "That after all those years of plotting how to avenge my mother's suffering, her premature death, I could not ruin Jacob."

He gave a soundless laugh. "He spoke today of his gray-eyed conscience. Well, you may congratulate yourself that you had become mine as well."

She stared at him. What did he mean? She moistened her parched lips. "You...you were not going to ruin him?"

He shook his head. "No. No," he repeated in a louder tone, staring into the grate. "Instead, I would allow him to make the profit he so craved."

"But how—?"

"By advising him when to sell. This venture was virtually risk-free."

"Why?"

He quirked a golden eyebrow at her. "You have to ask?"

Underlying the irony in his fire-lit amber eyes, Francesca read disappointment.

It smote her, convincing her more than anything else that day how truly she had destroyed any regard he had had for her.

"To gain your trust, 'Cesca.'"

The nickname mocked her.

They looked at each other a long moment through the flickering shadows. Every fiber in her desired to comfort him that night, knowing how much he must need it. But not from her, not anymore.

She bowed her head and quietly left the room.

Francesca stayed at the van Diemen residence only as long as she deemed absolutely necessary. She could not bear being under the same roof as Dirk, being the recipient of a distant preoccupation that his involvement with his newly acknowledged family brought about. She felt as if she were a stranger helping out.

She almost envied Lisbet, as Dirk's half-sister. At least Lisbet knew where she stood with him. Dirk offered her the protection of family and the material security of his wealth.

Precisely the things Francesca had turned down in running away from him.

She returned to Don Lorenzo's residence to pick up the rhythm of her life, a rhythm which had been shattered twice in less than a year. Something told her this time would be infinitely worse than the first time.

One day, when she could not run from her thoughts any longer, she went in desperation to the Bruin Biertje tavern.

"Hi ho! If it isn't Cesca! Where have you been keeping yourself these days?" Klaus greeted her with a broad smile. "Not too grand for the sight of this tavern, I hope? Though, 'twouldn't blame you for not wanting to associate yourself with the likes of some of these scoundrels," he added with a look at his current patrons.

"I am truly sorry I have not had a chance to come and visit you sooner. I have been away from Amsterdam, as you know." At his nod, she told him a little of the situation between Dirk and Mynheer Jacob.

"Yes, Dirk has already been by to tell me. My, my," he said with a shake of his head. "'Twouldn't have believed it possible, if it had been anyone else recounting it. I thought all he wanted was to see his father ruined and done for. Now it seems he's taken pity on the man."

"Yes," she answered, fingering the worn wooden surface of the bar. "It almost seems as if all the anger Dirk had inside him toward his...his father has evaporated." She looked up at Klaus, shuddering at the thought that occurred to her. "I am glad that Dirk did not carry out his original plan of revenge. The good Lord saved him from that fate."

"Aye. Vengeance is mine, doesn't He say? 'Twould've been difficult for Dirk to live with that had everything gone exactly according to his plan."

"Do you think that's why he's helping out his father? To relieve his guilt?" she wondered aloud, glad to have someone at last to talk to about Dirk.

Klaus furrowed his bushy white eyebrows. "Mayhap partially. There's a lot more to Dirk than that, however." At the look of interest in Francesca's eye, he elaborated, "There's the little boy who always wanted a father's love and notice. Oh, he's too practical to hope for Mynheer Jacob to give him more than the man's capable of. But a part of him probably wants to do right by his father, just because the man is his father."

Francesca remembered all Klaus had told her before about Dirk's youth.

Klaus leaned back with a long sigh. "Aye, all he needs now is the love of a good woman to settle him down and make him forget all thoughts of hatred and revenge." He shook his head. "I don't know what went through his head to go off on a sea voyage, when he had such a lovely bride waiting for him at home."

She didn't dare tell him it was in search of that very wife.

Klaus winked at Francesca and chuckled. "Ye should've seen him the first day back from sea, when I told him you'd been sitting here in this very tavern sketching everyone's portrait." Klaus's amusement deepened. "He looked like a seasick sailor, that green about the gills he was. And he staggered out of here like he hadn't yet realized he was back on dry land." Klaus slapped the counter and chortled at the recollection.

Francesca was feeling none too well herself as she bid Klaus farewell and returned to Don Lorenzo's residence. How much worse her own behavior appeared in light of Klaus's latest information. She pictured the scene as seen through the old salt's eyes.

What had she done to her husband but repudiate him at every turn? Would there ever be any way to bridge the wide gap she'd created between the two of them?

Twenty

Instead of being able to escape unnoticed to her room, Francesca met Don Lorenzo on the main floor. He motioned her to come and have a cup of wine with him.

"I have missed your company, mia cara, in these last few days."

"I'm so sorry—"

"Don't apologize. I have understood perfectly. Tragic news about your guardian, but thankfully, Signor Dirk was there to save the day, no?"

"Yes," she murmured. "He did indeed."

Don Lorenzo sighed. "I feel your days are numbered here among us." He smiled a smile of understanding tinged with sadness, which made his dark eyes look as velvety as a hound's. "Do not be alarmed, cara. Your work has satisfied me in all respects. But soon you shall have completed all you began, no?"

"I...I am still working on the group portrait." She wondered at her sudden nervousness. She had always known her time in the della Torre household would be short. It was not as if she had nowhere else to go. There was her apprenticeship with Master van der Helst, after all. So, why didn't the prospect fill her with more enthusiasm? Was it because she had become accustomed to being a full-fledged artist in these past few weeks under Don Lorenzo's patronage?

Or was it the thought of being alone again, belonging to no one?

"You seem far away, Francesca."

She shook her head with an effort. "I am sorry. I suppose

I was just thinking of what I shall do when I leave here." She couldn't quite manage a full smile.

"I thought that would be obvious."

"Well, yes, there is my unfinished apprenticeship to complete."

"Apprenticeship? Ah, I had forgotten about that." Don Lorenzo gave her a look full of meaning. "But there is another role that is much more important to you, I think, no?" He shrugged. "Francesca, cara, perhaps I am growing overly romantic with the years, but I always fancied I could detect the presence of love under my roof."

"Love?"

"The love between a husband and wife is the most beautiful love there is among lovers." Don Lorenzo laid a hand upon her knee. "When you find that you are blessed indeed."

"What is that"—she stumbled over the word—"love like?"

"Ah." Don Lorenzo's tone told her he understood much more than her question implied. "The union between a man and woman is as rich as one of our Florentine tortes, layer upon layer of discovery. Each encounter, each conversation, even the disagreements, bring about new revelations, which deepen the bond between the two."

Francesca listened, breathless at his description. For the first time, someone was relating to her all that she had imagined. "Have you ever experienced such things?" she whispered.

Don Lorenzo took her question seriously. "Yes, cara, with my beloved wife, Lucia."

Francesca looked down, saddened by the tenderness she saw in Don Lorenzo's eyes at the memory of his wife. "I'm sorry for your loss."

Don Lorenzo sighed and spread his hands. "So am I, cara, so am I. But life goes on. I thank the good Lord for all the years I knew with my dear Lucia. And for the two children still remaining me." He smiled at her tenderly. "It saddens me to see a young woman like yourself denying herself the joys of love with her new husband."

Francesca looked away. "I am afraid you don't understand. You see, I have hurt Dirk too deeply."

"And what did you do that was so terrible that cannot be forgiven?"

"I fear for a long time I did not trust him."

"And now?"

"Now I feel"—she put her head in her hands, feeling the weight of her loss—"he is a very honorable man."

"What then is the problem?"

"I've destroyed something very precious," she whispered. "All the regard he had for me."

Don Lorenzo chuckled. "I doubt things are so drastic. I would wager my favorite Rubens that Signor Dirk still wants his beautiful young wife. Why, at my house party, the man had eyes only for you."

Francesca gave a hollow laugh. "It is more than that. When I should have given him my loyalty and trust, I made another choice. I don't think he can forgive me for that. Look how many years it took for him to forgive his own father."

He patted her hand. "The two of you are young. He will forgive you. You are his wife. Any union between a man and a woman with as much passion as the two of you have is bound to be fraught with much anger. Anger that will be forgiven when there is love."

Francesca blinked away tears, afraid to let herself hope. "You are mistaken. Dirk doesn't love me."

"The intensity in his eyes when he looks at you tells another story, cara."

"'Tis only passion he feels—or felt. Now, I'm not even sure of that anymore. Not after what I did to him."

Don Lorenzo took her hands in his. "It is a hard thing to step on a man's pride. And this one, he is very proud, no?"

Francesca gave a wisp of a smile. "Yes."

Don Lorenzo patted her hand. "In that case, you must bend over double in asking his pardon. Men like that. This Dirk might appear hard at first, but believe me, if you are half the woman I think you are, you shall soon have him on his knees, begging you to come home again. Remember, you must allow him to regain his dignity before your eyes. Do not be offended by any coldness he may at first show."

Don Lorenzo stood and walked over to a cabinet. From a compartment he took something and came back to her. To her surprise she recognized the small inlaid box Dirk had presented to her a few days ago containing the sapphire earrings. "This is yours, no?"

She nodded, reaching for the jewelry box.

"I thought as much, when I saw it lying here."

When Francesca said nothing, he urged, "Go to him. Do not wait too long. Of all the men I have met here, he is the only one I judge to be worthy of your Florentine blood." He smiled at her with the appreciation of a compatriot. "Is he here in Amsterdam?"

"Katryn told me he was taking Mynheer Jacob and his daughter to his villa for a few weeks. He is there now."

"Perfetto. We shall leave tomorrow ourselves. After all, you have a family portrait to complete before you depart the della Torre family."

※

A few days had passed since her conversation with Don Lorenzo. Days in which she fretted and fussed inwardly, but in which she finally concluded it was better to brave the lion in his den than to live in her present state of uncertainty.

And now she found herself at Dirk's villa. Katryn, happily taking over the kitchens there, had directed her out to the farthest gardens at the edge of the woods.

Francesca stole upon her husband silently. He was with Willem and another man, bent over shovels, digging a new bed in the dandelion-dotted grass. They were shirtless, their back to her.

The artist in her drew in her breath in sheer admiration at the splendid ripple of muscle along his upper back and arms as he stooped to dig out another shovelful of dirt.

As she drew closer, the woman in her wept at the pale crisscross of scars against his sun-bronzed skin. Her heart went out to the youth who had endured those lashings. Her hand stifled a cry as she noticed the marking at one shoulder blade—the brand for a thief who had been convicted and sentenced to a flogging on the pillory.

Francesca longed to touch each wound and kiss away the memory of each slash. They had tried to destroy his dignity, but she knew, watching him now, how little they had succeeded.

In went his shovel, down went his booted foot, up went his bare arms, bringing his muscles out in strong relief. Francesca watched, dazzled by the steady rhythm of his pure, raw strength.

Willem spied her first, and with a touch to his forelock, he saluted her, before saying a word to Dirk. Dirk thrust his shovel into the earth a last time and turned slowly. He gave her no smile, but with a silent motion, dismissed the other two men.

"Are you here to see Jacob or Lisbet?"

Francesca recoiled at his sharp tone. Her attempt to gain his forgiveness would be more difficult than she had imagined. "I came to see you."

He raised one eyebrow, his hand resting on the shovel handle. "Well, don't just stand there like a frightened wren. If you have aught to say to me, approach."

Francesca took a few more tentative steps toward him, still keeping a safe distance between the two.

"I did not realize we had any unfinished business since we last parted, or are you in a rush for me to procure you a bill of divorcement?"

She sucked in her breath. Fighting down the urge to flee him, she stood firm. The hurt in his voice was there beneath the anger, she reminded herself. His eyes had a ferocious cast, the way they narrowed against the sunlight. Rivulets of sweat trailed down his face and chest, where it mixed with powdered dirt. The smell of freshly turned earth and pine resin from the forest at his back assailed her nostrils.

As he watched her, while giving no hint to his thoughts, Francesca almost lost courage. Only Don Lorenzo's encouraging words sustained her, when she would have turned and run. She moistened her lips and squared her shoulders. "You once told me forgiveness is for fools."

She saw that her words had startled him, as if they were the last thing he expected to hear. Then his gaze narrowed with suspicion. He left the shovel propped up in the dirt and took a few paces toward her. She stood her ground, her heart hammering in her chest, but he only walked past her, reaching for a linen towel draped across a shrub beside her.

"'Tis so. That was my opinion at one time."

Francesca met his gaze apprehensively, suddenly terrified because she could not read his thoughts behind the light mocking tone. Was he baiting her? Don Lorenzo's advice came back to her. Allow him to regain his dignity...bend over double in asking his pardon. Like a tonic, the words fortified her. She would bear anything, she decided, if it meant regaining her husband's regard.

"I suppose what I am asking then is whether you can be fool enough to forgive me."

His motion with the towel stilled. "In that case, 'twas brave indeed of you to come here today considering what I thought of forgiveness."

Her fingernails dug into the palms of her hands.

His golden eyes studied her. "I confess, you have me at a loss. What pardon have you need of?"

Francesca stared. She read no mockery in his eyes, but it was impossible he spoke seriously. "For several things." She took a deep breath. "Pardon for my rudeness to you when you came to see me at Don Lorenzo's with your gift."

His eyes flashed to her ears, noticing she wore the earrings now. She plowed on. "Pardon for not accepting it then. For not believing what you told me of my Florentine grandmother." Her throat hitched, and she dropped her gaze to his chest, sweat and grime against golden skin. "Pardon for putting everything before...my love for you." There, she'd said it.

The cicadas clattered in the hot afternoon.

"You did what you thought right," he said softly. "I had not earned your trust."

He would make her cry if his tone became any gentler. She dared not raise her eyes. "Somewhere deep down, a part of me always trusted you—ever since that night of my abduction." She gave a shaky laugh at the absurdity of the admission in light of the fact that he had been her abductor all along. "I suppose 'tis why your conquest of me came so easily."

He gave a dry laugh. "Easy? I had the devil's own time of it, I can assure you."

"But you had me, nonetheless," she reminded him. She looked up then, needing to know something for herself, and was caught by the tenderness in his eyes. "You wanted to prove I would capitulate, since you began your pursuit of me. You wanted me to lose my self-control, to prove I was not immune to your wooing." Had there been nothing more than that to his suit? She waited for him to deny it.

But he did not refute her assertions. "You forget, I intended to marry you. I would not contemplate that lightly."

"But your reasons were not enough to be taken seriously!" She almost cried out the words in her frustration. "Why should you want to marry me? Merely because my guardian would not admit me? You could have helped me in other ways—found me a husband, just as you are doing now for Lisbet, if that was your only concern!"

"I would think 'twould be obvious to you now, knowing my mother's history, that I would dishonor no woman and leave her to face the consequences." He made a harsh sound in his throat. "'Tis why it cut me to the quick when you thought I would dishonor Lisbet—my own sister. Nay, my only plan had been to keep her overnight and return her to Jacob with her reputation ruined. But I would not have permitted any of my men to touch her."

She gave a slight nod. "I understand that now."

His amber eyes studied her. "I never made a secret of wanting you. But I would only have you within the marriage bed. 'Tis why, when you ran away from me, I left the money with Pieter, in case you were with child."

She stared at him in confusion. Gradually his words sank in. "What money? You gave Pieter money for me?"

Dirk nodded, distracted. "Pieter knew you wouldn't take it from me, so he kept it for you, in case you should need it. I suppose he found a use for it, when you had the opportunity of your apprenticeship."

The facts cascaded into place. "You paid for my apprenticeship?"

Dirk shrugged at her disbelief. "You think I didn't understand how much your art meant to you? It makes no difference now. You have proved your worth as a painter many times over, since I commissioned you to paint my portrait." His eyes held faint amusement. "You know, you never did give me my money's worth. I paid for that painting fairly, yet you took it with you when you ran from me."

Francesca flushed, thinking of her unwillingness to relinquish the portrait. Afraid he would guess the special significance it held for her, she replied, "I shall give it to you, as soon as I get back to Amsterdam."

His eyes twinkled. "'Twill be no need of that. I acquired the painting despite your forgetfulness."

Francesca gasped. "You have the portrait? How did you get it?"

"From Pieter, though I had to pay twice for it—and dearly. I couldn't ever track you down at Pieter's, so perforce, I was obliged to deal with him. I must admit, he is not wholly the worthless man I first took him for." Dirk gave a wicked grin. "He did agree to sell me the painting."

"Pieter sold you my painting? He...he never told me," she said faintly, finding it hard to absorb all she was hearing.

He chuckled grimly. "I think Pieter realized rather quickly he did not have much choice in the matter. Since then, he has probably feared your displeasure too much to tell you who the buyer was. Though I'm sure he'll give you your payment when you tell him. He doesn't strike me as a dishonest sort."

She shook her head, still in a daze. "It doesn't matter about that. You shall have your money back, of course."

Dirk tipped his head. "I shall be keeping the painting, however." Francesca discerned the glitter of determination in his eyes. After a moment he continued more lightly. "I must admit, I am growing accustomed to it." His white teeth flashed down at her. "There, high above the mantelpiece for his heirs to admire, de Heer Vredeman surveying all his hard-earned wealth. A bit like my natural father, van Diemen, wouldn't you say?"

Francesca saw through the smile to the self-mockery beneath. "I marvel you can forgive him so easily."

"Easily? There was nothing easy about it. Mayhap after so many years I've just grown tired of my anger. Or, perhaps, the good Lord has shown me His grace." He shrugged. "At any rate, I do not intend to spend the rest of my life too closely associated with...Jacob." She noticed he would still not utter the word father.

"Until then, like a dutiful son, I am helping him reestablish himself." Again, irony underscored his words.

"I see. How is Mynheer Jacob?"

"Almost pathetically grateful for anything I do. I don't know how much more I can take, between that and Lisbet's constant carping. I shall have to set Jacob up in some business soon, so his natural avarice can have an outlet once more. I have discovered I prefer the shrewd, hard-nosed merchant to this broken shadow of his former self." Dirk looked pensive. "Mayhap I shall send him off to Batavia to oversee my plantation."

That last remark was enough to make Francesca overcome her own uncertainty enough to laugh.

"What is so funny?"

She shook her head. "I just cannot picture my guardian out there in the Indies. He is so...so stiff-lipped."

"You would be surprised how well people can adapt. In no time at all, he would have a score of slaves catering to his every whim and think himself a prince among men. It may be just what his pride needs. In the meantime, I already have a suitor lined up for Lisbet." He smiled meaningfully. "Not as grand as Bicker, by any means, but just the sort of iron-fisted man she needs to set her straight."

An awkward silence fell between them as their thoughts returned to the present. In the interval Francesca had had time to absorb Dirk's reason for wanting to marry her. It made perfect sense, she acknowledged. He was not the sort to want to dishonor a maiden. What encouraging words could Don Lorenzo give her now in the face of such frankness?

Dirk's next words interrupted her thoughts. "As soon as I clear up Jacob's financial affairs, I shall see about restoring your inheritance."

She blinked, then shook her head. "It doesn't matter about that." His charity was the last thing she wanted. Then she straightened her back and said in a brisker tone, "Anyway, if you can overcome your anger at Mynheer Jacob the way you have, perhaps you can be fool enough to forgive—" She couldn't summon the courage to say "wife," so ended with, "Me."

Dirk lifted her chin with a fingertip. His grin was broad, the smile reaching his eyes. "Haven't I proved a fool time and again with you?"

Francesca stood speechless a moment, unable to believe she was reading his words correctly. Finally she found her voice around the lump in her throat. "You have never seemed a fool to me. Cocksure perhaps, arrogant, prideful..."

"Which other of your suitors would go to Italy and back on some wild goose chase cooked up by a worthless painter—"

"I didn't know Pieter made up that tale until the deed was already done! And I never imagined you would take the trouble to come after me!" She looked at him earnestly. "Much less seek my family. You'll never know how grateful I am that you have reunited me with my father's family. 'Tis good to know—to know—" Her eyelids fluttered downward. "I belong to someone." Unable to bear his pity, she hurried on. "And I—I am also grateful for the money you gave for my apprentice fees. I shall repay you someday, I promise—"

She was startled when he pulled her face up to his again. Anger filled his eyes. "By all that's holy, woman, when will you get it through that skull of yours that 'tis not your gratitude or repayment I wish?"

Something long hidden away, or perhaps never tapped within her except on her wedding night, some ancient woman's instinct came to the fore, emboldening her enough to ask, "What do you wish, Dirk?"

The way she said his name was like a tender stroke on his body. Dirk took a while in replying, his own wants and needs jelling in crystal clear form for the first time since he had met her. "I want your whole-hearted devotion," he said fiercely. "I want you to forsake all other men—that hero-worship you have for Pieter, whatever it is you fancy for

Don Lorenzo, and any other wealthy art patron who might come along—"

"Very well."

"I want you to give me all the passion I know you are capable of. The passion you have bottled up inside you and only allow glimpses of in your painting. I want to know I am the only man that can bring it out of you—" He stopped in mid-sentence, narrowing his eyes at his wife.

Had he heard her clearly? Was she mocking him? But all he saw staring back at him was a pair of solemn gray eyes.

His speech at an end, he noticed for the first time how still she stood. Her lips were slightly parted, as if she was afraid to breathe. "What did you say?" he asked.

"I said, very well. But—" She spoke before he could respond, "What am I to have in return?"

He looked into those silvery depths, which were regarding him with gentle warmth. How had he ever thought their look prim and aloof?

"My love." It was the first time he had ever offered those words to any woman besides the woman who had borne him. Voicing them aloud to Francesca told him all at once what had been driving him mad for so long.

Now he waited, realizing he was more vulnerable than he had ever been. More so than when he had stood outside his father's fine mansion one winter day as a lad, waiting for a glimpse of the man. Getting his nerve up to speak to him and to ask help for his mother. Not for himself, by God! When the man in his fine black woolens and fur had finally descended with his small daughter by the hand, Dirk never even had the chance to open his mouth. The rich burgher had tossed him a stuiver, rapping out sharply, "Be gone now, boy. No beggars allowed on this street." And off Jacob had walked at a brisk pace, as if further contact with the ragged urchin might contaminate his daughter. Dirk's last sight had been of the man's tiny daughter trotting beside him on chubby legs, her butter yellow hair blowing out from beneath her little fur-trimmed cap.

Dirk put aside the memory, awaiting Francesca's reply, and knowing if there was one person capable of erasing the hurt of those memories, it was the woman standing before him.

Francesca did not speak. Instead, she lifted her hand to his cheek. All his focus was on her fingertips, feeling them against the springy fringe of his beard at his jaw line, moving upward to the portion of shaven cheek above it.

Dirk needed no other answer. He gazed warmly at her a second longer, reading the hope and fear in her eyes. He knew with a dead certainty that for the first time since he had lost his mother, he could risk exposing all his feelings to another human being. He knew Francesca would never again betray him.

As he reached for her, she came to him. At his touch, it was as if a dam broke forth. A sob escaped her lips, and she clutched the towel draped around his neck.

"Easy now," he whispered against her hair. But his gentle words made her cry the harder, saying brokenly, "I'm sorry, Dirk, I'm so sorry!"

He patted her on the back, telling her to shush, kissing the top of her head, murmuring endearments. But all to no avail. He began to realize how much she must have kept bottled up inside her. Her sobs also told him how much it must have cost her to come to him today. They reflected his own anguish up until the moment she'd appeared that day.

"Don't cry," he said above her head. "You'll make me feel worse than I ever did on that blasted trip to Tuscany and back. Believe me, I was not in the best of humors." He smiled in recollection and was relieved to hear a watery response, half-laugh, half-sob.

As he continued stroking her back, her breathing finally slowed, and when she began fumbling in her pocket for a handkerchief, he handed her his towel.

"Here, you'd better finish the job with this. You've got it half-soaked."

She took it and dabbed at her eyes and nose. "I'm sorry."

He gave her a stern look. "If I hear one more apology, I'll send you back to Amsterdam."

She answered with a tremulous smile. Her dark lashes were spiked with tears. Her nose was red and her lips deep crimson. She had never looked more beautiful.

Conscious suddenly of his soiled state, he lifted a palm gingerly to cup it around Francesca's nape and bring her face forward. All at once, he was a youth once more, kissing a girl for the first time. His lips barely grazed hers, his yearning growing immeasurably at the slight touch.

The instant their lips met, her lips parted and she brought a hand up to his shoulder to steady herself, then pressed against him in longing, unmindful of sweat and dirt.

Dirk's need overcame him and he crushed her to him. After long moments, he raised his head. "I'm filthy," he whispered hoarsely. "I must bathe."

Suddenly her eyes shone up at him. "Let's go to the sea!"

He loosened his hold and grabbed her hand. The two ran like children through the forest and to the dunes. By the time they reached the top, they were breathless and laughing.

"Do you dare?" he challenged her, the old familiar twinkle back in his eye.

She looked down the length of the beach both ways. The only figures were tiny specks far down the strip of sand. She nodded rapidly. "Yes!"

A long time later as the two lay among the dune grasses, the steady sound of the sea below them, she said, "Someday you must let me do your portrait...as a Greek god," she whispered, trailing a frond of grass along the sleek contours of one of his muscular arms.

His chuckle reverberated in his chest. "For you, Francesca, I would do just about anything."

Suddenly she faced a new fear. "You would not expect me to give up my painting for you, would you?"

She read the surprise in his eyes, as if the thought had never entered his head. "As long as your only art patron is your husband," he answered gruffly, kissing the tip of her salty nose.

"Dirk, I'm so ashamed that I ever made you believe there was something dishonorable between Don Lorenzo and me." She shook her head vehemently, sending her damp hair flying around her shoulders. "'Tisn't true! Don Lorenzo has been like a father to me, no more."

"I know, love. I was angry with you, to be sure, but I knew deep down you would never do anything dishonorable."

She cupped his cheek with her hand. "I do so love you, Dirk. You don't know how I missed you, when you thought I had gone off to Italy. I tried to convince myself I wanted you gone from my life. For the first time in my life, not even my painting gave me any satisfaction. My life was an endless series of gloomy days and sleepless nights." Her voice broke.

"Shush, my love. That time is past." He drew her to him. The two stayed embraced for some moments, as if aware of how closely they had come to losing one another. Then she felt Dirk's chuckle against her hair. "Anyway, 'tis your own fault for sending me chasing like a madman clear down to Italy for you. Your kin must think I would make a poor husband, half insane, clearly besotted. . ."

"You've met my family," she said in wonder, still finding it hard to believe he knew more about them than she did.

"I not only met them, but lodged and supped with them. They send you their finest compliments and anxiously await the day you can pay them a visit."

"I can scarce believe it after so many years of believing the contrary." She shook her head. "Why did my guardian tell me they didn't want me?"

"I believe by then his wife saw you as a convenient serving maid."

"And they truly want to meet me?"

He stroked the sand off her arm. "Truly."

"Tell me about them."

"Let's see, I can give you the names of your cousins, the latest crop of nieces and nephews to be christened, your grandmother, who says you need a good scolding—"

Her eyes widened in alarm. "Scolding?"

"For running away from me instead of settling down and giving me a dozen bambinos."

She would paint him, she decided with renewed determination. No clothing would mar his body this time. Perhaps he could pose as Samson bringing down the pillars with the Almighty's power unleashed. Or perhaps as Caleb scouting out the Promised Land for the Israelites. Whoever it was, he would be strong and noble, someone not easily cowed by life's circumstances.

As if sensing her scrutiny, Dirk opened one eye and regarded her. "What are you looking at?"

"My future painting."

"If you only mean to paint me you'll die a starving artist."

She opened her eyes wide, pretending astonishment. "You don't mean to pay me an honest wage?"

"Wage? What think you, woman? Isn't it enough that I shall set you up with your own atelier in town and one out here at the villa? I don't expect you to sit staring at my naked form all day." He grinned at her.

"I could do so quite easily," she murmured.

"I hope you'll allow me a robe in winter, else I'll soon catch a chill." While he spoke, he reached out and pulled Francesca towards him. When she rested in the curve of his arm, her chin propped in her palm, looking down at him, she asked, "Did you really mean it about my own atelier?"

"If it's what you want."

She stroked his cheek in response. "'Tis only one of the things I should like. There are a few others that come first."

He raised an eyebrow. "Such as?"

"Making you as contented as a cat."

His lips curved upward. "That you've already accomplished."

Her tone grew serious. "What would you have done if I hadn't come to you today?"

His answering look did not mirror her own concern. "Oh, I hoped you would come to me sooner or later, preferably sooner."

"Why, you conceited—"

His arm tightened around her. "Nay, my love, 'twasn't conceit. I needed you too much when you returned to Don Lorenzo to feel any conceit." The expression in his eyes made Francesca's heart contract.

"I'm truly sorry, Dirk," she whispered. "You seemed so preoccupied, so distant, I thought my presence could only add to your worries."

His hand squeezed her bare shoulder. "Never. I had so much on my mind then, that I needed your comforting presence more than ever. But I was afraid."

"You? Afraid?"

"Afraid you might reject me again if I reached out for you."

"Oh, Dirk!" Francesca stretched her arm across his chest, hugging him close, her head nestled in the hollow of his neck.

After a few minutes, she heard him chuckle. "I began to suspect a while back that you might care for me a little, so my hopes for your return were not completely extinguished. If I'd had nothing else, Katryn's unwavering faith in your love for me would have sustained me. So, I trusted you would soon come to your senses and return to your rightful place."

Francesca lifted her head to look at him again. She was beginning to know that teasing tone that masked far deeper sentiments. "And what if I hadn't come to my senses?"

He gave her a crooked smile. "I would have come up with another plan to bring you back willingly."

"I always knew you were a most resourceful man."

"So resourceful, in fact, that I plan to have you installed back in the villa by this evening."

Francesca leaned forward to kiss him tenderly on the lips. "It will be nice to come home."

In reply Dirk hugged her close.

Later she smiled indulgently at her husband, as he began to plan a honeymoon to Florence.

He would undoubtedly lead her an eventful life down through the years. 'Twould certainly be different to the life she had led up to then, she admitted with a shiver of anticipation. But it would never be dull.

She, in turn, would bear his children and paint her portraits and make a home for him such as he'd never known.

He thought he had been jesting when he'd said his portrait would look down upon his heirs from the mantelpiece. Aye, Dirk Vredeman would bear a clan, Francesca judged, and probably rule them like the royal lion he was meant to be.

ABOUT THE AUTHOR

Ruth Axtell knew she wanted to be a writer ever since she wrote her first story—a spy thriller—at the age of twelve. She studied comparative literature at Smith College, spending her junior year at the Sorbonne in Paris. After college, she taught English in the Canary Islands, then worked in international development in Miami, Florida, before moving to the Netherlands, where for the next several years she juggled both writing and raising three children. In 1994, her second manuscript was a finalist in Romance Writers of America's Golden Heart competition. Since then, Ruth Axtell has gone on to publish several historical romances, a novella, and a novelette. Her books have been translated into Dutch, Czech, Italian, German, Polish, and Afrikaans. Her second historical, *Wild Rose*, was chosen by the American Library Association's Booklist as a "Top Ten Christian Fiction" selection in 2005. Ruth lives on the coast of Maine where she enjoys gardening, walking, swimming, reading romances, and gazing at the ocean plotting her next romance.

OTHER BOOKS BY RUTH AXTELL

For a list of Ruth's other books, visit her website at http://ruthaxtell.com